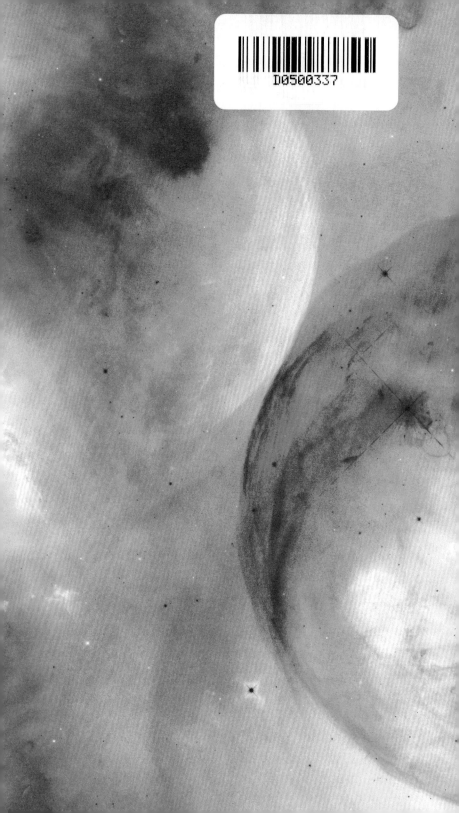

D0500337

UNDER
FORTUNATE
STARS

First published 2022 by Solaris
an imprint of Rebellion Publishing Ltd,
Riverside House, Osney Mead,
Oxford, OX2 0ES, UK

www.solarisbooks.com

ISBN: 978 1 78618 592 1

10 9 8 7 6 5 4 3 2 1

A CIP catalogue record for this book is available
from the British Library.

Designed & typeset by Rebellion Publishing

REBELLiON

Printed in the UK

UNDER
FORTUNATE
STARS

REN HUTCHINGS

SOLARIS

To M, *whose love and friendship*
have made me unbelievably fortunate.

JERETH

Deep Space Cargo Hauler *Jonah*

THE THING ABOUT luck, Jereth told himself, is that it always turns. Eventually.

He knew he was taking a foolhardy gamble when he threw the packet of oversalted snack cakes into the middle of the table—especially after he'd already lost two rolls of pepper-candy and a quarter-tin of spiced fruit. His chances of winning a game against Leeg were infinitesimally small. Still, there had been those few occasions when he'd snuck a win, when a particularly lucky run of tiles had thwarted Leeg's mathematical machinations.

He was almost surprised when Leeg turned over the winning tile again.

"Oh, what a shock," Leeg said drily. "Who could've predicted?"

"Damn it, I really thought I had you that time!" Jereth tossed his useless tiles on the table. "I had a wild three! Gods. I forgot how impossible you are."

"I can pretend you might win for a bit longer next time, if you like."

"Just shut up and take your winnings." Jereth laughed and shoved the pile of food toward Leeg. Given their current odds of long-term survival, it hardly seemed to matter that he'd just gambled away the last of his snacks.

Leeg picked up the packet of cakes from the top of the pile, examining it disdainfully. He tore open a corner, removed one salt-encrusted disc and bit into it with a grimace.

"Ugh. This stuff tastes like salted earwax. You got anything else you want to lose?"

"Forget it. I'm all out of snacks. And if you think I'm playing you for money, you're out of your mind." Jereth ran a palm over the table, rounding up the game tiles and sweeping them back into their pouch.

"Well... in that case, I guess I'll go to my bunk," Leeg said. He collected a stray tile and flicked the little hexagon in Jereth's direction. "Oh, wait... no I won't. I'll go lie down on the floor, because we haven't got bunks anymore."

The *Jonah* was a small cargo hauler that had seen too many years in space. The ship's tiny living area fit only the loosest possible definition of sleeping quarters: three cramped compartments in the wall, each hidden by a metal door with just enough room behind it for a narrow pallet and some shelving. It was uncomfortable at the best of times, but now that there were five people on the ship, the situation was downright claustrophobic.

Their hired engineer, Mendeg, had a contract that promised private sleeping quarters, so he had the compartment furthest from the bridge. The passenger they'd picked up, Keila, was paying a generous fee that warranted some semblance of hospitality. They'd given her the middle bunk, the one that used to belong to Jereth. The final bunk—Leeg's—was now occupied by their unexpected prisoner.

Leeg had argued that surely the *prisoner* should be sleeping on the floor instead of him. But the bunk doors, flimsy as they were, could be locked shut. So Jereth and Leeg were relegated to sleeping on a tattered red blanket in the bridge.

Leeg cast a miserable look at the three closed compartments where the others were sleeping soundly. "Must be nice to have a bed to sleep in, huh? Not that the beds in this junk-heap are that much better than the floor."

"Can you give me a break?" Jereth sighed. "It's only a couple more days. And I'm sleeping on the floor, too. What do you want me to do?"

"Would it matter if I told you? You never listen to me anyway," Leeg said. "I'm still trying to comprehend why you decided to pick up a hitchhiker."

"A passenger," Jereth corrected. "A very well-paying one."

"A complete stranger! Who clearly had some kind of run-in with the authorities—"

"She offered twenty-five thousand, Leeg. Come on. It's not like I could turn that down! We could use some extra money for insurance, in case we run into any more unforeseen circumstances."

"You mean like when we got hijacked?" Leeg rolled his eyes.

"*Almost* got hijacked," Jereth said. "I took care of it, didn't I? Everything's fine."

"Sure. Everything's fine, in the sense that we've now got a prisoner locked in my damn bunk," Leeg muttered. "This is a marginal improvement over the day I had a gun to my head. The only thing that's nearly killed me today is boredom."

"You'll get your bunk back, okay? I promise. As soon as we get to Zora Outpost."

Leeg nodded, but he was silent for a long time after that. He chewed quietly on the rest of the crumbling snack cake, his eyes distant.

Leeg wasn't much older than Jereth, but the years had worn heavily on him. His dark ponytail was shot through with silver now, his temples almost entirely greyed. His ash-pale cheeks were hollower, and his rare smiles seldom reached his eyes. But he was still the same Leeg who had risked everything with Jereth once.

The same Leeg who, despite everything, was willing to do it again.

Jereth glanced back at the airlock leading to the ship's hold. Beyond it loomed the ominous crates of their cargo: components for a black-market planetary defence system. Supplies bound for an unauthorized venture-ship heading outside Union space, away from this unwinnable war with the Felen, away from the inevitable collapse of human civilization.

It would be Jereth's final reckless gamble, if it wasn't already too late.

The word at the last outpost hadn't been good. There were whispers that a Felen fleet was holding Etraxas under siege, and he suspected it was true. There was a certain bitter satisfaction in the knowledge that even the Union's wealthy, self-serving capital wasn't invulnerable. Etraxas deserved the same fate as the fledgling worlds they'd left to wither under the alien onslaught. After the way the Union had forsaken the desert settlements, left them unprotected until it was time to raid the ranks of their young for more soldiers—

Jereth clenched his teeth, taking a moment to dispel the familiar rage before it had a chance to crystallize in his chest. Leeg's voice broke the silence.

"Hey... was that light up there always blinking? What is that?"

Jereth followed Leeg's gaze to the control console. An incoming message node was flashing, the pale-yellow hue indicating a sector-wide broadcast.

He went up the scuffed steps into the bridge to retrieve the message. It unfurled haltingly onto the viewscreen:

SECTOR ADVISORY—URGENT. Zora Outpost has been destroyed, lost to Felen hostilities. All civilian ships are strongly advised to avoid the area and use an alternate route.

Jereth swallowed hard, staring at the grainy screen. He balled his shaking hands into fists and braced them against the sides of the console.

"Jerry? You all right? What's it say?"

"Change of plans." Jereth didn't look back at Leeg. "Zora's out. We'll have to take a detour."

He tried to dismiss the message, but Leeg was already behind him, leaning over his shoulder.

"*Lost to Felen hostilities.*" Leeg punctuated the phrase with a long, defeated sigh. "Oh. Great."

Jereth forced his hands back to the controls. He called up the sector maps and started to piece together a new route, avoiding whatever might be left of Zora Outpost. At least a dozen new orange zones had bubbled up on the map, marking sightings of Felen skirmishers.

Jereth hoped Leeg wouldn't comment on how closely their new route dipped toward those swathes of orange. He glanced back at the three bunk doors, saw they were still shut, and exhaled. No need to discuss this with the others. Not yet.

"Look... think of it this way," he said, finally meeting Leeg's eyes. "Maybe we're getting all our bad news out of the way early on, right? Luck's got to turn eventually."

"There's no such thing as luck, Jerry."

The *Jonah*'s skim engines rumbled as the ship accepted Jereth's course change, and the navigation display spun to their new heading.

Jereth forced a smile. "Trust me. From now on, everything will go just fine."

His PREDICTION HELD for precisely eighty-seven minutes.

And then, every light, display and console on the *Jonah*'s bridge winked out at once as the skim engines stuttered and jolted into a sudden shutdown.

So much for luck.

SHAAN
Research Vessel RV ZC-2812 *ZeyCorp Gallion*

SHAAN SAT AT an empty table in the *Gallion*'s canteen, staring at the urgent message alert blinking on her bracelet. She weighed up the consequences of ignoring it like she'd ignored the first one, and the second. But this was Director Barnabyn's third message, and after three would come the voice-call. She didn't want to wait for that, not with the Director of Administration in such a foul mood.

She sighed and fished in her pocket for her ZeyCorp badge, wiping a smudge from one corner before she clipped it to her collar. The company logo gleamed brightly over her uninspiring title: *Facilities Coordinator*. Shaan hardly ever bothered with the badge unless she was leading a formal tour, but the captain's directive had been clear: full uniform, at all times. Everything had to be kept in perfect order for their diplomatic visitors.

As if a Felen Ambassador would care about a corporate badge. Shaan couldn't understand what the Ambassador was doing on a ship like this in the first place. The *Gallion* was a mobile research facility for hire, a corporate science ship that delved long months into deep space so the researchers who paid for ZeyCorp's services could run experiments. The decks usually teemed with people: scientists and their entourages, interns, engineers and equipment techs. But between rotations, there was a turnover when the ship was nearly emptied. Now, the *Gallion* was stripped down to its core crew, and the only guest apartment in use was the one occupied by the Ambassador.

The Ambassador was on the way to a summit in mainspace, and ZeyCorp had leapt at the opportunity for one of their ships to ferry a Felen dignitary. A hundred and fifty-two years had passed since the Peace of Etraxas and the end of the war, but Felen were rarely seen by human civilians. Diplomatic matters were normally conducted out in the border sectors—not on corporate science ships.

The week before the Ambassador's arrival had been filled with frenzied preparations. Everyone in the *Gallion*'s core crew got a lesson in Felen diplomatic protocols, and Director Barnabyn had insisted that they all recite the list of rules aloud.

Always address the interpreter, never the Ambassador directly.
Do not walk beside the Ambassador.
Do not turn your back to the Ambassador.
Do not touch the Ambassador.
Do not eat or drink in front of the Ambassador...

Shaan had repeated the protocols to Barnabyn's satisfaction, then promptly deleted the list from her lightpad. She intended to avoid the diplomatic visitors altogether. Even though she usually led the ship's tours, on this occasion Director Barnabyn wanted to take care of every detail himself, and Shaan had barely tried to feign disappointment.

This would be over soon. The *Gallion* wasn't far from its next scheduled stop, where more crew and new researchers would come on board. There, the Ambassador would disembark, and she'd never have to think about any of this again. Soon.

That is, if the ship's engines ever started working again.

Shaan pushed the thought of the Felen Ambassador from

her mind. She tapped her bracelet to acknowledge Barnabyn's message, then called the nearest lift and descended to the Engineering deck.

Some small part of her still hoped that the Engineering team had overlooked something obvious, that this engine malfunction wasn't as bad as it seemed. But hours had passed since the incident, and the ship remained disconcertingly silent. No one had uploaded an incident report yet, much to Director Barnabyn's chagrin.

Shaan emerged from the lift on the upper level of the Engineering deck. There was no one in sight. The consoles that controlled the ship's scientific arrays were switched off, and the oblong meeting-table sat empty, its projection surfaces dark. She walked to the edge of the upper deck's outcropping, looking over the rail into the Engineering pit.

Arranged around the lower level were more semi-circular banks of workstations, each with a garish purple seat that swung out sideways. Most of those seats were empty, too, and only a half-dozen consoles were in use. The engineers were engrossed in scrolling columns of glowing diagnostics, and no one looked up as Shaan walked down the stairs into the pit.

Uma Ozakka, Director of Engineering, was examining a stream of data at one of the main control consoles. The director perched on the very edge of the chair, tugging on a loose curl of her dark hair, twisting it around her finger the way she always did when she was deep in thought. Or when she was absolutely furious.

Shaan paused at the bottom of the stairs. Ozakka hardly looked in the mood to be delivered one of Director Barnabyn's pointless directives.

"I don't see why we can't connect to the gods-damned network," Ozakka said, shoving the wayward curl behind one ear. "And all these energy pulses... Dean, these numbers don't make any sense! We must have a sensor malfunction, too."

Dean, the *Gallion*'s AI, pivoted in the adjacent seat. The android's smooth, silvery face rearranged itself into a mildly annoyed expression. "There is no sensor malfunction, Director. The data is unusual, but it is correct. Four independent arrays all report the same fluctuations." Dean touched the side of the console with one finger, and a column of data bloomed from the projection surface in front of Ozakka. "Have a look."

The AI was embedded within the *Gallion*'s ship-net, and really didn't require an android body to interact with the crew. Still, all ZeyCorp vessels were equipped with a top-of-the-line android chassis. The company loved to brag about it, and Director Barnabyn insisted that Shaan mention it at the beginning of every ship tour. *Be sure to mention the top-of-the-line chassis, Shaan. Say it just like that. Tell them about the latest upgrades.*

Dean's chassis wasn't exactly human-looking—years of focus group feedback had shown that people were more comfortable interacting with androids that didn't look *too* realistic—but the current model was newly-upgraded with extra facial expressions and tones of voice. The glossy humanoid had articulated joints and round, emotive eyes that blinked more often when Dean disapproved of something.

"Your thoughts, Director Ozakka?" the android prompted.

The director was still frowning at the sensor data. "Recalibrate the whole sensor grid, Dean. Reset everything and start again. I want to double-check this."

"Yes, Director. I'll begin now." Dean paused for a beat, then blinked three times in succession. Shaan considered interrupting the conversation there, but before she could say anything, Dean emitted one of the high-pitched, electronic chirrups that preceded a corporate alert message.

"Director Uma Ozakka," the android said officiously,

"I must remind you once more that you haven't taken your company-mandated breaks today. You are currently in breach of ZeyCorp overtime regulations."

"Seriously?" Ozakka snorted a laugh. "This is hardly the time for company bureaucracy."

The android's head straightened. "I am quite serious, Director. You were warned about working extra hours without approval during the last rotation. The captain has not authorized overtime for you, so I'm afraid any further infractions will have to be recorded in the ZeyCorp system. If you haven't logged out and taken your break within the next—"

"I get it, Dean, thank you." Ozakka flicked off the console display and the glowing data abruptly dispersed. She held her hands up. "Look. I'm going, see? I logged out."

"A wisely considered choice, Director."

"I'll speak to the captain," she said with a sigh. "We'll be needing a few overtime authorizations today."

Ozakka started toward the bottom of the stairs where Shaan was standing. She stared at the floor, muttering under her breath with each long stride. Shaan couldn't quite catch the words, but she knew Ozakka well enough to guess at the string of curses hissing past her lips.

The director let out her breath with a long sigh, righting herself just before she ran into Shaan.

"Oh! Shaan, gods!" Ozakka gasped. "How long have you been down here?" She took Shaan's arm and turned her toward the stairs without waiting for an answer. "I'm on my way out for a *company-mandated* break. Come with me. We need to talk outside."

Shaan followed Ozakka up the stairs, back out the main doors and into the corridor. When the director turned to face her, Shaan's stomach knotted uncomfortably. She'd never known Ozakka to look this nervous. Her eyes were bright with anxiety, and there was a fevered sheen in the warm brown of her cheeks. She was tugging on her hair again, twisting that one beleaguered strand around her index finger. The rest of her hair was gathered up on top of her head, a flurry of dark waves caught in a hastily-placed hairband that looked as stressed as she did.

"What is it?" Shaan whispered. "Something's really wrong with the ship, isn't it?"

"I've never seen anything like this." Ozakka's voice was tight. "As far as we can tell, the engines are fine, but the cores aren't firing for some reason. It's like there's a damper on the core reaction." She dropped both her hands to her sides, rolling her shoulders. "Gods, talk about bad timing. Terrible luck. Of course the damn ship breaks down when we've got a Felen diplomat on board."

Shaan winced. "Uh, about that..." She glanced down at her bracelet. "Director Barnabyn's been trying to get a hold of Central, to get some official guidance about how to handle this situation. You know, with the... Ambassador." Shaan spoke slowly, steadying her voice over the last word. "We can't get through to anyone. All the external comms channels are dead."

"Yeah. We know. We're investigating that, too." Ozakka grimaced. "The sensors are picking up weird activity on the shields. It's like the ship's being hammered by some kind of anomalous subspace energy, dozens of small pulses. And we can't get our network connections back."

"Is that what caused the engine malfunction? These energy pulses?"

"I can't say for sure, but I don't think it's a coincidence," said Ozakka. "We were cruising in low skim, all systems normal... and the next second, bam! Everything went out. We lost the engines, the comms, the main power grid, all of it. We're on emergency power."

"Barnabyn wants me to remind you that you haven't submitted an incident report," Shaan said.

Ozakka made a face. "Oh, sure. I've got a fraction of a crew down here, working on a ship-wide breakdown, and your dear boss thinks we have time to fill out a report?" She looked down at her wrist, where her bracelet was flickering with urgent info-alerts. "No chance."

"I figured." Shaan sighed. "So… what do you want me to tell him?"

"What do I *want* you to tell him?" Ozakka's mouth twisted wryly, then she growled a brief volley of Anvaelian. She'd never taught Shaan this particular phrase, but a few of the choice words were familiar enough. Something about being turned into piss where one stood.

Shaan imagined the Director of Administration melting into a puddle in front of his desk, and she almost smiled. "Okay. Now, how about something I can say out loud without getting fired?"

"Tell him everything is under control," Ozakka said. "And that I'm on my way to deliver the incident report, directly to the captain. Right after the captain approves my damned overtime override, so I can get back to work—" She stopped abruptly and dropped her voice. "Shit. Don't look behind you. It just got worse."

Shaan glanced over her shoulder just in time to see Zel stepping out of the lift. Zel was the especially obnoxious Publicity Liaison that ZeyCorp Central had sent to oversee the Ambassador's visit. He was here to coordinate with the media when the ship arrived at its destination, and to approve any press releases. But the only thing he'd done so far was file several complaints about the food and beverage options in the *Gallion*'s vending machines.

"His royal highness, the publicity prince," Ozakka muttered. "What does he want?"

Zel had the kind of remarkable good looks and intimidating presence that immediately drew attention. He wore the same dull purple two-piece as the rest of the ZeyCorp staff, with the same corporate badge hanging at his collar, but he somehow managed to make it look striking. His glossy black hair was parted to one side, waxed and pinned back into two little coils; his flawless bronze skin shone over sweeping cheekbones in a perfectly-proportioned face.

As he approached, Zel flashed the kind of practised smile that would look more at home on an aristocrat's portrait. "Director Ozakka, ah! Might I have a word with you?"

"Sorry. I'm on a company-mandated break," Ozakka said, managing to sound at once annoyed and relieved. "You'll have to come back later."

Zel's expression clouded with confusion. He probably wasn't used to being rebuffed.

"Director, this matter is very urgent."

"Yes, well, so are the engine diagnostics. I'm on my way to ask the captain to approve my overtime, so I can get back to fixing the ship." Ozakka stepped past him. "Come back later."

"This concerns the engine diagnostics!" Zel said, stepping back into her path. "Any further delay is unacceptable. I'm running out of excuses." He inhaled sharply. "Director Ozakka, I'd like *you* to brief the Ambassador on the situation. In person."

Ozakka looked incredulous. "Me? I haven't got time for that!"

"I'll take one of your engine specialists, then," Zel insisted. "I need to reassure the Ambassador that we're taking this seriously."

Ozakka sidestepped him again. "Look, there's a grand total of eight engineers down there right now, and everybody is *busy*. Do you want the engines fixed or not?"

Zel's haughty jaw tensed, but his eyes were practically

pleading. "Director, I must insist that you accompany me. I can't express just how important this is!"

Ozakka sighed. She looked over at Shaan, then reached out and plucked the ZeyCorp badge from Shaan's uniform, simultaneously pulling off her own Engineering badge.

Zel's eyes widened.

"Here you go," Ozakka said, clipping her badge to Shaan's collar. "Here's your Director of Engineering, ready to brief the Ambassador. In person. With whatever update you want." And then, under her breath to Shaan: "Sorry about this. I owe you one."

Shaan's heart jerked into her throat.

"The Ambassador?" she whispered. "What? No, I... I can't brief the Ambassador—"

"You can," said Ozakka, patting her shoulder. "Just say the same thing you were about to say to Barnabyn. It's complete shit either way. Good luck, *Director.*"

SHAAN WALKED WORDLESSLY alongside Zel. Her heart was still pounding in her throat, and she had to quicken her step to keep pace with him when they exited the lift on the residential deck. He didn't slow down.

"Are you a good liar, Shaan?" he asked.

Shaan swallowed painfully. "I'm... I'm adequate."

"Good. It shouldn't be difficult. The Ambassador won't be interested in any technical details, so keep it simple."

She nodded. "Mm-hm."

"This whole endeavour is very important to me," Zel said. "Professionally and personally. I have a lot riding on this... as does the company. We can't make mistakes."

"Mm-hm." Shaan was scarcely breathing, but he didn't seem to notice her nerves.

"It's been a great honour for me to meet a Felen Ambassador," he continued. "My ancestors have such a long history of service to the Peace.... you know, it was my family who appointed the Negotiator to broker the truce at Etraxas! My great-grandparents stood in the Decipherer's presence! Can you imagine that? They might even have seen the *Jonah*!"

In the atrium on the *Gallion*'s Command deck, a commemorative plaque honoured the Peace between the Union and the Felen Starhold. *In Grateful Remembrance of the Peacemakers of the Great Ship Jonah,* it said. Above it hung an art piece representing the Fortunate Five, the unlikely saviours of humanity.

"Mm-hm," said Shaan, her eyes still on the floor.

"Well, perhaps you wouldn't understand," Zel said. "But as a Blessed Scion of Etraxas, there is nothing more humbling than to play some small part in the ongoing work of the Peace. We are doing the very work begun by the Fortunate Five!"

Zel stopped outside the guest suite where they'd installed the Ambassador. This was one of the ship's largest apartments, a multi-room space usually reserved for lead researchers. But even the *Gallion*'s best accommodation was barely the size of a modest room on a typical passenger ship.

"You've memorized the Felen diplomatic protocols?" Zel whispered, studying her anxiously.

She nodded.

"All of them? Remember, the Felen custom is to proceed into a room in order of rank. So I'm going to enter first, and then you'll—"

"I've got it, okay?" She tried to keep the nerves out of her voice.

Before Zel could reply, the door slid open, revealing the slender silhouette of the Ambassador's interpreter just inside the room. The young Voiced stood as still and impassive as a statue, as though she'd been in that exact spot all along. She wore a thin, floor-length robe in the Felen informal style, its pale sleeves covered with intricate rows of embroidery. Her black hair was scraped away from her forehead, tucked under a wide band of fabric that joined the neck of her robe.

"The Ambassador has been waiting for you," she said softly.

Her olive skin was unadorned with any holos or cosmetics, and she wore no jewelry except for the glittering kennai ornament suspended against her forehead. That symbol marked her as one of the Felen's chosen—genetically altered, no longer solely human. The Voiced all existed in that strange suspension between two identities, just as the Decipherer once had.

"Hello, Gida," Zel said, raising a palm to her. "It's good to see you again." He gestured toward Shaan. "I've brought the Director of Engineering to apprise the Ambassador of our situation."

"Hello, Director," said the Voiced, turning slowly toward Shaan. "Thank you so much for coming. Please... join us inside."

Most humans found the Voiced unsettling, if not downright disturbing. Over time, they all seemed to acquire the same serene, mask-like expression, a blank resting stare that concealed their true emotions while they were working. Still, this Voiced looked incredibly young, and was undoubtedly inexperienced. Despite her neutral expression, there was something skittish about her, like she was about to turn and take flight.

Gida beckoned them forward with a small motion of her hand, and Shaan took a step through the doorway, cutting in front of Zel.

"I'm a *director*," Shaan whispered, shooting him a look over her shoulder. "Order of rank."

Zel opened his mouth, then closed it again. He followed her into the room.

Inside the Ambassador's guest suite, not a single light was switched on. If it weren't for the engines stopping, the earlier power outage might have gone unnoticed here. It took a moment for Shaan's eyes to adjust to the low light before she could make out what was in front of her.

All the furnishings had been removed from the main room—quite some effort, since most of the ZeyCorp-issued furniture in these rooms was bolted down. There were indentations in the floor where the bolts had been, and the rectangular outlines of storage hutches and table fittings were still visible along the walls. Thick tapestries glowed with Felen designs. The floor was completely bare, with the exception of a small circular rug laid down in the centre of the room.

And on that rug sat the Felen Ambassador.

The Ambassador's back was turned to the door, layers of dark robes obscuring the spindly-limbed figure. The alien's elongated head and neck were ensconced under a huge beaded headpiece.

"I will speak for the Ambassador now," said Gida. "From this moment, my voice will become the Ambassador's voice. Do you understand?"

"We do," said Zel.

The room was heavy with an unnatural silence, and Shaan heard nothing but the sound of her own ragged breathing. Sweat beaded at her temples. There wasn't a flicker of motion from the pile of robes.

Gida turned and tilted her head toward the Ambassador. Then her irises slowly rolled back into her head as she transmitted a soundless, telepathic message to the alien. Her empty gaze remained fixed on some invisible point in the distance.

Goosebumps crawled along Shaan's arms.

"We grow concerned that we haven't resumed our journey," Gida said, her voice low and toneless. "It has been a long time since the engines stopped."

Shaan tore her eyes from the Ambassador, looking back at Gida as she replied.

"The ship is having some... minor technical problems." Shaan's shaking voice echoed in the empty room. "We've encountered an... anomalous energy field. It's preventing our engine cores from firing."

"We need assurance that you will fix this problem soon, and that we are not in danger."

"We're working on a solution," Shaan said. "We... we have state-of-the-art engine monitoring systems and diagnostics. And ZeyCorp has the highest safety ratings of any corporate fleet. You're very safe with us." Barnabyn would be proud of that one.

"You must advise us if this risks delaying our arrival at the summit," said Gida.

"That won't happen," Zel interjected. "We'll be back under way in one hour. And we'll pick up speed to make up the delay. Isn't that right, Director?"

Shaan bit her lip. "We... we'll do our best."

"There is one more thing," the Voiced said. "We are experiencing difficulties using our communication devices."

"Oh?" Shaan feigned surprise.

"We can't seem to reach the external network. Our messages all remain unsent."

"I apologize, Ambassador," Shaan said. "I'll, ah... I'll get someone to look into that right away."

"We give you our thanks, Director. Please keep us informed."

When the Voiced blinked and opened her eyes again, she looked genuinely relieved. She glanced at the Ambassador's back. The Felen still hadn't moved.

"I think that will be all," Gida whispered in her normal voice. "You may leave us."

When they'd exited the Ambassador's suite, Shaan leaned

against the wall in the corridor, her knees shaking. She closed her eyes and hugged her arms to her chest, trying to breathe deeply, but her heart felt like it was trying to tunnel out of her ribcage.

"Well done," Zel said. "I think they bought it. You can relax now."

"Relax?" Shaan blinked at him in disbelief. "And what happens in one hour, when the engines still aren't fixed? Then what? Why would you tell them that?"

Zel drew himself up to his full height. "We'll be under way by then," he said, as if he was willing the fact into existence. "In one hour."

UMA
Command Deck, *ZeyCorp Gallion*

UMA WATCHED AS Captain Olghan Fransk completed a slow, contemplative circuit of his office, his footsteps clicking over the purple tiled floor. Fransk was a tall, broad man, made even taller by the thick-heeled black boots of his dress-uniform. He usually carried himself with the kind of determined set to his wide shoulders that came with years of responsibility. But today there was a slump in his posture, and that made Uma almost as uneasy as the latest round of engine core diagnostics.

Fransk circled back to his desk. He adjusted the front of his formal purple blazer as he sat down, straightening the crisp collar adorned with ZeyCorp insignia. The company dress-uniform was reserved for special occasions and publicity ops, but the captain had been dressing this way ever since the Ambassador came on board.

"Olghan," Uma sighed, fighting to keep the exasperation from her voice. She didn't have a hope of keeping it together if Fransk couldn't. "Would you just take a breath and calm down?"

"That depends on whether you're here to tell me you've fixed the engines," he said flatly. "Please tell me you've got something. It's been hours, Uma."

He never addressed her by her given name, except in private. In front of anyone else, it was always *Director Ozakka*, it was brisk nods and strict business. He preferred not to get too personal with any of his staff, and sometimes she thought he resented the fact that they had a shared history. But in moments like these—when things went to pieces—he treated her the way he always used to, as his closest confidante and oldest friend.

She followed Fransk's gaze to the wide, oblong window. There was nothing out there, of course. Just darkness.

He looked back to her, his eyes hopeful. "Well? Anything?"

For an instant, she pictured Fransk as he'd been when they first met: the ambitious young student with his whole career mapped out, always in that blue jacket with their school's glyph on the back, his curly hair pulled into tight criss-crossed braids like most of the popular politicians were wearing. Olghan Fransk had the patience and tenacity to navigate a corporate bureaucracy. Her, not so much. She never would have imagined they'd end up working for the same megacorp.

"Sorry, no engine fix yet. We're still trying," she said. "We'll have to run more diagnostics on the cores, more tests on this energy field. I need you to give me another overtime override."

"Gods." Fransk's voice was hoarse with exhaustion. "How could this happen? We're supposed to have state-of-the-art monitoring systems, aren't we? That's what our adverts say."

"Well, we have a great record, all things considered," Uma said defensively. "This ship's gone years without a major technical incident. The *Gallion*'s one of the most reliable ships in the fleet."

"Exactly! Years without any issues... but now? Now, when we have a Felen Ambassador on board, we have... *this?*" Fransk squeezed his eyes shut. "Ugh. This kind of thing is exactly why I never wanted to go into space."

Fransk was more at ease with the intricacies of this company than anyone else Uma knew, but he was no spacefarer. Taking a captaincy in deep space had been an endurance test for him.

"I remember when you swore you'd never take a space posting under any circumstances," Uma said. "You told me they'd have to drag you into that captain's chair kicking and screaming."

"I guess I had some gods-damned sense back then," Fransk said bitterly. "They pressured me into taking this job, and you know it! A great career opportunity, they said. Just put in some time in space, make a few rotations with a flagship captaincy, and you'll be in line for a ZeyCorp chancellorship!" He sighed. "Just think... next year, I could've been sitting in a nice office at Central, planetside, with an ocean view."

"And you still will," Uma said. "Come on. ZeyCorp's hardly going to sack you because we had an engine malfunction! It's not even our fault; it's this energy field—"

Fransk's shoulders sagged. "No. This publicity stunt with the Ambassador... this was important. It had to go off without a hitch. If we don't make that summit, it'll be a PR disaster, and they'll have to find someone to blame. Central will have all our heads for this: you, me, Barnabyn..."

Uma frowned. "What's up with Central and this whole Ambassador-ferrying saga, anyway? You know anything you haven't told me?"

"Oh, just the usual ZeyCorp scheming from up high." Fransk gave another sigh. "Big money, of course. Apparently, they've got potential investors hanging on the idea of building a direct corporate relationship between ZeyCorp and the Alliance. The company wants to secure early access to any new Felen science tech. This was the first step... and now we've gone and screwed it up."

"Damn it. I'm sorry, Olghan."

He stared at the dark window for a while before he looked back at her again.

"Just tell me, straight up," he said. "How bad is it?"

Uma shifted her feet. "Well, the engine problem itself... that part's frustrating," she said, carefully selecting her words. "But the thing that's actually scaring me is how we've lost contact with the network. We've been trying all this time, and we can't get back online. We can't reach anybody."

Fransk's brow furrowed. "Because of the interference from the energy field?"

"It's not just that. Noussen found a way to filter out most of the interference, and we're picking up live data from our hover probes again. We should be broadcasting and receiving. But... it looks like there's nothing else out there."

"What do you mean, there's nothing else out there?" Fransk's frown deepened.

"There aren't any signals to pick up. It's like the whole network just vanished. And we can't detect any of the nearest stars where they should be. We can't detect any stars at all."

"But... then... where are we?"

"I don't know. Nobody likes that answer, but we have no idea. We weren't even at an eighth of our max skim speed when the engines went, and we didn't make any jumps. We shouldn't be more than a few hundred thousand klicks from where we last pinged the network! I can't explain it. It's like the ship just... slipped. And now we're somewhere else." She paused. "Or we're in some kind of gap between *wheres*."

Fransk shuddered visibly.

"We've started calling this place... the Rift," she said. The word felt foreboding in her mouth.

The captain mumbled something low under his breath that sounded like an invocation. He wasn't a particularly religious sort, and the last time Uma had ever seen him pray was when he'd forgotten to study for a university exam. But now he flicked his fingers in a quick gesture of prayer, just under the edge of the desk, as if he thought she might not notice it.

"Look, we'll solve this, Olghan. We'll get through it." She leaned across the desk to rest her hand on his purple sleeve. "But it might take a bit more time."

"Time is the one thing we haven't got." He twirled open a virtual console on his desk and keyed in two passcodes, looking pained. "There. You have your overtime override, Director Ozakka. Take a short break, and you can get back on the system in one hour." His gaze met hers. "This is the last override the system will let me give you, so... please, for the love of all the gods, make this one count."

UMA'S FOOTSTEPS ECHOED strangely as she walked down the deserted corridor. The ship was always unsettlingly silent when they were in turnover, and it was worse than ever without the calming hum of the engines.

She seethed at the indignity of being ordered to take a break at a time like this, when Engineering had less than a quarter of its usual complement. The odds that they'd find a fix before the overtime overrides ran out were slim-to-none. But a tired crew was an unproductive crew, and they all desperately needed rest.

When Uma unlocked her apartment on the residential deck, the music track she'd been listening to picked right up where she'd paused it. The instrumental medley sounded almost mockingly cheerful now, chirping along as if nothing had changed since she'd left for work. She dismissed the music and turned on the ambient lights, illuminating the single rectangular room of her living-quarters.

There was little space for sentiment in the *Gallion*'s crew apartments. Each staff member had the same average, utilitarian room: a bed, a few storage compartments, a table and chairs. The rooms all had the same tacky furniture, bolted firmly to the floor so it couldn't be moved. Most of it had a ZeyCorp logo emblazoned somewhere on it. This ship was never meant to be a place you got emotionally attached to. And yet, over the years Uma had spent here, the *Gallion* had started to feel a bit like a home.

She zipped off her boots, arching her feet as she shook them free. Her muscles were taut with tension; her head was pounding. She contemplated throwing herself face-down on the bed, but first she went to the low shelf where she kept her few personal effects.

There were her half-dozen fragile old books, their faded spines facing out, each book enclosed in an airtight clear container to preserve the delicate pages. Beside those stood the miniature model spaceship that she'd built long ago—a scale model of the Fortunate Five's famous ship, the *Jonah*. And next to that was the last gift her father had given her before he died, a rare bottle of Etraxan agnathe on a gold-brushed stand.

She touched each of the items in turn, running her fingers over them. Everything felt oddly brittle to her since they'd entered the Rift, like it was all a breath away from disappearing.

At the end of the shelf was a picture of her father in a heavy wooden frame. She brushed her fingers over her father's face, staring intently at the picture. Every detail was already burned into her mind: her father's wide, dark eyebrows sweeping over serious eyes, a strong nose so much like her own, waves of thick hair that fell to his shoulders, his smooth brown skin unlined except for a scattering of wrinkles around his eyes. He wore his work uniform, a navy blue shirt with silver constellations embroidered on the sleeves. A slim lanyard bore the badge that identified him as a curator of Anvaelia's branch of the *Jonah* Museum. The lanyard itself was peppered with colourful pins from the various historical societies he'd belonged to.

Uma could remember everything about this picture perfectly. But could she remember *him* as clearly as she once had? Could she recall the sound of his voice echoing in one of the Museum's long halls? Could she remember what Papa had looked like in motion, striding through the door to his office? She tried to call his image to mind, but the memory felt as fragile as those crumbling books.

There was a time when she used to speak aloud to her father whenever things went wrong. She had often held half a conversation with this picture, asking for Papa's advice, pretending he was still listening. But she hadn't spoken to the picture in a long while, and she couldn't think of anything to ask him now.

Instead, she lay back on her bed, closed her eyes, and let her mind grow as blank as possible.

And then, her bracelet chimed.

"Director Ozakka, I'm sorry to interrupt," came Dean's voice. "But we've just picked up a transmission."

"Oh!" Uma's heart leapt with relief. "Thank the gods. What kind of transmission? Is the network back?"

"I'm afraid the network is still unreachable, Director," the AI said. "But we are receiving a broad-band local distress call from another stranded ship. I've already alerted Captain Fransk."

"A distress call..." She exhaled slowly. That wasn't exactly good news, but it was reassuring to know that the rest of the universe hadn't vanished entirely. Of *course* it hadn't. "Play the transmission back for me, Dean."

"Certainly, Director. Here it comes."

The back of Uma's neck prickled as a crackling, garbled recording began to play.

"Calling all channels, we have an emergency! This is the civilian cargo hauler *Jonah*. Is anybody out there? We've had a complete systems failure... ran into some type of... unusual energy field... no power. If anyone's receiving this, we need immediate assistance. This is an emergency. I repeat, this is Eldric Leesongronski of the *Jonah*, requesting assistance."

There was a long silence, and then a second voice: "Ah, fuck. Give it up. I'm telling you, Leeg, there's nobody else out here."

The recording hissed, clicked twice, and the transmission ended.

JERETH
Pilar Deep Space Outpost
1 week before the Rift

JERETH SAT IN a dingy bar, ensconced in a small booth near the back. The place was populated with the usual cargo-outpost denizens: a mixture of hauler crews, scrap dealers, repair engineers, and a handful of merchants that fit various definitions of the word 'unscrupulous.' Half of the overhead lights were burned out, and the floor was sticky under Jereth's feet.

Still, for the first time in a long while, Jereth might have described his mood as 'relaxed.' His business on Pilar Outpost was all but completed. A docking token bearing the *Jonah*'s berth ID rested in his jacket pocket, alongside the card that contained his newly-validated cargo permits. There had been no problems clearing his cargo; the official who'd scanned the permits had barely glanced up.

A hundred and twenty crates—purporting to be a shipment of live squid—had already been loaded onto the ship. Miraculously, the cargo had all fit. Jereth smiled to himself.

"What're you smiling about?" Leeg grumbled, returning to the table with two glasses of agnathe in his hands. He wrinkled his nose. "Gods. I thought you said this was the best bar on Pilar."

"It's the *only* bar on Pilar, unless you go down to the lower level," Jereth said. "And trust me, you don't want to go down to the lower level."

As deep space cargo-stops went, Pilar was unremarkable: five stacked docking rings, held together by an off-kilter cylindrical core that had seen better days. The top two levels glowed with lights from mismatched hab-cubes occupied by the locals. Only a few cubes would be vacant, ready to be rented out at cutthroat prices to anyone desperate enough to get off their ship. The middle level was the marketplace, with its hodgepodge of supply shops, food stalls, traders and news terminals, and this one ramshackle bar. Below it were the cargo docks, and below that was a second marketplace, the one with wares of a less legal variety. Jereth knew the place well enough, but he was quietly relieved that he'd arrived with his counterfeits already in order.

Leeg put his elbows on the table as he sat down, then pulled them back abruptly, wiping at a streak of grime that stained the sleeve of his black jacket. He shoved one of the glasses toward Jereth, then sniffed the liquid in his own glass.

"They call this agnathe?" he muttered. "I thought I'd be glad to get off that garbage-ship, until I saw this place."

"Would you stop it? There's nothing wrong with the ship!" Jereth's mild annoyance didn't erase his smile.

"It's junk, Jerry! It's salvage, and it's falling apart."

"It *was* salvage," Jereth corrected. "It's been refurbished."

"I'll be shocked if we even survive this trip, never mind the rest of it. I seriously can't understand how you're not dead."

Jereth drew his shoulders back and laughed. "Same goes for you." His hand shook as he held his glass aloft, agnathe dripping inelegantly over his thumb. "Here's to us, huh? Still alive. Still undefeatable."

"To us. Still fools." Leeg swallowed a mouthful of spirits and grimaced. "Ugh. It's good to have you back, Jerry, but your judgement has not improved."

They sat mostly in silence after that, both of them lost in their thoughts, sipping slowly at the eye-watering drinks until they'd drained their glasses.

Jereth was contemplating getting up to order another, but before he could move, a stranger strolled over to their booth and casually sat down next to him.

"Hey! There you are!" the stranger said, one gloved hand closing over Jereth's arm. Her voice was loud, overly familiar, but it shook with nerves. "You been waiting for me long? I'm so sorry I'm late!"

Her face was surreal, its expression obscured by heavy cosmetic mods. Pale, reflective eyes gleamed from their sockets like small moons, with a pair of unnaturally sharp cheekbones jutting beneath them. Where her eyebrows should have been, a row of iridescent fish-scales gleamed bright as frost over her deep brown skin. A thick cold-weather coat concealed the rest of her shape, its high collar meeting the edges of a formless hat that was tied down over her ears. Her coat-sleeves were tucked into matching dark gloves.

"Pretend I'm with you," she whispered. "Please..." She glanced furtively behind her, and Jereth followed her gaze to the door.

There were two Union soldiers standing at the bar's entrance. Mid-ranked UWDF officers, by the look of them. Both deffies wore light body armour and carried at least one visible weapon, and an uneasy hush had fallen over the tables nearest the door.

The taller of the two officers remained by the door, bulky arms folded. Meanwhile, the second soldier entered the room and started walking among the tables, peering from side to side, like a predator watching for things that scurried.

"Jerry," Leeg said through his teeth, "*do* something."

Jereth turned back to the stranger. She was a problem he hadn't anticipated, but he certainly didn't owe any favours to the United Worlds Defence Forces.

"All right," he whispered to her. "Listen. You're with us... but since you're so late, you'll have to buy us a round to make it up to us. We're drinking agnathe." He gestured toward the bar, then held up his empty glass and wiggled it. "Drinks. Got me?"

The stranger blinked. Clearly, standing up again and walking across the room—right through the line of sight of the UWDF officer—hadn't been in her plans. But after a moment's hesitation, she nodded. She stood up from the bench, adjusted her hat and started toward the bar.

Leeg's eyes flashed. "Jerry..."

"What? I got her away from us, didn't I? Besides, we don't have any drinks." Jereth tilted his head in the direction of the officer still prowling among the tables. "I don't suppose the deffies came in here for a drink, though."

By the time their new friend started walking back toward them, three glasses of agnathe clutched in her hands, the officer was almost in front of their table.

The stranger looked back toward the door, where the other soldier was still standing guard. Then she took another step, and another one, her eyes fixed on Jereth and Leeg. She kept walking purposefully toward their booth, holding the drinks straight and steady until she clambered onto the bench next to Jereth.

Jereth pushed one toward Leeg, and they all lifted their glasses in a silent toast.

The officer stopped directly in front of the table.

Glanced at them once.

And then moved on to the next booth.

Whatever the deffies were after, they hadn't found it. The three of them sat huddled over their glasses, breaths half-held, until the officer had finally examined the last row of tables and loped back to the main door again. The two soldiers exchanged a few words, turned and left. A moment later, the hubbub of conversation and clinking glasses returned to the bar.

Beside Jereth, the stranger pulled off her lumpy hat, shaking out a mass of tiny silver-white braids. Then she turned her high coat-collar down, revealing the full extent of her cosmetic mods. The small fishscales above her eyes extended into bigger blueish ones that ran down her temples and along the sides of her neck. The tips of her earlobes were as long and slender as fingers, each ear dividing into six or seven points that stood out from the sides of her head. Her eyes glowed, their ice-pale irises ringed with smaller circles that slowly changed hue as she blinked.

In some cities, her mods would be unremarkable, just your usual oddities in fashion. A few tweaks of trendy genetic modification wouldn't have turned heads on Sëgra. But on a deep-space cargo outpost like this one, they didn't do much for her chances of blending in.

"Thanks," the stranger whispered. "I thought you looked like good people."

"I wouldn't be so sure," Leeg said. "You find many good people in bars like this?"

A brief look of worry crossed the stranger's face, but then she folded her gloved hands in front of her with a shaky smile. "I said you looked like good people, not *reputable* people."

Jereth smirked at that.

The stranger leaned forward. "I bet you have a ship docked here, don't you? And that you know how to keep your heads down... how to avoid getting searched? See, I really need a lift to the next outpost, and I thought maybe you—"

"No," spat Leeg. "We have no room." He shoved his half-finished agnathe aside. "Besides, the ship we've got is a junk-heap. It's unfit for human habitation."

"Don't listen to him. There's absolutely nothing wrong with

my ship," Jereth said, laughter in his voice. "We might be able to negotiate a price, if you need a ride. What're you offering?"

Negotiate a price? mouthed Leeg, livid.

The stranger exhaled with relief. "I, uh... I could pay you... three thousand creds?"

Jereth arched an eyebrow. "Three thousand?"

Passage on a low-budget carrier transport to the next outpost might cost half a thou, but that would require an ID check-in. Biometrics, most likely, and an image capture. And a tracking mark on her transit permit, which he'd be willing to bet she didn't have in the first place.

"What about four thousand?" she said quickly. "Or five. How about five?"

"Whoa, there!" Jereth chuckled. "I didn't even say no yet! You do understand how negotiation works, right?"

"Jerry, this is ridiculous! We don't have room for a hitchhiker," Leeg hissed.

"Please," the stranger said. "You have to help me. Five thousand is all I've got left on chits. And I don't know how to get a fake transit permit."

Aha. So he was right. No permit. There was a guy in the lower level who sold cheap but decent counterfeits—fakes that would probably do for an in-sector hop—and Jereth briefly contemplated telling her where to find him. But he didn't say anything.

The stranger peered at Jereth, her odd face imploring. "I can't withdraw any more chits here, not with the UWDF all over the place. But if you can get me off this outpost, to somewhere safe... then I'll pay you another twenty thousand when we get there," she said. "I promise."

"Oh... well! Now, that's a little better!" Jereth stroked his chin, holding back the huge grin that pulled at the corners of his mouth. This could be his lucky day after all. "I want the first five up front, though. Deal?"

"Deal," she said, beaming. "I'm Keila, by the way."

Jereth held up his hand. "That's great. I don't need to know any more than that," he said. "Whatever you're running away from, whatever you did to piss off the deffies... you can keep all that to yourself, understand? I don't want to know anything. Once you pay me, I'm gonna forget I ever saw you."

"Thank you," she whispered, fixing him with her ice-pale gaze. "I knew it. You *are* good people."

They left the bar with Keila walking between them. Her hat was tied on again, her coat pulled up tight to her chin, her shoulders hunched.

"This is a terrible idea," Leeg muttered. "We already have illegal cargo and now we're harbouring some kind of fugitive?"

"What can I say?" Jereth lifted his shoulders with a grin. "I'm always gonna be a gambler. Look at it this way, if that ship gets searched, we're fucked anyway, so what's the difference?"

Leeg just glared.

They made their way through two scarcely-staffed checkpoints, walking as fast as they dared without looking like they were in a hurry, and then took a capsule up to the docks.

Jereth stood in front of Keila as the capsule ascended, shielding her face from security cameras. She was taller than he was, but she slouched low in her big coat, her face turned against his shoulder. Leeg stood morosely beside them, both hands shoved in his pockets.

The capsule rose through the docking rings, passing between gaps in the leviathan metal scaffolds that made up the ship berths. The shadows of varyingly-shaped cargo haulers, shipping-tugs and salvage trawlers loomed large over their heads. There were three sleek UWDF cruisers docked side by side, their hulls gleaming as bright as mirrors under the floodlights, and Jereth clenched his jaw.

At last, the capsule slowed to a stop in front of the *Jonah*'s berth. The squat, sturdy ship sat lower on its anchors than it had a few hours earlier, resting at a slight tilt under the docking ring's erratic artificial gravity now that the cargo bay was fully loaded.

"That's my ship over there," Jereth said, pointing it out for Keila. "My engineer's probably still checking the systems over, but we'll take off shortly."

Dargo Mendeg, the ship's engineer, had been hired for this trip only. Mendeg wasn't privy to the contents of the cargo, or the full details of their journey. He wasn't exactly what you'd call pleasant-mannered, but he minded his own business and he'd been competent enough to hold the *Jonah* together so far.

Keila's gaze went up the *Jonah*'s patched, pitted hull, but she didn't say anything as they exited the capsule. There was no one on the concourse, not even one of the so-called inspectors who sometimes wandered around, threatening an extra permit check until you handed over a few chits.

The three of them started toward the ramp that led up into the *Jonah*'s berth, but stopped short when Leeg let out a strangled yelp.

"Stop! Hands behind your heads!" came a voice from Jereth's left. He whirled, and his spirits sank. To one side of the ramp stood a lone UWDF officer, brandishing a plasma pistol.

The officer wore a fancy Union blazer, her stiff collar piled with rows of military insignia. Her dark hair was closely shorn, like most high-ranking military types, and her forehead gleamed with a faint sheen of sweat.

She yanked Leeg's sleeve, pulling him off the ramp and motioning for him to get against the low wall behind her. "Hands behind your heads!" she repeated. "All of you, line up over here!"

Keila was trying to wriggle away from Jereth, wrenching herself out from under his arm. He tightened his grip on her coat, cursing under his breath. She would only attract more attention if she bolted.

"Don't," he whispered. "Don't run. Trust me."

"Move!" the deffie shouted. "Over here! Now! How many times do I need to tell you?"

Slowly, Jereth let go of Keila. He raised his hands and flashed the officer an unassuming smile. "I think there's been a little misunderstanding here. See, we're not—"

"Shut *up!*" the officer growled. "Shut your mouth unless I ask a question!"

Keila slouched against the wall next to Leeg, her shoulders sagging in defeat beneath the giant coat. Jereth followed.

He studied the deffie's face as he complied: small, wide-set eyes, a high forehead, olive skin, a softly rounded nose. There was an indentation above one of her nostrils, as though she'd recently removed a decorative piercing there. But most importantly, she had no visible implants, and no active communication devices clipped into her ears. There was a small chance she was up here on her own, but her companions wouldn't be far behind. Jereth didn't have much time.

The officer patted down Leeg's black jacket with her free hand, checking him for weapons, but her gun stayed trained on Jereth.

"We don't even know this person," Leeg said, bobbing his chin toward Keila. "I've never seen her in my life. She just sat down at our table, back at that bar. I've never—"

The officer jammed the gun against Leeg's throat. "Which part of 'shut up' didn't you understand? Gods almighty! Look... I'm not with the deffies, okay? I *am* the reason this place is crawling with them, though."

The officer peeled aside her military blazer, revealing three more weapons harnessed to her side—none of them regulation UWDF arms.

"What?" Leeg frowned in confusion.

Jereth examined the officer's uniform more closely. From the waist down, she was wearing plain clothes: light grey trousers that tapered at the ankles, a pair of short, square-toed blue work boots, and what looked like a mechanic's satchel clipped to her belt.

All civilian clothes, aside from the blazer.

Not a uniform. A disguise.

Jereth weighed up his options. He did have the small gun he always carried when they disembarked in a place like this, but he doubted he could get it halfway out of his jacket before the false officer took a shot. She was still brandishing her own weapon, her finger tense over the trigger.

"I heard you say that's your ship over there?" She jabbed her gun in the direction of the *Jonah*. "So here's what's going to happen. We're going to walk over there, all four of us together, like I'm escorting you for a cargo search. As soon as we're on board, I want you to unclamp immediately, launch your ship and get me off this outpost. Otherwise, you all die. Got it?"

"Right," said Jereth, nodding. "I think I got it."

"Don't try anything unwise," she said with a thin smile. "Start walking to the ship. Hands where I can see them."

"Well, this is just great," Leeg muttered. "Just fantastic, Jerry."

"No talking. Walk."

They walked in silence, single file, up the ramp to the ship. Jereth let the hijacker in first without further protest—not that he could do much else with that gun pressed to his cheek. With any luck, Mendeg would be on the other side of that door, and effectively armed.

As soon as the *Jonah*'s main door had hissed shut, before Dargo Mendeg had even noticed the extra people who'd climbed on board, the false officer charged into the ship and kicked the burly engineer hard in the knee.

Mendeg was a big man, stocky and broad, and he went down

with all the subtlety of a falling boulder. He grunted in shock as he hit the scuffed metal floor. "What the...?"

"Stay down, and show me your hands!" she shouted. "This is a hijacking!"

Mendeg rolled into a sitting position, his expression confused as he took in the hijacker's blazer and insignia. "Wait... we're getting hijacked by the UWDF?"

"Just do what she says, Mendeg," Jereth said with a sigh. "I'll explain later."

Jereth wasn't quite sure *what* he was going to explain later, but he wasn't about to explain anything right now.

The hijacker looked back again, her eyes lingering over Keila's bulky coat.

"You!" She pointed the gun at Keila. "Take off that coat and drop it. Then kneel down on the floor. All of you, get down!"

Keila hastily pulled off her gloves and unfastened the coat. She shrugged it off and let it fall, revealing bare shoulders and arms glistening with gold holo-tattoos that extended all the way down to her fingers. The coat clattered to the floor, its pockets heavy with whatever her worldly possessions might be.

"The hat, too," said the hijacker.

Keila tugged off the hat. Her multitude of silver-white braids spilled down her back, and those odd, many-pointed ears unfolded from her head as she dropped to her knees between Mendeg and Leeg.

Mendeg's eyes widened when he got a closer look at her. "Who in the five hells are you?"

"It's fine, this one's fine," Jereth said soothingly, kneeling on Mendeg's other side. "This one's all right. She's a paying passenger."

Mendeg looked bewildered. "A passenger?"

"Looks like this other one's trying to steal our ship, though," Jereth continued. "Hang on. I need a second to think."

The hijacker upended Keila's rumpled coat, shaking its contents out onto the floor, then stomped over it with the heel of her boot. She kicked at the scattered items with disinterest until she picked up a thick card-block full of credit chits.

"Hey!" Keila protested. "That's mine!"

"You mean *mine*," Jereth said. "Five thousand creds, right? Is there five thousand in there?"

The hijacker ignored him. She flipped through the card-block with one nail, then shoved it into her satchel.

"Start the procedures to unclamp this thing!" she ordered. She peered up into the dimly-lit bridge. "If this junker is even spaceworthy. Gods. Your ship looks like shit."

"Told you," Leeg muttered to Keila.

"I want you to stand up one at a time, understand?" the hijacker said. "When I tell you to, you'll walk into the bridge and go to your usual station."

Jereth's eyes flicked over to Leeg. Leeg was leaning forward slightly, giving Jereth a familiar, piercing look. A look they'd perfected years ago: *Ready. Give me a sign, Jerry.*

"I need to unlock the controls," Jereth said in the calmest voice he could manage. "I'm the only one who can do it. The ship's locked to me."

"Great," snapped the hijacker. "You first, then. Stand up."

Jereth moved with painstaking slowness, pulling himself from his knees into a crouch. He smoothed down the front of his jacket and stood partway up, surreptitiously feeling for the comforting shape of his gun. The hijacker's eyes were glued to him.

Then, in one fluid motion, Jereth plunged his hand into his jacket, pulled out the gun and threw it toward Leeg. Before the hijacker could react, Jereth dove forward, grabbed her around the waist and tackled her to the ground.

She screamed, and her weapon fired into the ceiling. A force field sparked angrily where the shot grazed the wiring. And then Mendeg was scrambling up to help, holding the hijacker down, wrenching the weapon out of her hands while Leeg stood over them with Jereth's gun.

Jereth sat back on the floor and slowly let out his breath. His hands were shaking.

Mendeg tore the UWDF blazer off the hijacker's back and used it to tie her arms firmly behind her. She spat in Mendeg's face, swearing at him the whole time as he dragged her to the wall and dropped her unceremoniously against it. He patted her down and relieved her of the rest of her weapons, then fished the card-block of chits out of her satchel.

"Damn well better be five thousand creds in there," Jereth said to Keila. "Don't think I won't count it."

"Ugh," Leeg groaned. "This trip is actually going to kill me."

"Hello. My name's Keila," Keila said, raising her palm to Mendeg with a hesitant smile. "I'm, uh... I'm the one that's *not* trying to steal your ship."

Mendeg said nothing back.

Keila retrieved her big coat, then started crawling over the floor on her hands and knees, collecting the things the hijacker had shaken out of her pockets.

Jereth reached out to pick up the nearest item. It looked like a child's toy—a shiny synthetic cube, every side identically smooth and white. He started to turn it over to take a better look, but Keila snatched it from his shaking fingers before he could get a grip on it.

"That's, uh... that's a souvenir. It's sentimental," she mumbled. "Thanks." She shoved the cube back into her coat pocket without looking at him.

Jereth shrugged, then scrambled up to his feet and motioned to Mendeg. "C'mon. We're gettin' out of here. Start prepping for ship launch."

"You're still dropping me off somewhere... right?" Keila asked quietly.

"We'll be passing Zora Outpost in a week or so, I reckon," said Jereth. "I can let you off there, if that'll do for you? Not that you've got much choice."

Keila nodded. "Sure, yeah. Zora's good. Anywhere's good."

"Great," said Jereth. "At Zora, we part ways. You get off my ship, you get me the rest of the money, and after that, we don't know you. None of this ever happened."

UMA
Engineering Deck, *ZeyCorp Gallion*

DESPITE ALL THE empty seats around the Engineering pit, Uma stood next to the captain as the rest of the crew filed in. With everyone assembled in one place, there was no denying just how tiny the *Gallion*'s turnover crew was.

The captain, two directors, eight engineers, Shaan, and Zel. Thirteen people and one android, that was everyone on board.

No. Fifteen people, Uma corrected herself. The Ambassador and the Voiced interpreter remained oblivious in their guest apartment. Uma couldn't imagine how anyone was going to tell the diplomatic contingent about *this*.

She looked around at the crew. Wazar, the equipment team lead, was clutching a steaming hot beverage to her chest like some kind of elixir, her shock of blue-grey hair in disarray. The Cordero siblings, both of them engine techs, looked dazed and bleary-eyed after hours of repeated engine core resets. Even Zel was out of sorts, hovering anxiously at the edge of the pit. His usually-perfect coif was flat on one side, as if he'd slept on it.

By the time Director Barnabyn appeared—dressed in his formal blazer, just like the captain—the crew was abuzz with speculative conversation. Outside of a drill, Captain Fransk had never invoked an emergency Full Staff Assembly.

"Crew of the *Gallion*," Fransk began. He drew in a long, laboured breath. "It's been many hours since the event that knocked out our engines, and we haven't yet restored our connection to the network. We don't know if our signals relaying our position have reached anyone. We have no idea where we are." He paused. "We have a long list of serious problems. But none of those are the reason I called this assembly."

Fransk's gaze lingered on Uma for a moment, and she gave him a small, encouraging nod.

"The *Gallion* has picked up another ship's distress call," Fransk continued. "Dean alerted me and the directors. But... as our current crew is so small, I want to share what we know with all of you before we make any decisions."

A confused whisper rustled through the room.

"The transmission we received is of human origin, albeit using an antiquated comms protocol. It is the only external signal of any kind that we've received since our ship entered the energy field." Fransk turned to the android. "Dean? Show us the ship scan."

Dean tapped two smooth fingers together to call up a projection. As it unfolded above the android's hand, the image slowly resolved and enhanced, and the outline of a ship appeared.

An unsettlingly familiar ship. The back of Uma's neck prickled again.

"I've isolated the source of the signal and located the ship, eighty klicks away," the android said. "You will note that this image quality is unusually poor. That is due in part to the interference from the energy field, but the ship also has two scan-jamming devices mounted on its cargo bay. The devices are of an extremely old make and quite inefficient, so this hasn't prevented us from mapping their hull."

The image zoomed in and rotated. "It appears to be a small civilian ship," Dean continued. "The hull profile suggests a short-haul freighter, 00Y class—a common war-era vessel. The best-known ship of this type is undoubtedly the one that carried the Fortunate Five to Etraxas at the end of the war. The *Jonah*."

Uma thought of the small, silvery model of the *Jonah* that sat on the shelf in her apartment, and a chill squirmed down her spine.

"Of course, the *Jonah* was a very ordinary ship for its time. There were thousands made exactly like it." The android paused. "Most of them would be long out of service by now, but a few may still be spaceworthy if they were well-maintained. This could also be a modern replica of the *Jonah*."

"Replay the transmission, Dean," Fransk said.

The android's head bobbed, and the crackling recording began to play.

"Calling all channels, we have an emergency! This is the civilian cargo hauler *Jonah*. Is anybody out there? We've had a complete systems failure... ran into some type of... unusual energy field... no power. If anyone's receiving this, we need immediate assistance. This is an emergency. I repeat, this is Eldric Leesongronski of the *Jonah*, requesting assistance."

A garbled pause, then that second voice: "Ah, fuck. Give it up. I'm telling you, Leeg, there's nobody else out here."

No one made a sound for a solid minute after the recording had ended.

And then Wazar spoke for them all, her voice low and breathless. "Um... what the fuck?"

Fransk was fidgeting with the collar of his purple blazer. He didn't say anything.

"Surely we can't take this seriously!" said Barnabyn. The Director of Administration was a peevish man with an immaculately groomed beard and sparse black hair that he kept combed flat to his head. He had the demeanour of a perpetually disappointed schoolteacher. "Is this meant to be some kind of prank?"

"The authenticity of this message is doubtful, Director Barnabyn, for obvious reasons," Uma said. Her voice came out a lot shakier than she'd expected. "But there *is* a ship out there, eighty klicks away. And if it's anywhere near as old as it looks, their life support systems are probably failing. They won't have enough shielding to survive this energy field."

"How do we know there's really a ship there at all?" said Barnabyn. "I'm not sure I trust our instruments anymore."

"Well, someone must have sent that transmission." Uma gestured at the glowing image of the ship. "And what about the hull scan? Look there. That's a ship."

A chatter of voices erupted from the crew, all interrupting each other, their exhaustion forgotten as they shouted out increasingly outlandish theories.

Maybe all of this was an elaborate hoax. Maybe it was some kind of secret psych experiment being conducted by ZeyCorp. Maybe it was a hallucinogenic experience that the crew were all sharing. Maybe everyone on the *Gallion* had actually died hours ago during the initial incident, and they just hadn't accepted that they were dead yet. That last theory was from Macey the engine tech, ever the pessimist.

Fransk looked exasperated.

"Stop!" the captain said, clapping his hands together. "Everyone! Stop. That's enough. Nobody in this room is dead. I assure you, we are all alive right now, and we need to be doing something constructive."

"Captain, have you considered the possibility that the transmission might be... authentic?" said Zel, rising out of his seat. "Everything about what we're experiencing is already strange. First we can't find any stars, then we can't figure out where we are... and now we have a ship from the wrong time?" He looked around uncomfortably. "If we have no idea where we are... can we be sure *when* we are?"

"That's absolutely absurd. You're not seriously suggesting that ship could be the real *Jonah*?" Barnabyn shook his head emphatically. "Impossible."

Wazar looked intrigued. "Hmm. If we ran into some kind of rare anomaly, I guess we could have travelled back in time. I mean, it's unproven, but it *is* theoretically possible to find space-time irregularities in the subspace layer. We could even be completely outside the flow of time."

Macey made a horrified face.

"Or... maybe we're just seeing an echo of events that already happened ages ago, playing back."

"There's nothing like this in the historical accounts of the *Jonah's* voyage," Uma said. "No mention of the *Jonah* running into an anomalous energy field, or losing power, or making a distress call... I suppose it's possible, given how unreliable the records are, but—"

"I'm sorry to interrupt, Director," Dean said, "but I've continued to intensify our scans, and the vessel has only a single backup power cell. It's nearly drained. Their life support systems appear to be struggling. I'm afraid anyone on board won't survive much longer."

"What can we do?" Fransk looked agonized. "Could we get over to them with a shuttle?"

"The engines on our smallest shuttlecraft should fire up. They won't be affected by the energy field, since their propulsion systems don't depend on a core reaction," Dean said. "However, their shielding is very minimal. It would not be safe to traverse that distance."

Uma glanced at the Rift telemetry that was skipping along

on her bracelet display. "Dean's right. And even if we could boost the shields enough to survive the ambient field, there's no chance a shuttle would withstand those big energy pulses. A single hit would fry the nav and knock it right out."

"Well, what if we could bring the other ship over to *us*?" Wazar said thoughtfully. "We could focus our tractor beams directly on the hauler's position and try to drag them over. The *Gallion* can probably manage a weak pull from eighty klicks."

"That sounds reasonable," said Fransk, looking entirely unconvinced of his own words.

"Captain, I wouldn't advise that," Barnabyn said. "This situation is awfully suspicious. Whoever's on the other end of that transmission seems to have no problem lying to us, so why should we stick our necks out?"

"But the ship's in distress!" Noussen protested, pointing at the projection of the little hauler. "Those people on board could die!"

Noussen was a short, round-faced girl with hair styled in elaborate beaded twists. She barely looked old enough to be out of prep school, but she was more than halfway through a second university degree. She'd recently become the *Gallion*'s youngest junior engineer, promoted to Communications Specialist after finishing her internship. It was Noussen's work on restoring the comms grid that had allowed them to pick up the transmission.

"Come on, Noussen. This is obviously a scam," said Barnabyn. "We have a diplomatic contingent on this ship; we can't take risks that might endanger them. If there's any chance this is a hijacking attempt, or worse, some kind of plot to kidnap our Felen Ambassador—"

Fransk's face was a mask of utter horror.

"But, Director... why would a kidnapper send a nonsensical transmission like that?" Wazar squinted at the projection that was still spinning next to Dean's hand. "It sounds like they don't even know we're here."

"Nonetheless, we have to take precautions," Barnabyn said. "ZeyCorp protocol calls for a full risk assessment to be filed—"

"There's no time!" Uma cut the Director of Administration short. "That ship's running on a sliver of emergency power. People's lives are at stake here!" Her heart was pounding. "Captain?"

Captain Fransk turned to Barnabyn, then back to Uma again, looking torn.

"Captain," said Barnabyn insistently. "The risk assessment is mandatory."

Oli, please, Uma mouthed when Fransk met her eyes. "If we want any chance of saving them, we need to start those tractor beams right now. Captain—"

"Do it," Fransk said. "Engineers, start pulling that ship in. Tractor beams are authorized."

Uma let out her breath, avoiding Barnabyn's glare.

Fransk motioned to the android. "Dean, can we send a reply back to... this so-called *Jonah*?"

"Certainly," Dean said. "Go ahead, Captain. I'll record and transmit it on all channels."

Fransk cleared his throat. "We hear you, *Jonah*. This is Captain Olghan Fransk of the deep space research vessel *RV ZC-2812 ZeyCorp Gallion*. We've received your distress call, and we're going to attempt to rescue you. We're pulling your ship toward us with our tractor beams."

He paused, then added: "Please note that any acts of violence or piracy against us will not be tolerated. This ship is corporate property, and ZeyCorp will take the strongest possible legal action if the *Gallion* or anyone aboard comes to harm. Thank you."

* * *

THE SMALL HAULER fit into the *Gallion*'s largest cargo bay—but only just. When it came to rest, the widest part of the little ship sat nearly against the far wall. If the *Gallion* hadn't been in turnover, this bay would have held six short-range science vessels. But now, it contained the *Jonah*.

"It's not the *Jonah*, for the gods' sake," Barnabyn kept repeating as they waited for the bay to re-pressurize. "We don't know what this is. Let's stick to facts."

The *Gallion* crew clustered around the narrow window that looked from the service corridor into the cargo bay, all crowding forward and craning their necks for a look.

"We need to stay rational about this," Fransk was muttering next to Uma. "Be reasonable, be calm, be professional. Keep it together."

Uma wasn't sure if the captain was talking to the others or to himself.

She studied the ship on the other side of the window. It was a three-engine hauler, a classic war-era design, with a rugged hull that had seen better days. Some attempts seemed to have been made to improve the condition of the ship's body, but these ministrations had been purely functional, with no thought given to the aesthetics. The hull was visibly patched in several places, and the repair job had made no effort to match the original hue of the panelling. The patches were a dull silver-grey, their edges uneven and bubbled where they'd been sealed to the hull. The rest of the ship's body was a dark, rust-coloured red, and its hexagonal cargo pod perched over the top like a shell.

"That ship barely looks like it's holding together," Barnabyn said disdainfully. "They couldn't have found a nicer replica?"

Uma had seen nicer ones, that was for sure. The War History Society she and her father had belonged to once worked on a *Jonah* replica, and that ship was an absolute marvel when it was finished. They'd sourced a genuine antique hull from the same production line as the *Jonah,* and they'd restored it to a gleaming reddish-bronze.

"I'm pretty sure that's a real vintage hull," Uma whispered to Fransk. "See those seven ridges along the top? Most bad replicas try to make it symmetrical, but the uneven number was a hallmark of the Nilsom shipyard. That's the only place these hulls were manufactured."

Fransk nodded silently, his mouth a taut line of tension. The corner of his eye was twitching.

Just then, a battered panel on the hauler's side started to slide open. The crew behind Uma pushed forward to get closer to the window as a metal platform slowly extended from the ship. A rickety boarding-ramp unfolded from the end of the platform and clattered down to the bay floor.

Uma held her breath.

After a moment, a man appeared at the open door and ducked out onto the platform. He wore no uniform, just a simple pair of baggy brown trousers and a plain grey shirt with a jacket over it. He had an unruly mop of auburn hair, and the tawny complexion of a Latter-Worlder. He looked around the bay, one hand resting on the open hatch as he waved over his shoulder to someone behind him.

And then out came a second man, tall and pale, dressed entirely in black from his slim trousers to his bell-sleeved shirt. His greying dark hair was held back in a ponytail, tied at the nape of his neck.

"Eldric Leesongronski," Uma whispered breathlessly. "That's the Pathfinder."

"You mean the *alleged* Leesongronski." Barnabyn's face was pressed against the window beside her, his breath fogging the pseudo-glass. "Stick to facts, Director Ozakka."

The two companions stood for a while just outside the *Jonah*'s open hatch. They glanced behind them into the ship, then leaned their heads together in conversation, deliberating something briefly before they started walking down the ramp.

When they reached the bottom, the first man went around to the side of the ship, where he stood looking up into the maw of the nearest engine. Meanwhile, the man in black walked slowly along the bay floor, coming closer to the window where the ZeyCorp crew were watching.

He turned in a circle, both hands stuck in his pockets. And then he looked up at the window, his eerily familiar eyes meeting Uma's through the pseudo-glass. He peered at her curiously, as though trying to discern exactly who or what she was behind the tinted pane.

Uma brought a hand to her mouth. "Oh my gods... Olghan, that's *him,* that's really the Pathfinder!"

Fransk still said nothing. His eyes were fixed on the ship, where a third figure had appeared on the platform: graceful, tall and lithe, with a fountain of tiny ice-white braids cascading from the top of her head. Rows of fishscale glinted up the sides of her neck and across her face, and her strapless shirt revealed a web of elaborate holo-tattoos weaving down her brown arms. A pair of long, many-pointed ears fanned out from the sides of her head like stars.

She stepped down the ramp cautiously, holding what looked like a bulky cold-weather coat.

"The Voicegiver," Uma gasped. "Look at her! She looks exactly like *Keila Kva-Sova!*"

The tattooed woman looked back to the top of the ramp, where a stocky man in coveralls had just lumbered out onto the platform. He had a large, bushy moustache, and a thick grey beard that obscured most of the lower half of his face. The man reached back through the hatch and roughly tugged a fifth reluctant figure out of the ship. He held the furious-looking woman by one wrist, and she flicked him an obscene gesture with her other hand as she stumbled through the door.

This last newcomer had close-cropped hair shaved into a military style, and wore clothes that looked much too big for her. The bearded man scowled and shoved her forward, taking hold of her oversize sweater. He kept a firm grip on the back of her collar as they walked together down the ramp.

"See there, the one with the shaved head?" Uma whispered, nudging Fransk's shoulder. "I think that might be Charyne Jaxong, the Inventor. Her hair is different, but..."

The corner of Fransk's eye was still twitching. "I don't see it, Director Ozakka," he whispered. "None of these people look much like the Fortunate Five to me."

"Besides the fact that it's *completely impossible*," Barnabyn muttered under his breath.

Uma turned back to the window, alternately watching the people and the ship, trying to steady her breathing. The Fortunate Five were as unlikely a group of heroes as humanity had ever known, and the events at the end of the war had always fascinated her—the history, the remaining mysteries, the wealth of conspiracy theories. She'd soaked it up since she was a child, reading every word she could find about the Negotiator, the Pathfinder, the Voicegiver, the Inventor and the Decipherer.

The hauler's hatch was still standing open, but no one else had exited the ship. Uma frowned. None of them wore anything like the Negotiator's diplomatic regalia. And where was the ethereal Decipherer in her famous green cloak? Every time the *Gallion* crew walked through the Command deck, they passed by the Five's richly robed likenesses, shining boldly from the painting in the atrium. But these people were in casual attire, stumbling out of a junk ship. It was little wonder the captain didn't find them convincing, even if three of them were dead ringers for members of the Fortunate Five.

"Ahem... so, ah, how should we proceed from here, Captain

Fransk?" Zel asked. His stance was as arrogant as ever, but his usual self-assurance seemed shaken.

"Well, I suppose we'd better go in there and introduce ourselves," Fransk said grimly. "Captain and directors only, we don't want to overwhelm them. Directors, you're with me. The rest of you wait here."

There was a murmur of disappointment from the crew. For a brief moment Zel looked like he was going to say something else, but then he stepped back with an indignant look on his face.

Fransk swiped in an access code and unlocked the service door, and Uma followed him into the brightly-lit cargo bay. Behind her, Barnabyn was mumbling something that sounded like 'waste of time' and 'fixing the engines.'

The five visitors turned in unison to look at them.

"Well! Hello, there!" the auburn-haired man said, raising his palm with a cordial smile. "You must be our rescuers, huh? I'm Jereth Keeven. Captain and owner of the *Jonah*."

"Wait, what? *That's* the captain?" Uma whispered. That wasn't right. Everyone knew Eldric Leesongronski had been the *Jonah*'s captain. Barnabyn stared straight ahead, pointedly ignoring her.

Fransk cleared his throat. "Ah! Welcome on board, Captain Keeven." He adjusted his dress-jacket before he raised his hand and returned Keeven's greeting. "I'm Captain Olghan Fransk of the research vessel *Gallion*, representing ZeyCorp Research Support. I trust you received our message?"

"Sure did!" Keeven laughed irreverently. "Just in time, too. We're real grateful for the rescue, but don't worry, we shouldn't trouble you too long. My engineer reckons our engines aren't damaged. We just ran into some kind of fluke energy field, and that gave us a massive power failure." He shrugged. "Real bad luck, huh?"

"Our ship's misfiring, too," Fransk said, worry clouding his face. "We're running on emergency power with all our engines spun down. And we've lost contact with the network."

"Damn." Keeven's smile faded. "Same for us. Engines down, network links out. It's a miracle you caught our hail when you did. Our backup power cell was almost dead."

"Turns out it's a bad plan to head into deep space with just one backup cell," the bearded man said gruffly. "We used to have more, till *somebody* asked me to take the rest of 'em out to make more room for the cargo." He glared in Keeven's direction, but Keeven ignored him.

Fransk looked behind him, motioning Uma and Barnabyn forward. "Ah... come, I'd like to introduce you to the *Gallion*'s directors," he said, looking flustered. "Here we have our Director of Administration, Aldwim Barnabyn... and this is our Director of Engineering, Uma Ozakka. Some of ZeyCorp's finest. We hire the best and brightest in every field."

Uma winced. Leave it to Fransk to fall back on the ZeyCorp publicity lines when he was put on the spot. This was exactly why Fransk was a sure bet for that company chancellorship.

The alleged Leesongronski raised his left palm. "Hello. I'm Eldric Leesongronski, and I am never, ever getting back on *that* thing." He threw a disdainful glance over his shoulder at the *Jonah* before he looked back at Fransk. "You don't happen to be hiring, do you? How exactly does one go about applying to ZeyCorp?"

Fransk blinked. "Uh... I... ah..."

"That's enough, Leeg," Keeven said, patting Leesongronski on the shoulder with a good-natured chuckle. "Our ship's perfectly fine."

Leesongronski looked back at the *Jonah* again with a grimace. "Oh, sure, it's fine," he muttered. "These people have eyes, you know."

Uma stared at Leesongronski, unable to shake the chill of recognition every time he spoke. That was the Pathfinder's low voice, with his soft, distinctive lilt. How many hours had she listened to Leesongronski's lectures? How many long journeys had she spent watching recordings of the talks he'd given all over the United Worlds? Surely no impersonator could be this convincing.

It wasn't just the uncanny familiarity of those haunted eyes burning from Leesongronski's pale, hollow-cheeked face. It wasn't just the particular way he stood with his shoulders pulled together, both hands deep in his pockets, rocking back on the heels of his feet like he'd done every time he stood at a lectern. It wasn't just the clothes he wore, so accurate to the vintage cuts of Leesongronski's perpetual black ensembles. No, he mimicked Leesongronski in his very *essence*. Uma couldn't shake the certainty that she was somehow staring through history at the real Pathfinder.

"Right... so... is this all of your crew?" Fransk said after an awkward silence, motioning behind Jereth Keeven at the three others. "We haven't been introduced yet."

"Ah! Well, Keila over there is a passenger." Keeven indicated the tall, tattooed woman with the pointed ears. "And this here's my engineer, Mendeg." Keeven gestured toward the big, bearded man. "And next to him... that's... uh..." He squinted at the short-haired woman Mendeg was still holding by the collar. "That's... uh..."

"My name is *Charyne*," the woman spat.

Mendeg tightened his hold on the back of her baggy sweater, scrunching the folds of woolly material in his fist.

"Right. Charyne! Of course!" Keeven said. "Charyne's our... other passenger."

Uma looked up into the *Jonah*'s still-open hatch, a growing unease coiling in her chest.

"Is this everyone?" she asked. "You haven't got any other... diplomatic passengers?"

"Diplomatic passengers? What? Hells, no!" Keeven laughed heartily, raking a hand through his messy hair. "You've got to be kidding. I've got too many people on board as it is. We're sleeping on the damn floor, and I haven't heard the end of it. I *was* planning to drop off my two extras at our next stop, but... ah, well. What can you do, huh?" He shrugged again. "At least we're still alive, so let's thank our lucky charms for that. Gods damn it. Half this sector's nothin' but detours around orange zones."

Uma froze. "Wait... hang on. You're definitely not picking anybody else up?"

"Why? You asking for a ride?" Keeven grimaced. "In case you haven't noticed, we're not movin' anytime soon."

Uma forced a smile. "Sorry, ah... could you excuse us for just a moment?"

She tugged Fransk by the sleeve of his purple blazer, leading him a few paces away. Director Barnabyn followed them.

"Something's off about their story, isn't it?" Fransk said when they were out of earshot.

"You mean besides the fact that Leesongronski's apparently not the captain? Oh, yeah. It's way off," said Uma. "First of all, they should have picked up the Decipherer and the Voicegiver together. But the Decipherer isn't here at all! And they'd have to be on their way to rendezvous with the Negotiator now, but instead they're—"

"It's a scam, then." Fransk looked relieved. "They've got the story all wrong. So this couldn't possibly be the real ship."

"I told you it's a hoax, and a bad one at that," Barnabyn said smugly. "I knew it."

"I'm not so sure," Uma whispered. She glanced back at the *Jonah* crew and felt chilled again. "I'd know Eldric

Leesongronski anywhere. You can't imagine how many times I've watched his lectures and his documentaries. That man over there has the voice, the same inflections when he talks... even the mannerisms. The way he stands with his hands in his pockets like that, he's—"

"A skilled impersonator," Barnabyn finished for her. "Obviously."

"If only we had our network connection," Fransk said mournfully. "Dean might be able to check for a bioscan match in some historical archive, or maybe..."

"I don't need a bioscan to know this is ridiculous," Barnabyn hissed. His sandy cheeks had been flushing redder and redder, and now even his ears were turning crimson. "Think about what you're implying! Even if we had somehow... *fallen through time* and run into the crew of the *Jonah*... how could they possibly be missing the Decipherer? And if they aren't picking up the Negotiator, there could be no Peace! That would alter the course of history!"

The words settled uncomfortably between the three of them, and Barnabyn looked very much like he wished he hadn't said them.

"We have to ask them more questions," Uma whispered.

"What we *need* to do is fix our engines," Barnabyn said.

"And we all need to get some sleep," said Fransk, rubbing at his twitching eye. "We have to clear our heads. I can't even think straight right now."

Uma glanced back toward the *Jonah* crew, who were all looking at them curiously. "This is too strange to be a coincidence. It's all connected somehow," she said. "The engine problem, the Rift, that distress call... it's all linked. And we need to figure out *how* if we want to get out of here."

SHAAN
Common Deck, ZeyCorp Gallion

SHAAN SEETHED. SHE could hardly believe that Barnabyn had actually sent her to do this. The rest of the *Gallion* crew had been sent back to their apartments until further notice, but Shaan? Shaan was to stay, to finish the guest induction for these... people, whoever they were.

Any shred of sympathy she might have had for her visibly rattled boss had evaporated. She hated Barnabyn, she hated this ship, she hated all of this. Guest inductions were a pain at the best of times, but this was beyond ridiculous.

Ozakka and Fransk had taken the alleged Eldric Leesongronski and the junk ship's captain elsewhere, leaving Shaan to deal with the rest of them—the duo masquerading as Keila Kva-Sova and Charyne Jaxong, plus the bearded engineer. Mendeg, was it? They trailed behind her as she led them down the corridor, all looking as miserable as Shaan felt. The visitors had briefly gone back on board the ship to collect their personal effects, and when they'd returned, Mendeg was carrying a small travel-bag. The other two didn't appear to have any baggage at all.

Kva-Sova was still clutching that bulky coat to her chest as she walked, cradling it in a bundle like a baby. Up close, her facial mods were even more striking. Her glowing eyes phased slowly from white to honey-yellow as she blinked, the scales along her forehead and neck catching the light like tiny jewels.

Jaxong hadn't said a word to anyone since they left the cargo bay. As soon as Mendeg had relinquished his hold on her, she'd kept a visible distance from the others. She shuffled along silently in her ill-fitting sweater, a pace behind the rest of them, avoiding eye contact.

"Even a new-fangled ship like this one didn't detect that energy field in time to avoid it, huh?" Mendeg was saying. "See, I knew it wasn't a fault in our instruments. That ship might be in rough shape, but I did all the major safety checks. I'm no fool."

"We're all so unbelievably grateful that you found us," Kva-Sova chimed in, smiling warmly as she caught up to Shaan. "We really didn't think anyone was out here! But then you answered our distress call, just in time."

"Yes, well... we're having a little trouble believing it ourselves." Shaan sighed. "Come on, I'll have to take you over to the Registration office and print up some guest bands."

Shaan completed the guest induction process as she'd done countless times before, following the prompts from the ZeyCorp system. She added five new temporary accounts to the ship's manifest, linked each of them to one of the empty guest apartments, and assigned access permissions for the visitors.

The system blinked at her:

Add Guest Access to ZeyCorp Knowledge Bank and Full AI Support?

She deliberated for a moment, then unselected that one. No. They'd have no access to the ship's knowledge banks or any archives. No internal network permissions at all, and only the most basic query permissions from Dean. Whatever they were up to, they certainly didn't need to be given easy access to more information.

When she'd finished, the system unleashed a now-familiar screed of errors.

External network not found.
Restoring network connection to ZeyCorp Central...
Please wait...
External network not found.
Restoring network connection to ZeyCorp Central...
Please wait...
External network not found.
Restoring network connection to ZeyCorp Central...
Please wait...

At last, it relented:

Printing guest bands in offline mode.
Please upload guest data later.

Five slender purple guest bands dropped out into the collection tray, each emblazoned with the ZeyCorp logo.

"All right, please fasten your guest band to your left wrist, and keep it on for the duration of your stay," Shaan said, lapsing easily into her orientation speech. "You'll find your apartment number displayed when you first awaken your band. The door to your apartment will unlock with proximity. If you lose your guest band, please notify me immediately."

She handed out the guest bands, slipping the last two into her pocket.

"I've given you all unlimited access to the vending machines, so you can dispense any food you want, free of charge. You can use your band to access the ship's comms system and talk to us, or to each other. You may also direct any basic questions or requests to Dean—that's the AI that runs our ship-net." She didn't bother mentioning any of the android's latest upgrades.

"AI, huh?" Mendeg's bushy eyebrows knitted together. "Damn fancy ship you got here. You've got to be well-armed, right? There'll be a target on your backs, flyin' this close to an orange zone. Dangerous place to be stranded." He narrowed his eyes. "Or... wait, I bet you've got some of that new stealth tech, haven't you? Is this a nightship?"

"Um..." Shaan shifted her feet uneasily.

"Fuckin' Felen vermin. You better be stayin' alert for 'em. I'd do a long-range scan for skirmishers every quarter-hour, at least... they're all over this sector now." Mendeg made a disgusted sound low in his throat. "Your ship might be fancy, but those things'll tear your nice shiny hull clean apart. No shields can stop 'em."

Kva-Sova was staring at the floor, still clutching her coat, her bottom lip quivering like she might be about to cry.

"An' if they get in here, you can bet they'll do the same to us," Mendeg continued, lowering his voice like he was telling a ghost story. "When they capture a civvie ship in deep space... they take you alive. They rip you to shreds, an' they do it real slowly, to make sure it hurts. Sometimes, they'll even carve out your—"

"Enough," Kva-Sova choked out. "That's... *enough*. Thank you." Her many-pointed ears had retracted tightly against the sides of her head.

Jaxong wasn't paying attention to the conversation. She had snapped on her ZeyCorp guest band, and was studying the virtual display curiously, turning it on and off, rotating her wrist to make the projection expand and contract while she waved her other hand over it.

Shaan cleared her throat. "Look, why don't I take you over to the vending machines and we'll get you some food?" she said. "Then I'll show you where your apartments are. Come with me."

The others filed obediently toward the door, but Mendeg lingered behind. When he caught Shaan's eye, he motioned her off to one side.

"Hey, listen," he whispered. "I've gotta tell you something. For your own damn good, since you did save our lives, after all." He pointed furtively at the back of Charyne Jaxong's head. "You need to keep an eye on that one. She's big trouble, got me?"

"What, unlike the rest of you?" Shaan gave him a dubious stare. "I don't know what you're doing here, but I'm pretty sure you're *all* big trouble. Every single one of you is another problem we don't need. So don't make this any worse. Okay?"

Mendeg looked offended, but before he could say anything else, she turned and started down the hall.

"The canteen's this way," she said without looking back. "Let's get this over with."

UMA
Command Deck, ZeyCorp Gallion

UMA STOOD NEXT to the desk in Fransk's office, shifting her feet uneasily. Fransk was in his chair, drumming his fingers against the edge of his lightpad the way he did when he was thinking. Barnabyn had absconded quietly to update the Ambassador alongside Zel, and Uma dreaded to think what they could possibly be saying. But for now, there was a much more pressing problem right in front of her.

Jereth Keeven, the *Jonah*'s captain, was leaning back in his seat with one scuffed, unlaced boot crossed over the other, casually spinning the bowl of glossy ZeyCorp adver-tags that sat on the corner of Fransk's desk. Beside him, the alleged Eldric Leesongronski sat in an identical purple seat with his chin resting on one hand, dark eyebrows furrowed. Leesongronski had his bell-sleeved black dress-shirt buttoned all the way up to his neck. He'd arrived with his black formal jacket folded over one arm, like he was on his way to a dinner-party, and had hung the jacket neatly on the back of his chair.

"You've got some pretty weird high-tech shit around here," Keeven was saying. He took one of the adver-tags and held it up to his eye, peering through the hole in it before he threw it back into the bowl. "You're a science ship, huh? What's your company worth? Got to be a fortune."

Uma and Fransk glanced at each other nervously.

Keeven was undeterred. He pointed at Fransk's lightpad. "Hey, can I see that thing? What is that? New make?"

Fransk ignored the question, nudging the lightpad just out of Keeven's reach. "Captain Keeven, I've discussed your situation with my directors," he said. "The five of you are welcome to stay with us for as long as you need to. As soon as we repair our engines and we're back under way, we'll be glad to have a look over your ship, too. Our engineers can help you with any repairs, if you need—"

"Nahhh." Keeven waved his hand. "Thanks, but we'll be fine. My ship might not be pretty, but it's solid. Once we've cleared this energy field, if you can just boost our backup power cell back to full, I'm sure we can take care of ourselves from there."

"Actually, I think you might be able to help *us* out with something," Uma said. "I'd like my team to examine the *Jonah*'s sensor logs, to compare them to our readings. Whatever data you gathered when you hit that energy field, it's bound to be useful."

"Sensor logs, hmm?" Keeven gave a noncommittal shrug. "All right. I'll ask my engineer about that." He swivelled in the chair and looked over his shoulder toward the closed office door. "Where'd you take the rest of my folks to, anyway?"

"Our Facilities Coordinator is showing them to their guest apartments," Fransk said. "I hope you'll all find our accommodations comfortable."

Keeven laughed. "You kidding? This ship's a palace." He ran a palm over one of the rounded projection surfaces that lined the edge of Fransk's desk. "It's incredible. I've never seen anything like *any* of this."

"I actually won't be sleeping on the floor tonight. There's the real miracle," Leesongronski muttered, half to himself.

"Unbelievable accommodations. An actual bed."

"Listen... I, ah... I'd like to ask a few more questions before you leave us for the night," Uma said. "I hope you don't mind. Some of them might seem a bit... strange."

"Oh, I do love strange questions," Keeven said. He leaned toward her, planting his elbow on the desk. "Go ahead. Question me. And for the record, I don't mind a little force." He smirked suggestively.

Uma ignored the quip. "Where did the *Jonah* last dock, and when was that?"

"Pilar Outpost," Keeven said. "It was... about a week ago, I reckon?"

"What did you do at Pilar?"

"Do?" Keeven arched an eyebrow. "We made a cargo pickup."

"And... is that all?"

Keeven didn't answer that one. The ghost of a frown flitted across Leesongronski's face, and Uma tried not to stare at him.

"Where did you get the *Jonah*?" She looked back at Keeven. "Have you had the ship for very long?"

Keeven sat up straighter in the chair, his demeanour changing abruptly. The charming smile vanished, and he narrowed his eyes. "All right. You wanna tell me what this is really about? Why in the five hells would you need to know any of that?"

"I know this seems unusual," Fransk said. "But your answers could help us a... a great deal. If you could just answer Director Ozakka's questions..." He looked at Keeven imploringly. "We saved your lives, didn't we?"

Keeven paused a moment, then shrugged. "Fine. I got the *Jonah* not too long ago, from this little deep space scrapyard. I can't remember the name of it, if it even had a name. Wasn't exactly my first choice, but my ship needed repairs and I didn't have time to wait. So I had to trade my ship for that junker, straight up." He looked over at Leesongronski. "It was fully refurbished and it's certified spaceworthy, before you say anything smart."

"So the *Jonah* wasn't even your original ship? You just... found it at a scrapyard?" Uma frowned.

"Yep." Keeven sighed dramatically. "Lot of good that trade did me, huh? There's pretty much no chance I'll make my delivery on schedule now."

"I see." Uma took a deep breath. "And your delivery... is it by any chance a delivery for the Geminus Initiative?"

"The what?" Keeven stared at her blankly.

She looked over at Leesongronski, trying to steady her voice. "The Geminus Initiative. Are you affiliated with the Peace Project, Professor Leesongronski? You're on a mission for them right now, aren't you?" Uma searched Leesongronski's face for a reaction, her heart pounding. "It's all right if you tell us the truth. You're completely safe here. We know you've been working with the peace activists—"

"Peace activists?" Leesongronski recoiled. "No, of course not! Absolutely not!"

"Listen, I don't know who you think we are, but we've got nothin' to do with any peace activists," Keeven said sharply. "I might be a lot of things, but I'm no traitor to the Union. And neither is Leeg." He shoved a hand into his jacket and fished something out of an inner pocket. "Here. You wanna check out my cargo permits?"

He tossed a flat, antique mem-card onto the desk.

"Go ahead. Check it," he said. "The *Jonah* is hauling a shipment of live deep-water squid, bound for Fedraya. My cargo clearances are in order."

"I... That's okay. I believe you." Uma slid the card back to him, wondering if the *Gallion* even had the means to get any data out of a card that old.

Leesongronski gave a short, bitter laugh. "You don't look like you believe him."

Uma glanced over at Fransk. His eyes were half-closed, and he was wincing, holding the bridge of his nose between two fingers.

"Well, we're... just a little surprised," Uma said. "See, our... our, ah, records show that the *Jonah* should be on the way to Etraxas."

"To Etraxas?" Leesongronski's eyes went wide. "Etraxas is under Felen siege, in case you hadn't heard."

"We're not going anywhere near Etraxas." Keeven's fist clenched on the desk. "Look, how about you tell us who you're working for, and what you really want. Are you with the government or something? Are you UWDF ops? Special service agents?"

"What? No! We work for ZeyCorp Research Support." Fransk held out the corporate badge on his collar like a tiny shield. "Administration. See? We run a science ship, nothing more." He reached for the bowl of adver-tags, took one out and held it toward Keeven. "Look. Research support and serviced deep-space accommodation, for teams of up to one hundred and twenty scientists. The highest safety ratings in the field. That's what we do."

Keeven got to his feet, his scowl deepening. "Well, you're askin' some damn funny questions," he said. "We're not gonna be interrogated without cause, so unless you've got some kind of a warrant, I think we're done here."

"But—"

"Come on, Leeg," Keeven said, pulling on Leesongronski's sleeve. "Thanks for the rescue and all, but we're leaving. Immediately." He looked at Uma. "Tell your engineers to prepare to release my ship, right now."

"I'm afraid that's out of the question," said Fransk.

"Oh, what, so you're holdin' us hostage?" Keeven's hands shook against the desk. "We're prisoners here? Is that it?"

"Of course not," Uma said. "But the *Jonah* doesn't have the shielding to withstand that energy field. Your engines aren't working. And your backup power cell is dead."

"Then you'll recharge my cell first. And I'll take my chances with the shielding."

"You still can't start your engines! You'll be going nowhere!"

"Well, at least I'll be going nowhere under my own command. You have no grounds to hold us here. Release my ship!"

"Captain Keeven... please." Fransk leaned heavily on the desk as he stood up, exhaustion in his voice. "We've all had an incredibly trying day. And none of us are out of danger yet, not until we can find a way out of here. Please. We really need to cooperate, and our engineers need your ship's sensor logs."

Keeven locked eyes with the *Gallion*'s captain, his jaw tensing visibly. Both his fists were clenched now, and he was holding them tight to his sides, his arms shaking. He didn't say anything.

"Your crew and mine all need to get some rest. We're too exhausted to think," Fransk said with a placating gesture. "Let's get you settled in your guest apartments, and we can discuss this later... when we're all in a better state of mind."

Keeven leaned down and picked up the two well-used travel bags they'd brought from the *Jonah*. He slung them both over one shoulder. Then he snatched his antique mem-card off the table and slid it back into his pocket with difficulty, his trembling hand catching on the edge of the fabric. Meanwhile, Leesongronski wordlessly collected his black jacket from the back of the chair and folded it back over his arm.

"Fine. We'll talk later," Keeven said through his teeth. "But no more weird questions."

Fransk sighed with relief and tapped his bracelet. "I'll call our Facilities Coordinator, and she'll come show you to your apartments."

"We'll wait outside," Keeven growled.

SHAAN
Command Deck, *ZeyCorp Gallion*

WHEN SHAAN ROUNDED the corner, Captain Fransk's office door was closed. A thin orange bar glowed along the right side of the door: *Do not disturb. Meeting in progress.* Two figures were standing in the corridor just outside the door, leaning against the wall.

The taller of the two was the impersonator posing as Eldric Leesongronski; the smaller one was Jereth Keeven, the dishevelled auburn-haired captain of the junk ship. There were two utilitarian carry-bags sitting on the floor at their feet.

Shaan gritted her teeth in silent rage. It was beyond comprehension how they thought anyone was going to buy this charade. What was their angle? Why would a group of con artists want to impersonate three of the Fortunate Five, with a makeshift *Jonah* so ridiculous that it was falling apart? What did these people *want*?

Keeven was focusing intently on a small red ball, throwing it from one hand to another. The process seemed to be taking all his concentration, and he dropped the ball more than once, muttering to himself each time he bent down to retrieve it. Leesongronski was staring at the floor, his hands stuck in his pockets, looking deep in thought as she approached.

"Excuse me... uh... Eldric Leesongronski?" It was absurd, but she didn't know what else to call him.

Leesongronski didn't react, just continued to gaze forlornly down at the floor tiles. Next to him, Keeven pocketed the red ball, shoving his unruly hair back from his face.

"What do you want from him?" Keeven snapped.

Shaan shoved down her simmering rage as she held out the purple guest bands. "I'm here to take you to your apartments," she said rigidly. "Fasten this to your left wrist, and come with me. I'll give you the rest of your orientation on the way."

Leesongronski finally looked up just enough to give the guest bands a disdainful glance.

"No, thanks," Keeven said. "Whatever those things are, you can keep 'em."

"They're your guest bands." She rolled her eyes. "You'll need one for access to the vending machines in the canteen, and to unlock your apartment. And to log into the comms system."

"Nice try. I'm not wearing your surveillance leash," Keeven said with a smirk. "That's a tracking device."

"It does track your location, yes. For the nefarious purposes of locating you in the ship if there's an emergency," she said. When they stood side by side, Shaan was almost as tall as he was. She pulled back her shoulders and stood up straighter. "Look, you want to eat and sleep, right? So just take your gods-damned guest band, or you'll be sleeping in the corridor."

That was enough to prompt Leesongronski to take one of the bands. He clipped it to his wrist without looking at the display, then wandered a few steps away, his gaze already shifting down the hall toward the *Gallion*'s atrium.

Keeven still didn't take his guest band.

"Well?" Shaan held the purple bracelet up to Keeven's face. "I'm not waiting here all night."

He leaned over and peered at the ZeyCorp staff badge hanging on Shaan's collar—her own badge, this time, complete with her hated title. "*Facilities Coordinator*, hmm?" he said in a mocking tone. "Damn. I thought you were the prison warden! Isn't there something in your job description that says you have to be polite to guests?"

"Guests, maybe. Stragglers we rescued from floating space garbage? I don't think so."

Remarkably, he cracked a half-smile. "Fair enough," he said. "So, what's a Facilities Coordinator do around here?"

"It's not that hard to figure out. I give orientations and tours. Make sure all the research teams get the equipment they ordered. Collect feedback and deal with complaints." She sighed. "At the moment, I don't do much of anything, because we're in turnover. The ship's practically empty."

"Hmm." Keeven looked back at Fransk's closed office door. "Say... do you know Uma Ozakka? The Engineering director?"

"Uh, yeah."

"And the captain? Fransk?"

"Yeah. Of course I know them. Why?"

Keeven smiled from the corner of his mouth. "Seems like you ZeyCorp people desperately want something from me," he said. "And I want something from you, too. Sounds simple, right? So we should be able to come to an... agreement." He gave a determined nod, then snatched the purple guest band out of her hand. "How about you help me strike a deal? I bet you know how to talk to 'em, how to say the right things."

"Uh... what kind of deal, exactly?"

"Your Director Ozakka wants me to hand over my ship's sensor logs. Me, I want to get out of here as soon as possible. I want them to release my ship, and those logs are my only bargaining chip." He looked thoughtful. "How about this? I'll give you *one* log file as a show of good faith, and then I'll give you an encrypted drive with the rest of the logs. I want Ozakka to charge up my backup power cell and release my ship. Once we're clear of the *Gallion*, I'll send over the decryption key for the rest of the logs. That sound okay to you?"

"Does it sound okay to *me*?" Shaan laughed incredulously. "I don't know. I don't usually negotiate blackmail terms on behalf of ZeyCorp."

"Trust me, it's a really good deal." He grinned.

"Why should I trust you? All you've done is lie from the minute your ship sent that distress message." She glared at him. "Save your nonsense."

Keeven's smile faltered. "Look, I don't know what it is you think I lied about, but I just want my ship back. That's it. I'm being honest with you!"

"Great. And now I'll be honest with *you*," said Shaan. "Whoever you really are... if you've got any scrap of integrity, you'll give Director Ozakka those sensor logs. No 'deals,' no messing around. We're running on emergency power, we still can't reach the network, and we're all getting fucking scared. None of us want to die here in some deep-space hell-void; so how about you stop being an asshole and help out?"

Keeven was silent for a long moment after that, his expression inscrutable.

"Wow," he finally said, recovering his mocking tone. "Well. Honesty appreciated. Thank you for the insight, Facilities Coordinator."

"My name's Shaan. Not that it matters."

"Shaan." He repeated the single syllable, drawing it out much longer than necessary. "All right, then, *Shaan*."

"You know, if your friend really wants to pass for the Pathfinder, he might reconsider the kind of company he keeps," she said.

Keeven frowned, and what looked like genuine confusion clouded his eyes. "Pass for who?"

She threw him an exasperated look. "Ugh, forget it. I'm way too tired for this. Let's go find your apartments."

"I have no idea what any of you people are talkin' about," Keeven said. "You've obviously got us confused with someone else." He looked over his shoulder. "Hey, Leeg! You coming?"

The alleged Eldric Leesongronski had already meandered most of the way across the half-lit atrium, and was looking around at the artwork. Like all the ZeyCorp ships, the *Gallion* had a large open space at the centre of the Command deck that doubled as a gallery, the curved walls lined with pictures and portraits of the Worlds' greatest philosophers and thinkers, explorers, scientists and adventurers. To remind everyone, Captain Fransk always said, on whose shoulders they all stood. Shaan seldom looked at any of the portraits, but she knew exactly where *that* one was. The one representing the Fortunate Five—a framed reproduction of the famous painting, *The End of Our Days of War*. And Leesongronski was standing directly in front of it. Damn it.

Keeven had already started walking in Leesongronski's direction before Shaan could stop him. Leesongronski kept his eyes fixed on the painting, not moving until Keeven joined him and followed his gaze up the atrium wall.

Shaan knew the artwork well. In the middle of the frame, a regal Eldric Leesongronski struck a heroic pose, his shoulders back, his chin tilted upward. The artist had outfitted the Pathfinder in bright blue robes and livery. To his left stood the similarly-outfitted Jaxong and Kva-Sova, the Inventor and the Voicegiver, their heads turned reverently in the same direction. To Leesongronski's right stood the Decipherer—the first successful Voiced—in her distinctive green cloak. One of her gloved hands rested on the noble Negotiator's arm, lost in the flowing sleeve of his diplomatic finery. The Negotiator and the Decipherer were angled away from the others, their faces unseen, their hands outstretched toward the imposing figure of the Felen Starhold's Envoy on the opposite side of the canvas. Below the painting, the commemorative plaque gleamed. *In Grateful Remembrance of the Peacemakers of the Great Ship Jonah.*

The alleged Leesongronski reached out with one finger and gingerly touched the edge of the painted Pathfinder's robes. His already pallid face had turned an unhealthy shade of grey when he turned back to look at Shaan, his mouth half-open in shock.

Keeven's hand slowly balled into a fist as he took in the alien figure and the likenesses of his companions. "What in the *fuck* is this supposed to be?"

Shaan studied them, a sliver of doubt edging into her mind. Keeven's outrage seemed anything but insincere, and Leesongronski truly looked like he was about to be sick.

Her voice dropped low. "*The End of Our Days of War.* One of the most famous artworks of the age," she said. "It's the sealing of the truce with the Felen! You're seriously telling me that *neither of you* have ever seen this painting before?"

"Is this a joke?" Keeven growled. "Whatever weird scam you're trying to pull here, I've had enough. And we don't know any gods-damned peace activists, okay?" He turned abruptly and spat onto the floor. "The only way this war's ever gonna end is when there's no one left alive to fight the Felen. Believe me, it's a lost cause."

Shaan sucked in a painful breath, her vision blurring slightly. She steadied herself against the wall. "No. The war with the Felen ended a hundred and fifty-two years ago," she whispered. "And *they* stopped it." She pointed back at the Leesongronski in the portrait. "That's the Pathfinder. Professor Eldric Leesongronski, the captain of the great ship *Jonah*. The Fortunate Five sealed the truce with the Felen at Etraxas and ended the war."

There was a long, awkward silence. Keeven and Leesongronski looked at each other.

And then, Keeven burst out laughing.

JERETH

Some Crappy Little Bar, Hanioch Inner System
16 years before the Rift

JERETH COULDN'T REMEMBER exactly how he'd ended up in this particular dingy bar. He didn't even know where the place *was* exactly, or what this town was called. He remembered storming off the UWDF cruiser and onto the Hanioch orbital base, then grabbing his stuff and jumping onto the first planet-bound transit he saw. He'd ridden the ground train to the end of its route, where he supposed he'd probably marched into the first bar he came across and started drinking.

He was in the mood to destroy something—anything, everything, starting with himself.

Empty shot-glasses littered the counter in front of him, but he couldn't recall what he'd been drinking. He grabbed the one closest to him and sniffed it. Bitters. Damn it, he didn't even like bitters.

"Another one?" said the barkeep, reaching for the bottle.

Jereth raised a hand. "Actually... no. No more for me. I'm leaving."

He threw a handful of loose credit chits onto the countertop, staggered to his feet and shuffled to the door.

He had no idea where he'd go next, but it didn't exactly

matter anymore. He'd officially been dumped out of the UWDF, stripped of his command and unceremoniously dismissed. The deffies were bloody fools, the whole lot of them. He was probably the best pilot in the whole damn sector, and they really wanted to assign him to another useless patrol tour in a Prime system?

Problems with authority, said his dismissal record. *Unable to follow orders. Unsuitable for further military duty.*

So maybe he hadn't taken the demotion from Squadron Leader particularly well. And he may have accidentally started a fistfight with a higher-ranking UWDF officer. *You're finished, Keeven. You'll never fly a UWDF ship again. You're a disgrace.* Well, so what? If they hadn't sacked him this time, he would've quit anyway. Jereth Keeven was done with the United Worlds Defence Forces, for good.

Screw the UWDF, screw the Felen, and screw this gods-damned war. This had never been Jereth's thing anyway. Becoming some kind of UWDF hero had always been his brother's dream. But Ludyth Keeven was long dead, buried in a desert on Desmoën, without ever having left that dusty rock. And for some reason, Jereth was still alive.

Jereth blinked back angry tears as he stumbled out of the bar, trying to get his bearings. Nothing looked familiar. There were a few squat, flat-roofed residential compounds nearby. Most of the windows were dark, but a couple of cheap food-markets at street level still looked open. In the distance, he spotted a flickering sign for a ground train stop. That must've been where he came in.

How long had he been in that bar? The planet's fat orange sun had long ago set, and a few hazy stars now glowed over the horizon.

Gods damn it, his head was spinning. Maybe looking up at the sky hadn't been a great idea.

He looked back down, steadying himself against the wall—and then he saw the low archway leading into the building across from the bar. The symbol for 'chance' was embedded over the door.

Jereth laughed to himself. It figured that the bar was right next door to a gambling-house. An age-old combination: either you'd get drunk and go waste all your money, or else you'd lose it all first and come to drown your sorrows.

All terrible ideas seemed like good ones at that moment. Jereth took a deep breath of cold, sharp night air before he pushed open the door, hoping he wouldn't look so inebriated as to be thrown right back out again. He stumbled over the low step on the way in, despite his best efforts to walk as straight as possible. But no one looked twice at him as he entered, and he slouched into the gambling-house unnoticed.

The whole place was one long, shabby rectangular room, with a few tables for dice running along one side. About half the seats were occupied, mostly by bored-looking locals. At the very back stood a brightly-coloured double roulette wheel; he'd seen the same kind in gambling-houses back on Desmoën.

Jereth knew enough half-decent cheats to swindle a win at some games, but games of pure chance were a foolish waste of money. Still, he found himself walking toward that back corner, where a roller in a stiff, gaudy uniform was spinning the nested wheels. Two balls bounced around in the gold-rimmed maze in the centre. Jereth stared dizzily at the hypnotic pattern.

The group of players around the table watched as the balls tumbled round and round until the wheel gradually slowed. Each small globe made a final revolution and then clinked down through the maze, until it fell through a hole and dropped into the painted grid below.

The roller whistled softly as the balls came to rest in the grid.

"Well, well. Another win to you, my friend," the roller said.

The victor sat at the far side of the table, just out of Jereth's view. The rest of the players all looked annoyed, their expressions tight-lipped and dour. No one liked to lose, but this bunch seemed particularly tense, their eyes darting furtively from the roller to the victor. No one was saying anything.

Jereth stepped closer to the table, circling casually toward the other side. The recipient of the winnings was in view now: a pallid, serious-looking man about Jereth's age, with jet-black hair pulled back into a long, neat ponytail. He was wearing black from head to foot, and a thin cigarette was stuck behind his ear. With his milk-pale complexion and strangely formal clothes, he could not have looked more out of place.

The man in black glanced at the winnings displayed on the panel next to him, looking unperturbed. He steepled his hands in front of him as the roller placed the gold and silver balls back into the wheel and gave the contraption another spin.

One by one, the players placed their betting disks into the grid to secure their bets, and the board filled up quickly. Jereth nudged his way forward. There was a nervous energy around the table, a lingering tension, like things were about to get interesting.

The man in black was the only one who hadn't placed his bet yet when the roller let go of the wheel, but players still had a few seconds to add a disk to the board after the spin had started. Everyone's gaze lingered over the man, and the roller watched him closely as the balls started clinking down into the maze.

Jereth also watched him. Bizarrely, he was just sitting there staring straight ahead, unmoving, unblinking, completely still—like he was looking right *through* the spinning wheel. The balls in the maze were a blur now, tiny streaks of silver and gold, glinting as they bounced around.

"Bets down in three…" said the roller. "Two… one…"

Still the man in black didn't move... and then, an instant before a high chime sounded to cut off the bets, he stuck out his arm. He dropped his disk into the grid where a flower symbol and a star symbol intersected, then yanked his arm back, steepled his hands again, and waited.

The wheel slowed to a stop, the balls jingling down toward the grid. Jereth watched in fascination as the gold ball settled in the row with the flower symbol. There was a murmur around the table. The silver ball clinked along behind, dropping through the hole above the star.

"Lucky... yet again," said the roller, scowling.

The whispers around the table were unmistakable now; all eyes were on this man who seemed about as indifferent to his winnings as he was to the rest of the room. He made no expression of joy or surprise. He didn't speak. He just pressed the button in front of him to collect his winnings, then resumed staring straight ahead.

"Bets on the table!" said the roller, rapping two knuckles against the side of the wheel. "Next round!"

Then Jereth saw the roller's hand dart briefly under the table and flick a hidden switch.

Almost instantly, three bulky figures in matching staff uniforms peeled away from the side wall and started moving toward the table.

Security.

The roller spun the wheel, watching the approaching security guards. The bets were counted down. Again, there was no move from the man in black until the very last moment before the chime sounded, when he briskly dropped his disk onto the intersection of a ship symbol and a feather symbol.

The wheel crawled to a stop, and the balls started to fall. Everyone at the table stood up in unison, eyes fixed on the dropping spheres. A loud gasp went up from the table, and a moment later the ship and the feather glowed on the screen suspended above.

The man in black picked up his betting disk and reached out to collect his winnings, but the first security guard was already there, wrenching his arm abruptly behind his back.

"What do you think you're doing? Are you cheating, you little gutter-rat?"

"Whoa, easy!" protested the man in black. He looked around in bewilderment, as if he'd only just become aware of the other people in the room. "I didn't do anything wrong!"

The guard grabbed him roughly by the chin, digging thick fingers into his cheek and forcing his head to one side. "How'd you do it, huh? How'd you rig the game? Are you aware of the consequences of tampering with our equipment?"

"I didn't tamper with anything! I didn't—"

The second security guard grabbed the collar of his black shirt and smacked the back of his head. The cigarette fell from behind his ear and rolled away over the dirty floor.

The guard pointed at the wheel, then at the winnings displayed next to his spot at the table. "Don't tell me that's luck. Looks like cheating to me."

"You want to read our policy on cheating?" The other guard grinned, holding up a clenched fist. "I've got a copy... right here."

Maybe Jereth was too drunk to think straight. Maybe he was still desperate for a fight. Maybe it just felt like the right thing to do. But it was at that point that Jereth reached out and grabbed the nearest security guard by the arm.

"Hey! Let... let 'm go," Jereth slurred.

The guards smirked, turned to look at each other, then looked back at Jereth. One of them shook the man in black again. "Oh? Friend of yours?"

Jereth was suddenly aware that everyone in the room was

staring at him. Games at the neighbouring tables had stopped; all eyes were on the unexpected spectacle.

Jereth squared his shoulders. "Yeah. Sure. He's my friend... an' ... an' he said he didn't do anything... so let 'm go!"

He took a stumbling step forward and shoved the guard.

And before he could get his balance back, a fist struck him right in the chin.

THE NEXT THING Jereth knew, he was lying on the dry patch of grass between the gambling-house and the bar he'd been in before. He must have blacked out for a few seconds after he took that punch. There was a thundering pain in his skull.

He probed at his aching jaw—nothing felt broken, thank the gods. Jereth opened his eyes and tried to sit up, instantly regretting it as the alcohol-laced contents of his stomach rushed up into his throat. He rolled over and spat out a mouthful of blood before throwing up over the grass.

"Well, *that* was some extraordinarily bad judgement," said a voice from beside him.

Jereth turned his head and saw the man in black lying on the grass next to him, flat on his back. His ponytail had come undone, and blood was streaming from a cut below his eye.

"What did you do a daft thing like that for?" The man shook his head. "You're a fool."

"Hey, I was defending you!" Jereth protested. "They were gonna punch your face in!"

"Yes, well, you didn't exactly stop that from happening, did you?" The man wiped the blood from his face with the edge of one dark sleeve, then sighed heavily. "I guess I should give you some kind of reward, to thank you for the effort... but my money was all in that betting disk. I don't suppose you want to go back in there and ask them for my winnings?"

Jereth looked at him incredulously, not sure if he was joking or not. "...No."

"Ah. Well, maybe you're not a complete fool, then." The man in black reached his arm out and offered a palm. "My name is Eldric Leesongronski."

"Leeg-*what?*" Jereth mumbled. "I'm not gonna 'member *that,* even if I wasn't six hours from sober." He raised his palm in return. "Name's Jereth."

"Jereth, the not-quite-complete-fool." His new acquaintance smiled distantly.

Jereth raked his hair back from his face. "Y'know, if you wanna talk about being a complete fool, Leeg... here's a tip. When you're cheating in a gambling-house, it's not a great plan to win the same game a dozen times in a row."

"But I wasn't cheating! There aren't any rules against predicting where the balls will drop. Only against tampering with the machines," Leeg said.

Jereth frowned. He felt like he might be sobering up, but his spinning head hadn't caught up yet. "Predicting? What, like... you're sayin'... you can foresee the future or something?"

Leeg laughed glibly. "That *is* what predicting means, yes."

Jereth rolled his eyes. It hurt.

"I know... about... games of chance," Jereth said slowly, trying not to slur his words. "An' I... I know a lot of good gambling scams, too. I grew up in a dust town on Desmoën—there wasn't a hell of a lot else to do." He paused and pondered. "That game you were playing, that wheel... that game's pure luck. The wheel moves on more than one axis... each spin's totally unique..." He rubbed his eyes, sifting through his blurry thoughts for the words he wanted. "So how'd you get your guesses that accurate? You got some kind of special implants or something?"

Leeg shrugged. "No. Mathematically speaking, it's a closed

system. As soon as those balls drop and the roller lets go of the wheel, that particular future is sealed. Unless something interferes with the machine itself—which, as we've just established, is against the rules—it's just a matter of observing the system to calculate each ball's most probable trajectory."

"Observing," repeated Jereth. "Trajectory... right. So... you're..."

"A mathematical genius, yes. A cheater, no. I didn't break any rules."

"I don't think they're interested in what you did or didn't break," Jereth said, gesturing back toward the gambling-house. "They were pretty damn keen to break your bones." He dragged himself up onto his elbows and clutched the grass with both hands, trying to convince himself that the ground wasn't actually moving. "We should—we should prob'ly get out of their yard soon, huh?"

Leeg scrambled to his feet, brushing dry grass from his dark trousers. Then he leaned over and—with considerable difficulty—hauled Jereth up by the shoulders.

"Wow. You're *really* drunk, aren't you?"

"You're a genius, all right," muttered Jereth, leaning on Leeg for balance. "So, what're you doin' in this hole, anyway? Shouldn't you be at a... at a university or something? Or gettin' your brain probed for science?"

"I was just passing through on the way to a job," Leeg said with disinterest. "My last job didn't pay me, and I ran out of money. I needed to get to the outer system by tomorrow, though... but I guess I'm stuck here. I sank the last of my money into that game."

They were walking now—well, more like stumbling arm in arm—with Leeg struggling to compensate for Jereth's erratic steps. Jereth didn't know where they were going, and he couldn't recall asking Leeg to follow him. But at the same time, he was currently relying on Leeg to keep him standing upright, so he probably shouldn't complain. Leeg was also carrying Jereth's backpack, Jereth noticed with a start.

"So, uh... what's your job?" asked Jereth, his eyes fixed on the pack that contained the sum total of his own money.

"I'm a subspace navigator." Leeg stopped walking. "A commercially-certified jump architect."

"Huh. We still have those?" Jereth swung around to look at Leeg, and nearly lost his balance. "I thought nav computers did all that fancy jump calculation stuff now."

"Navigational computers are fine for known jump paths," Leeg said, "but they're useless for working out new ones. Turns out that when there's an interstellar war going on, there's suddenly a market for finding new jumps and looking for new navigable subspace streams. You've got to calculate it all from scratch, and no computer can reliably do *that*."

"But *you* can do it? Reliably?"

"You'll never meet an unreliable jump architect," said Leeg drily. "Only reliable ones."

"Ohhh... because... because the ones who screwed up... they're all dead, right?" mumbled Jereth after a pause. "That's a joke. I got it. You're funny, Leeg."

"Yes," said Leeg, patting his shoulder. "That's right. They're dead."

"So, how many new subspace streams have you found?" Jereth asked.

"Ummm..." Leeg stared up at the starry sky. "Well... technically... zero. I haven't discovered any totally new streams. Not yet." He took a deep breath. "I've done more than a hundred and forty halvers without losing an envelope, though."

"Halvers?"

"Yeah. Jumping new routes through known subspace streams. That's hard enough to do. One wrong move and your envelope collapses, and that's it—ship's gone. One blink and it's over."

Jereth nodded. "Huh. So... who's payin' you to do that? The UWDF?"

Leeg laughed derisively. "No. Big multi-system shipping companies, mostly. Apparently business is terrible right now because of all the restrictions on trade, with the war and everything—and when a company does get a permit, it's usually only good for a few weeks. They want to maximize their delivery times, get in as many runs as they can while the permit lasts. Better jumps mean less time wasted, so they're investing in finding new shortcuts. It's good for company profits."

"But... the last company you worked for didn't pay you," Jereth pointed out. He was inordinately proud of himself for having remembered that fact—he *must* be sobering up.

"Well," Leeg said with a sigh, "it's a risky business. When two out of their three architects lose ships in the same week, what do you think happens? The company folds... and the third architect doesn't get paid."

"Shit," Jereth muttered.

"Yes," Leeg said. And then, after a pause: "Speaking of navigation, have you given any thought to where we're going right now? You're still drunk, and I'm still broke."

"Well... just as well you're sober an' I've got some money in here, then," said Jereth. He reached to retrieve his pack from Leeg's shoulder. "I think... we should prob'ly stick together for a bit."

UMA
Command Deck, ZeyCorp Gallion

UMA SAT IN Fransk's office, idly flicking at the Rift data on her lightpad. She'd slept so fitfully that she felt like she'd barely closed her eyes. Every muscle in her body was tense, and the scant rest had done nothing to alleviate the knot of anxiety in her ribcage.

The captain seemed fragile, exhausted and vulnerable. He looked older than she'd ever seen him. There was an ashen hue to his brown skin, and his eyes were bloodshot, shadows forming under them. She wondered if he'd slept at all.

Fransk had probably hoped that getting some rest would make it all go away, that it was all some strange awful dream. But, no—the *Jonah* was still sitting in their cargo bay. Their five mysterious guests were still on board. The *Gallion*'s engines still wouldn't start.

And somehow, things had gotten worse.

"What was Shaan thinking? She was only meant to take them to their apartments, not on an art tour of the atrium!" Barnabyn blustered. "What did she tell Leesongronski about the Fortunate Five? Now I've got this to worry about, on top of all the lies we've been telling the Ambassador?"

"Would you calm down?" Uma said. "You keep telling me they're just scam artists, that our Leesongronski is an impersonator, that this is all a hoax. So what does it matter if Shaan told him things about the Fortunate Five? Hmm? You can't have this both ways, Barnabyn."

Barnabyn looked taken aback.

"We didn't exactly confine our visitors to quarters," Fransk said with a grim nod. "I suppose they could just as easily have gone into the atrium and read the plaque on their own. They're our guests, Director Barnabyn. This ship isn't a prison."

"Gods! They could all be out there right now, sitting around in the canteen, talking to our crew," Barnabyn protested, his brow furrowed. "Let's get a full staff memo out, immediately. I want this situation locked down. No one on the *Gallion* crew is to speak to the visitors without explicit permission from the administration. And under no circumstances will any of us tell them that we have a Felen on board. We need to keep the Ambassador out of this."

"Fine." Uma bit back her frustration. "I'll tell the engineers. But we still need to figure out what's really going on here." She set her lightpad on the edge of Fransk's desk, flicking away the relentless, harrowing rows of figures still coming back from the *Gallion*'s hover probes. "I want to get a closer look at the *Jonah*. If that hauler isn't a genuine antique, then it's the best fake I've ever seen. I could take some samples from the hull... we could analyze the materials, and run a few tests to check the—"

"Director Ozakka, remember that you're an engineer on this ship, not a historian." Barnabyn sniffed indignantly. "We still need an engine fix."

Uma's shoulders stiffened. "And we are *working* on it. But we also need to find out for sure who these people are! Can't you see how this might be important?"

"You know, I think I did a school project about the Fortunate Five once," Fransk mused thoughtfully. "But I can't say I actually remember all that much about them."

Barnabyn grimaced. "Me neither. I must've been asleep when we covered the *Jonah* mission in history class. It's kind of embarrassing, actually... I know all their nicknames and what each of them did for the Peace, but only if I sing that *Flight of the Jonah* song to myself."

"Embarrassing, maybe, but not surprising," said Uma. "The Union went to a lot of trouble back then to make sure people didn't learn too much about the Five's origins. I mean, it wouldn't have looked very good if humanity's Peacemakers weren't the most *reputable* of citizens. A lot of the details about their lives were... quietly forgotten."

"Ah! You're talking about Leesongronski's shady past, aren't you?" Barnabyn's face lit up with some distant memory. "I remember now! He was wrongly accused of stealing from a bank or something, wasn't he...? But then he was exonerated. His name was cleared."

"Oh, sure. His name was cleared, they arrested somebody else," said Uma. "As for whether he was actually innocent or not, well, that's a whole different story. There's loads of convincing evidence that Leesongronski was behind one of the biggest banking hacks in history. It was part of this years-long cybercrime spree that happened while he lived in Sëgra City, a whole bunch of hacks attributed to a notorious hacker called the Jetsetter."

"Really? Leesongronski was in Sëgra City?" Barnabyn wrinkled his nose. "I don't remember any of that from history class. Apparently *somebody* was paying closer attention than me in school."

"Gods, no, no, none of this was taught in school," Uma said. "You won't find it on the knowledge banks, either. You've got to dig deep, read all of Leesongronski's unauthorized biographies, to find the good stuff."

"Right. And you read all of those? Since yesterday?"

"I've been interested in the *Jonah* voyage for years. Ever since I was a child, I've read everything I could find about the Fortunate Five. Including the, uh... more unofficial sources," Uma said.

Barnabyn made a disdainful noise. "You mean the conspiracy theories."

Fransk rubbed at the worried crease between his eyebrows. He didn't say anything.

"Well, I've just always found it fascinating how these people could be so damn important to humanity, but we're happy to know so little about them," said Uma. "And that's exactly why I think we need to ask more questions about our guests before we—"

"But what is the *point* of all this, Director?" Barnabyn interrupted. "I don't mean to be rude, but what is this going to accomplish in regard to *getting us out of here?*"

"I... Well, I guess... I don't know," Uma conceded with a sigh. "I just feel like we're on the edge of figuring something out, don't you? Like there's a missing piece here, something that can explain all of this. They have the answers. I feel it."

Fransk sighed. "They said they aren't answering any more strange questions. I doubt you'll change Keeven's mind, and Leesongronski didn't seem eager to chat."

"We haven't tried talking to any of the others yet!" Uma said insistently. "What about Keila Kva-Sova? Maybe she can tell us something... like how she even got on the *Jonah* in the first place. Think about this. If Eldric Leesongronski *isn't* working for Geminus, then what is the *Voicegiver* doing on his ship? How come the Voicegiver is there, but not the Decipherer? Who in the hells are Jereth Keeven and Dargo Mendeg, and why is

Leesongronski not in command of the mission? It doesn't make *any* sense! None of this matches the historical record."

Fransk had flicked open his lightpad and had brought up an article about Keila Kva-Sova in the *Gallion*'s knowledge bank. He flipped curiously through some pictures, then selected and enlarged one. The Voicegiver's serene, strange-eyed face peered from the projection, rows of silvery blue scales glinting up her ridged neck—indistinguishable from the stranger they'd met the night before. "Hmm," he said thoughtfully. "So... hang on. How was Kva-Sova connected to the others in our history? It says here she was working on the Voicing procedure under the Geminus Initiative's protection."

Uma nodded. "Yes, that's right. Kva-Sova worked for years on the Peace Project, which was *incredibly* illegal. The Geminus Initiative was building secret observatories in deep space, trying to send signals to the Felen. They thought peace was possible if only they could find some way to communicate with the Felen... but at the time, any civilian attempt to contact alien intelligence was considered an act of treason."

Barnabyn was slowly sinking lower into his chair as she spoke, as if the weight of all this information were literally pressing on his shoulders.

"These mods, all these scales on her face, the long ears... these are all gene tweaks?" Fransk flicked to the next picture, zooming in on one of Kva-Sova's pointed ears. "Huh. It looks... so old-fashioned." Hardly anyone wore cosmetic mods anymore.

"Extreme tweaks like this were in style back then. It was high fashion in some cities," Uma said. "Kva-Sova was one of the best cosmetic geneticists of her generation. She made her living doing all kinds of those animal fashion mods, editing foreign things into people. Extra ears, fish-scales, whiskers with feeling in them, tails that twitched. But she was actually using her cosmetic lab as a cover for the work she was doing for Geminus. Experimenting with splicing Felen cells into the human brain, trying to activate telepathic speech. Researching the Voicing."

"Gods," Fransk whispered.

"Well, we can hardly just walk up to her and *ask* her about all that, can we?" Barnabyn said. "Even if she is the real Keila Kva-Sova—which she obviously isn't—do you really think she'd tell you about it? 'Oh, excuse me, are you a traitor to the Union? Have you illegally inserted any Felen genes into human brains lately?'"

Fransk's frown deepened. "They got awfully defensive when they thought we were calling them peace activists. We need to tread carefully here."

Just then, an insistent buzz sounded at Fransk's office door.

No company picture flashed up on the inner ident-panel. It was a visitor without a ZeyCorp staff ID.

The three of them looked at each other for a moment, then Fransk wordlessly twirled out his virtual console. His right hand flicked a quick prayer gesture before he touched the door release.

And there stood Jereth Keeven, wearing the same rumpled trousers and scuffed jacket as yesterday.

"Great, you're all here," Keeven said. "We need to talk."

THE CONFERENCE HAPPENED in the meeting-room on the Command deck. Uma had an abiding aversion to this room, its walls all patterned with symmetrical designs in airy shades of violet. A ZeyCorp logo shimmered high above a polished white table, and the ceiling was sheathed in strips of pale ambients that vaguely suggested daylight. A few arti-plants wound their way up the walls, the kind with leaves that moved and rustled as if they were cavorting in some invisible breeze. Standard corporate chic, and the opposite of soothing. The place called up memories of long, droning speeches from visiting corporate stiffs.

On the few occasions Uma had been trapped in this room, she'd seen a good deal of cringe-inducing formalities and awkward pleasantries. But today, the room hosted the strangest meeting any ZeyCorp administrator would ever attend.

Along one side of the table—the side where visitors to the *Gallion* usually sat—were the crew and passengers of the *Jonah*. Uma realized with a chill that the three had happened to arrange themselves in the same order as they appeared in the famous painting: Jaxong at the far end, then Kva-Sova, then Leesongronski. Keeven and Mendeg sat in what should have been the Negotiator and Decipherer's positions. Uma shivered again.

Her eyes drifted back to Leesongronski. He wore another bell-sleeved black dress-shirt, slightly different from yesterday's, neatly buttoned up to the top. His black formal jacket was laid over the back of his chair again. Leesongronski looked up, sensing her gaze on him, and she quickly looked away.

Captain Fransk cleared his throat. "Well. Thank you all very much for coming," he said. "I hope we can... ah... clear some things up with an open dialogue."

Fransk had taken his usual spot: in the middle of the table, facing the visitors, flanked by his two directors. The lightpad in front of him glowed faintly in sleep-mode, as though it were waiting to be woken for a boring introduction to some new company policy. But Uma had never seen Fransk look this nervous presenting a policy. His forehead glistened with sweat.

"I apologize that we started off on the wrong foot yesterday," Fransk continued. "Perhaps we could've been more forthright." He tugged at the collar of his blazer. "If there's anything we can do—"

"Look, Captain, we're real grateful for the rescue," Keeven said, cutting him off. "But we can't stay here any longer. I'm running on a tight deadline, understand? I need to negotiate some kind of deal with you, whatever'll get me my ship back, with a full energy cell." He gestured down the table at Jaxong and Kva-Sova. "How 'bout we compromise? You give me my ship and charge my energy cell, and those two can stay with you. I don't have room for 'em anyway. You can have a nice long chat, ask each other any questions you like. But not us." He indicated Leesongronski, Mendeg and himself. "The three of us really need to go."

Kva-Sova and Jaxong glanced at each other, but neither spoke.

Worry flashed across Fransk's face. "I'm afraid that won't be possible. Like we told you yesterday, your ship's shielding won't hold against the Rift energy. Your engines won't start. There's nowhere to go. And as of yet, we're uncertain how we'll get our own ship out of this... this 'Rift-space.'"

Keeven's eyes narrowed with suspicion.

"There's a second problem," Uma said. "We haven't got any power spare to recharge your energy cell. The *Gallion*'s emergency cells will run out soon. With our engines down, we can't generate more power, and every attempt we make to reboot our engine cores is draining us. It's a matter of *days* before this ship's depleted."

"Oh, yeah?" Keeven sat back in his chair. "I'm not sure I buy that, Ozakka. See, I watched that little safety demonstration that came on in my room, and it said this ship's equipped with enough emergency power to last for six *months*."

Uma almost laughed. "You mean that ZeyCorp safety reel? Sure, we could survive for six months if we shut down all our systems and sealed ourselves into the isolated emergency chamber. We'd make it even longer than that, since there's so few of us on board. That chamber runs on a sliver of power, just enough to keep us from freezing and to maintain a bare minimum of air and water recycling... until help comes." She bit the inside of her lip. "But, see... we have no idea if our distress signal even reached anyone. We still can't connect to the network or determine our location. It's likely there *isn't* any help coming."

Out of the corner of her eye, she saw Barnabyn slump in defeat.

"These are the facts," she said. "We're off the grid out here. The gods alone know where we are... or even *when*. If we shut down our instrumentation, black out this ship and go into that chamber, we'll just be waiting to die in there slowly. Waiting to starve to death or suffocate. We need to find a way out of here while our main systems are still operational."

Fransk nodded gravely. "Director Ozakka is right. Like it or not, we need each other. We saved your lives by pulling in the *Jonah*. And now we're asking for your help."

Keeven's gaze darted warily around the room, like he was searching it for some threat, or perhaps a hidden camera. "Right. But whoever you think we are... this is a big misunderstanding," he said. "We haven't got anything to do with this Geminus Initiative you keep talking about."

"I know that," Fransk said. "But our Engineering team still needs access to your ship's sensor logs. We need to run a comparison, yours to ours. It's possible that your logs hold some clue about the makeup of this anomaly—"

"Oh, come on!" Mendeg interrupted, elbowing Keeven hard enough to make him flinch. "Keeven, we don't have to talk to these people, or give 'em anything! This is nonsense!"

"Of course you don't have to." Fransk kept his cool, dropping his voice into the same pacifying tone he took when the research teams squabbled over equipment allocations. "We're simply asking for a civil dialogue. To see if we can cooperate."

Mendeg curled his lip, practically baring his teeth. "Civil dialogue? What the fuck's that supposed to mean? How about you give us our bloody ship back, how's that for civil dialogue?"

He started to stand up, but Keeven held up one hand, motioning the burly engineer back into his seat. "Let me handle this, Mendeg. Keep calm."

"*Calm?* Really?" Mendeg shoved Keeven's arm away. "Not only have they been tellin' us they're from the damn future, but they're implyin' we're all traitors!" He slammed his palms on the table and whirled toward Fransk. "That's what you think, right? These three over here, they're all workin' for that Peace Project? Contactin' the Felen?" He pointed down the table at Jaxong, Kva-Sova and Leesongronski.

Fransk edged his chair back from the table. "That's what the history texts say. Now, clearly there's some sort of mist—"

"I don't care!" Mendeg got to his feet again. "This whole business has fuck-all to do with me and Keeven. We're not in your 'Fortunate Five.' So the two of us can leave, right? They stay, we go."

"Go where? Out an airlock?" Keeven said. "We aren't going anywhere without Leeg. Would you just sit down, Mendeg?"

Mendeg did not sit down.

"You know what? I'm not takin' orders from you anymore, Keeven," he snarled. "You want to sit in here and negotiate with these degenerates, when they told you they're allied with the Felen?" He jabbed a thick finger toward his companions. "You all have a choice. If you *collaborate*, you're all traitors to the Union. Me, I'm getting the fuck out of this room."

He whirled and stormed to the exit.

The door opened and Mendeg stumbled into the corridor. His stomping footsteps receded as he barrelled away in the direction of the lifts, a string of unintelligible curses echoing behind him.

Keeven lifted his head. Beneath that unkempt mop of hair, his eyes were grim. And when he went to push his hair back from his face, his hand was shaking. From this angle, Uma glimpsed a perfectly round, knotted scar on the side of his neck. *Stasis scarring.* That was how they did it in the old days when they put you down—they'd stick you with one port in the neck and two in the spine. Jereth Keeven must have served time in a stasis prison.

"Well?" Keeven said. "Anyone else got somethin' smart to say?"

Eldric Leesongronski sat motionless, steepling his hands in front of him. Keila Kva-Sova was watching Keeven, her sharp ears pointing straight up, alert and quivering, like prey sensing danger. At the end of the row, Charyne Jaxong slouched sullenly in her chair, arms crossed. She still wore that oversized sweater, a poorly-manufactured garment that looked more like it would have fit Mendeg.

None of them spoke.

"This is not going very well," Barnabyn muttered to himself.

Keeven let out a long sigh. "Fine, how about this? If it'll settle things up, I'll get you those sensor logs off my ship. But I want a little something in return."

"Certainly," said Fransk, sounding anything but certain.

"You claim you've talked to the Felen, right? So... you must know a lot about 'em?" Keeven scrutinized the captain opposite him, gesturing at the lightpad on the table. "And you've got a lot of weird gadgets around here. I have a friend who collects Felen tech. You happen to have any of that lying around? Weapons, maybe? Military tech to trade?"

Any scrap of intact Felen tech would have been worth a small fortune on the black market in Keeven's time. And weapons, a large fortune.

"We don't carry weapons of any kind," Fransk said. His

voice was slow and measured, as if every syllable required a superhuman effort. "We are a law-abiding civilian vessel. And we are at peace with the Felen. We have no need to be armed."

Keila Kva-Sova emitted a muffled gasp, and everyone in the room turned to look at her.

A lone tear had escaped from under her unnaturally long eyelashes. It slid over the jutting angles of her cheekbone, following the ridges in her face all the way down to her chin.

"I... I have a question," she whispered. The glow in her eyes flared like a tiny amber flame. "If the Union really did make peace with the Felen a hundred and fifty-two years ago... does that mean the Peace Project succeeded?"

Fransk nodded solemnly. "It did, yes."

Her hands flew to her mouth, and when she lowered them again, her voice grew in confidence. "Captain Fransk... it's not true that none of us are involved with the Geminus Initiative," she said, pushing her chair back. "I am a member of the Peace Project. And I have been working with Geminus for years."

"You *what?*" Keeven nearly choked on the word, his eyes wide. "You—you're a gods-damned *peace activist?* I let you on my damn ship! I *helped* you!"

Beside him, Leesongronski's face was turning a sickly shade of grey.

"Oh, please," Kva-Sova shot back. "You knew I was running from something. You said you didn't want to know about my problems."

"Yeah, well, I thought you had *normal* problems! Like maybe you stole something from the wrong person, or you were hopping out-system without a permit!" Keeven shouted. "Excuse me if I didn't immediately jump to *high fucking treason*. Gods damn it. We never should've picked you up."

Leesongronski muttered something under his breath, too low for Uma to hear properly, but it sounded a lot like 'I told you so.'

Charyne Jaxong sat in silence. She was fiddling with a loose loop of synthetic fibers on her sleeve, winding the thread around her finger and then unwinding it again, not looking at the others. Uma hadn't heard Jaxong utter a word since she'd told them her name in the cargo bay.

Kva-Sova looked away from Keeven, turning her pleading gaze back to Fransk. "Please, Captain Fransk. I need to know what happened. How was the Peace made, in your history? How did we get through to the Felen? Was it the signals? Did we finally get them a message?"

"Um... ahem..." Fransk swallowed, his jaw working. He glanced at Uma. "Director Ozakka, ah... how should we...?"

"Captain," Barnabyn interjected. "Do you think it's wise to discuss this right now?"

"It was the Decipherer!" Uma blurted out before the captain could respond. "She was your success story. You performed your gene splice on her, and she acquired the telepathic sense, learned the Felen language. She translated the truce negotiations."

Kva-Sova let out a high-pitched keen. Her tattooed shoulders heaved, then she buried her face in both hands and started sobbing.

"Wait. Do you know who I'm talking about?" Uma whispered, her heart pounding in her throat. "Where is the Decipherer? The one you Voiced? Why isn't she with you?"

The Decipherer's identity had always been shrouded in mystery, even more so than the Negotiator's. Uma's skin prickled with the possibility of an answer. Where had the Decipherer come from? What did she look like? How old was she? There were dozens of theories, but no historian had ever come close to a conclusive answer. Historically speaking, the Decipherer was a ghost.

Kva-Sova lifted her head, her amber-hued eyes still shining

with tears. "I have no idea who you mean," she mumbled. "All my gene splice experiments failed. I thought we were getting close, but then the Peace Project was disbanded. We had to destroy our computers, we shut down our labs, we took all the signal hubs offline. The UWDF infiltrated us. Anyone with links to the Geminus Initiative is being arrested on treason charges—'unauthorized contact with alien intelligence.'" She glanced tearfully at Keeven. "That's why I was hiding from those soldiers on Pilar."

Keeven was glowering at Kva-Sova with revulsion.

"So... I guess you definitely don't all know each other through the Geminus Initiative," Uma said aloud. She wasn't entirely sure for whose benefit.

Kva-Sova shook her head. "No."

"'Course not! I told you I don't know any peace activists." Keeven grimaced. "She's just a hitchhiker! She paid me to get a ride off Pilar Outpost. Speaking of which, she still owes me twenty thousand creds."

"Wait, then what about... you?" Uma looked down the table at Charyne Jaxong, who still hadn't spoken a word. "How did you get on the *Jonah*, if—?"

"You mean our 'hijacker'?" Keeven interrupted with a brusque laugh. "Hah! We didn't even know her name until we got here! That wise-ass pulled a gun on me at Pilar and tried to steal my damn ship."

Jaxong remained engrossed in her synthetic string, still winding it around her finger.

"I wonder if we could return to our discussion about the sensor logs," Fransk said cautiously. "Captain Keeven?"

Keeven slumped forward in his chair, both trembling hands pressed to his forehead. He stayed that way for a few seconds, his expression unreadable. Finally, he swung his chair toward Leesongronski and motioned him closer.

The two of them put their heads together and had a short, whispered conversation. Then Leesongronski nodded resentfully, and Keeven turned back to the group.

"Fine," Keeven said. "You'll get the sensor logs. But there's one condition." Keeven clapped a hand onto Leesongronski's shoulder. "Leeg's gonna go with you to your Engineering deck. Anything you're doing, the numbers you're running, the data you're pulling from that Rift, you show *everything* to him. No more secrets."

Fransk glanced at Uma and Barnabyn in turn. "That... would probably be all right," he said. "Director Ozakka?"

"Of course! Yes!" Uma said, barely keeping the nervous excitement from her voice at the thought. Eldric Leesongronski, the Pathfinder himself, in the *Gallion*'s Engineering pit—

Suddenly, Charyne Jaxong sat up and straightened her shoulders. "I'll go to Engineering as well." She said it calmly, almost casually, like it was a perfectly reasonable statement. "I can help you."

"What are *you* going to help us with?" Leesongronski said. "Unless we happen to need another gun held to our heads... and you weren't even much good at *that*."

Jaxong paused a beat, then pushed up both sleeves of her oversize sweater, exposing her slender olive-skinned arms. "Well, I do happen to be a theoretical subspace physicist. Good enough for a top job with the UWDF, before I... took a leave of absence from the military science unit." She fixed Leesongronski with a disdainful stare. "Look me up. Professor Charyne Jaxong of the Samouga Research Institute. I'm probably the most useful person here."

Uma's heart jumped. Jaxong—the Inventor—had been one of the most qualified theoretical physicists the Worlds had ever seen, and that fact seemed to be unchanged in this somewhat divergent history. Whatever else had shifted in their timeline,

Jaxong had still been involved with the Samouga Research Institute. That had to mean something.

"Captain—" Barnabyn began.

"I think we could really use Professor Jaxong's expertise," Uma interrupted. She turned back to Jaxong. "We've been picking up some form of anomalous substrate energy in the Rift. Substrate energy research was one of your specialties at Samouga, wasn't it, Professor?"

Jaxong looked surprised. "Yes. So you *do* know of me! I'm impressed."

"Your theories are still fundamental to modern research," Uma said. "I don't think there's a subspace engineer or a physicist alive who doesn't know of you."

Keeven opened his mouth to say something, but Captain Fransk had already stood up from his chair with a decisive nod.

"Fine. Take them both to Engineering, Director Ozakka. They're on your team, starting now," he said. "Please ensure that you're sharing Rift-related data only, and nothing else." He shot Uma a pointed look. "No access to our systems, are we clear?"

"Clear. I'll take care of it, Captain."

Barnabyn heaved himself to his feet, looking shaken. "Gods," he muttered. "I sure hope this is a better idea than it seems."

SHAAN
Common Deck, ZeyCorp Gallion

SHAAN HAD NO destination in mind when she exited the lift. The *Gallion*'s power-conservation mode had been enacted ship-wide, and the ship's passageways were dark except for the tiny lights lining the corridors. The ambients along the ceiling flickered to life one by one as they sensed motion, then waned again as Shaan passed. She followed the familiar triangles of bright yellow that always pointed toward the front of the ship.

Everyone had been unsettled by the eerie silence since the engines stopped, until one of the techs had come up with the brilliant plan to pipe a low-volume recording of an engine hum throughout the ship. That had improved things slightly, but the illusion was a hollow one. There was still something wrong— the weight of a stillness that shouldn't be there, and a feeling of cold dread and finality that Shaan couldn't shake off.

In the canteen, everything was dark except the faintly pulsing neons of the vending machines, their chirpy displays still suggesting beverage options. For a brief moment, Shaan wondered how long they'd keep blinking after everyone on board was dead, but she pushed the morbid thought away.

Days, the Engineering team had said. They had a matter of

days left before it was too late.

How many days? How many hours? And too late for *what*, exactly? It wasn't as if anyone had a clue how to get the *Jonah* back to wherever it came from. Director Ozakka seemed convinced that Professor Leesongronski, at least, was the real thing. That the *Jonah* had somehow been transported here through time. But how could that be possible?

Maybe Macey's outlandish theory was right, and everyone on the *Gallion* was already dead. Shaan certainly felt as insubstantial as a ghost.

She walked toward the vending machines, pondering the likelihood that this could get any worse, when her foot caught on something soft in the dark. She jumped back with a yelp and looked down.

Gida, the Ambassador's Voiced, was sitting on the floor, tucked halfway under one of the tables. She had curled herself as small as possible, her knees pulled up to her chin, as if she'd been hoping to escape notice. The folds of her voluminous Felen robes were bunched up under her elbows, save for the single trailing edge that had snagged Shaan's foot.

"Oh my gods! Gida? What are you doing there?" Shaan's heart pounded, and she struggled to catch her breath.

"I—I'm so sorry, Director!" Gida stammered. "I didn't mean to startle you!"

Director?

The word jarred in Shaan's bleary mind, until she remembered the deception they'd wrought in the Ambassador's apartment. Was that really only yesterday? This poor, deluded girl still thought Shaan was the Director of Engineering. Gods damn it.

Before Shaan could say anything, Gida pulled herself up, her long, layered robes splaying over the floor as she stood. The kennai jewel on her forehead glinted in the dim light, swinging hypnotically on its delicate chain.

"I was hoping someone might come in... that I might overhear something about what's happening," Gida said. "No one will answer my calls over the comms. The Ambassador has been anxious for an update." Her voice was thin and plaintive—so unlike the low monotone that came out of her when she spoke for the Ambassador. "Please, Director. Tell me what's going on."

Shaan briefly considered maintaining the deception, but to what end? All she really wanted was for Gida to stop talking to her. For her to go away. For all of this to go away.

"I hate to tell you this, but I'm not actually the Director of Engineering," Shaan said. She tapped a fingernail against the ZeyCorp badge hanging on her collar. "See? I'm the ship's Facilities Coordinator."

Gida's expression clouded with confusion. "You're... the what?"

"I gave you that update yesterday because the director was too busy," Shaan said, her eyes skirting away from the girl's wide-eyed stare. "But I don't know anything about the engines. I don't even work in Engineering."

Gida's face crumpled fleetingly, but she quickly smoothed her expression, recovering the emotionless composure her training demanded.

"Oh," she said in a near-whisper. "I see."

"I'm sorry if that's disappointing," Shaan said. She hadn't meant for it to sound quite as cold as it did, but the Voiced didn't seem perturbed.

"I heard some of your crew talking earlier," Gida said. "They were saying that you haven't been able to make contact with anyone. That we're... lost. I have no idea what to tell the Ambassador. This was my first solo assignment, and I feel like I'm all alone out here..."

Shaan startled back. Her *first* assignment? Why hadn't Geminus chosen a more experienced Voiced, or sent so much as a single human adjunct to support her? It hadn't occurred to Shaan to wonder until now, but it did make perfect sense. This journey on the *Gallion* was some publicity op that ZeyCorp had cooked up, not a serious diplomatic endeavour. Geminus wouldn't have sent anyone important; they'd send a nobody, a minor guest at the summit. An Ambassador who didn't even merit a full escort, accompanied by a Voiced who was practically still a novice. Who else would the Starhold agree to saddle with a human-run corporation's ridiculous publicity stunt?

"Help me," Gida said. She reached out for Shaan's arm, her fingers brushing the edge of Shaan's uniform sleeve. "Please. I'm scared, and no one will tell me anything—"

There was something about Gida's earnest, trusting stare that went through Shaan like an arrow. She recoiled and pulled her arm away, suddenly nauseated.

Gods, *why?* She had held it together when the Ambassador came on board. She had held it together though Barnabyn's endless protocol rehearsals, and even through that damned Engineering update Zel had forced her into, but this was too much. Seeing a Voiced again, up close, had dredged up everything she'd spent so much effort burying, and it was all she could do not to bolt from the room.

When she looked at Gida's pleading eyes, all she could see was the last young Voiced who had begged her for help.

Ashlish's eyes. Ashlish's terrified face. Ashlish's bloody hands as she crawled away over the floor, Ashlish screaming and screaming, her fingers scratching helplessly at Shaan's throat as Shaan held her by the wrists and—

Shaan stepped back, away from Gida.

No. *No.* She shoved the memories to the back of her mind. Nobody here knew about what she'd done six years ago. And no one would ever find out. Not ZeyCorp, not her friends and colleagues on the *Gallion*, and certainly not Gida. Shaan was a different person now.

"Leave the past in the past," she mumbled to herself, steadying herself against the table. "Leave the past in the past."

"You don't like me very much, do you?" Gida whispered. "I make you nervous?" She sighed sadly. "That's all right. Lots of people feel uncomfortable with the Voiced. We must seem so strange if you're not used to being around us, with the whole... alien sense thing..." She gestured vaguely toward the glittering kennai symbol on her forehead.

Shaan swallowed hard. "I have to go. I'm sorry. You should really be back in your apartment, with your Ambassador."

Before Shaan could take another step to leave, Gida reached out to grab her arm again.

"Wait, please!" she pleaded. "Please. Before you go... I have to tell you something."

Shaan stopped, her throat tightening. "Tell me what?"

Gida pointed across the canteen, at the vending machines. "I... I saw someone. About half an hour ago, standing right over there by that machine. A person who wasn't wearing your company uniform. She had a lot of facial mods... like those old-style animal gene tweaks..." Gida looked searchingly into Shaan's face, her voice scarcely more than a whisper. "If I didn't know better, I'd swear it was the Voicegiver herself."

Shaan froze. The pulsing neons were enough to have illuminated anyone standing by the machines, and Kva-Sova's face would be unmistakable at this distance: those eyes that glowed like pale flames over her unnatural cheekbones, those rows of fish-scales gleaming along her brow, those huge fan-like ears.

"Who is she?" Gida whispered. "We were told there would be no other guests during the Ambassador's stay. It was an explicit condition of our transport."

"You'll need to ask our Publicity Liaison about that." Shaan took another unsteady step back. "Go back to your apartment, Gida. Right now. You shouldn't leave the Ambassador alone. Go!"

Gida stared at Shaan in stunned silence. And then, without another word, she ran from the canteen. Her robes swirled behind her as the dim corridor swallowed her.

Shaan sank into the nearest chair, tears stinging sharply in her eyes as she choked back her horror.

SHAAN

Geminus Base, Border Zone Sector W1F
6 years before the Rift

SHAAN HAD BEEN in the detention centre for several weeks. At least, that's what they told her; she'd had no real sense of the passage of time since the shuttle crash. She hadn't been able to recall much of what happened at first. And when it started coming back to her, she only wished she could forget it again.

Whenever she closed her eyes, Shaan relived those last seconds before the crash—the awful moment when Ashlish, momentarily lucid, had realized what was happening to her. Over and over again, Shaan felt the instant she'd lost control of the shuttle, that sickening roll as she overshot the docking clamps, Ashlish frantic against the safety restraints, thrashing and screaming. So much blood everywhere.

After that, everything had gone black.

They said Shaan had been unconscious when the ruined shuttle was hauled into the evac ship. She'd woken hours later in a brightly-lit med-bay, her bones fractured, her internal organs crushed and her memories of the accident hazy. But she *had* woken, and that made her the lucky one. Ashlish never would.

Ashlish had died instantly on impact, they said. *Died instantly.*

And it was all Shaan's fault.

The medics were still resuscitating Shaan on board the evac ship when more bad news had come: Verkhoy Station had been destroyed, in a bizarre incident that would confound investigators for months and defy any logical explanation.

Verkhoy was an impressive, ultra-modern facility, anchored deep in a border sector. It had a rotating complement of six hundred and twenty-four inhabitants—mostly human adjuncts and administrators, alongside a handful of Felen and nearly five dozen Voiced.

The station served as the administrative hub for the Geminus Peace Alliance in the sector: an occasional diplomatic base, but mostly a showpiece, a small cog in the beautiful workings of the Alliance. Such little jewels of cooperation between the Union and the Felen Starhold dotted the border sectors like a glittering chain, underlining the achievements the Alliance had made in the years of the peace. *In Peace as One,* proclaimed the Geminus standard.

Until Verkhoy Station disappeared without a trace.

By all accounts, the unoccupied station had vanished from long-range scanners shortly after being emptied by the evacuation order, and no part of it had been recovered. There was no wreckage, no debris. Even the station's power supply, its Jaxong drive, had disappeared. It was as though an entire chunk of space had just turned in on itself like some cosmic sink-hole, sucking the station out of existence.

Shaan had been one of the last two people on board Verkhoy, disobeying the Governor's direct order to evacuate at once. Her actions were immediately deemed suspicious, and the addition of a dead Voiced to the matter didn't make things any simpler.

Not just any Voiced, either, but Ashlish, the most astonishing young prodigy that Verkhoy's program had ever seen. Ashlish was only an *ailukh*—a Voiced in training—but she was one of the most promising novices in recent memory. All her potential and talent had shattered along with that shuttle, along with her young life. She would never receive her cloak and kennai now. She was gone.

The autopsy confirmed that Ashlish died as a result of Shaan's unsuccessful docking with the evac ship. But Ashlish had other injuries, too—defensive injuries, signs of a struggle. Deep scratches on her arms and wrists. Finger marks on her neck. Slash wounds that couldn't be attributed to the shuttle crash. What exactly had happened on that ill-fated station? Everyone wanted to know.

Shaan couldn't believe anyone actually suspected her of Ashlish's murder, much less of sabotaging Verkhoy Station. Yes, she had breached the evacuation order, and she had lied to the Governor, and she had made some terrible, inexcusable mistakes... but of course Shaan hadn't done anything to the station, and she certainly hadn't killed Ashlish on *purpose!*

Still, Shaan wasn't allowed to leave her room in the detention centre without an armed escort, and whenever she was called to testify in the inquest, she was accompanied by a full Geminus security detail. Four guards would arrive to fetch her, their weapons primed behind the pale-pink shimmer of their body shields. It was ridiculous. She obviously wasn't dangerous; sometimes she needed to lean on one of the guards just to make it down the corridor.

Your detainment by the Deep Space Security Unit is just a formality, it's only until the inquest is concluded, she'd been told. *No one thinks you're responsible for what happened to the station, Shaan. And the crash will probably be ruled an accident. We just need to complete the investigation.*

Some days, Shaan was interviewed for hours on end. Other days, she might have thought they'd forgotten her entirely, if not for the cold meals thrust through the door. Sometimes, she was taken to be assessed by the medical examiner, who would fill out another report on the state of her injuries. She was given another battery of tests, then another psych exam. People wouldn't look her in the eye when they spoke.

And then came more questions from the Council. Questions about what happened on the station. Shaan never seemed to give the answers they wanted, and the words thrown about in the Council Hall struck at her like so many barbs: *potential terrorist* and *rule out nothing* and *lacks any credible explanation*.

She answered dutifully, mechanically, until she couldn't possibly imagine what more there was to say. Afterwards, she was taken back to the confinement room, where she lay on the narrow bed and stared at the ceiling. Waiting for it to be finished.

On the night before the verdict was to be read, Shaan sat in her room, slumped over on the bed with her back against the wall. She closed her eyes, trying not to think about what would happen next.

And then she heard the click and whirr of her room's secure door unlocking. Someone was opening the *whole* door. Not the food delivery hatch, and not the slit she had to slip her hands through to be cuffed. Her heart raced.

She sat up quickly, dropping her bare feet to the floor and smoothing her rumpled clothing. So far, every time she'd entered the Council Hall, she'd still worn a Geminus uniform; but now she was wearing the wrinkled civilian one-piece they'd given her, a clumsy grey garment that gaped at the neck and bunched up at the knees.

Shaan was shocked to recognize a senior Geminus officer in the open doorway, carrying one of those fancy geometric cases emblazoned with the official Border Security seal.

"Hello, Shaan." The officer flicked one hand, and a Geminus identification holo hovered over her palm: *Geminus High Commander K. Sifyer, Border Security.* "May I speak with you in private?"

Behind Commander Sifyer, the long corridor was deserted. No security detail. She was completely alone.

"Oh! Yes, of—of course," Shaan managed. "Come in."

Sifyer motioned Shaan toward the tiny table and chairs in the centre of the room. "Please, sit down."

Shaan had only ever seen Commander Sifyer from afar, in the Council Hall, sitting among the other human security officers assigned to observe the Verkhoy case. Each day of the inquest, Sifyer had been there behind a thick plate of pseudo-glass, listening to the proceedings, her gaze steady and serious.

The Commander normally wore the deep green blazer of her security detail, with the Heart of Geminus logo and the Border Security seal hanging at her collar. But not today. Instead of Geminus green, she wore plain grey trousers and a beige shirt that buttoned from the shoulder. Every fold in her clothing was perfect, as if it had been hot-pressed only moments before. Her hair was pulled back, covered by a brightly patterned canvas wrap.

"I apologize for my casual attire," Sifyer said, "but this is an... unofficial visit. I'm catching a transit out of here in a half-hour, so I'll have to make this quick."

The Commander set her bag on the floor and folded herself elegantly onto the opposite seat. Up close, she looked younger than Shaan would have imagined for such a high-ranking officer. Her uncreased brown skin shone under the room's low-hanging light, and she had a dramatic, sculpted arch to her eyebrows that gave her an inquisitive look.

"Our deliberations over the Verkhoy matter have concluded," Sifyer pronounced. "You will receive a formal verdict tomorrow, with the details of the Council's decision. But... after all you've been through, Shaan, I thought you deserved to hear this news in person."

"The inquest is over?" Shaan whispered. "Commander

Sifyer... you do believe me, don't you? I didn't murder Ashlish! And I didn't have *anything* to do with what happened to the station..."

Her voice faltered. It was irrelevant now, either way. The Commander was looking at her with genuine concern, looking her right in the eye, like no one had since the accident.

"I've always believed in your innocence, Shaan," the Commander said gently. "I've never thought for a moment that you killed Ashlish deliberately, or that you sabotaged the station. I think it was obvious to everyone in that Council Hall that you simply found yourself in the most unlucky of circumstances."

Hope welled in Shaan's chest. "So... the Council... they've cleared me?"

Commander Sifyer shook her head. "I'm afraid it's not that simple, Shaan. Losing a station in the border zone is serious, as you can tell by the number of senior officers and security specialists involved here." She gave a deep sigh. "Relations with the higher workings of the Felen Starhold are complicated at the best of times. The Starhold wants answers that we don't have, about the events on Verkhoy Station. This whole affair has been extraordinarily delicate."

Shaan nodded silently.

"As for your professional misconduct in the weeks leading up to the incident, that's a separate matter entirely," the Commander said. "That kind of thing is not usually the jurisdiction of Border Security. However, I did make my opinion known to the Council."

"It's bad news for me... isn't it?" Shaan could hardly get the words out.

"The Council exonerated you in regard to the station's disappearance," Sifyer said. "But your involvement in the death of an *ailukh* would always have carried serious consequences."

She looked pained. "There was sympathy in the Council due to your unusual situation, and I did suggest that they might find an appropriate position for you elsewhere in the Alliance's operations. Unfortunately, my suggestion was not well-met by the Council."

"Then... what's going to happen to me?" Shaan's voice quivered.

"You won't work for Geminus again," Sifyer said. "The Council has ordered your immediate and permanent dismissal. I'm sorry, Shaan."

"No!" Shaan choked, a dry sob escaping her throat. "No! But... but I—"

"Your service to the Alliance will be struck from the record. You'll be cleared to leave this base tomorrow, after a final psych assessment and exam. But, Shaan, from the moment you leave, you will be forbidden to ever discuss the fact that you were involved with Geminus. You are never to have any further contact with the Felen, or with the Voiced, or with anyone else affiliated with the Geminus Peace Alliance. These are the terms of your dismissal." The Commander paused. "This is a good thing, Shaan. No prison sentence, no criminal record. No record at all, as long you don't get into any more trouble. Think of it as a clean break."

"No... please..." Shaan whispered.

"As far as anyone outside of Geminus is concerned, you were never here. This never happened," Sifyer continued. "We've introduced a new record of employment to your profile in all public systems. It says you've been working in corporate administration for a few years, with glowing performance reviews. You shouldn't have any problems finding a new job."

Tears ran freely down Shaan's cheeks now.

"But—Geminus was my *life*, Commander. I don't know anything else."

"There are other ways to serve humanity, and to uphold the values of the Peace," Sifyer said with a reassuring nod. "I'm certain that you'll find a new calling, Shaan. You know... I believe all things happen for a reason, even if we can't see it at the time."

"*What* reason?" Shaan brushed tears from her cheeks with the back of her hand. "What purpose could *any* of this serve? Ashlish's death was *pointless!*"

Sifyer was quiet for a long time. "I'm sorry, Shaan," she finally said. "It's difficult to come to terms with a tragedy like this one. There are no words of comfort that can undo the pain." Her eyes never left Shaan's. "But the workings of destiny are not ours to unravel. The truth is, you and I will probably never understand why this happened, and we have to accept that."

"I don't *want* to accept it."

"And yet, as with all things we lose... as with all things that break our hearts... eventually, we must." Sifyer unfolded herself from the tiny chair and picked up her bag. "I wish you the very best in whatever you choose to do next, Shaan," she said. "Go in peace."

"Thank you, Commander," Shaan whispered.

Sifyer started to head for the door, then paused and looked back. "May the gods grant us solace from this tragedy. And may we strive to leave the past in the past."

UMA
Engineering Deck, *ZeyCorp Gallion*

IT TOOK THE Engineering team the better part of a day to get anything useful out of the *Jonah*'s sensor logs. Keeven had returned to his ship and produced a giant old data drive, containing all the logs from the outboard sensor grid. The thing was enclosed in a heavy, warped metal case that had to be pried open, and the format was so antiquated that Uma couldn't think of a way to retrieve the data at first. Dean had to hunt through every archive the *Gallion* had, until something finally worked.

They had settled Charyne Jaxong at a console and shown her how to stream the data comparisons. Jaxong had picked up the *Gallion*'s systems comfortably, marvelling at the precision of their instruments, and soon she was offering suggestions alongside the other engineers as easily as if she'd been there all along. After a few hours, the thought that Charyne Jaxong— *the* Charyne Jaxong, the Inventor—was sitting in the *Gallion*'s Engineering pit, flicking casually at a lightpad, almost seemed normal.

Almost.

Eldric Leesongronski, on the other hand, wasn't doing much except pacing around in the upper level of Engineering, glaring down into the pit with thinly-veiled suspicion. Occasionally, he came down to glance over someone's shoulder and mutter under his breath, but mostly he just perched on the railing at the top of the stairs, watching them. It was incredibly disconcerting.

Every quarter-hour, Uma would walk slowly up the stairs with a lightpad in hand, pretending she needed something at one of the equipment control consoles. It forced her to walk past him, hoping this time she'd think of something to say to him.

He must have noticed her looking, because this time he snapped out of his reverie and turned to face her.

"What're you staring at?"

"Oh! Sorry!" she mumbled, nearly dropping the lightpad. "I, ah... Professor Leesongronski, I... I was just wondering if I could possibly... talk to you?"

"About what? You got some new data?" He gestured at the lightpad in her hand.

"Well, no. I was actually wondering if I could talk to you about... yourself."

His eyebrows went up, and his mouth made a shape like he wasn't sure he'd heard her correctly. "What?"

"I know so much about you, Professor Leesongronski," she blurted. "I've read all your biographies. I've listened to every lecture you ever recorded, and all your academic talks... and I've read just about everything you ever wrote. I actually feel kind of like... I *know* you."

And you're my favourite. Please don't turn out to be any more of an asshole than I already know you were.

"Oh?" Leesongronski frowned. He rearranged himself on the railing, hooking the pointed toe of one shoe around the bottom rail. "What do you know about me, exactly?"

Her heart skipped as she contemplated condensing a life history she knew almost as well as her own. "Well, I know a lot of things. Like... you were space-born, but you went to study at the university on Anvaelia. You were the first person in your family to move planetside in three generations."

He shrugged, looking away. "So what?"

"While you were at university, you were chosen to apprentice as a jump architect, so you went back to space," she continued. "Then you found work as a commercial jumper, and you were working for a shipping company before you moved to Sëgra City..."

Leesongronski flinched almost imperceptibly at the mention of Sëgra, but he didn't look at her. He took a thin cigarette out of one of his jacket pockets, lighting the end of it with some sort of compact silver pen. He closed his eyes tightly as he inhaled, and a plume of hazy, blueish smoke coiled toward the ceiling.

"I know you fell in love on Sëgra," Uma said quietly. "With Dafnë Valay. She was a dreamhouse performer in the Dome Theatre, right?"

Leesongronski's head snapped up. He slowly removed the cigarette from his mouth, his eyes finally meeting hers. "And do you know all about how the Felen killed Dafnë, too?" he asked, his voice tight. "What about that part?"

Uma winced. Dafnë Valay had been killed in a Felen incursion on the Dylham settlement, seven years before the end of the war.

Seven years *ago*, for the man in front of Uma. For him, it wasn't a historical event. For him, the grief was still as fresh and real as Uma's grief for her father, almost seven years gone.

"I'm so sorry," Uma whispered. "I didn't think. I didn't mean to bring up..."

The sweet-smelling smoke snaked around Leesongronski's head like a halo. He stared into the distance.

"It only took them seventeen minutes to level the settlement," he said. "Seventeen minutes from when the Felen hit atmo, till the last comm link on Dylham blinked out." He took another slow drag from the cigarette. "I used to think about that, wondering if she died in the first minutes before anyone knew what was happening... or if she lived till the last minute, knowing exactly what was coming. Some people managed to record messages before they died, and sent 'em up into the info-sats... but she didn't leave one."

The last missives from Dylham were in the war archives. Uma had searched through the transcripts before, scouring for Dafnë's name in the tags and not finding it. She'd been curious if any of the other messages were from people Leesongronski might have known on Dylham. But she couldn't ask him that.

Before she could think of anything to say, an indignant yell echoed from the pit below.

"Hey!" shouted Nack, jabbing his finger in Leesongronski's direction. "Where's that smoke coming from? Is that thing actually on *fire?*"

Nack had been with the *Gallion* longer than anyone else on board. The curmudgeonly skim engine specialist had worked every rotation since ZeyCorp commissioned the ship, and word had it that he got grumpier with each one. In the time Uma had known him, that had certainly borne true.

She rubbed at her eyes, suddenly acutely aware that she had a pounding headache. "Don't worry, Nack. I've got this."

"This equipment is extremely sensitive!" Nack yelled. "We have regulations, you know!"

"Professor, ah... I'm sorry, but you can't have that in here," she said to Leesongronski. "It's just company policy, and I have to... um, hello? Hello, Professor?"

Leesongronski didn't seem to hear her anymore. He was holding the lit cigarette aloft, twirling the fingers of his other hand through the smoke, staring into the swirling patterns. Like he was looking at something else.

She touched his shoulder. "Professor Leesongronski?"

"What?" Leesongronski's head turned, and he peered at her curiously, as if he'd only just remembered that she was there. He stuck the cigarette back into his mouth.

"You can't do that in here." She motioned apologetically at the cigarette.

Without saying a word, Leesongronski hopped down off the railing, pausing to straighten the hem of his jacket before he turned around and walked calmly out to the corridor.

"...or anywhere else on the ship, probably... but... all right," Uma said. Her shoulders slumped.

She leaned against the rail where Leesongronski had been sitting. *Fuck, damn, shit, godsdamnit.* Of course she would say something foolish the first time she actually tried to talk to him. What must he be thinking now? And she hadn't even had the chance to ask him anything about how he pulled off the Jetsetter hacks.

He probably wouldn't ever talk to her again, and she couldn't exactly blame him. She tilted her head back and watched the last blue tendril of smoke dissipate toward the ceiling.

SHAAN
Common Deck, *ZeyCorp Gallion*

SHAAN WALKED THE corridors, lightpad in hand, completing the end-of-day facilities check. She didn't know why she was bothering, but having nothing to do made her uneasy. The last thing she wanted was too much time to think. The ship's walls already felt like they were closing in on her; every footfall sounded unnerving.

But what greeted her when she turned the corner near the *Gallion*'s staff lounge was even stranger: a chorus of uproarious, unbridled laughter. The door to the recreation space was open, bathing a section of the corridor in flickering light.

Shaan looked around the corner into the lounge. It was a small semi-circular room, with its own vending machine, a beverage dispenser, and a mismatched assemblage of seating that could accommodate about a dozen people. There were a few entertainment consoles, and a little virtual projection set that ran multiplayer sim games.

Noussen, the *Gallion*'s junior comms specialist, was sitting cross-legged on the floor with her back to the door. The other two junior engineers, Syru and Mikolai, were huddled on the overstuffed sofa behind her, their arms twined around each other. Everyone was looking up at the glowing game projection that shimmered in the air just below the ceiling.

High over their heads, the game's final score was ratcheting up. Pale green numbers danced into the projection, their reflections flickering over the room's curved walls.

"Argh! Wasn't even *close* that time!" Noussen laughed, the beads in her hair jangling softly as she shook her head. She let herself drop back onto one of the floor cushions, slapping her knees. "Your score's unbeatable, Mik!"

Shaan blinked. How could anyone on this ship possibly still have so much enthusiasm for anything?

"Oh, hey, Shaan!" Noussen turned around, squinting at Shaan in the semi-darkness. She flicked the game's wire-thin targeting eyepiece off her face, catching it neatly in one hand. "We got kicked out of Engineering, did you hear? Apparently, we're still supposed to log off after we max our hours. Rules apply, life-or-death crisis or not."

"Company-mandated breaks, huh?" Shaan rolled her eyes. "I can't believe they're actually enforcing that right now. Director Ozakka must be thrilled."

"You ever tried pleading with Dean?" Noussen laughed. "No chance. Even the captain can't override this anymore. We're under orders to take a rest."

"None of us could sleep, so we're playing *MeteoRacers Ultimate* instead," said Syru. "And, big surprise, I'm losing again. Badly."

Syru was an academic from U Tel's Engineering department, doing a year's work experience to fortify his research on shield harmonics. He had the clipped, precise accent that came from being schooled in mainspace, and his wheat-coloured hair hung wispy and pale against his sandy complexion. He was slight of build, small and slender-limbed, but he carried himself with all the brash confidence of someone accustomed to being at the top of his class. He'd asked questions at every single stop when Shaan had given him the orientation tour a year ago, and Shaan often joked that he hadn't stopped talking since.

Syru was an oddly complementary match for Mikolai, the soft-spoken junior who'd come on board a few months after him. This was Mik's first time in deep space, after completing an award-winning research thesis in theoretical subspace physics. Mik was the Engineering liaison to the science teams now, preparing reports and assisting the visiting researchers with experiment setup. Like Shaan, Mikolai hadn't had much to do during turnover—though he'd evidently spent his downtime practicing his space-racing skills. The high score was several thousand points higher than she remembered it.

"Face it, you just can't beat me at this!" Mikolai said, a triumphant grin dimpling his brown cheeks. His cloud of dark curls bobbed around his face as he leaned in to kiss the top of Syru's head. "You're cute, Sy, but you are incredibly terrible at this game."

Syru shoved him playfully, looking over his shoulder at Shaan. "You wanna play a round, Shaan?" He dangled one of the game's targeting eyepieces in the air. "C'mon, get over here."

Shaan winced. She didn't even like *watching* this game. Every time a space-racer started to spin out of control, a familiar panic would rise in her gut. And when an opponent's racing pod slammed into hers and exploded violently into splinters, she always had to look away. She clenched her teeth.

"Hey... you okay, Shaan?"

"I'm fine." She composed herself quickly. "But, gods, I really don't understand how you're all sitting in here calmly playing games at a time like this. Talk about a disaster!"

"Disaster?" Syru's eyes widened, a smile breaking onto his face. "Well, a PR disaster for ZeyCorp, maybe. But I'm having a great time! I think I've found a way to adapt one of my experimental shield modulations to work on a shuttle. And tomorrow, I'm gonna run some tests to see if we can get an exploratory shuttlecraft out into the Rift!" His smile widened. "I thought work experience in corporate would look good when I apply for my research funding next year... but here we are doing actual *groundbreaking science.*"

Mikolai nodded in effusive agreement. "Yeah. Can you believe I got to talk physics with *Charyne Jaxong* today? The real live Inventor?" He sucked in a reverent breath. "Gods. It's like, we've got to be dreaming, right? One of the greatest physicists of all time is reviewing some of my calculations right now!"

"And I'm working on improving our scan range, so we can see further into the Rift," Noussen said perkily. "Director Ozakka's letting me access the *entire* array and make any changes I want! Nack says juniors usually don't get to touch that stuff until they've done at least three rotations."

"Eyyy, I wouldn't let a junior be layin' a hand on that shit without the proper training, Director!" Syru said in an exaggerated imitation of Nack's gruff baritone. The three of them dissolved into giggles again.

"Okay, one last race for me and then I gotta sleep," Noussen said, stretching her arms over her head with a yawn. "Log into the sim, Shaan. You can take my spot."

"No thanks. Really. I'm... I'm just not a great pilot," Shaan mumbled.

"Not a great pilot? Hah! Well! You'll never get a better opportunity to learn from an expert!" said Jereth Keeven.

Shaan jumped back in shock as Keeven suddenly sat up from the floor. He'd been lying just out of her view, leaning against the sofa next to Noussen. One of the game system's targeting eye-pieces glinted above his right eye. "You want a piloting lesson? I used to be a squadron leader for the UWDF—top of my unit. You won't find better than me. First lesson's free, but after that I'll have to charge you."

"What the—?" Shaan gasped. "Keeven! What're you doing in here?"

Keeven held up his wrist, brandishing the ZeyCorp guest band. "Why so surprised? You mean you haven't been keeping track of my location? Haven't got my vital stats? Look, I'm wearing your leash an' everything!"

The others giggled.

Shaan folded her arms, forcing herself to some semblance of composure. She pretended to check her own bracelet. "Oh, yep, there we go," she said. "You're right. I just got an alert that you've exceeded the maximum ZeyCorp limits on being a pain in the ass."

Keeven laughed, raking his unruly hair away from his face. "Wow, ouch. Is this how you treat your esteemed guests? I expected higher standards from ZeyCorp. Can I speak to your supervisor?"

"That's enough, Keeven. This is a staff-only lounge, you shouldn't be in here." Shaan pointed to the open door, relief flooding her at the excuse to dodge her turn on the game. "Get out. I'm escorting you back to the residential deck."

Keeven stood up as slowly as possible, then picked up his scuffed jacket from the arm of the sofa. "All right, all right. I'm *goin'*." He looked over his shoulder at the juniors. "Remember, corporate life's a prison, kids! Fight the rules! Get out of the machine! Be free!"

Noussen, Syru and Mikolai collapsed into laughter again, all three of them waving to Shaan as Keeven ambled unhurriedly to the door. They kept their hands up, grinning, until Keeven had exited into the corridor.

"Go." Shaan pointed toward the lift and started walking. Keeven followed.

"They seem like nice kids, huh?" he said. "Real fun bunch. I like them."

She walked faster, staring straight ahead in silence. What *was* Keeven doing here? He was up to no good, obviously. Suddenly he was fine with hanging around playing games with ZeyCorp staff? What happened to his blackmail schemes?

Keeven kept pace with her, and kept talking. "Hey, listen. You know that sim game they were playing in there... what do you call that? That thing is bloody incredible! Your game tech's way more advanced than any military sim I've ever seen!"

He tapped the targeting eyepiece still stuck to his face, and its turquoise ready-light flashed off and on. The heads-up display sparkled briefly over his face before it retracted again, and he blinked in wonder.

"You know, I was thinking... maybe your people could give me one of these game systems as an extra thank you gift, hmm? What do you say? It'd be worth a fortune to the right people, but to you, it's just a silly video game, right? I bet no one would even notice if you gave it to me, and—"

Shaan stopped abruptly, and he nearly walked into her. She reached out and snatched the eyepiece off his face.

"Enough! Stop!" she hissed. "Stop this. I want you to tell me what you're really doing here."

Keeven opened his mouth in feigned shock. "What, you mean in the lounge? They invited me to play! Is there some kind of company rule against guests having fun?"

"Oh, spare me. The other day you were up on the Command deck trying to blackmail us, and now you're joking around, playing sim games like nothing's wrong? You're up to something. I want to know what it is."

He shrugged. "I adapted my strategy, that's all."

"Your *strategy?*"

"I need allies, Shaan." His face was serious. "I need information sources I can count on. As long as your people won't release my ship, I'm stuck here. So it wouldn't hurt to make a few friends, build a little circle of trust... get it?"

"No, I *don't* get it! You act like this whole thing is a gods-damned joke to you!" Shaan's voice rose, fury burning in her cheeks. "You honestly expect anyone on this ship to trust you after all the lies you've told? After you tried to scam us into believing your rust-bucket ship is the *Jonah,* that your friend is Eldric Leesongronski? Come on. Nobody's falling for any of this. You're just some selfish asshole."

"Oh, really?" Keeven took a step back, and his expression darkened. "*I'm* the one who's selfish? Let me ask you something about this so-called history of yours, Shaan... since you all seem to know so damn much about it." His eyes narrowed. "Don't you think it's funny that there was no rush to make a truce with the Felen until Etraxas came under siege?"

She frowned. "What do you mean?"

"Think about it. The Union wasn't scrambling to make peace deals when the Dylham settlement was levelled. They weren't in any hurry when the Felen started blowing up all those deep space outposts. People've been dying in this war for *generations.* But, oh, gods forbid Etraxas should fall! Not the crown jewel of the Union! So now it's time to beg, to get desperate, to bend our knees to the enemy? Whatever it takes to save the Capital, is that right?"

Shaan didn't say anything.

"You think the Union ever gave a damn about the rest of us?" He lowered his voice. "Do you even know about what happened to the Desmoën settlement?"

Desmoën. He pronounced the name of the planet the old way, with the emphasis on the O. Something tugged at her memory, but she couldn't quite bring it into focus.

"Desmoën... I know a little, I think," Shaan whispered. "It was one of the dust worlds."

The dust worlds were a group of human settlements that had been left isolated during the war, their terraforming programs unfinished, the planets not quite habitable. Settlers had been stranded for years without resupply in decaying temporary infrastructures.

"Just one of many places the Union abandoned," Keeven said bitterly. "'Middle of nowhere' doesn't even begin to cover it. Where I'm from, the Felen were a *myth*. When I was a kid on Desmoën, there were rumours about some alien war going on, sure, but folks figured it was all made up. Thought maybe the Union was just lookin' for excuses why our supply ships never came... why our sanitation equipment never got replaced... why we still didn't have clean water..."

He trailed off. When he looked back at her, his eyes were wet.

"The Union ships finally came back into orbit when I was fourteen years old," he said. "But d'you think they were coming to help us? To fix our water systems? To give us medicine?"

Shaan shook her head slowly.

"'Course not. They came looking for recruits to take to war. Picking up young soldiers to go fight the Felen." His face twisted into a grimace. "And after those recruiters left... how many UWDF warships do you think they left in orbit around Desmoën? How many fighters do you think they ever sent back there, to protect my homeworld?"

Shaan looked at the floor.

"That's right. Zero," Keeven said. "Because the Union's only ever been interested in protecting the Prime Worlds. Fuck everyone else! So much for the *United* Worlds of Humanity, huh?" He shoved his arms into his jacket. "I'm sorry if I'm not more worried about the precious aristocracy on the Capital, but this war's lost already. If Etraxas is under siege, it's too late. The Union's finished."

"No," breathed Shaan. "No... it wasn't too late! The siege

of Etraxas was withdrawn! The Union survived because of the Fortunate Five! Humanity was saved when the Negotiator—"

"Look, I think we've already established that I've got nothing to do with your damn Fortunate Five," he interrupted, his voice thick with emotion. "You said it yourself. I'm just some selfish asshole, right? So why don't you leave me the fuck alone?"

They walked the rest of the way to the lift without saying anything else.

The lift doors opened automatically as they neared it, and when Keeven stepped inside, Shaan didn't follow. She let the door close on him, the pseudo-glass pane slipping shut between them.

His stormy eyes stayed locked on hers through the transparent door, and she didn't break the gaze until the lift slid away with its little musical chime.

Shaan put her back to the wall and slid slowly down to the floor. For a while she stared into the empty lift, her eyes welling up with tears. She needed rest, but her head was too full, her thoughts too chaotic. Instead of getting up and going up to her apartment, she woke her lightpad and opened the ZeyCorp knowledge bank.

Even in offline mode, the ship's encyclopedia was phenomenal. She wasn't surprised to see the list of the most recent searches— there were only a handful of people on the ship's internal network, all looking up the same things.

ZEYCORPnet KNOWLEDGE BANK

CURRENT POPULAR SEARCHES
Jonah Voyage
Eldric Leesongronski
Fortunate Five
Voicegiver
Contact War

Shaan cleared away the suggestions and entered a search of her own. She navigated through the blocky boxes of data that unfurled over her lightpad.

Planet: Desmoën

SEARCH RESULTS
Desmoën Settlement
Wartime Decline and Supply Crisis

In the latter stages of the war, the <u>Desmoën settlement</u> was almost entirely cut off from Union commerce and offworld communication. The population endured a number of deadly crises including the collapse of the <u>hydroponic farming ecosystem</u> and the water contamination that occurred when the <u>filtration systems</u> fell into disrepair, due to lack of replacement parts for maintenance.

Many settlers perished at a young age from health problems related to poor air quality and ongoing issues with water and sanitation. Others lost their lives in one of several mass <u>outbreaks</u> of preventable diseases, when supplies of routine immunizations and common medicines ran out. During the worst of the crises, the <u>average life expectancy</u> on Desmoën dropped below sixty years, and disease-related deaths among infants and young children rose as high as one in four. Basic medical supplies and water purification tablets became some of the planet's most profitable black market goods.

Controversy surrounded the UWDF's <u>recruitment of young soldiers</u> from among the settlers of Desmoën and other so-called 'dust worlds,' with many critics expressing anger that the Union did not also send supplies to replenish the stores of the settlers left on the surface. The official government stance was that sufficient supplies could not be delivered, and that delivering only a small amount of supplies risked triggering deadly riots and unrest on the surface—

"Shaan? What're you still doing here?" Shaan looked up to see Mikolai's round face staring down at her with concern. "I thought you were taking Keeven back to his apartment."

She minimized the article, letting the lightpad rest on her knee. "No. Keeven... left without me."

"You coming back to the rez deck with us? We're heading up now." Mikolai glanced back at the lounge door just as Syru bounded out into the corridor, followed by Noussen.

Shaan leaned her head back against the wall. Usually, the juniors' cheerful faces and bubbly chatter would have comforted her; they were the closest thing she had to a family. But tonight, Shaan just wanted to be alone. Tonight, after everything, seeing her friends and shipmates only reminded her of how little they really knew about her. They understood about as much about her past as she did about Keeven's.

"Hey, did you see the popular search list in there?" Syru grinned, noticing the ZeyCorp knowledge bank prompt on Shaan's lightpad. "Too bad none of those history entries have anything *interesting* in them, huh? It's mostly just boring old facts."

"He knows because he's tried every single permutation of '*Jonah* conspiracy theory' and 'Leesongronski hacker coverup' and 'Fortunate Five true history.'" Mikolai laughed. "We literally couldn't find any of the stuff Director Ozakka was talking about." He looked down at Shaan's lightpad again. "It's so weird what's actually in the history trove, isn't it? Director Ozakka's right... there's not much info in there about any of them. It's like almost everything about their pasts got wiped out."

"Well... maybe it should stay that way. Maybe some things are better left buried," Shaan said bitterly. She held out the targeting eyepiece that she'd snatched from Keeven, and pushed it into Mikolai's hand. "Go on without me. I need to be alone right now."

When the lift doors had closed behind them, she flicked back to the knowledge bank article. Something tugged at her thoughts again. There was something about the Desmoën settlement...

She returned to the search prompt.

Desmoën + Fortunate Five

The search returned just one result. A single paragraph, buried on the thirty-sixth page of a dry article listing various monuments and memorials to the Five across the United Worlds.

> While no records exist to confirm the origins of the Union's Negotiator, his homeworld has long been listed unofficially as <u>Desmoën</u>. At the former site of the core settlement, a monument to the Fortunate Five can be found, alongside a plaque marking the Negotiator's supposed birthplace.

JERETH
Desmoën Settlement
28 years before the Rift

ON ONE OF the hottest days of the year, Jereth followed Ludyth up the dusty ridge that overlooked the desert. A storm was gathering in the distance, and a flock of small birds circled and shrieked on the horizon, their erratic flight patterns foretelling the coming dust cloud. The brothers sat on a flat rock with their bare feet hanging over the edge, throwing pebbles off the cliff toward the enormous scaffolds that held up the water delivery system.

The scorching wind raised pillars of reddish dust into the air, stinging Jereth's eyes. Everyone was meant to keep their breathing mask on, especially when the dust rose, but Ludyth sat defiantly with his mask hanging loose around his neck. And if his older brother hadn't put a mask on, then Jereth certainly wasn't about to do it first. He coughed into his sleeve when Ludyth wasn't looking, and stubbornly ignored the burning in his throat.

Ludyth had reached the age of sixteen standard years this season, old enough for the UWDF Academy. He spoke of little else lately except fighting in the war, and he had already decided that he wanted to become a military strategist. Ludyth was planning to become a UWDF hero—maybe even the one who worked out a way to end the Felen threat for good.

The Desmoën system had so far been completely untouched by the war, and the settlement lay far from any sector where alien ships had been sighted. If it wasn't for the occasional news report trickling in from mainspace, no one in the dust-bowls would have known about the space war at all. Desmoën was the only world that Jereth had ever known, and the thought that there were other worlds out there—worlds with people on them—seemed almost as fanciful as the idea that there were aliens.

The war had been going on for two generations by the time the Keeven brothers were born, but there'd still been some old folks in the townships who insisted that the whole thing was a lie. There was no war, they'd scoff, and there sure wasn't any such thing as aliens. But then the deffies had arrived to start recruiting for the war academies. These days, the jokes and dismissive laughter about the 'so-called space war' had died down to a nervous whisper. The Felen were real, and they were deadly.

When the UWDF recruiters came, they brought flight-training sims and aptitude tests, and promises of glory and triumph over the alien threat. They'd been taking more young recruits away every month. So far, no one that had been taken by the deffies had sent any messages back to Desmoën. Jereth tried not to think about that. Ludyth had already received his UWDF intake code, and he was due to be shipped off to mainspace any day now on the next departing transit.

Whenever Ludyth got hold of an offworld news report, he would read out loud the horrific tales about the war, repeating each one several times with morbid fascination: Felen attacks on Union ships and outposts, impenetrable alien shields, disgusting experiments, biological warfare. More and more, the stories coming in were grim and fatalistic. The aliens had technology far more advanced than anything the Union could muster, and it was only a matter of time before things got worse.

Jereth didn't like to imagine the hideous fate that might await his brother when the deffies took him away—out of his sight, somewhere out in space. The two had never been separated for so much as a day before. They even shared a room in their minuscule, weather-beaten hab-cube. But Jereth wasn't old enough for the UWDF Academy yet. He was a whole standard year younger than Ludyth, though the brothers looked enough alike that they were sometimes mistaken for twins.

Ludyth was lost in thought now, staring at that reddening horizon, swinging his feet over the edge of the precipice. Dust gathered in his eyebrows.

"Hey... Ludyth?" Jereth said, poking at his brother's leg with one toe. "You okay? Why're you being so quiet?"

"I'm just thinking," Ludyth said. "When I go away... I might never come back here again."

Jereth picked up a pebble and flung it into the distance. He thought of Ludyth out there in the cold depths of space, out where those horrible things were, and he shuddered despite the heat.

"Don't say that. When the war's over, and the Felen are gone, then you'll come back."

Ludyth shrugged his thin shoulders. "Doubt it."

"Why?" Jereth whispered. "Do you think you're gonna die?"

"What? No, 'course I'm not gonna die! The Union's gonna win, don't worry." Ludyth grinned, slapping Jereth's back. "But, Jer, there's so much more out there than this planet. All those places we read about? I'm not gonna spend the rest of my life on this dustball."

"Where will you go?" Jereth asked.

"When the war ends? Anywhere I want!" Ludyth hurled a big rock into the distance, shielding his eyes with one hand as he watched it sail out into the canyon. "When the Felen are gone, the travel restrictions'll get lifted, and then we can go see all the worlds."

"But... what if the Felen win the war?" Jereth whispered.

Ludyth managed half a laugh before he inhaled and choked on a mouthful of dust. He coughed and sputtered, still smiling even as he choked.

"Naaaah. Don't be silly, Jereth," he said between coughs. "We'll annihilate them! Blow 'em all up. Boom! No more aliens."

Jereth coughed, too. His lungs were aching, and his tongue was parched with the acrid taste of the inhospitable air.

"Yeaarrrrrrgh!" Ludyth gave a hoarse roar, his voice echoing out over the gorge. "Listen up! I'm gonna be a Union hero!" he shouted into the desert. "That's right! And all you aliens out there better run, 'cause I'm UWDF now! I'm gonna be a deffie!" He turned to Jereth. "An' next year, so will you!"

Jereth thought about putting his breathing mask on, but instead he just grimaced and spat a mouthful of red dust onto the ground. Dusty tears welled in his eyes as he stared out into the gathering storm.

"I'm scared, Ludyth," he said. "The aliens—"

"It's the aliens who should be scared! We're brave." Ludyth thumped his narrow chest. "Strength to the Union, right? Victory for Humanity!"

"You've always been *way* braver than me," Jereth said. He pulled his dusty, scabbed knees up to his chin. "I'm not much good at anything."

"Oh, shut up, Jereth." Ludyth slapped the back of Jereth's head. "You're gonna be a damn good fighter pilot. Remember when we stole that old hover-tractor from the construction site? Hah! You were what, ten years old? You were flyin' that thing like a pro. You got almost halfway to the town limits before you crashed it!" He grabbed Jereth's arm and hauled him to his feet. "Hey. How about we go do the water tank dare, for old times' sake? You've *got* to. Just once, so I can see you do it before I go."

Jereth cringed. Ludyth had always loved playing that water tank game, but Jereth *hated* it. Every quarter-hour, a tank would come sliding along the cables suspended over the gorge, bringing brackish water from the distant wells into the township reservoir. Just before a tank came down, the settlement kids would all squeeze through the gate and climb the fence into the maintenance works, daring each other to balance on the thin spar that ran under the cable system.

They'd purposely wait until a tank was halfway down the ridge before they started crossing. They would run as fast as they could across the spar to the support tower and then back again, trying not to look down at the long drop into the gorge below. But Jereth was terrified of heights, and something about that endless, dusty chasm made him nauseated with fear. He'd managed to dodge the water tank dare for his entire childhood, and thankfully, Ludyth finally seemed to have given up pushing him to do it.

Until now.

"C'mon," Ludyth said. "There's a storm coming in, so we've gotta hurry. But you're doing it."

Jereth didn't utter a word of protest. They marched in silence along the curve of the ridge, following it until they reached the locked access gate. Beyond the gate was the maintenance spar, jutting out into the gorge like a flat knife.

Jereth wiped his watering eyes and looked up. The thick, silver-grey cables were rising and falling with the gathering wind. Ludyth shielded his eyes and looked into the distance. There was no water tank in sight, and there was no one on the platform.

"I reckon we've got a few minutes before the next tank. So let's do a practice run first, while there's nothing coming," Ludyth said. "Follow me."

Ludyth got down onto his stomach and crawled through the small gap underneath the metal gates. He hoisted himself up onto the second security fence inside, and—an added defiance—got his foothold by curling his toes over the top of the sign that said *Danger: No Unauthorized Access*. When he'd dropped down on the other side of the fence, he gestured theatrically toward Jereth.

Jereth wriggled under the gates after his brother. He clambered up the inner fence and dropped onto the maintenance platform. The dusty metal under his feet was burning hot, and he wished he had worn shoes. But Ludyth hadn't worn shoes, so Jereth had left his behind, too.

"I'll go first, then you come right behind me. Got it?" Ludyth said. "You can do this. Look!"

He bounded off down the spar, running lightly toward the support tower on the other side. Jereth watched, chewing his lip, as Ludyth ran all the way down to the end without stopping, his long auburn hair streaming behind him.

When he'd reached the small platform at the other end, he slapped one palm victoriously against the tower and whooped with triumph.

"There, see?" he shouted. "It's easy!"

More than once, Jereth had seen Ludyth run this spar when the incoming tank was close enough to make the platforms rumble. He felt sick thinking of it. He'd once watched one of Ludyth's friends cut her run so close that the hot rush of air from the passing tank had knocked her right off her feet. She'd only just made it back to the main platform, and when the others had hoisted her back over the fence, her face and clothes had been covered with desert-dust, blood streaming from her elbows and knees. The older kids had collapsed into jubilant laughter, congratulating her on how close she'd come to death.

"C'mon!" Ludyth shouted. "Just do it! Run across, and don't look down!"

Don't look down.

The spar was less than a pace across, but it was pocked with small ridges to help workers' boots keep their grip. It shouldn't be all that hard to walk along it.

Dust-streaked sweat was dripping into Jereth's eyes as he set one foot onto the spar, then took a small step... then another.

"Yeah!" Ludyth yelled. "You're doing it! Go on!"

Jereth fixed his gaze on Ludyth and stepped a little faster. *Don't look down. Don't look down. Don't look down.*

He'd made it about a third of the way across the spar when he felt a slight rumble under his feet. He turned his head to look over his shoulder, his stinging eyes straining to see if there was a tank on the cable. But his body turned too quickly for his unsteady legs, and he felt himself losing his balance. His vision blurred as he dropped to one knee. And then, he accidentally looked straight down into the gorge, and everything around him started spinning.

He gripped the edge of the spar with both hands.

"I... I think I'm gonna go back, Lu!" he shouted. "I can't get any further!"

"Oh, come on, don't give up now!" Ludyth yelled back. "Just do it!"

Jereth tried to move, but he couldn't. His knees had locked; his fingers were tiny vises hooked over the edge of the spar. He looked down into the gorge again, and the world tilted around him.

"There's a tank coming down!" Ludyth shouted. "You've got to move! Stop messing around!"

Jereth's stomach turned, his heart pounding in his throat. He couldn't make himself stand up again. Instead he started to crawl back toward the first platform on his hands and knees, the hot metal burning into his bare legs.

Behind him, Ludyth's voice was getting panicked. "Jereth, you hear me? There's a tank coming! You have to get up!"

The platform he'd started from seemed unbelievably far away, but Jereth pulled himself up to a crouch, then somehow got back on his feet. He could feel the whipping heat of the oncoming air. The tank was getting closer, its mechanical wheels crunching as they rolled along the dirt-encrusted cables. The ominous rumble grew under his feet.

Ludyth was screaming now, his voice raw with dust and fear. "Jereth! Just do it! Move! Go!"

Jereth staggered toward the platform. The dust was so thick he could hardly see where he was going. He clenched his eyes shut, struggling to take in a breath of dusty air.

And then he felt his brother's hands on his back.

Ludyth had launched himself across the spar at a breakneck run. He collided with Jereth at full speed, giving him a fierce shove between the shoulder blades and pushing him the rest of the way back to the platform.

Jereth fell face down. The impact forced the air from his lungs as he skidded hard onto the platform. He looked back just in time to see the tank strike his brother.

Ludyth had almost made it. His left hand clutched at the low rail around the platform, but the rush of hot air sucked him back as the tank passed. He lost his grip and was dragged back over the spar, pulled right under the oncoming tank.

Less than two seconds later, it was over.

When the tank rumbled away, Ludyth was lying on the spar, his body as limp as a doll. One of his arms was bent behind him, and his legs were splayed out like the limbs of some strange dried-out insect. Blood was pooling under his head.

"Ludyth!" Jereth screamed. "No, no!"

He scrambled to his hands and knees, his chest tight with panic. He crawled frantically back over the spar toward Ludyth's crumpled body.

"Lu? Can you hear me?"

Ludyth's tangled hair was whipping around his head like a crop of desert-grass, and Jereth reached over to push it out of his face. Fine red dust was settling over him, filling the cracks in his chapped lips. Blood snaked slowly from his nostril.

"Ludyth!"

Ludyth's eyelids fluttered open, and he made a small, weak choking sound in the back of his throat. But his stare was unfocused, like he was looking right through Jereth, and the whites of his eyes had turned crimson.

"Lu! Can you hear me?"

"J... Jereth?"

Ludyth's lips had hardly moved, the sound so lost in the wind that Jereth wondered if he'd imagined it. But then Ludyth shifted slightly. He stretched out his good arm, reaching toward Jereth. For a moment, his fingers brushed against Jereth's shirt-sleeve.

And then Ludyth's head tilted back, and his arm dropped back to the spar. His bloodshot eyes stared skyward, empty. His body slumped to the side and rolled over the edge of the spar.

Jereth knelt on the spar and screamed, but his brother was gone. Ludyth plummeted into the gorge, disappearing into a cloud of red dust as the Desmoën desert swirled up to take him.

SHAAN
Common Deck, ZeyCorp Gallion

SHAAN STARED DOURLY into a half-finished carton of breakfast mash. A small bunch of crew sat at one long table, eating breakfast together. It should have felt congenial, but the mood was subdued. The new ship-day had hardly begun, but everyone already looked either exhausted or preoccupied.

Next to her, the Cordero siblings were both nodding off, their eyes half-closed. Beside them, Macey sat with his head resting on one elbow, staring at the tabletop and looking barely conscious. To Shaan's other side, Wazar and Noussen were busily scrolling through a knowledge bank entry about the Fortunate Five as they slurped at their breakfast.

"Damn. There's hardly anything in the history trove about the fun stuff," Wazar said, scrunching up her face. "There's only, like... two paragraphs here about Leesongronski's time living in Sëgra City. And it doesn't say anything about him being suspected of hacking a bank!"

Noussen laughed. "Well, if you want to read the juicy biographies, Director Ozakka said she's got a bunch of them."

"That's right." Ozakka grinned. "You've got to know where to look if you want to read the good stuff. Let me tell you, the history texts are *not* your best source when it comes to true history."

"Did any of you know the Negotiator was supposedly born on Desmoën?" Shaan said, swirling her spoon over the top of her mash.

"Yeah, I've definitely heard that." Director Ozakka looked thoughtful. "There are a few reliable contemporary sources that mention he was from a dust world. A couple of them name Desmoën specifically. Seems legit enough. But of course, there'd be no official record since we don't even have his real name, so he could've been from anywhere." She tapped her spoon. "You know, if you want some fascinating history about the dust worlds, there's a great documentary that—"

"Right! Must be about time to get started on some real work," Nack abruptly announced from the other end of the table. He stood, shovelling the last of his mash into his mouth as he got up. "I'm going down to Engineering to set up another core reset. How about we give up on all this sensor log shit and move back to looking at the engines today, hmm, Director?"

"No, absolutely not. I said no more core resets, Nack," Ozakka said. Her smile faded, her face all business now. "The resets are draining too much power, and nothing we're doing on the engines is working. We need to run more long-range scans."

"I did ask Dean to schedule some more scans after Noussen's last tweaks on the array," Wazar said. "I'll be sending out another round of hover probes today, too."

"If we keep scanning, we'll find *something* out here," said Ozakka confidently. "We probably just haven't looked far enough yet."

"And there must be a rescue-ship searching for us by now," Shaan said, willing herself to believe it. "ZeyCorp would have reported us missing as soon as they saw us drop off the network. They'll send someone."

"Yeah, except they'll send the rescue-ship to our last known location," Macey said dejectedly. "Which, face it, probably isn't anywhere near where we are right now."

"If a rescue-ship was coming, we'd have picked up their signal already," grunted Nack. "You all know damn well there's nobody lookin' for us. And there's naught out there in this void for us to find, either. These sensor logs an' long-range scans are completely pointless! We've got to start the engines, or we're done for!"

Macey's face fell. "Guess we're all gonna die, then."

Wazar pulled a sachet of dried alga out of her pocket, tapping it against the edge of the table to break up the pieces before she tipped it into her ZeyCorp-branded mug.

"Nah, mate. We'll get rescued," she said confidently. "Eventually. We've still got that six-month danger-chamber, right? Highest safety ratings in the field, folks!" She winked. "The company might not care much about our replaceable asses, but this ship's too expensive to lose. And with a Felen Ambassador on board? That would be a publicity nightmare! Central will *have* to find us."

As if on cue, Zel swept through the main entrance into the canteen. *Damn it*. Shaan dropped her eyes to her breakfast mash, feigning great interest in watching it ooze off her spoon. He was already making a beeline for the table.

"Well, look who's here," Ozakka muttered under her breath. "The publicity prince himself. Gods, you just have to say the words 'publicity nightmare' to summon him, huh?"

"What's he *wearing*?" Macey hissed. "Is that a *cape*?"

Zel had donned some kind of ceremonial sash over his uniform. A wide band of rich maroon cloth was draped over his left shoulder, the colour clashing spectacularly with the ZeyCorp purple beneath it. The ends of the sash were pinned together with a jewel-encrusted emblem, and a silver-white cape hung from the back of his uniform collar.

"We havin' a costume party?" Nack said loudly.

Zel strode the last few steps to the table, his indignant look leaving no doubt that he'd heard. The silky cape swung behind him as he walked. It might have looked elegant in another context, but over a ZeyCorp two-piece it looked nothing short of ridiculous.

"For your information, this is the regalia of the Blessed Noble Houses of Etraxas, not a *costume*," Zel said icily. When he held his chin high, a glittery cosmetic sparkled along his cheekbones, heightening the gloss of his perfect bronze skin. "I brought this outfit along for my speech at the press junket. And... well, it seemed like the appropriate time to put it on."

Wazar looked bewildered. "Why's that?"

"Why? Because Etraxas is under siege, back in their time," Zel said. "Aren't you concerned about all this? That there might be some kind of a... a disturbance to the events of history?"

There was an edge of frustration in his voice, and his Etraxan accent seemed more pronounced than Shaan remembered it, almost as if he were deliberately emphasizing it.

"You should all be worried, but especially me!" he said. "My ancestors were on Etraxas a hundred and fifty-two years ago; every single one of my great-grandparents lived in the Etraxan system during that siege!"

"Ohhhh. Right," said Wazar, cracking a smile. "I get it. You're worried about blinking out of existence, huh?"

Zel's handsome face contorted. "It's not funny! If history's been changed somehow... if the *Jonah* didn't make it, and we never sealed the Peace with the Felen, then the fall of Etraxas would be inevitable! My grandparents would never have been born! Nor my parents... nor... me."

Wazar stirred the green liquid in her mug, looking unconcerned. "Don't know what to tell you, mate. I mean, can history even *be* changed? I figure we'd all have disappeared by now if we were going to, no?" She shrugged.

"Maybe this is some kind of alternate universe or something," Macey said. "We don't know how this works."

"That is my *entire* point!" Zel's dark eyes widened. "Nobody knows how this works! If we don't fix this, we could all be erased! Think about that!"

Wazar reached into her pocket, pulled out a second sachet of alga and tipped it into the mug. She stirred it contemplatively, popping the bubbles around the edges.

"Well? Are you thinking about it?" Zel demanded.

"I'm thinking... we should throw a raging party," Wazar said. "If we're all about to blink out of existence, then we should all log out, quit work early and make an absolute mess in here. Not like ZeyCorp Central will ever find out, huh?" She screwed the lid onto her mug, flipped her blue-grey hair, and took a sip.

Zel's glare was frosty. "I find nothing amusing about that," he said. "Billions of lives are at stake, including ours! We need to take action! We need leadership!" He drew himself up to his full height. "*I'm* the only Blessed Scion of Etraxas here, so it's obvious who should take charge. Don't worry. I'm taking steps to set this right."

"You mean like dressin' up in a cape?" Nack asked, wiping food from his chin.

Zel huffed. "We need to ensure that the Peace mission goes ahead. Imagine if the Peacemakers had never arrived to seal that truce, and Etraxas was annihilated! The rest of the Prime Worlds would've fallen soon after. The entire Union would've crumbled if the *Jonah* didn't make that journey! We need to make these people understand that the Peace really is possible. Just in case it makes any difference."

"I think... I might actually agree with you," Ozakka said slowly, setting down her spoon.

Shaan gaped. Gods, if the publicity prince and Ozakka were

coming down on the same side, maybe this really was an alternate universe.

Zel looked no less surprised. His sweeping eyebrows leapt toward his hairline, and he blinked like he might not have heard properly. "Really?"

"Yes. I'm listening." Ozakka folded her arms. "I am seriously hoping you've got more in mind than just the cape, though. What are you planning on doing?"

"I'm not *planning* on doing it. I've already done it," he said, inhaling deeply through his nose. "See... last night, I took Keila Kva-Sova to meet our Felen Ambassador."

UMA
Command Deck, ZeyCorp Gallion

UMA SAT IN her usual seat in Fransk's office. Absolutely nothing had changed since the last time she'd been in here. There was a coaster sitting next to the bowl of adver-tags on the corner of Fransk's desk—one of the dozens of tacky free coasters they'd acquired from ZeyCorp conferences. For some reason the sight of it almost made her smile. The idea that their lives would ever be that mundane again seemed absurd.

"Are you out of your mind, Zel?" Barnabyn was shouting. "You took her to see the Ambassador? Without consulting any of us?"

"I took action when no one else did," Zel said defensively. "I am a Blessed Scion of Etraxas! And in my capacity as the ZeyCorp Publicity Liaison in charge of this diplomatic visit, I decided we should tell them the whole truth—"

"Zel, we made an agreement not to tell the *Jonah* crew that there's a Felen on board," Fransk interrupted. "This isn't something we should take lightly." His eye twitch was back.

"We need to do damage control," Barnabyn said. "What are the consequences here?"

"Telling Kva-Sova was probably safe enough," Uma said.

"She believes in the Peace Project. She's the only one of them who was actually working for the Geminus Initiative."

"But the others are... so unpredictable." The captain rubbed a hand over the back of his neck.

"Not to worry," Zel said, almost smugly. "I'm no fool, Captain. I took only Kva-Sova to the audience, in complete confidence. I asked that she not disclose what she saw to any of the others. But I needed her to see it for herself, don't you understand? She has to see that her Voicing procedure *can* work, that it *has* worked, and that we truly can speak to the Felen. How is she meant to become the Voicegiver if she thinks her procedure was a failure?"

"So, ah... what did the Ambassador say about all of it?" Fransk asked. "And Gida? What did they say about the... the time travel, or whatever we're calling it? Did they even believe it?"

"About as much as any of us." Zel sighed. "But I... Well, I actually don't know *all* of what they said, because they asked me to leave the room."

"They *what?*" An indignant flush had crept into Barnabyn's face, his sandy cheeks gradually turning crimson. "You left Kva-Sova alone in there? With the Ambassador?"

"Er, well... yes, and with Gida. I believe the Ambassador's exact words were... *Leave us, we would like to discuss some matters in private with the Voicegiver.*"

Fransk buried his head in his hands. "Gods, this just gets worse and worse."

"What was the alternative, Captain?" Zel demanded. "Tell none of the *Jonah* crew anything? Let them leave, so they can go back to using the great ship *Jonah* to deliver some... some crates of squid or whatever it is they're hauling?"

"Live deep-water squid, that's what Keeven said," Fransk lifted his head, his eyes meeting Uma's with something like resignation. "While we're on the subject, Director Ozakka... did you manage to get a full scan of their hold?"

Uma bit the inside of her lip. "We did. And I was really hoping you wouldn't ask about that, because you aren't going to like it."

Something shifted in Fransk's face then, like some last vestige of hope had just drained out of him. "It's not squid in there, is it?"

"Not even close. That cargo hold is chock full of weapon components." Uma reached for her lightpad and called up the report. "Looks like they're hauling diffractor charges—we've got signatures consistent with high yield C9D8 cubical blast cells. And reactive lenanium filament, weapons-grade. They've got about a hundred and twenty crates, as many as could be crammed in there. That's why they only had room for one backup energy cell. The other cells were removed to make more cargo space."

Barnabyn looked horrified. "B-but what's all that stuff for?"

"War supplies, maybe?" Zel said. "Could those be arms for the UWDF?"

Uma stifled a laugh. "Definitely not. The UWDF didn't use this type of thing. This is contraband." She flicked at the lightpad. "You know, permits for aquatics were one of the hallmarks of a good war-time smuggler. It was a pretty hard permit to get, but ideal because containers of live sea life were scan-exempt on most outposts." She smiled wryly. "That shipment belongs to a black market arms dealer. Probably bound for a ditch ship."

Three blank looks.

Uma sat back in her chair, resting the lightpad on her knee. "Okay, so... super quick history lesson. Toward the end of the war, a lot of weapons were being smuggled up to the Baedenoch system. They were arming the ditch ships—you know, all those rogue venture-ships that were taking off, claiming to be heading out of Union space? It was a total scam, these flights with no known destination, but even an almost-certain slow death in space seemed better than sitting around waiting for the Union to lose the war and the Felen to take over. People were willing to pay exorbitant sums of money for a chance to escape."

"So that's what you think the *Jonah*'s hauling?" Fransk frowned. "Weapons for a ditch ship?"

"No doubt about it."

Zel's eyes flashed disbelief. "But the *Jonah* was supposed to be on a peace mission! They can't be hauling arms, this is *awful*." He looked close to tears. "How can all these... differences even be possible?"

"I don't know, Zel. I don't understand it either." Uma shook her head. "So much of what they say happened isn't right. And yet so much of it stayed exactly the same. Think about this: Keila Kva-Sova says her Voicing experiments never succeeded, so she didn't bring the Decipherer to Pilar Outpost... but she still hitchhiked on board the *Jonah* at Pilar anyway? And somehow Charyne Jaxong ended up on that ship by chance, too, even though none of them knew each other? Even though Leesongronski wasn't even working for the Geminus Initiative?" She fixed her eyes on Fransk. "It's so strange how they're *almost* the Fortunate Five, but not quite."

"Without the Decipherer or the Negotiator, they're not the Fortunate Five at all," the captain said. "They're just three people without a single clue how to talk to the Felen or carry out a peace mission, even if they wanted to."

"Which is exactly why we must convince them it *is* possible!" Zel said. "That's why I had to let Kva-Sova see the truth! She believes in the mission, and now she's seen proof that her Voicing procedure can succeed! She knows she *could* Voice someone successfully when they get back. Maybe history had it wrong, and she just... hadn't quite done it yet?" He stroked the jewelled crest that pinned his sash, his expression mournful.

"And what about the Negotiator, then?" Barnabyn said. "I suppose you think they'll just find him somewhere, waiting to hitchhike along too?"

"The Negotiator was the last of the Five to be picked up," Uma said. "After they collected the Voicegiver and the Decipherer at Pilar Outpost, the *Jonah* stopped to rendezvous with him at—"

"Look, it doesn't matter how history says it happened," Zel interrupted. "What matters is what we're going to *make* happen, understand? We'll do whatever we have to, and so can they. It's not too late to save Etraxas. It can't be."

"Well, let's pray that's true," Fransk said. "And that it's not too late for all of us."

SHAAN

Common Deck, ZeyCorp Gallion

KEEVEN WAS STANDING at one of the vending machines when Shaan found him. He was staring at the screen, lost in thought, making no move to select any of the beverage options. He stood with his thumbs looped through his belt, his chin raised, his head tilted back so his shaggy auburn hair just grazed his shoulders. He looked calm, almost serene. Probably because he wasn't talking.

She leaned against the nearest table and watched him.

At last, Keeven grabbed a cup from the dispenser, shoved it into the vending machine, swiped his bracelet and selected a beverage. As the hot drink started trickling into the cup, he turned and looked over his shoulder.

"Well, well! If it isn't the ZeyCorp prison warden." He gave her a sarcastic grin. "Checking up on me? Am I allowed to stand here?"

"I'm just here to get a drink." Shaan stepped toward the vending machine and reached past him for a cup. "Carry on."

Keeven lifted his full cup to his mouth and took a sip. "Mmm! Not bad, this one. You've got some good stuff in here."

"Seriously?" Despite herself, Shaan laughed. "You must be

the only person ever to give favourable reviews to the ZeyCorp refreshments. Don't forget to fill in a guest feedback form."

"Yeah, sure." He took another sip, looking at her over the edge of the cup. "It's a deal. I'll give you top marks on the refreshments if your people let me out of here."

"Gods. Would you stop acting like we're holding you hostage?" Shaan rolled her eyes. "You can't start your engines. If we let you leave in that junk-heap, you'd die. You should count yourself lucky that we're keeping you here."

"Oh, believe me, Shaan, I don't want to die any more than you do. But thanks for the advice." He pointed at the empty cup she was still holding, then smirked. "I thought you were here to get a drink."

She scowled and pushed her cup into the dispenser. The mix he'd selected was still onscreen, and she didn't bother changing it.

While her cup slowly filled with the same dark pink plant brew he was drinking, Keeven wandered a few paces away. A moment later, he pulled that little red ball out of his pocket and started bouncing it off the nearest table, catching and releasing it with his free hand.

Thump. Thump. Thump.

Shaan collected her drink, circled the table and sat down.

Thump.

He threw the ball right in front of her, landing it a hand's width from her drink before he scooped it back into his hand. She glared.

"Why're you always doing that, huh? Did you look up a list of annoying habits and decide you needed them all?"

Thump.

"What, you mean this?" He bounced the ball higher this time and caught it over his head. "It's therapeutic, if you have to know. Kind of a personal story."

Thump.

"Right. I'm sure it's fascinating."

He snatched the ball out of the air and slid into the seat across from her.

"When I got out of stasis prison, I couldn't even feed myself," he said. "I couldn't lift my hand to my damn mouth. No one knew how bad the damage was going to be." He held up the ball. "This? This was part of my recovery training. Helped restore my coordination."

"Stasis prison... wow." Shaan fidgeted with her cup. "We don't do that anymore. It was banned years ago. It's barbaric."

Keeven rubbed the knot of scars on his neck. "Well, I got sent down for twenty-four years in a high-security orbital. How's that for barbaric?"

Shaan frowned. "But... how could you even survive for twenty-four years?" Anything more than ten years had always basically been a death sentence. Neurological damage was a standard side effect, even for short-term suspension. And the longer you stayed down, the smaller your chances of coming back at all.

Keeven tossed the ball from one hand to the other. "Hah. Well, luckily for me, I only served six of them. I got an early release." He winked. "Not entirely legally, of course. Friends in high places. And by that, I mean friends with lots of explosives."

"Gods. No wonder your ship's hauling a hundred and twenty crates of weapon components," she said. "You're obviously some kind of an arms dealer, right? That's why you don't support the peace movement?"

Keeven blinked at her for a moment, as if weighing up how to respond.

"There's no point lying about it," she said. "Ozakka scanned your hold. We know you aren't carting live squid."

"Now, first of all, let's get a few things straight," he said.

"One, I'm not an arms *dealer*. I only handle the transport. And two, this has nothing to do with the UWDF—I'm not exactly supplying the war effort here, am I? All the weapons I move go directly to the venturers. People about to go lookin' for new worlds. They all want planetary defense systems, to protect themselves when they get there."

"Call it whatever you want, it's still arms dealing," she said. "And... to protect themselves when they get *where* exactly?" She eyed him suspiciously. "Director Ozakka says all the ditch ships that left during the war were bogus. Those venture-ships didn't find any new worlds, and they were never going to. The people building them knew it, too—they knew all they were selling was false hope. Those venturers all died in deep space, if they didn't just explode."

"Hey, hey, hey." Keeven raised both hands. "First of all, everybody who gets on a ditch ship knows the risks. We're talking about desperate people here, Shaan. They *want* false hope! You could tell them right to their faces that the ship isn't going anywhere and they'd still get in it." He paused. "And... hang on, if that's what you think, why does it matter that we supplied them with weapons they never used? If they just died in deep space, if all the ships exploded, then what's it matter if we armed them?" He sat back with a self-satisfied look. "Maybe you should decide what it is you want to hate me for, hmm? I don't know what you take me for, but I'm not a monster."

"Well, you haven't given us a lot of reasons to trust you," she said. "You don't exactly seem like the honest sort."

He laughed. "Oh, gimme a break. *I'm* the dishonest one? And what about all the secrets *you've* been keeping, hmm?"

Shaan's mouth went dry. "I—what do you mean?"

"Ohhh, I know all about your Felen Ambassador," Keeven said smugly. "And I know about your telepathic interpreter that you've got on board. That girl who's been genetically altered into some kind of a half-Felen... thing?" He looked genuinely revolted.

"Oh, my gods," Shaan whispered. "Who told you? One of the juniors?"

"As if! I couldn't get a damned useful thing out of them. Luckily, Keila was more than happy to spill it." He crushed the empty cup between his hands. "Apparently, one of your ZeyCorp cronies took her to *see* the thing, and then tried to swear her to secrecy! Like that was ever going to work. She's a peace-activist fanatic, what did you think she was going to do? She told me everything."

Shaan's mouth dropped open.

"Ever since Keila came back from seein' it, she won't leave me alone." He grimaced. "She thinks she'll convince us that a truce with the Felen could actually happen. When we get out of here, she wants us to help her track down some of her Peace Project people, if any of 'em haven't been arrested yet."

Shaan stared at him. "But—"

"In case it wasn't obvious," he said, "my answer was no. Absolutely no gods-damned way."

UMA

Engineering Deck, ZeyCorp Gallion

IT WAS LATE at night by ship-time when Uma sat down in the upper level of Engineering. Most of the engineers had just cycled out on a break. Charyne Jaxong had retired to her apartment. Eldric Leesongronski had never returned after that nauseatingly awkward conversation yesterday.

In the pit below, only Wazar and Noussen were still tinkering with something on the equipment simulator. Macey was asleep at his console, his head tucked into the crook of his arm, his face illuminated by a still-spinning projection from a lightpad he'd dropped onto his lap.

Uma switched on her own lightpad, spun out a shimmering key-pad and started to compose the day-end report for the captain.

SUBJECT: *ENGINEERING UPDATE, ZeyCorp Gallion*

Work continues on the analysis of sensor log data from the hours after we entered the Rift. We can now conclusively rule out a sensor grid malfunction on the *Gallion*.

If our instruments were defective or compromised, we would have expected to see significant discrepancies in our data when compared to the *Jonah*'s. However, the data collected by our ships was almost perfectly synchronous. Any divergence can be ascribed to our instruments being more precise than the *Jonah*'s.

The words peppered out in front of her and tumbled into the projection, so many neat rows of letters in ZeyCorp's blocky bespoke font. She wondered how many of these updates she'd written since she first stepped onto this ship. And how many she had left to write. Shrugging off the chill that crept down her spine, she flexed her hands and carried on.

We've picked out a stable, low-level energy fluctuation in the Rift—a persistent pulse, like a heartbeat. We're using that pulse to synchronize the logs. During the initial hours in the Rift, before we hauled in the *Jonah*, both ships recorded the exact same number of pulses. From the point of view of the Rift, we can thus deduce that our ships arrived here simultaneously.

Mikolai is working with Professor Jaxong on a more detailed analysis of the anomalous Rift energy. Their working theory is that we're looking at a type of transmuted substrate energy, something from a deeper subspace layer than we've ever sampled. This might be possible through a theoretical phenomenon called a substrate fracture. I've asked Mikolai to prepare a short presentation on this tomorrow, using simplified language that can be shared with the entire group.

Syru has been testing a modification for our shuttle shields. The engines on our smallest shuttles will be functional in the Rift, as they don't rely on a core reaction.

However, their shielding is minimal, making them currently unusable. Syru is calibrating a shield pattern specifically to resist Rift energy. This might allow us to use a shuttle on autopilot to explore further into the Rift than our hover probes can go. Testing will resume tomorrow, with assistance from Wazar.

Noussen and Wazar have continued to work on improving our comms reach and long-range scanning capability. They are experimenting with a 'relay chain' of hover probes, to see if we can use them as repeaters and get our signals to reach further. More on this tomorrow.

Nack and the engine team have been redirected to supporting each of these projects as needed. No further engine core resets are planned at this time. We continue to conserve energy and hold off on any more core resets until we've gathered more information.

Uma Ozakka

Director of Engineering

She read the text once over and hit 'send.'

A new image bloomed in its place: the projection she'd pinned as her background, so she'd see it every time she switched on her 'pad. A rolling time-lapse of Rift telemetry. It was a thing of grotesque beauty, like some huge, gelatinous mass. It moved like a wave that never crested, but instead turned in on itself. Each wave became three other waves, spiralling away into a sea of fractals.

She was still staring at it when Wazar's excited voice echoed up from the pit.

"Awww, yeah! Director Ozakka, come look! Our long-range scan's coming through!" Wazar shrieked triumphantly. "It's a real beauty!"

Against the far wall, Dean's android body purred to life in

its charging port. Two round eyes blinked open, the android's cheeriest expression already on display.

"Long-range scans are now complete!" the AI chirped. "I am happy to report that we've picked up an object of interest!"

Macey had also snapped awake at the shouting. He looked around in confusion, rubbing at his eyes. "Wazar? What's going on?"

"Check it out!" Wazar said. "We sent out another volley of long-rangers, using the hover relay chain aaaand... we got something! Looks like we found another ship!"

"You are fucking kidding me," Macey intoned.

"See for yourself." Noussen flicked the scan up to the main projection screen, where it resolved from a blurry, indistinct shape into a slightly less fuzzy one.

"Wow. It's... a blob," said Macey. "What is that?"

"Large object, looks symmetrical, about eight hundred and forty klicks out. We've also got some energy signatures..." Wazar layered in several other scans as the object's outlines continued to sharpen. "Damn! Good work, Noussen!"

Uma walked down the stairs, squinting at the column of measurements alongside the projection. "Huh, you sure that scale's right? That's a pretty big ship."

"Roughly twenty times our size, yeah," said Wazar. "Could be some kind of passenger liner? The shape's real weird, though."

"You said we've got energy signatures? Let's see if they match any known core halos," Uma said. "That should tell us their engine type, even if the engines are down. Dean, could you run that check?"

"On it now, Director," the android said.

"Whoa... What *time* do you think this one's from?" whispered Noussen. "I wonder how long it's been out here."

Wazar tapped her chin. "Well, the *Gallion* and the *Jonah* have both been here for almost four subjective days, even though we're from different times. So I'm guessing that ship's been here for about four days, too? From their own point of view. Right?"

Noussen shrugged. "Sure. Probably."

"As for what year they think it is, I guess we'll have to ask 'em!"

"Gods, I can't believe we're sitting here talking about this like it's normal," said Macey. "We are literally about to hail a ship to ask them *what year it is.*"

"We've already been hailing them," Dean said. "Repeatedly. Our distress call is still on a loop, on all channels. There's been no response."

"Maybe they heard us, but they don't want to reply," said Wazar. "Don't forget how suspicious we all were about answering the *Jonah*'s distress call."

"Or maybe everyone on board is dead," said Macey dejectedly. "Just like we will be soon."

Noussen shuddered. "Macey, would you *please* stop saying that?"

"This ship's way out of our tractor beam range," Uma said. "We were struggling to do a weak pull at eighty klicks, and this is more than ten times that distance. If they don't answer our hails, I'm not sure what else we can do."

"You know... I'm not so sure this thing's actually a ship." Wazar leaned forward, studying the projection. "There's more than one object here. See this little structure? What's that?" She reached up and pinched the projection, zooming in on a blurry oval smudge near the bottom of the scan. "That little dot could be a remote power annex."

"Power annex..." Uma frowned. "Then it's a space station."

"I think so." Wazar pointed out a fuzzy protrusion around the larger of the two objects. "This bit here could be a docking ring."

"Dean, cancel that request to identify engine core halos,"

Uma said, her frown deepening. "Match for an anchored drive signature instead."

"Understood, Director. Checking now."

Uma paced around the console, one palm pressed to her head, twirling a strand of hair with her other hand. She walked all the way around Engineering, glancing up the stairs every so often to reassure herself that no one new had arrived. The railing where Leesongronski had sat remained empty.

At last, the android's silvery head tilted to one side, then straightened with a gleeful chirp. "Success, Director!" Dean said. "The signature is consistent with a ring-annexed anchored Jaxong drive. I can surmise that the drive is currently deactivated, but the annex has approximately six standard power cells, all of them full."

"Full power cells!" Wazar squealed. "Oh my gods!" She jumped up from her chair. "Director Ozakka, we've got to find a way to get out there! What about Syru's shuttle shields? If we could send a shuttle out, we could retrieve those power cells, and then we could—"

Uma held up one hand. "Hold on, hold on. Let's not get ahead of ourselves yet." Anxiety gnawed at the edges of her mind. There was something too unnerving about this. A *space station*, out here?

"Director Ozakka's right. We don't know who they are, or if anyone's on board that station," Noussen said. "We can't just fly over there and start lifting their energy cells. Shouldn't we check if they need help?"

"Well, if they won't answer us, there's not much else we can do, is there?" Macey said.

"I do have one idea." Noussen turned in her chair. "What if we sent them an ident-request? That reply should be automated, so we ought to get *something* back."

Wazar grinned. "Brilliant, mate!"

"Dean," Uma said. "Please send a local ident-request to that station."

"Sending now," said the android. "It may take a few tries, Director. Communications at this distance are fragmented."

It took six minutes before the station returned a reply. Six breathless minutes, during which absolutely no one spoke. A feeling of foreboding was steadily building in the room, and Uma's skin crawled.

Then, Dean's expression switched abruptly to one of intense concern.

"Oh! Reply received," the android said. "The docking protocol codes are... 555, 200B, 0X. That's *Danger Do Not Board, Secure Facility, Unoccupied.*"

"Shiiit," said Wazar, whistling softly.

"Their unique registration number is 322-1095-3A," Dean continued. "And the registering company is... the Geminus Peace Alliance."

Uma sank into the nearest chair. "Geminus!"

"I've queried registration number 322-1095-3A against the *Gallion*'s knowledge bank," Dean said, "and I can find only one match. That number was mentioned in an update we got from the Deep Space Registration Directory."

"Tell us, Dean."

"Six years ago, the *Gallion* received a standard update ping from the ship-net, refreshing our navigation databases," the android said. "Among other corrections in that update, this station's record was expunged from the Directory. Registration 322-1095-3A was invalidated."

"Invalidated why?"

"It was marked as a status L5, Director. *Structure confirmed dismantled or destroyed.*"

Wazar gestured at the projection. "And yet somehow, we're looking at it."

"I have its former coordinates on record," Dean said. "It seems this station was anchored quite far into a neutral sector, out on the border between Felen and Union space."

Uma slowly shook her head, still blinking in shock.

"It was called Verkhoy Station," Dean added, switching back to a disappointed expression. "And until we regain access to a network connection, I'm afraid that's everything I know."

ELDRIC
Sëgra City, Sëgra
11 years before the Rift

ELDRIC LEESONGRONSKI STOOD on his glassed-in balcony, looking down at the City of Neverending Night from his palatial lodgings. From up here, it was difficult to imagine that he'd made any bad decisions. He did wonder sometimes why he hadn't made different choices, or why he hadn't turned out to be a better person. But the longer he lived in Sëgra City, the less often those questions troubled him.

Perhaps it just wasn't a place for that kind of contemplation.

Sëgra City was a domed metropolis, a glowing globe of lights that clung like a bright barnacle on frigid black rock. It was deep in an outer-system asteroid belt, where the distant, pallid sun was nothing but a faint smudge in an endlessly dark sky. The cold reaches of space were held back only by the centuries-old dome: one big spherical protrusion surrounded by several smaller ones that had been added as the city sprawled out.

The settlement had once been a mining base, but the Sëgran rock had long ago been plundered of all its natural riches. Its hollowed shell now overflowed with wealth of an entirely different kind. Now, it was a city where dreams were made real as easily as they were shattered. *No consequences until morning*, so the saying went. But the sun never rose on Sëgra. Hours, days and years blended into one long intoxicating night.

The city had no shortage of interesting people. There was business, some of it legitimate, the vast majority of it not so much. There was entertainment, each neon-soaked street replete with virtual and visceral pleasures. Crucially, there happened to be a proliferation of gambling-houses, betting rings and virtual games. There was the lure of anonymity, too—the City of Neverending Night was as good a place as any to disappear.

For the first time in his life, Eldric felt like he could do anything he wanted.

And then, he met the wood-nymph.

It happened in the Dome Theatre, the city's biggest dreamhouse, where dozens of performers animated an endless series of immersive virtual reality shows. Sëgra City had some of the best VR tech ever made; expansive experiences that took hours to walk through and felt as real as dreams.

Whenever Eldric walked through a show, he spotted some of the same performers. The animators would switch places from day to day, but he couldn't help but recognize their patterns: the order in which they deployed their flourishes and twirls, the speed with which they switched colour palettes, the angles at which they held their real limbs to generate these motion-captures. It became a little game to him, something to pass the time. Eldric had no idea what any of the animators really looked like, but their patterns were unmistakable.

And then one day, quite by chance, he saw one of them *outside* the show.

The animator was making her way through the dreamhouse lobby after drifting out of the performers' backstage entrance, and she was still in her animation gear. Her hair was tucked into a flat cap, and her body was encased in a shimmering suit from her shoulders to her feet. Her bare brown arms were still flecked with the tiny round nodes that tracked her movements when she worked.

Eldric looked at the dots as she moved and immediately knew he'd seen her before. In one show she'd played a wood-nymph in the midsummer scene: a ghostly sprite with leaves and vines growing down twig-like arms, a face carved from tree bark with sharp birdlike features, four trailing gossamer wings. Next she was a sea creature, a silver-finned fish with a long coiled tail and scales as bright as mirrors. In another show, she was a winged sun-apparition, an ethereal form cloaked in blinding fractals. But the way she moved was unmistakable.

Before he could think about what he was doing, Eldric was already elbowing a path toward her. The place was overcrowded, and his progress through the crowd was slow, but the animator paused halfway across the lobby to rummage through her bag. She tugged out a dark robe and pulled it over her head, covering her VR suit.

When she straightened up and lifted the bag back onto her shoulder, Eldric was in front of her.

"Hello," he said.

The animator stared at him. She had an expressive heart-shaped face, with deep brown skin and long-lashed eyes set over a wide nose. Something about her felt immediately familiar. Eldric hadn't really considered who the performer might be when she wasn't a sprite or a fish, yet the face seemed to suit her perfectly.

"Can I help you?" She spoke with a melodic accent, each syllable a high, clear note.

"You work here... right? You're a dream-play animator in the Dome."

She shook her head, and started to step past him. "Sorry. I'm not allowed to talk to patrons." She quickly pulled down her silk sleeves, hiding the nodes on her arms.

"Well... I just wanted to tell you I saw you in the show," he said. "You're one of the best animators in there."

She gave a short, sarcastic laugh. "Sure, yeah. I'm sure you saw me. Me and the sixty-odd other backup animators, huh? Nice line, but I'm not a lead."

"I know you're not. I can always pick you out, though."

She looked at him dubiously. "Right."

"You were a wood-nymph in the forest show. You came in at the start of the second act, except on the last day of the week, when you also animated a rock spirit and two of the bird-creatures in the first half. For the ocean show, you do the silver fish—in the main pattern, you're the third one, and the seventh one, and the fifteenth. In the show just now... fractal sun designs, upper level, second from left for most of the middle act." He smiled.

She stared at him, her mouth slightly agape. "You're, um... wow. You're incredibly observant. Do you always memorize the backup animations?"

"Only the memorable ones."

A small smile played at the corners of her mouth, and she looked him slowly up and down. He was wearing a red-striped jacket, half-buttoned over a lightly patterned shirt. The sleeves dripped with an absurd amount of gold-shot embroidery. His long hair was braided off to one side, pinned back with an ornate jewelled clasp. After five years in the City, Eldric still thought most of these Sëgran fashions looked ridiculous, but he'd started to get used to them.

"Well... thanks for noticing me," the animator said. "Too bad you're not the producer. Getting promoted to lead here is all about house politics, who you cozy up to. No one cares about *skill*. This whole city's so fucking fake."

Eldric nodded. "Yeah. It's like they say, if you want something here, you have to buy it, steal it, or win it."

"I guess I just haven't been lucky yet," the animator said. She reached up to her neck and pulled a slender chain out from under her collar, tapping the small gold sphere that hung at the end of it. It was a fortune-charm, embossed with the old-world symbol for *luck*.

"There's no such thing as luck," Eldric said. "Chance and luck aren't the same thing."

"Oh, I know." She laughed. "But it doesn't hurt to keep one of these just in case, does it? It's worth a shot." She nudged his arm like she'd just told him a secret. Then she tapped the symbol on the fortune-charm once more, and dropped the twinkling orb back under her collar. She shifted her bag on her shoulder. "I should go. It was nice meeting you."

She had one of the most fascinating voices Eldric had ever heard. Suddenly, he didn't want her to walk away.

"Hey," he said. "Wait. Do you want to get a drink with me?" He pointed across the lobby at the concourse that led out to the dreamhouse bar. "We could keep talking over there."

"Sorry. I can't. I told you, we can't talk to patrons in the theatre." She glanced over her shoulder. "It's actually written in my contract."

"No breaking the illusion, huh?"

She grimaced. "Something like that."

"Well, what if we went for dinner, then? Outside the theatre?" He motioned toward the exit. "There's no illusion to break out there."

"For real?" She blinked twice, looking surprised. "You're asking me to dinner?"

"Sure," said Eldric. "There's a nice restaurant on top of the Night Palace. It's got a great view."

She laughed then, touching his arm lightly as if he'd just told a hilarious joke. "Mm-hmm."

"No, really," he said. "We can go right now. I've got a permanent reservation."

Her eyes widened incredulously. "A permanent reservation... at the *Night Palace?*"

"Yeah." He smiled. "I live there, actually."

"I... um, right..." A strange look crossed her face, and she looked him up and down again, her gaze lingering on his expensive jacket. "I'm not exactly dressed for the Night Palace. Would you mind waiting while I run backstage and change?"

"Take your time," Eldric said. "I'll stay right here."

Her eyes met his, and she didn't move to go. She just kept looking at him.

"My name's Eldric, by the way," he said, tentatively raising his palm. "Eldric Leesongronski."

She returned the gesture, and her smile returned. "Hi, Eldric. I'm Dafnë Valay."

UMA
Command Deck, *ZeyCorp Gallion*

When Uma came into his office, Fransk was standing by the window, gazing out into the impenetrable blackness beyond the pseudo-glass. A steaming ZeyCorp-branded mug sat untouched on his desk, and he wore a heavy cardigan half-buttoned over his uniform.

"Director Ozakka," he said, turning to face her. "Uma... come in." His eyes were hollow, his brown skin lustreless.

"Gods. You look awful, Olghan."

"I can't sleep properly, not with all this hanging over us. And now this Geminus station..." He shuffled to the desk, sat down and pulled the mug toward him. "I don't even know what to think anymore."

"Well, how about some good news?" Uma forced a smile, setting a lightpad on the desk. "See this scan? That's a ring of six power cells around the Jaxong drive, on that small annex a few klicks out from the station. The Jaxong drive isn't active at the moment, and we don't know if it can work in the Rift... but those energy cells? All signs point to them being *full*."

Fransk frowned down at the lightpad. "Mm-hmm."

"Are you hearing me? We can replenish our power!" she said.

"If we collect these cells, we can buy ourselves more time to examine the Rift phenomenon and find a way out!"

Fransk pushed the lightpad aside.

"It's eight hundred and forty klicks to that station, Uma," he said. "Can we even autopilot a shuttle at that distance, with all the interference?"

"Well... not exactly," Uma said. "Noussen's hover relay extended the reach of our signals, but comms are fragmented. The shuttle would have to be piloted manually."

"What?" Fransk's frown deepened. "No! Out of the question. If we send somebody off this ship, we could lose them out there."

"And if we don't, we could lose everybody," Uma said. She sat down and leaned across the desk toward him. "There's no other way to do it, Olghan. It's a live pilot or nothing. Comms will be too patchy for a remote docking." She paused. "We'd also need the pilot to go out in a space-suit, to undo all the power cell couplings so they can be towed back."

"What?" Fransk recoiled, nearly choking on his beverage. "We don't have anyone with the proper training for that. I don't think anyone on board even has manual flight experience."

Uma paused, weighing the words up before she said them. "I think Jereth Keeven could do it."

The captain's eyebrows shot up. "*Keeven?*"

"He told us he used to be a military pilot. He was apparently a squadron leader in the UWDF. And he has EVA experience. If anyone can land a shuttle out there in dangerous conditions, he can." She took a breath. "I've, uh... I've actually talked to him about it already. He agreed that he'd do it for us."

Fransk still looked suspicious. "Agreed at what price?"

Uma sighed. "He wants a guarantee that we'll let him keep two of the power cells we recover," she said. "*And* he wants that video game system from the staff lounge."

"The sim-player? Good gods. What for?"

"Who cares?" Uma said. "I told him he could have it. What's the difference?"

Fransk was silent for a long time before he looked up again. "Have you finished testing those shuttle shield mods Syru was working on?"

"We're getting there," she said. "Syru's still fine-tuning the modulation patterns. We should be good to run final tests within a day. Maybe less." She took the lightpad back, switching it off as she folded it away. "So... do we have your approval to launch a shuttle?"

"I want a full report on those shield tests," Fransk said, tapping the desk. "I need to know this is safe. Then we'll talk about it."

She bit back her annoyance. This was a better response than she'd anticipated. Olghan Fransk was many things, but he was *not* a risk-taker.

"Got it," she said. "I'll send a report across as soon as we're done testing."

She started to get up.

"Wait. There's one more thing." Fransk motioned her back, his expression serious.

"Yes?" Uma lowered herself slowly back into the chair, a sinking feeling in her stomach.

Fransk pinched the bridge of his nose, his expression grim. "You know... Nack told me you let Charyne Jaxong see the specs for the Jaxong drive. Did it occur to you to talk to me before you did that?"

"Oh, shit." Uma looked away again. "I... I did mean to tell you."

"You *meant* to tell me? Uma, we had an agreement!" The captain wasn't given to raising his voice, and this was as close as she'd heard him come to shouting in a long while. "Jaxong and Leesongronski were to be given access to the Rift data and *nothing* else. Was that not what we agreed?"

"Gods, calm down." Uma sighed. "Look, I know Professor Jaxong can help us. She was one of the most brilliant scientists of the age, Olghan; she's the gods-damned *Inventor!* And she's the one who designed that drive, so maybe she can come up with something—some theory, or some way to make the drive draw power in the Rift, or—"

"No," Fransk's voice cracked. "We can't seriously be letting her look at her own future work, letting her see things she hasn't actually invented yet. There is *Felen technology* involved in that drive! Did you think about that?" He swept his hand over the desk, nearly upending his mug. "If we keep messing with things this way, then we... oh, gods, Uma, what are we doing here? We have to stop."

"Oli, believe me. I am trying to do the right thing." Uma softened her voice. "It's not like we're giving Jaxong completely new information, okay? That drive doesn't contain anything she hasn't already seen. She said she worked as a physicist for the UWDF, so she was probably studying Felen tech already."

The corner of Fransk's mouth twitched nervously. "Are you sure? I thought we didn't have technological exchange with the Felen until well after the Peace."

Uma sighed. "Look. Our history says that Jaxong was researching renewable deep-space energy, right? And then, after the Peace, once there was open knowledge exchange with the Felen, she invented the Jaxong drive with a combination of human and Felen tech. She revolutionized renewable energy for space stations, found a way to draw power directly from the subspace layer. That's what you know. Right?"

Fransk nodded tentatively.

"Wrong. If you dig into the sources a bit, the Fortunate Five actually showed the original prototype for that drive to the

Felen *during the Peace negotiations*. Olghan, she must have already had the basic concept finished *way* before free tech trade!"

"How is that possible?"

"It's possible because Jaxong was already studying Felen tech, trying to reverse-engineer it. She definitely wasn't working on renewable energy. No. The UWDF hired Jaxong to develop new weapons during the war. The Samouga Research Institute was working on the S-bomb. A weapon of mass destruction, a bomb that could tear through subspace by subverting Felen transit-gates."

Fransk inhaled sharply, pursing his lips. "Did you read that in one of your *Jonah* conspiracy books? Because I thought the Union wasn't even close to developing subspace weapons during the war."

"Well, you sure won't find any official records saying the project existed. And yes, most people would call it a conspiracy theory, which is exactly why I didn't bother to mention it to you before," Uma said. "But when you think about it... it makes sense that the UWDF would've funded something like that. There was no hope of ending the war. The Union was so desperate, they would've tried anything."

"Subspace warfare... gods," he whispered. "The one line we've never crossed."

"Look, whatever your opinion on conspiracy theories, I can tell you this. Her Jaxong drive idea damn sure didn't come out of nowhere. It's actually based on very similar energy principles to the ones she would've needed for the S-bomb. Any subspace physicist or engineer can tell you that the Jaxong drive shares the same structures as a hypothetical bomb."

Fransk sighed. "It still doesn't seem right, involving her this way."

"She understands what's inside that drive better than anybody else on this ship," Uma said. "We're running out of time. We *need* her."

"Fine," Fransk said at last. "Show her what you have to. But for the love of all the gods, tread carefully. No showing her things from the future. Promise me."

Uma stood up from the chair. His eyes met hers, and for a brief moment, she saw that bright, handsome, headstrong young version of him, the Olghan she'd known at university. He had always liked promises a lot more than she did, but she still hated breaking them.

"If we want to stay alive, Oli... we might not have any choice."

SHAAN
Residential Deck, *ZeyCorp Gallion*

SHAAN MOVED AIMLESSLY through the ship, walking faster and faster. She didn't know where she was going, and she didn't care. Only a few hours had passed since Engineering found that station, but it felt like a lifetime. And all she wanted, with every fibre of her being, was to *run*.

Everyone else had been too preoccupied in the aftermath of the discovery to notice that Shaan was gone yet. Of course, Syru or Mikolai would probably message her the next time they were heading to the canteen. They always checked in, always happened to pop by Shaan's apartment to see how she was doing on days when the research teams had been insufferable. Even now, with everything that was going on, they had never failed to include her. She had better friends than she deserved, that was for sure.

On the residential deck, Shaan swiped open the access to a utility corridor and unlatched the hatch to the emergency stair shaft. Then she slipped through and descended into the dark, climbing down stair by stair into the narrow passage beyond, her clammy hands clutching the rails.

She came to a stop on a triangular landing two decks down,

in front of the door that connected this escape shaft to one of the research decks. Red floodlights illuminated the access point.

Beyond the pseudo-glass window in that sealed door, the overhead lights and ambients were all out. The researchers' office rooms and labs were cold and deserted. A glowing symbol over the door warned that life support systems on that deck were switched off—Director Ozakka had sealed off all the unused decks on the first day.

Having run as far as she could get from anyone else on the ship, Shaan sat down on the landing. She stared through the pseudo-glass into that empty hallway, acutely aware of just how *alone* she was down here. She thought of Ashlish, running alone through the long, empty corridors on Verkhoy Station, with the evac announcement blaring behind her.

Verkhoy Station. It was here, after all this time. How was that possible? When one of the engineers had spoken its name aloud, it was as though her soul had fractured into pieces, shards of grief lancing through her body.

She couldn't shake the creeping certainty that this was the end of the line, for all of them. Verkhoy Station was a bad omen. *Death, darkness, only death*, Ashlish had said.

Shaan willed herself to be calm. There was no reason anyone would suspect that she knew more about that station than she let on. She wasn't the only one who was out of sorts. Everyone was stressed and tired, and they were all acting at least a little bit weird.

She closed her eyes and focused on the artificial engine hum. *Leave the past in the past.* The only past she had now was on the *Gallion*. She let her mind linger there, over six years of memories on this ship.

She thought of some of the less-insufferable researchers who had done rotations on the *Gallion*, remembering as many of their names as she could, wondering where they were and what they were doing now. She thought of Wazar's famous turnover parties, of laughter and silly drinking games and inside jokes. She thought of that long month of awkward, hilarious flirtations between Syru and Mikolai when Mik first came on board, both of them somehow oblivious to the other's feelings until Wazar finally convinced Syru to make a damn move.

Shaan smiled to herself for a moment. If she tried hard enough, she could almost make herself believe that she'd imagined the last few days. She could will it all to disappear.

But even things that disappeared could return.

Her smile faded. Behind her eyelids, she saw the looming spectre of Verkhoy Station.

And she saw Ashlish.

Always, always Ashlish.

UMA
Engineering Deck, *ZeyCorp Gallion*

THE MOOD ON the Engineering deck was fragile. Uma paced the pit floor, watching the bleary-eyed crew bent over their consoles. She walked to one side, looked at the scan of the station again, walked to the other side, looked at the Rift numbers again. Her thoughts raced.

A Geminus station. The Jonah. *The Rift.* Somehow, that station had to be the missing piece of the puzzle. But how?

The team had already determined that it wouldn't be feasible to enter the station. It was a highly-secured Geminus facility, and unoccupied, so there wouldn't be a safe way to get its airlocks open. Still, Uma couldn't help wondering what was inside. Had its sensors collected any additional data? Could any of Verkhoy's comms equipment still be working? Once they retrieved those power cells and bought themselves more time, finding a way into the station itself was a tantalizing prospect.

Deep in thought, Uma walked up the stairs and sat down at the oblong table on the top level. She opened her lightpad and reviewed the test results that Syru had sent through. The junior had done an unbelievably thorough job on the shield mods. Not a single breach had been recorded across the first forty-seven simulated situations, with eight sim runs each. Every result was annotated with lengthy technical readouts and stats from Dean.

The test schemas were each marked with a bright blue *SUCCESS* symbol. All but one.

Uma opened the forty-eighth schema, the final test Syru had carried out. This one simulated close exposure to a burst of the highest recorded intensity of Rift energy. As with the others, the same sim had been run eight times in slightly variant situations.

FAILED [CRITICAL]
Result: Potential shieldform collapse.
Simulations run: 8.
8 / 8 severe breach in third band
8 / 8 secondary systems critically damaged
7 / 8 full shieldform collapse and immediate life support loss

Gods damn it. Something always had to go wrong.

Uma tugged out her hair elastic and shook out her hair. She focused on her breathing as she slowly gathered her hair back up into a knot on top of her head. Then she picked up the lightpad again, scrolling the details of that last test back and forth.

Potential shieldform collapse. Immediate life support loss.

It was an edge case, the unlikeliest of events. Nothing to worry about, really, she told herself—but seeing it laid out like that was disconcerting nonetheless. She was poring over the data for the third time when she suddenly became aware of someone watching her.

She turned around.

Eldric Leesongronski had returned to Engineering at last, and he was standing right behind her, his dark eyebrows furrowing into a frown as he looked at the open report on her 'pad. Her hand froze, midway through flicking the projection.

Leesongronski said nothing. He just stood there, staring at her hand, twirling a small gold orb on a chain between his fingers.

Uma's heart jumped into her throat. She quickly swiped the projection away, shoving the lightpad to one side. "It's only a simulation, Professor Leesongronski," she said defensively. "We haven't finished testing yet. It's still a... a work in progress—"

But Leesongronski wasn't looking at the lightpad. When she moved her hand, his piercing gaze followed it. She had rolled her sleeves partway up today, and he was staring at her wrist.

"Sëgran soul-bond," he said quietly, almost to himself.

"What?"

He pointed at the sun-shaped scar on the inside of her left wrist. "That's the sun-seal of the Temple of Everlasting Light on Sëgra. Isn't it? A Sëgran soul-bond."

"Oh! Um... yeah. It is."

"Bound and sealed until the Great Suns burn out..." Leesongronski dropped the orb's slender chain back under his collar, then slowly rolled up his own sleeve, exposing the raised lines of an identical sun-shaped brand on his wrist. "How about that?"

Uma gasped aloud. "Oh my gods. It really is the same!"

He held his pale arm out toward hers, their hands nearly brushing together as he compared their scars—the mark of what Sëgra called a soul-bonding ceremony. Uma's sun-seal was perfectly aligned on her brown skin, the lines all the same width, each ray coiling off neatly from the central circle. Leesongronski's scar was off to one side of his wrist, and some of the rays trailed off slightly. One of the coils was doubled, as though the brand had been set down twice.

"Dafnë got real nervous when we got in there. She was afraid it was gonna hurt... didn't press it on straight." He ran a finger over the lopsided rays on his wrist. "Damn. Sëgra City. I can't believe they're still doing that same old shit, with the fire-branding and everything."

"They'll keep doing it as long as the Great Suns are shining, right?" Uma smiled.

Leesongronski didn't smile back. He shook his shirt-sleeve back down.

"What were you doing way out on Sëgra, anyway?" he asked. "You didn't *live* there, did you?"

"No. I was just... visiting."

"Hm," he said. "So how's the City doing these days? Still a trashy hell-pit?"

She laughed. "Yeah, I guess. A lot of it's still the same. I saw a lot of the places you went... and I saw where you lived. The Night Palace is still there. And the Temple of Everlasting Light, obviously." She took a deep breath. "You know, it's probably kind of strange to tell you this, but we only went up into the Temple district because I wanted to see the spot where you and Dafnë made your soul-bond."

"What?" Leesongronski nearly choked.

She couldn't make herself meet his eyes. "We got all the way up to the top of those big steps in front of the Temple, and I wanted to get a look inside. But they said we couldn't go into the chambers where the oaths were made unless we were planning to do the ceremony ourselves, so... we said we would do it. We paid the fee and we went in. They put these flower garlands on us and threw glow-dust over us, then walked us through the circle of fire. We went all the way up into the chambers and we did it. We made a soul-bond, fire-brands and all."

"Ugh," Leesongronski said. "That place isn't even a real temple. It was so tacky."

"Oh, I know. It just... it seemed like a great idea at the time. We made our oaths, we branded each other, then they tied ribbons on us..." Uma half-smiled at the memory. "Afterwards, we got a token for a free drink."

"We got a free drink, too," Leesongronski said, shaking his head. "Soul-bonds, tch. What a joke. Dafnë thought it was romantic, though. She said it was a nice idea, you know, like a symbol that we really meant what we said."

"It *was* romantic, in its own way." Uma sighed. "I was so madly in love... Tacky or not, it seemed perfect that we made those promises, right there, right then."

"Hm," Leesongronski said. "You two still together, then?"

"Nope." Uma pulled her sleeve down, tucking it over her ZeyCorp bracelet and covering her scar. "I wouldn't undo it, though. We had some good times. No regrets, that's my policy."

"You're doing better than I am, then." Leesongronski made a sarcastic congratulatory gesture. "I've got plenty of regrets."

Just then, a loud yell from the Engineering pit startled them both.

"This has gone far enough!" Nack shouted. "I swear, you kids'll fall for anything!"

Uma bolted up from her chair and looked over the rail. Down in the pit, Macey, Noussen and the Cordero siblings were clustered around Charyne Jaxong, who was seated at a console next to Mikolai.

"I'm sure Professor Jaxong knows what she's talking about," Noussen protested. "And she says Mikolai's right!"

Nack made a disgusted noise low in his throat, gesturing at Jaxong. "Oh, does she work for ZeyCorp now? Who made her the authority here?" He jabbed a finger at Macey and the twins. "As far as I'm concerned, you three are still part of the engine team and you still report to me. Go back to your consoles and stop wasting time!"

"Nack!" Uma shouted from the top of the stairs. "What in the five hells is going on?"

Nack's eyes flashed fury as he pointed at Jaxong. "Director, do you know what she's saying? She's got half your team sold on some pseudo-scientific nonsense!"

Jaxong didn't say anything. She just stared down at the lightpad on her lap.

"All right, Nack," Uma said. "Take a deep breath. I'm coming down."

She looked back at Leesongronski, motioning him to follow her down the stairs. The small group watched her in silence as she walked down, like they were waiting for her to pronounce some kind of judgement.

"Mikolai. You want to tell me what happened?"

The junior ran a hand over his dark curls, glancing nervously at Nack before he spoke. "Well... Professor Jaxong reviewed my presentation on the properties of the Rift," he said. "The presentation you asked me to make, about the potential substrate fracture?" He flicked open a projection on his console, and several intertwining shapes lazily spiralled out. They twisted and spun rhythmically as the projection expanded.

"I made this model based on the Rift energy fluctuations," Mikolai said. "See? Here's the fracture, expanded and realized as a multidimensional shape. I think we're looking at a form of energy that's theoretically possible, but was never expected to exist outside the deepest subspace layers."

Mikolai opened a second projection, one Uma recognized. It was the map plotting the locations of the most powerful Rift energy bursts. "When we started to haul in the *Jonah*, their outboard sensors were still recording," Mikolai said. "According to their logs, when we had the *Jonah* about halfway over to us, the energy bursts started intensifying. See, our two regions of the Rift are separated by a kind of seam—like a fault-line. And all along that line, that's where our hover probes have been detecting the biggest energy anomalies."

"We call it the 'boundary zone,'" Jaxong said, finally looking up. "There's another one just like it that separates the *Gallion* from Verkhoy Station, too. A second seam."

"It's not a straight line, though... nowhere near it," Mikolai said. "I started plotting it out, based on the origin points of the strongest energy pulses. And when we unfold that graph into 5D, we get... this." He gestured at the undulating shape again. "Based on this data, I proposed that a violent event of some kind could've caused an aberration in space-time. Something like a high-energy subspace explosion could've triggered this fracture."

"And I say Mikolai is right," Jaxong said. She paused, her eyes lingering on Leesongronski before she cleared her throat and continued. "I've worked on subspace weapon prototypes. A subspace weapon could absolutely have caused that fracture."

Uma sucked in a breath. "I knew it," she whispered. "You were on the UWDF's S-bomb team. Project Last Shot."

"How do you know that?" Jaxong's head snapped around, her eyes wide. "Project Last Shot was highly classified."

"People talked, after the war. They said the Samouga Research Institute was developing a superweapon for the Union. That you were trying to subvert Felen transit-gates, to set off a deep-layer rupture that would make subspace channels permanently unnavigable. To make a star system unreachable forever." She studied Jaxong's haunted eyes. "Is... is that right?"

Jaxong looked down at her hands. "Yes," she whispered. "That's all true."

Uma couldn't read the expression on Leesongronski's face. He was nodding his head slowly, regarding Jaxong with something that might have been newfound respect. The other engineers just stared.

"The UWDF did fund my research company," Jaxong said. "My team and I worked on Last Shot for years. But when they started pressuring me to test the prototype... I thought it was too dangerous to attempt. The results were unpredictable, the consequences of a mistake were... unimaginable." She shuddered. "I made up my mind to run, before they could find a way to force my hand."

"You know, to this day the Union denies that they were *ever* planning to test a subspace bomb, or that they had anything close to a usable prototype during the war," Uma said quietly. "The UWDF's superweapon was never tested. We don't know exactly why, but... it was probably because you defected before the prototype was completed. The Geminus Initiative gave you sanctuary, and you joined the Peace Project instead."

"I guess I did defect," Jaxong said, tilting her head as though she were only just realizing it. "But I've never had anything to do with the Geminus Initiative, or the Peace Project, or any of that. What help would Geminus be? They're all under arrest, or else in hiding with bounties on their heads." She pursed her lips. "The UWDF put a bounty on me, too. Sixty million creds for my capture. They were hunting me by the pack."

Behind Uma, Eldric Leesongronski cursed under his breath.

"Enough of this. How about you tell Director Ozakka the rest of it?" Nack said, glaring at Jaxong and Mikolai. "Tell her what you said before."

Mikolai took a long breath, gazing up at the undulating shape in the projection. "Well... Professor Jaxong suggested that a subspace detonation could potentially invert the Rift again," he said. "A violent explosion from *inside* the Rift could force space-time to fold itself back out again, and punch out that fracture."

"What?" Uma frowned.

"I told you," Nack sneered. "It's pseudo-scientific garble."

Jaxong gave a laboured sigh. "Look, I simply said that if we *are* in a semi-stable bubble of deformed space-time, then a disruption from inside the bubble could push that deformation back out into normal space. That's a scientific fact, whether *you* understand it or not. Hypothetically, if we could improvise something like an S-bomb, we might be able to force these Rift segments back to where they came from."

"Or we might just blow ourselves up," said Macey glumly.

"But... how could we improvise a subspace bomb anyway?" said Noussen. "We're trapped in a void with nothing except what's on this ship."

"Or out on that station," Mikolai pointed out, his face beaming. "Verkhoy Station has a Jaxong drive on its power annex! With the right alterations, we could do it. We have Professor Jaxong, and we have all her knowledge—"

"You're out of your mind," Nack said. "Director, this is nonsense."

Uma held up a hand. "Professor Jaxong, do you really think something like this is feasible?"

Jaxong shrugged. "By looking at the drive specs... yes, I could certainly use the drive as an improvised bomb core. The technology involved is similar. But I'd have to make some changes to the drive's programming, and we'd have to reverse three of the four draw fields. We'd also need to examine how the drive is affected by the unusual conditions out here."

The engineers looked from Jaxong to Uma, a glimmer of hope in their gazes.

"But even if everything was ideal, we'd still have a *lot* of work to do," Jaxong said. The engineers' faces fell as quickly as they had brightened. "We'd need to build a primer first—a detonator to set off the initial reaction. That ring of full power cells would probably work for the primer fuel, but we'd need to set off a diffractor charge load of at least nineteen thousand mitzwols per cell. And we'd need weapons-grade lenanium cabling to wire it up. So... unless any of you happen to build black-market space weaps in your spare time, I think we're out of luck."

Nack grumbled something undoubtedly unpleasant under his breath.

Uma's heart was suddenly racing. "Professor Jaxong... what if we had some C9D8 diffractor charges? Could you use those?"

Jaxong shrugged. "Sure, if you had enough of them. Are we talking individually cached charges, or dual? And what kind of connectors?"

Uma slowly turned to face Eldric Leesongronski. "Professor Leesongronski... I think it might be time we inspected those crates of live squid."

ELDRIC
Sëgra City, Sëgra
11 years before the Rift

Deep below Sëgra City, the old mining shafts wound their way into the planet's core. Some of the abandoned tunnels had long ago collapsed. Parts of them were inhabited, but Eldric rarely ventured that far below the middle city.

As he boarded the transit that would take him as far into the City's core as public transport would go, he tried not to think too much about how much rock was over his head. It was ridiculous to be this nervous. He had jumped starships into the unknown abysses of subspace hundreds of times, but *this* unnerved him beyond anything he'd ever felt in deep space.

He kept his eyes fixed on Dafnë, memorizing the planes of her face, the warm brown glow of her cheeks, the way her hair moved when she turned her head, the way she always looked slightly downward when she laughed. He'd met her less than a month ago, but it already seemed perfectly natural that he would follow Dafnë Valay pretty much anywhere she went.

She had linked her arm into his, easily resting her head against his shoulder as the transit-capsule descended. She didn't look the least bit worried, even when they disembarked at the poorly-lit hub at the end of the line. She swung her bag gleefully over one shoulder, pulling him along.

Eldric followed her down a narrow alleyway into a tilted, ramshackle-looking building that jutted straight out from jagged rock face. At the end of a jet-black corridor, Dafnë punched in an access code and called a tiny hyperlift, a mesh-covered pod that hardly looked big enough to hold two people.

He hesitated, eyeing the tiny space. "In that? Both of us?"

"Come *on*. There's lots of room!" Dafnë bounded inside, motioning him in with a laugh.

She reached for his arm and pulled him forward until the curved door could slide shut behind him. Her back was already against the limits of the mesh wall, and she stood with her arms around him, entirely comfortable. He couldn't see her face from here, but he knew that she was smiling.

The pod lurched downward with unsettling speed as he clutched her, her dark curls spilling over the bright green of his jacket. He rested his chin on the top of her head, his teeth clenched together.

When the door opened abruptly, Eldric nearly lost his balance. He stuck one foot out into the corridor to steady himself, and looked around. The space they were in looked residential, almost quaint. They'd stepped into a wide corridor with bright, geometric artwork painted along every wall: a soothing pattern of polygons in yellow and green and blue cascaded from the ceiling to the floor.

Dafnë grabbed his hand and pulled him along, passing three identical panelled doors before they reached the corridor's end. She swung the last door open without taking out a key or inputting any codes.

"My place!" she announced dramatically.

"What—you—you don't *lock your door*?" Eldric's voice came out more incredulous than he'd meant it to.

"Lock it from what?" She laughed merrily. "Who's going to

come all the way down here? And anyway, the top entrance is secure."

"What about the other residents?" He gestured out at the other doors. "Other people come in here. We're still in the City—"

She shook her head, her sea of long dark curls bouncing around her. "It's different here. I know everybody who lives in this compound. And anything I have, they're welcome to take."

She pushed aside the patterned curtain just behind the open door, and Eldric blinked in surprise. Beyond it was a small square room, and what could have passed for sunlight was streaming from two square ambients in the ceiling. Along the walls hung all kinds of plants, vines and ferns, and flowering greenery. Every surface was covered with them, with the exception of a narrow wardrobe door and the small, stowaway bed built into one wall.

"Like it?" She beamed. "Sit down. It's comfortable." She pointed at the edge of the bed.

Eldric sat down slowly, reaching out with a tentative hand toward the vine dangling overhead. The leaf was cool and smooth to the touch—and it felt unmistakably *alive*.

"Whoa. These plants are *real*?" He couldn't remember when he'd last seen a living plant anywhere in the City. "Where did you get all of these?"

"Oh, lots of places... I get seeds and cuttings from the offworlders, usually. Then I search the 'net to find out what kind they are. I look up how much water and light they need..."

He looked at her in astonishment. "Don't they die? We're so far underground."

"Yes." Her voice was soft. "They die. Even with the lamps, sometimes it's not enough. But... even if they don't make it, Eldric, they still mattered. They made me happy while they were here." She sat down on the bed next to him, her hand resting on his arm. "Don't they make you feel better?"

Sitting here, next to her, Eldric *did* feel inordinately better than he had on the surface. He leaned his head back, listening to the stream of gentle noise that floated in from the direction of the hallway: footsteps, distant laughter, the fumbling sounds of someone learning a musical instrument in a neighbouring apartment. There was nothing of the thundering chaos that usually permeated the city. Instead, there was a stillness that was difficult to describe.

He broke the silence. "I can't believe how quiet it is here. It's like another world."

"I know. I love it," she said. "The lower city's got a bit of a... reputation topside, so hardly anyone comes down this deep. I suppose at least it keeps all those overdressed fools from the dreamhouse crowd out of here—" She stopped herself as her gaze flicked to his embroidered jacket, and her eyes went wide. "Oh! Gods, sorry, I—you know I didn't mean to imply that *you* were—that you're one of the—"

Eldric shifted to look at her, suddenly aware of how out of place he looked down here. The fancy collar on his ornate shirt felt oppressively tight.

"You're not one of them, Eldric, I know. You're like me. Just waiting to get out." She raised one hand, and her fingers brushed lightly over his cheek. "I don't understand why you're still here. You can afford to get out. Why haven't you left?"

He looked away, not letting his mind linger overlong on the reasons. "Everything I... Every*one* I care about is here," he said. "This is my life. And... you're here."

I don't want to leave without you. That was what he wanted to say. The words surprised him as they formed in his mind, but he bit them back.

Dafnë sighed wistfully. "Well, I don't plan on staying here forever, Eldric. Someday, I want to go somewhere with a real sun, and plants, and rain... somewhere far, far away from here. I want to die on a green world."

We could leave here together.

He didn't say anything.

She was quiet for a long time after that, staring up at the hanging plants, before her face brightened again. She sat up and straightened her shoulders.

"You're going to meet my friends today!" she said cheerfully. "And I want to take you to see the Collectors—the people who run the Vault. I think you'd like them a lot."

"The Vault?" Eldric's eyebrows rose. He'd heard talk of it, of course, but it hadn't occurred to him that it was actually real. "The art bunker? They're really doing that?"

"Of course! And it's going to be so amazing. Imagine, a whole archive of humanity's art and creation! The data banks will be housed down here in the deepest tunnels, just in case the worst happens. Even if the City crumbles, even if we all die, the records will still be safe." She shuffled closer to him. "The Collectors are trying to preserve everything they can get a copy of: art, books, music, any media they can find. I've just started helping with one of their campaigns, asking people to contribute things through the online portal."

"Huh." He shook his head slowly. "Wow."

"Do *you* want to upload something?" Her voice rose excitedly. "Like a song, or a poem, or a copy of your favourite novel, or—?"

"I don't know about that." Eldric shrugged. "Who are you saving all this stuff for, anyway? If the worst happens, like you say, then everybody's gone. Who's going to listen to all those songs?"

"Well, hopefully not *everybody* will be gone," Dafnë said. "Humanity's resilient, Eldric. We've already been through so much. We've gone into space, we've explored dozens of worlds... We're survivors, right?" She reached up and touched the dangling vine above her head. Her eyes glittered with emotion, staring into his. "You do believe we're going to make it, don't you? That humanity will go on beyond this war?"

"Sure," he said, his voice entirely unconvincing. "Probably."

She grinned playfully. "Guess you'd better find something to put in our archive, then."

If most of humanity was wiped out, Eldric doubted anybody left would care about a cache of shitty electronic novels, or whatever passed for the City's taste in music. The Vault would perish here, buried in neon lights and tacky jackets and all the City's false pretense, right along with the residents. What difference would it make?

"Please. Please upload something." She clasped his hand. "It would make me happy if you did."

"Fine," he said at last. "I'll find something. But only because *you* asked me."

"It does matter, Eldric." She reached up, cupping his chin in both her hands. "It does."

And when her lips met his, for a small moment he let himself believe that it really did.

UMA
Engineering Deck, ZeyCorp Gallion

UMA JOINED THE group of engineers clustered around the big table on the upper level of Engineering, watching Charyne Jaxong. Even Zel was at the table now, still wearing his Etraxan finery, his cape trailing behind his chair.

Jaxong sat in the centre, unaware of the crew's rapt gazes. She had finally taken off that misshapen woolly sweater, and someone had given her one of the short-sleeved purple sport shirts with the ZeyCorp logo on the front. There was only so long anyone on the *Gallion* could escape that logo.

Jaxong's face was screwed up in concentration as she sketched complicated diagrams on a virtual board. She worked in silence, filling the left side of the board with equations, labelling each of the device's components by hand with a small white stylus. Every so often, Jaxong would stop writing, lift her head and motion to Mikolai. The junior would hold a lightpad up to her, pulling up a new batch of calculations or bringing up a new view of the Jaxong drive schematic.

The whole board glowed with Jaxong's tightly-clustered handwriting, and a chill crawled down the back of Uma's neck: she was outlining the Last Shot bomb spec. From memory.

When Jaxong set her stylus down, her face was serious.

"Director Ozakka, I'm glad you're back," she said, sounding genuinely relieved. "Do you know when I'll be able to get back on board the *Jonah* to examine those diffractor charges?"

Uma sighed. "Well... I've just been discussing that with our... uh, weapon supplies department. Directors Keeven and Leesongronski." She rolled her eyes. "They're deliberating outside. They'll let us know when they have a decision."

"Well, I hope they're quick about it. I really need to check the casing type and charge loads before I can finish this spec," Jaxong said disdainfully.

A minute later, Jereth Keeven came striding through the main doors, with Eldric Leesongronski trailing close behind him. When they reached the table, Keeven didn't say anything. Leesongronski, dour-faced and black-clad as usual, stopped just short of Jaxong's chair and dropped a folded lightpad in front of her.

"All right," Leesongronski said grudgingly. "I've checked out your calculations, and I admit you might be on to something with the substrate fracture thing." He raised a finger. "But this subspace bomb of yours... I'm not convinced. Where's your documentation? You got a spec?"

"Working on it," said Jaxong. She jabbed her stylus in the air, pointing at the scribbles that covered her v-board. "It's missing the fine details, but feel free to look. If you can understand it." She threw him a glare.

Leesongronski squinted at Jaxong's handwriting floating in the projection. "Wait... this is *it?*" His face was somewhere between incredulous and horrified. "You're writing it out by *hand?*"

"I'm used to working on paper, actually," Jaxong said. "But they didn't have any. So this'll do."

"Paper!" Leesongronski exclaimed. "Are you serious?"

"No computer system is secure enough for information this dangerous," Jaxong said. "My team worked on paper for the schematics. Our calculations were all done with offline devices, and we didn't keep a single coherent digital record. No one person besides me knew what all the inputs were, so when I defected, all they had left was the results of my sims." She tapped her temple. "They couldn't test the bomb without me. Everything they needed was up here."

"Damn. No wonder the deffies were so keen on hunting you down," Keeven said, sliding into the chair across from Jaxong. "You stole their secret weapon!"

"More like... she *was* their secret weapon," Uma said quietly. "Professor Jaxong was the key to all this research. Her ideas are still considered revolutionary in our time."

Jaxong grimaced. "Revolutionary or not, that bomb wasn't ready for a live test. I told the UWDF that a test gone wrong could be disastrous. But given the circumstances... they didn't care about the risks. They didn't care how dangerous it was."

"So... you thought your bomb was too dangerous to try *winning the war* with it, but you want us to set it off *here?*" Keeven said, arching an eyebrow. "That makes sense to you?"

"Well, at least here, we're only risking lives that are already lost," Jaxong said. "If my Rift theory's correct, then even starting our ships' engines wouldn't do any good, because there's no way back to normal space. We either try Last Shot while we can, or we'll die here."

The whole table fell into a sombre silence. Jaxong picked up her stylus and resumed her scribbling.

Leesongronski was still frowning at the glowing spec, muttering something to himself.

"So? What do you think of it, Leeg?" Keeven asked, nudging Leesongronski. "Spec look any good?"

Leesongronski didn't take his eyes off the v-board. "Well,

the math checks out. Her 5D equations look solid," he said slowly. "Thing is, Jerry... I don't know shit about subspace weapons. This is specialized theoretical physics. Not my area of expertise." He studied Jaxong, his gaze suspicious. "She's asking us to put an awful lot of trust in her."

"Yes. Yes, I am," Jaxong said, whirling to face him. "And that's exactly what *you* do, every time you jump a ship. Isn't it? Who checks your jump calculations? Every person on your ship just has to trust that you're going to twitch your fingers the right way, and that the ship isn't going to be crushed to the size of this pen!" She stabbed at the air with the stylus, and Leesongronski jumped back a little. "So if you want to live, you'd all better let me work. And someone will need to take me out there, so I can see that drive up close."

Uma looked at Keeven. "Professor Jaxong needs to examine the diffractor charges you've got on the *Jonah*. As soon as possible," she said. "Our crew is meant to be making a decision on these plans soon, so I need a finished spec to present to the captain."

"Hang on a minute, Ozakka," Keeven said, holding up one hand. "*Your* crew is making the decision? Funny that, since *I'm* the one you need to pilot that shuttle. And now you're asking me to give up part of my cargo, too. Which isn't exactly easy to replace, lemme tell you." He smiled sarcastically. "I think *I'm* the one who's gonna be making the decision."

"It's a bad idea, Jerry," Leesongronski said. "Not that you ever listen to me."

"How about this?" Keeven said, leaning forward conspiratorially. "I'll fly out and tow back those power cells for you like we already agreed, and we'll buy ourselves a little more time. And *then* we can negotiate about—"

"No!" Jaxong interrupted, startling everyone at the table. "No! You can't remove those power cells. We need them!"

She held out both hands in fists, then brought them together. "Power cells. Diffractor charges. Together. That's how we're going to build that primer."

Keeven leaned back. "You seriously want to blow up the full power cells? As in, our only source of power out here?"

"Yes," said Jaxong, looking mildly exasperated. "Exactly."

"All of them?" said Keeven hopefully. "Maybe we could remove *my* two cells first—"

"All of them," Jaxong said. "Six full cells should be enough, if Dean's estimates on their yield are correct. But no less. If you remove a single one?" She flattened her hands and smacked them loudly onto the table. "The primer reaction wouldn't be strong enough."

There was silence around the table again, everyone exchanging anxious glances. Uma's heart sank.

"We'd be giving up our last chance to recharge," Noussen whispered. "We could run out of power."

"The S-bomb is our *only* chance!" Jaxong snapped. "What good is more power when you can't get out of here? Have you all been listening to what I'm saying? Unless we can set off that bomb, we're trapped here!"

Keeven made a dramatic show of stroking his chin, like he was deep in thought. "Lemme get this straight. If we go with Charyne's plan, we blow everything up. Not only do I lose part of my cargo, but I don't even get my full power cells! Two of which happen to be part of my *payment* for doing that shuttle run. If the bomb doesn't work, we're totally screwed... like, insta-dead. Now, that doesn't sound like a good Jereth-deal, does it?" He smiled slowly. "But on the other hand, going with Charyne's idea could have... certain advantages."

Keeven tilted his head toward Leesongronski, locked eyes with him and stayed that way for a few seconds, his expression unreadable. No one said a word. Keeven swung his chair from side to side, looking back at Jaxong, then around the table, then back at Leesongronski again.

"Jerry," Leesongronski began, "I don't think—"

And then, Zel got to his feet, drawing himself up to his full height. "Captain Keeven, please. This is a matter of life and death. We are trying to save our future here. You simply *must* cooperate."

"Oh?" Keeven swung his chair back around. "And who are you, exactly?"

"I am a Blessed Scion of Etraxas, that's who," Zel said, overenunciating every syllable, his aristocratic accent more exaggerated than ever. His bronze skin shone with that iridescent cosmetic, and he had underscored his eyes with a dramatic black line of kohl that swept all the way up to his temples.

"You're Etraxan, huh?" Keeven leaned all the way back in his chair, looking Zel up and down, his eyes lingering over the cape and sash. A cheeky grin was spreading across Keeven's face. "Y'know... if they're all as good-looking as you, maybe Etraxas *is* worth saving."

Zel stared at him, his composure rattled. "I—uh..."

Keeven winked. He held up his ZeyCorp guest band, tapping it to flash up his apartment number. "If you wanna try to convince me... I'm just sayin'. You know where to find me later."

Zel looked affronted and flustered at the same time. He glanced incredulously at the others around the table, like he wasn't sure he was hearing correctly. Apparently, he had no eloquent pre-rehearsed responses for this particular diplomatic situation.

"Keeven." Uma sighed. "Can we get back on topic, please? The diffractor charges?"

"Awww, don't get jealous, Ozakka," Keeven said with a smirk. "Don't worry. You're also invited." He flashed her a grin. "Got any plans after this meeting?"

"Director Ozakka, I'm sorry to interrupt," Dean said. The android was walking up the stairs from the pit, wearing a deeply concerned expression. "I'm afraid I've discovered a serious problem."

Uma winced. She hadn't seen this particular expression on display since Dean informed her that all four of the *Gallion*'s engines had shut down. "What is it, Dean?"

"It's regarding Professor Jaxong's proposed modifications to the Jaxong drive," Dean said. "I was asked to do a little research on that drive model in our knowledge banks, to determine how we could get into the drive's systems to reprogram it. But from what I've found, it looks like we won't be able to access the drive very easily."

"Why not?" Jaxong tapped her stylus against her temple.

"Because the power annex is heavily secured," said the android. "The Jaxong drive is a volatile piece of equipment, very dangerous if misused. To access the drive's internal systems, you must first initiate 'scheduled maintenance mode.'" Dean's marble-round eyes flicked downward, looking as downcast as a vaguely-humanoid robot could. "And it appears scheduled maintenance mode can only be initiated from inside the structure the drive is paired with. You would need to do it from inside Verkhoy Station."

SHAAN
Common Deck, ZeyCorp Gallion

SHAAN HAD WAITED until the *Gallion* had shifted into night-cycle before she ventured out from her escape-shaft hideaway. Despite her nerves, she was getting hungry, and there was only so long she could remain unaccounted for. Mikolai and Syru had already sent her several messages, all of which she'd swiped away without reading. Ozakka had sent one too, and Barnabyn, of course. She'd ignored them all.

The ship's day/night cycle meant almost nothing now, not with the engineers working around the clock, taking as many shifts as they could manage without collapsing. But Shaan still felt safer under the dimmer ambients. She felt like she was disappearing, turning invisible.

The canteen was as deserted as the corridors, except for the two people sitting at a table in the far corner. Jereth Keeven and his surly-faced engineer were deep in conversation, oblivious to her presence. The two were bent across the table over a pair of ZeyCorp vending-machine beverages, speaking in whispered tones just too low for Shaan to overhear.

She lingered in the doorway for a moment before she moved any closer, walking in as quietly and casually as she could without looking like she was sneaking. She briefly contemplated ducking under a table like Gida had, but she didn't dare do it. Instead she held her breath, trying to listen in. Their voices were nothing more than unintelligible murmurs from here. They still didn't see her.

Mendeg was scowling, as always. He was wearing his faded coveralls, looking slightly more dishevelled than when he disembarked from the *Jonah*. He reacted to most of whatever Keeven was saying with thinly veiled contempt, tugging on one end of his moustache as he listened. Keeven was doing most of the talking. He was waving his hands animatedly, drawing shapes in the air, spreading his palms apart like an entertainer who'd just made his big reveal.

Then Mendeg started nodding slowly. Something like agreement seemed to pass between the two, and Keeven reached out to pat Mendeg's bulky shoulder. Mendeg's scowl had melted into a toothy, unhinged grin, and he thumped the table with one fist.

Keeven grinned back conspiratorially. He held his drink aloft and tilted it toward Mendeg.

The engineer reciprocated, that manic grin still plastered over his face, and they touched the plastifoam cups together. The gesture might have looked at home in some back-alley bar, but against the backdrop of the *Gallion*'s crisp, sterile corporate canteen, it was so incongruous that Shaan almost laughed out loud.

There was another minute or two of whispered conversation, and then the massive engineer collected his cup and stood up. He leaned down and fished around inside his boot, pulling out his purple ZeyCorp guest band and snapping it back onto his wrist. Shaan frowned in confusion as Mendeg lumbered back out of the canteen, leaving through the opposite door.

Keeven stared after Mendeg, a smug smile on his face, sipping his drink with an expression that looked almost triumphant.

"Hey!" Shaan shouted before she could think. "Keeven! What're you doing?"

Keeven's head whipped around. His smile faltered for an instant when he saw her there, as if he was worried about what she'd overheard. But he recovered his composure quickly, his nonchalant grin returning almost before she could register his alarm.

"Well, well. Good evening to the prison warden!" he said. "Don't you worry. I'll put my leash back on in a second. I'm assuming that's why you're here?"

"You'll... *what?*"

Keeven reached down into his own boot and extracted his purple ZeyCorp guest band. "There we go," he said, fumbling to snap it back onto his wrist. "See? It's back. Happy now?"

She stared at him in confusion. "What in the five hells? Why'd you take your guest bands off?"

"We were having a confidential conversation," he said. "We're private citizens, you know, not members of your staff to be monitored."

"Keeven, for the last time, the bracelets don't record—" She sighed. "Oh, never mind."

He tipped the last of his drink into his mouth and crumpled the cup. "Mmm. This stuff isn't bad, I'm telling you. You still want me to fill out that feedback form?"

She ignored the question, arching an eyebrow at him. "You managed to get Mendeg talking to you again," she said. "How'd that happen? Director Ozakka said he refused to speak to anyone. Last anybody saw him, he wanted to thrash you."

"Expert-level people skills, right here," Keeven said, jerking one thumb at his chest.

"Right." Shaan rolled her eyes. "So... what were you talking about that's so damn secret?"

Keeven gave a sly smile, tapping the band of his bracelet. "And you wonder why I took this thing off. Where's your warrant?"

"Keeven."

"Look, I was just convincing him to help me unload some of those cargo containers off the *Jonah*," Keeven said. "I've got the access codes, but he's the one who usually works the loading system."

"You're unloading those weapon components?" She frowned. "What for?"

An amused look crossed Keeven's face. "Oh, you haven't heard the latest? Apparently, we need some spare parts. We're building a weapon of mass destruction. As you do."

Shaan's shoulders seized. "You're... what?"

"Hey, don't look at me like that. This is fully sanctioned by your very own *Gallion* administration," he said. "You'll be shocked to discover that *I'm* the one who was against it." He motioned her into the chair across from him. "C'mere, sit down for a bit. I wouldn't mind running something past you. How well do you know your Captain Fransk?"

"Hold on," Shaan said. "Back up. Who's building a weapon of mass destruction? And *why?*"

"Charyne's pitching this weird idea about inverting the Rift with a bomb, to get us out of here," Keeven said with a shrug. "She needs some of the supplies I've got on board to build it. Then we'll be going out to the power annex and wiring up that Jaxong drive, to turn it into an S-bomb." He pointed at Shaan's face with a laugh. "Aha, see, that face right there? That was my first reaction, too. Wild, right?"

"You're actually going along with this?" Shaan said. "Seriously? When you got here, your engineer was warning us to watch her, acting like she was some kind of threat... and now you want to help her build a *superweapon?*"

"Well, I got some new information," Keeven said enigmatically. "I told you, I'm real adaptable."

"Keeven—"

"Only thing is, we need to convince your Captain Fransk that this plan's good," Keeven said. "Ozakka's supposed to present the plan to him, and we need him to agree, else we're going nowhere."

"Well, that's the end of your plan, then." Shaan said, relief washing over her. "Fransk won't agree to anything half that dangerous. This one time, we had a science team that wanted to launch two deep space probes simultaneously, and that argument dragged through a week of meetings because it was *technically* against regulations." She sighed. "I'm pretty sure there's no ZeyCorp policy covering the safe assembly of deadly weapons, so he'd probably need Director Barnabyn to write one first. And Barnabyn's going to want to assess staff consensus levels, or something like that..."

Keeven barked a laugh. "Well. Good to know, I'll mark that down in our show notes here." He pretended to type a note into a nonexistent handheld device. "So... we probably shouldn't mention the explosives we're gonna use to get into the station, hmm?"

"Into the *station?*" Shaan froze. "Wait. Is someone boarding Verkhoy?"

"I am," Keeven said. "Turns out we need to flip some kind of maintenance switch in their control room before Charyne can reprogram the drive. We're still figuring out the details."

"Verkhoy Station is a Geminus facility. It's highly secured," Shaan said, her heart pounding. "There's no way you'll get in there, much less all the way up to the control room."

"Wanna bet?" Keeven grinned. "I've got a couple of scarabs on the *Jonah* that should do the trick. They're pretty damn expensive, but nowhere near what this lost cargo'll already cost me. So I guess if I'm in, I'm all in. For the cause, huh?"

"Scarabs?" Shaan frowned.

"Scarab grenades. Tiny but mega-powerful explosives. A half-dozen of those little fuckers could take out a whole ship.

A friend of mine used to use 'em to break into orbital prisons."

"No..." Shaan whispered.

"Not much'll hold against a scarab," he went on. "One blast should punch a hole in that station about four paces wide." He raked back his hair, still grinning. "It'll make a hell of a mess... but I doubt Geminus'll be coming after us for the repair bills, hmm?"

"You can't do that, Keeven. The security system will detect a break-in."

"So? Who's it gonna alert out here, the time travel police?" he scoffed. "Lemme let you in on a secret. Maximum security only works if there's someone watching that gives a shit. It's gonna be fine."

"No, it won't!" Panic rose in Shaan's throat. "If you try to break into that station, I promise you, it won't be fine. You're going to *die*."

"Oh?" Keeven's grin faded. Her terrified expression must have rattled him. "Why's that?"

"Because Verkhoy Station had a grey destruct protocol. Nanotech immolation," she said. "That station's been in an emergency lockdown; the grey destruct would have been auto-engaged when the last person evacuated. And if everything stayed exactly like it was when Verkhoy disappeared, then nothing's changed, Keeven! Nobody ever turned that system off!" She fixed her eyes on him, hoping fervently that he'd believe her. "If you try to break in there, that station will implode."

"Okay..." he said sceptically. "But how can we tell if it was in an emergency lockdown?"

"I know it was." Shaan took a deep breath, forcing herself to choke out the words. "Keeven, I know. Six years ago, right before that station disappeared... I was on Verkhoy Station."

His face was stunned. "What?"

"I... I used to work for the Geminus Peace Alliance."

Excerpt from the
Geminus Inquest Proceedings
into the Verkhoy Station Incident

Official Transcript Committed to Record
Witness: Shaan Norte
Inquest Session 81

—Thank you for rejoining us, Shaan. Do you acknowledge that anything you say in this room will become part of the official record of this inquest, and that you are still bound by your oaths to the Geminus Peace Alliance and your commitment to the Geminus values?
—I acknowledge it.
—Then we'll begin. We would like to return to the matter of the evacuation procedures. On the day of the incident, were you aware that an evacuation of Verkhoy Station might be imminent?
—Yes.
—How did you become aware of this possibility?
—I overheard some of the watchfleet tech team talking about sensor malfunctions. I asked them about it. They said we might need to evacuate.
—Was Ashlish with you when this conversation took place?
—Yes.
—Would it be correct to say, then, that both you and Ashlish should have been prepared to leave the station when the evacuation order came? Since you had advance warning?
—Yes. We should have been more prepared.
—Were you afraid when you heard the Station Governor's decision to call an evacuation? Nervous?

—**No. I didn't think there was any real threat.**

—Did you question your Station Governor's judgement, in the matter of the potential threat posed?

—**No.** [Witness is silent for four seconds.] **Not directly.**

—But you did question his judgement privately, did you not? And you expressed your displeasure at Ker Marecc's decision to several of your colleagues.

—**I was annoyed, that's all.**

—You said the evacuation was 'a waste of time,' is that correct?

—**I did, but so did everyone else. Everyone thought Ker Marecc was being over-cautious.**

—What reason did you, personally, have to disagree with the Station Governor's decision?

—**No reason. I was... just wrong, I guess.**

—Would it be correct to state that you did not get along well with Ker Marecc? That on previous occasions you had not shown the Governor the appropriate respect?

—**I found him difficult to work with. But I did show him respect.**

—Let's go back to the evacuation, now. From the time you were ordered to evacuate until the time your vehicle departed the station, approximately twenty-one minutes had elapsed. All accounts place you no more than three minutes from an evac point at the moment the order was given. You stated that you spent the missing minutes following Ashlish to another level in the station. Can you explain this?

—**Ashlish ran in the opposite direction. She was running the wrong way, away from our evacuation point. I followed her.**

—Under a level four alert, your instructions were to proceed to the nearest evac point, immediately and without exception. Why did you pursue Ashlish instead of following the order given by Ker Marecc?

—I felt that Ashlish was... [Witness is silent for seven seconds.] **I thought she was in danger. I had to help her.**

—You said you didn't think there was 'any real threat.' Why, then, did you feel that Ashlish was in danger?

—**Ashlish was disoriented. She... wasn't thinking clearly. She told me she needed help.**

—If Ashlish wanted your help, why would she run away from you when you pursued her?

—**I don't know.**

—Why did Ashlish flee to the upper levels instead of proceeding to the evacuation point?

—**I don't know.**

—Several witnesses reported having seen Ashlish in a state of extreme panic. Ashlish said: "death, darkness, only death." What did she mean by that?

—**I don't know.**

—Shaan, did Ashlish have any reason to fear that you intended to harm her?

—**No! No!** [Witness begins sobbing.] **The crash was an accident. Just an accident!**

—Ashlish had wounds on her body that were not the result of the shuttle collision. After the accident, you were also observed to have deep scratches on your arms and face. Can you explain this?

—[Witness is silent for fifteen seconds. Interviewer proceeds to next question.]

—Did you have a physical altercation with Ashlish on the station?

—**She was already bleeding when I found her. I had to force her into the shuttle, to get her off the station. She was struggling. Scratching me. She tried to choke me. I had to defend myself.**

—What caused you to crash your vehicle after you launched it from the station?

—Ashlish kept attacking me, hitting and scratching me in the shuttle. She was screaming. I couldn't *think*. I activated the manual controls by mistake, instead of the pre-programmed descent. I lost control of the shuttle, and... I misaligned the docking clamps. Came in too fast.

—Had you ever seen Ashlish behaving in this way before?

—[Witness is silent for twelve seconds. Interviewer repeats question.]

—Please answer the question. Had you observed any prior signs that Ashlish was becoming unstable?

—[Witness is silent for six seconds.] **Yes.**

UMA
Command Deck, ZeyCorp Gallion

"How in the five hells is this possible?" Captain Fransk repeated for what felt like the dozenth time. Uma watched him stand up and circle his desk, pacing again. He was pacing more and more lately. "Shaan not only worked for the Geminus Peace Alliance, but she was stationed on *Verkhoy?* The exact same station that's out there now?"

Barnabyn had the staff database open on his lightpad. He was frantically flipping through Shaan's ZeyCorp employment record, scouring each line of text. Uma leaned over to look at the photo on Shaan's ZeyCorp file. Her straight, dark hair was a little shorter back then, and her eyes perhaps a little sadder, but she was mostly unchanged. Below the picture was her date of hire. Six years ago—the same rotation when Uma had first come on board the *Gallion.*

"It's my name on her hire," Barnabyn muttered. "Gods! I was the one who ran her background checks. I would definitely remember something like this. And I most certainly would've checked the public record... Let me check my notes on the interview—"

"Director Barnabyn," Fransk said. "Calm down. I'm sure you

did your job thoroughly. No one's accusing you of any less."

"Geminus did this," Uma said. "They must have replaced Shaan's profile, and they gave her a false background to cover the years she worked for them. Obviously."

Barnabyn stroked his beard, staring at Uma like she'd just sprouted a second head. "You're saying they doctored her residence history? And her *employment records*? On the *public net*? Those are both corroborated with the tax and citizenship bureaus. Only the highest levels of Union government could even begin to falsify something like..." He trailed off. "Oh."

"No government bureau is better at this than Geminus," Uma said quietly. "They could probably delete someone from the record entirely, if they wanted to. Switching an employment history, tweaking a place of registered residence... that would be nothing to them. And anyway, nobody who works for Geminus has an ID that actually *says* they do." She inhaled through her nose, locking eyes with Fransk.

Fransk nodded. "Director Ozakka's right. There's no way we could've known Shaan's background was falsified."

"Did anyone ask her what she's *doing* here, though?" Barnabyn asked, wide-eyed. "I mean, if she was working in some cushy government job for Geminus, then why leave and apply to ZeyCorp, of all places? Why not move to another Union agency? Those government types don't usually hop into the private sector."

"I don't know," Uma said. "Everything I know right now came from Keeven. When I found out, I came straight here to update you."

That was almost true. Uma had stayed in Engineering for an hour and half, talking through the implications of this latest revelation with the rest of the team. And then she'd gone to her apartment to regroup. And *then* she'd gone straight to Fransk's office.

"Keeven told you all this?" Barnabyn folded his lightpad away with a huff. "How do you know he's telling the truth? He's a charlatan."

"Well, for starters, he knows a *lot* of things that he didn't know before," Uma said, folding her arms. "Like the exact location of the control room on Verkhoy... and the way their security system works, and where the shuttle docking points are..." She trailed off. "He and Professor Leesongronski are working with Dean on an action plan. Keeven wants permission to take Shaan with him out to the station."

"An *action plan?* Which they somehow managed to pull together in the time it took you to come up here and see me?" Fransk gave her a knowing look.

She shrugged sheepishly.

"Who else knows about this already?"

Uma avoided his eyes. "Just me. And Professor Jaxong... and the Engineering team. They were all there when Keeven came to tell us."

"So, basically everyone." Fransk worked his jaw, looking more upset than she'd seen him in years. "Well, I'm glad I was informed so promptly. I'm only the captain of this damned ship!"

"Oh, come on! What's the point of keeping secrets now?" Uma's voice rose. "We should be sharing information with the crew!"

"Yes, but—" Fransk glanced at Barnabyn, then back at her, with a look that said he would definitely have finished that sentence if they had been alone. Barnabyn was dead silent, staring at his closed lightpad like he wished he were anywhere else.

Gods, please let this be the right thing to do. Uma pressed a hand to her head. Of course it was the right thing. Keeven was a skilled pilot. Jaxong was the most acclaimed physicist of the age. And Shaan... Shaan had worked for the Geminus Peace Alliance, on that very station. Everything was lining up to make this mission possible, to make it successful.

"What is it you're waiting for, Olghan? Are you really still trying to convince yourself that we shouldn't be doing this?" Uma whispered, leaning across the desk toward the captain. "Last Shot *is* going to work! I know it."

The captain sighed. For once, he didn't correct her for addressing him by his familiar name in front of Barnabyn. He just shook his head.

"I'm waiting for those shuttle shield tests you promised me, for one thing," he said. "I want those results on my desk *today*."

"And we'll need a full staff meeting," Barnabyn said. "If you want to authorize a mission to that station without a proper risk assessment, then we should at least evaluate staff consensus levels."

Uma bit back a curse. *Evaluate staff consensus levels.* On the use of an archaic superweapon as a means of escaping a temporal anomaly, which may or may not affect the course of history. She wondered how exactly Barnabyn was planning on submitting that issue summary to ZeyCorp Central.

"Fine," she said through her teeth. "Syru's running the last round of sim tests now. I'll have him send the results directly to you, Captain."

"Good. And... Director Ozakka?"

"Yes?"

"I want hourly reports." Fransk tapped the desk, fixing her with a warning look. "Inform me immediately when something happens. I do mean *immediately*."

SHAAN
Emergency Stairwell, ZeyCorp Gallion

SHAAN SAT ON the landing in the emergency stairwell, listening to the artificial engine hum. Keeven had told all of them, she was certain. Ozakka must know by now. And Barnabyn, too... and the captain, and everyone else on the entire fucking ship. Mikolai. Syru. What did they *think* of her?

What had they said when they found out her employment history was a lie? How could she explain that? How could she look any of them in the eye, ever again? No matter what they said, she couldn't tell them the whole truth. She couldn't ever tell them that Geminus had dismissed her, thrown her away without a second thought. And that she'd deserved it. She'd deserved worse.

Ashlish was *dead* because of her.

Some part of her still couldn't believe that Verkhoy Station was floating somewhere out in that void, haunting her from afar. Like it *wanted* her to face what she'd done. She leaned her aching head against the railing, willing the tears not to fall.

And then she heard booted footsteps clanging down from above.

Someone had just climbed into the escape shaft on the residential level, and was taking the metal stairs two at a time.

Under Fortunate Stars

"Shaan? Shaan! Hey. I need to talk to you."

Jereth Keeven.

He climbed the rest of the way down the stairs and sat on the landing next to her. There wasn't much room, and their shoulders were nearly touching when he sat down.

"Hi."

"How did you find me here?" she snapped.

He pointed up the stairs with a half-smile. "You left the emergency access door cracked open. Didn't take a genius."

"Well, I don't want to talk to you," she said. "I already told you everything I know. Leave me alone."

Why had she told him anything? Of course she couldn't have let him fly out there and *die*, for the gods' sakes. But she could have found some other way to convince him it was too dangerous, to stop him from boarding the station. Instead, she'd gone and blurted that out. *I used to work for the Geminus Peace Alliance.*

There was no taking it back now. She cursed under her breath.

"C'mon," Keeven said, nudging her shoulder. "Remember when your people needed my sensor logs, and you said we had to cooperate?"

She scowled. "What does that have to do with you following me here?"

"Honestly?" He leaned forward. "I need your help. I helped you with the logs, didn't I? Now I need you to help me."

"How?" She looked at him dubiously. "I told you everything I know about that station. There's nothing else."

"Ahhh." He tapped his temple with one finger. "See, knowing is good... but there are some things only you can do. I have an idea, but we'll need to work together. Come with me to Engineering."

"There is no 'we,' Keeven. I'm not going to Engineering. Go away." She buried her face in her crossed arms. The last thing she wanted was to answer any questions from the rest of the crew. The thought of facing them made her stomach turn.

Keeven didn't respond, but made no move to leave. When she looked up a half-minute later, he was still staring at her.

"What do you *want*, Keeven? I said go away!"

"I need you to come with me," he said quietly. "Out there. To board that station."

Her mouth dropped open. "What? You're out of your mind!"

"Look, just hear me out." He looked almost earnest. "You're right. I'd be out of my mind to go alone. But with you? That's a game-changer. Think about it, Shaan. From the point of view of that station, you only left it a few days ago, right? Nothing changed since it disappeared. You'll still have all your permissions, your passcodes, your auths; here in the Rift... *you still work there.* You can get us in."

She took a painful breath. "Keeven, no. Even if I went with you, it wouldn't help. I didn't have the kind of security clearance you're looking for. I don't have permissions for the control room, or access to put a damn Jaxong drive into maintenance mode. I don't even know how. You'd need a high-level technician to authorize that, or the Station Governor—"

"Hold on," Keeven said. "Forget about the control room for a second, and start smaller. Could you open an airlock to get us inside, without me having to blow anything up?"

"Probably," Shaan whispered after a long pause. "I could open an airlock on the lower level. But we wouldn't get much further, because the security doors will be down. The control room is dozens of decks up."

"But if you can get us inside, we're making progress, right? We're further than we were before." He reached out and took her hand, holding it imploringly between his palms. "Please. I *need* you to do this, Shaan. And... I kind of already pitched this plan to Ozakka. C'mon. What's it gonna take?"

Close up, she could see that the deep brown of his glittering irises was flecked with amber. His stare was unwavering, but there was a tremble in his lower lip, and his hands shook slightly against hers.

Was he being sincere? How could she possibly tell? He was a con artist.

"What's the point of going over there if we can't reach the control room?" she finally asked.

"Leave that to me. Open the airlock, and I'll take care of the rest. Trust me."

"Trust *you?*" She barely suppressed a laugh. "Of course I don't fucking trust you!"

He flinched when she yanked her hand away from his, and for a moment she thought he looked genuinely hurt.

"Lemme ask you something, Shaan," he said. "If you're the trustworthy one here... how come you never told your crewmates that you used to work for Geminus? Huh? If being a peacekeeper or whatever is such a *noble* profession these days, why in the five hells didn't you want anybody to know?"

Shaan swallowed hard. "That is none of your gods-damned business."

"No, I'm curious," he persisted. "Your crewmates looked real shocked when they found out. Kinda sounded like none of 'em knew *anything* about your past until today. Weird, right?"

"Look who's talking," she shot back. "Do you go around telling everyone the details of your oh-so-interesting past? Like how you ended up in that stasis prison, for example?"

To her shock, he didn't react with anger, or even annoyance. Instead, he grinned. "Coincidentally, that is *slightly* related to the plan."

"Your crimes just happen to be related to getting us into that station?" She rolled her eyes sarcastically. "Right. Okay."

"Can you keep a secret?" He winked. "Now. Have you ever heard of a crypto-hacker called the Jetsetter? Tell me history remembered that, at least."

ELDRIC
Sëgra City, Sëgra
11 years before the Rift

ELDRIC LOOKED FURTIVELY over his shoulder before unlocking the heavy door in front of him. His hand traced the keypad by instinct, and he felt the familiar click under his palm as the security door receded, then slid open.

In the dimly-lit corridor beyond, he climbed three shallow steps, then attached an authorization device to the panel on the inner door. He entered a second sequence of codes, and let himself into the space he and Jereth called The Apartment.

When they'd first arrived on Sëgra, they hardly had a chit to their name. Jereth's meagre savings had been just about enough to get the two of them from that bleak transit-hub on Hanioch to Sëgra City, and they could only afford a single room in the lower reaches of the middle-city. But before long, using Eldric's particular skills, they'd made the rounds of the neighbourhood gambling establishments and cracked a few game tables. They collected their winnings with more subtlety than Eldric had applied to that first catastrophic attempt, never winning too much, never visiting the same table twice in a row.

Then Jereth had discovered how the electronic tabs in the hotels worked, and that the food dispensers in one of the entertainment complexes were connected to a central computer system. The encryption was surprisingly simple for Eldric to break, and Jereth created a false employee login, giving himself a small rolling credit balance to dispense free food.

They hadn't needed to hack free meals for long before Jereth came up with another exploit, and another. Soon, they could afford two rooms, and then bigger rooms, and then a temporary flat. Jereth looked after the logistics: he talked to people, he scouted things out, he researched their targets. Then Eldric would do the math. He just had to find the patterns. *Break this game, Leeg. Crack this security code, Leeg. Open this file, Leeg.*

By the time Jereth and Eldric moved into that lavish suite in the Night Palace Hotel, they were pulling in more money than even Jereth could spend. But they'd kept their old flat in the middle-city: a couple of smallish semi-circular rooms at the back of the most nondescript building in its block. They'd converted The Apartment into a base for their hacking operations. It housed their remote network setup, Eldric's computers and everything relating to the *jobs* they did. By standing agreement, they never discussed business in the Night Palace, or anywhere else except at The Apartment.

Now, when Eldric slipped through the inner door into the windowless room beyond, he found Jereth already there, sitting in front of the computer console.

"Hey! Get off of my desk, Jerry!" Eldric's tone was only half-amused.

Jereth spun the chair around, his mouth full of food he was eating out of a foil bag. "What's the problem? I'm not touching anything!"

Eldric snatched the bag out of Jereth's hand and pushed it across the desk, away from the console. "I've asked you a dozen times not to eat next to the console."

"Aren't you even going to look and see what's in there?"

Jereth pointed at the foil bag, grinning. "I got something for you too." Jereth pulled the bag back toward him and took out a triangular pastry. "This is the one you like, right, from that place uptown?" He held it up to Eldric's face, scattering pink sugar crystals over the edge of the desk.

Eldric couldn't quite suppress a smile. He took the pastry and bit into one corner, catching sugar crumbs with his other hand. "You want something, don't you?" he said. "We're here because you're about to tell me something I won't like."

"Ah, damn. Stop knowing me so well!" Jereth's grin widened. He stuck out his foot to pull another chair up to the desk. "Sit down. I have a new lead on the Grenobal Bank job. I think it's time for the Jetsetter to go *bigger*."

Eldric wiped sugar from his face and grimaced. "Oh, come on, don't start with that again. I told you, it's way too risky. The banks have layers and layers of safeguards. It's not like you can transfer a large amount to some random account without any record of it."

"You say that, but wait till you see this." Jereth shoved the rest of his pastry into his mouth, then reached into his pocket and pulled out a small silver card. "Look."

Eldric brushed off his hands, then delicately lifted the little square up to the light and swiped a finger across the surface to activate the tiny display.

"*Antiem Holdings SCC. First-rate brokerage and escrow services for Sëgra City,*" he read. "Never heard of it."

"Let me tell you the story." Jereth took back the card and held it in front of him dramatically. "Behold: Antiem Holdings, registered as a City company for the last ten years. This one guy, Antiem—complete slimebag, by the way—he's the whole business. He takes on a few high-end property deals here and there, but mostly, all he does is hold the stakes for big-ticket private games. Four of the biggest casinos recommend him, and at least one of them doesn't work with anybody else. He's their sole escrow partner."

"Escrow partner?" Eldric frowned. "Which means...?"

"Not often I get to be the one explaining something to the genius, huh?" Jereth shook his head, grinning. "He's a third party—the neutral front, so to speak. The casinos don't want to get involved in any money disputes for private games, so that's where Antiem comes in. Sometimes he puts up the cash to back someone who doesn't have their whole stake available, but his main service is to hold the money from all the buy-ins, to make sure the entire pot is accounted for. When the game's over, he pays it out to the winner. Of course, he keeps a cut, not to mention the interest he earns while he's holding it."

"Hm." Eldric had a sinking feeling that he wouldn't like the rest of this story.

"I didn't have an angle at first, but then I thought, hey, maybe this guy's useful," Jereth went on. "So I decided to do a bit of recon. I've seen him around the VIP lounges, so I had a chat with him. I told him I was interested in running a private game. Me and nine other players, with a stake of half a million each—"

Eldric's stomach lurched. "Half a million? On one game?"

"I'm not actually *doing* it, Leeg!" Jereth laughed. "I was just gathering info. But I had to make something up, make it look like I was serious. He was asking me for details about the game, the buy-in rules and so on... I just made it all up! I guess he was convinced, though, because he gave me a contract to review."

Jereth set the little silver card down in front of him and tapped the logo embossed on the front. One edge of the square peeled back, and a contract document unfurled onto the desk.

"Check out this agreement. Most of it's just legal jargon and ass-covering... as you'd expect..." Jereth dragged his finger over a few paragraphs of small, tightly-packed text. "Boring, boring, boring... Antiem Holdings is not responsible if you bankrupt yourself, blah blah... screw you if you don't pay your fees, blah blah blah... but look down here!"

He highlighted a line: *Funds held in escrow are secured by Grenobal Bank and will be released to the winner one standard week after the game's conclusion.*

"The money's held in a Grenobal account," said Eldric. "So?"

"He holds it for a week after the game ends! The stakes he holds go up to five million per player. Shit, think about how much money must be sitting in his business accounts! He's the one, Leeg. Transferring huge chunks of money to random people is his expected behaviour. He could transfer *millions* without setting off any warning bells at the bank."

Eldric leaned back in his chair, exhaling slowly. "I don't know, Jerry. We've never done anything this extreme."

"Well, if you're going to rob a bank you have to go big, else what's the point?" Jereth grinned. "You already know how to crack Grenobal, right? The identity swap."

"I said I *might* be able to crack Grenobal." Eldric steepled his hands. "I saw one possible loophole in their identity system. But cracking into the bank isn't the problem," he said. "I can probably break their transforms, I can do the identity swap... breaking the encryption's the easy part. The real headache will be covering our tracks afterwards. They have a lot of redundant logging systems—"

"But you *can* do it," Jereth said.

Eldric shook his head. "I don't know. Millions... it's too much, Jerry."

They'd done such inconsequential things at the beginning, nothing that really mattered to anyone. When Eldric thought about all the things he'd done since, it seemed inconceivable that he'd once worried about stealing a few mediocre cups of broth and some stale bread-sticks.

Jereth laughed. "What, you think if we just took *one* million they might not notice? Nah. Soon as we do it once they'll close the loophole, and we'll never get in there again. We have to take as much as we can in one shot, and *this* is the rich asswipe we're gonna take it from." Jereth tapped the logo on Antiem's card again, and the contract folded itself neatly away. He pocketed the card.

"There's no chance the City will let this one go. Not if we mess with the banks. We'd have to be damn sure they can't trace it to us." Eldric leaned back, checking the time on the wall behind him. "Look... can we talk about this later? I need to get going soon. I have plans."

"What? You just got here!" Jereth said. "What plans?"

"I'm going to meet Dafnë at the dreamhouse. We're going out with her friends later."

"Dafnë?" Jereth looked confused. "Really? You're *still* seeing her? How come I haven't met her yet? You should bring her to the Night Palace."

"Uh, I have brought her over. You've met her."

"Oh," said Jereth with a shrug. "Maybe I did. I dunno, I meet a lot of people."

Eldric sighed. "I really wanted her to like you, Jerry. I can try to bring her over again... if you think you could manage to act half-decent so she could actually get to know you this time."

"Hey, what's that supposed to mean?" Jereth looked indignant. "Why *wouldn't* she like me?"

"You were completely wasted when you introduced yourself, and you gave her one of your fake names. Of course you don't remember any of it. Not like I told you it mattered a lot to me." Eldric rolled his eyes. "You never listen."

"Um... okay..." Jereth looked up at the ceiling. "Ohhh, wait! I think I *do* remember, actually! Dafnë from the dreamhouse! With the long curly hair, right? I talked to her a bit when we had that party. She seemed nice."

"Oh, really?" Eldric fixed Jereth with a sceptical look. "Tell me one single thing she said, then."

"Hm. Uh... well... lemme think. She said... she said she's an animator... and she works at the Dome Theatre... Shit, yeah! I do remember that! I was talkin' to her all about the Dome's network security!"

Eldric frowned. "What?"

Jereth sat up straighter. "Yeah! I was askin' her some stuff about the headsets, an' about their VR system... and how they lock down the network when they..." He grabbed Eldric by the shoulders. "Oh my gods. I think I just had an absolutely *incredible* idea."

"That's great, Jerry. Hold that thought," Eldric said, peeling Jereth's hands away. "But I really need to go now, or I'm going to be late."

"You're a fucking genius, Leeg, you know that? And I'm the mastermind!" Jereth grinned, clapping a hand onto Eldric's shoulder as he jumped to his feet. "Trust me. This Grenobal job is the big one. And when the Jetsetter pulls this thing off... We're gonna be running this whole city. You and me."

SHAAN
Engineering Deck, *ZeyCorp Gallion*

SHAAN FOLLOWED KEEVEN into Engineering, relieved to see only a tiny group working up top. Charyne Jaxong was scribbling away on a v-board while Director Ozakka and Mikolai watched, but the rest of the upper level was vacant.

The three of them looked up as soon as Shaan came in, their eyes immediately focused on her with those awful, searching stares, like they didn't quite know what to say to her. Like all the people at the Verkhoy inquest.

So much for becoming invisible.

Thankfully, Keeven didn't take long to engage his theatrics. Before anyone could question her, he sat down at the table next to Mikolai and swung his booted feet up over the adjoining armrest, sitting in his chair sideways.

"Greetings, ZeyCorp friends!" he announced, motioning melodramatically for Shaan to sit down. "I call this meeting to order, and I bring excellent news! Not only has Shaan here agreed to go with me to the station... but I've got another big idea." He clapped his hands. "Let's work on this pitch!"

"Keeven, slow down." Ozakka's eyes darted to Shaan, her expression concerned. "The captain has a lot of questions right now, and I don't think he'll—"

"Don't worry, Ozakka, we've got this," Keeven said, waving his hands dismissively. "But right now, I have a new question for you. We've got more than one of those little shuttles that can take Syru's shield mods, right?"

"Yes," Ozakka said, looking puzzled. "We have two of them."

"Fantastic. So, change of plans. We're actually gonna take *two* shuttles to Verkhoy." Keeven held up two fingers, throwing the words out as casually as if he were telling them what he was having for dinner. "Cool?"

Ozakka blinked. "What?"

"Hear me out. See, Charyne needs to get to the power annex, and somebody needs to help her set up those diffractor charges to wire everything up for the S-bomb," Keeven said. "That's a two-person job. But before Charyne can upload the state changes to the drive, we *also* need to go flip that maintenance switch, which is inside the station. Everything would go a lot faster if we work in two teams and do it all at once. One shuttle goes to the annex, one to the station."

"Except you're the only qualified pilot on this ship," Ozakka said.

Keeven gave a slow smile. "Ah! Well, luckily, we have another talented pilot."

"We do?" asked Ozakka. "Who?"

"Mendeg?" ventured Jaxong anxiously.

"Tch, 'course not. *Him*." Keeven pointed across the table at Mikolai. "You wouldn't believe the moves I saw this kid pull off in that space-racing game! He must have thousands of hours of flight sim experience!"

Mikolai gave an awkward laugh. "What, *MeteoRacers Ultimate*? Captain Keeven... that's just a video game." Worry flickered across his round face. "I've never even done basic flight training."

"Well, you're a natural!" Keeven smiled. "What you were doing in that game was flight manoeuvres, no question about it. You were looking at a heads-up display, making a judgement on speed, on distance, on space—and using manual controls! All you need is a control configuration that you already know."

"Keeven," Ozakka began. "I don't think—"

"Dean said you could customize the shuttle controls to work in a configuration like I'm used to," Keeven said. "Couldn't we rig up the other shuttle with the control system from that racing game? Turn the game motions into shuttle controls, so Mikolai can fly the shuttle the same way."

"I don't know." Ozakka sighed. "I mean, yes, the controls are customizable, and we could probably rig that up pretty easily. But sending a junior engineer with no flight training out there? This isn't going to make Captain Fransk any happier."

Keeven's face was unworried. "Listen, Mikolai's a pro. I'll vouch for him. Set him up with the right controls, and he'll be as good as I am out there." He turned to Mikolai. "This won't be half as hard as that game, kiddo. Nothing's going to be shooting at you. All you have to do is avoid those energy pulses and make course corrections. That's it."

Just then, Syru came up the stairs from the pit, clutching a lightpad.

"What's happening?" he said, immediately noticing the stunned expression on Mikolai's face. "Something wrong?"

"Big news, Syru!" Keeven grinned. "Your boyfriend's about to become our new hero!" He slapped Mikolai on the back. "Behold, our second shuttle pilot!"

Syru froze on the top stair, his step faltering. "W-what?"

"You heard me!" Keeven said. "Mikolai's gonna fly Charyne to the annex, so he can help her lay out those diffractor charges and wire things up. Meanwhile, Shaan and I will get to the station and find that damned maintenance switch."

Jaxong's face had visibly brightened. "It *would* be good to have someone else out there with me who has the faintest clue what they're doing," she said. "Mikolai could really help me out with the technical setup."

Keeven looked triumphantly in Ozakka's direction. "See? That's what I call consensus. I hear your captain likes that."

Mikolai still looked shocked. "You really want my help, Professor Jaxong?"

"Mikolai, you are a promising theoretical physicist," Jaxong said. She motioned at Keeven, who was still sitting with his booted feet over the next chair. "Let's just say it'll significantly improve our odds if I have someone *competent* to help me on this."

Mikolai's shy smile gradually returned. "Well... if Captain Keeven thinks I'm good enough to fly..." He looked at Syru, beaming proudly. "You believe this, Sy?"

Syru didn't look enthused at all. In fact, he looked rather ill. He slowly approached the table, sinking into the chair next to Mikolai with a thump.

"Sy?" Mikolai put his hand on Syru's shoulder. "Hey. What?"

"I... you... don't..." Syru stammered, his eyes panicked. He glanced furtively at Director Ozakka. "The thing is, Mik... those shuttle shields—"

"Passed all reasonable safety checks, I hear," Keeven cut in. "Good work, Syru."

Shaan was struck by how young Syru looked at that moment. He was still clutching his lightpad to his chest, his mouth half open. A few loose strands of wispy hair framed his thin, heart-shaped face, and he looked... fragile.

Fragile, and terrified. And so very, very desperate to believe what he was hearing.

Shaan dug her nails into her palms as the unbidden memory clawed its way to her conscious mind. Ashlish. *Death, darkness, only death.*

"Trust me," Keeven said, flashing that half-smile of his. "Everything's gonna be fine."

Before Syru could say anything else, Charyne Jaxong shifted in her seat, turning toward Shaan. "If you don't mind... I have a question now," she said. "For Shaan."

Shaan wiped her clammy palms on the hem of her uniform. "Me?"

"Jereth said Verkhoy Station is empty because of an emergency lockdown. He said you told him the Geminus staff were all evacuated, not long before the station vanished." Jaxong tapped one end of her ubiquitous white stylus against her temple. "How did they know they needed to evacuate? Did they have advance warning about the Rift?"

Shaan picked at the edge of her fingernail. "It was just a glitch," she mumbled. "The monitoring system had some kind of technical fault, so we were evacuated as a precaution. There *was* no reason."

Jaxong frowned. "You're telling me... this mass evacuation of an entire space station was unrelated to the Rift?"

"Geminus never quite got to the bottom of it, but the inquest ruled that the two things weren't necessarily related." Shaan's voice was unsteady. "The fact that we happened to execute an evac order right before the station disappeared was just very—"

"Fortunate?" Jaxong finished for her. "You're kidding."

"Well... fortunate for some." Shaan inhaled slowly. "The station was never recovered, so there was no conclusive evidence of what happened. All they had was theories."

"Theories," Jaxong said, chewing on the word. She twirled her pen. "Hmm. Tell me about this monitoring glitch."

"The station techs said the sensor grids were malfunctioning," Shaan said. "They were detecting faint subspace eversion, like some nightships might be surfacing nearby. But there were no ships out there. The Station Governor sent out patrols with lightnets.

They swept the whole area, but they didn't find anything."

"Whoa! You can detect nightships now?" said Keeven, sounding amazed. "Fully cloaked?"

"With Felen tech, yes," Shaan said. "The Felen have always been able to detect them. But anyway, that doesn't matter, because there were no nightships there. It was just a sensor malfunction. It kept happening, so eventually the Governor decided to evacuate us as a precaution." She dropped her eyes to the table. "Most people thought the evac was a waste of time. We didn't take it too seriously."

"But then the whole damn station disappeared," Keeven said. "With nobody on board."

Shaan nodded. "The inquest afterwards went on for months. They thought it might've been some new weapon... or a new kind of cloaking, or some sort of terrorist attack, using tech even the Felen didn't know about. Problem was, there was no evidence left to look at. No debris, no sign of a recent grey destruct. It was like the station had never *been* there at all. Even the power annex with the Jaxong drive on it was gone."

"Of course... because it's all in the Rift!" Mikolai exclaimed. "The drive, the station, all of it is here!"

"I'm not so sure Verkhoy Station had a sensor malfunction," Jaxong said softly. Her forehead furrowed. "If they had sensors capable of detecting nightships, those sensors would have to be very sensitive to small fluctuations in substrate levels. So what if... what if that substrate eversion they were detecting...?"

She reached over and pulled up a fresh v-board from the table, as deftly as if she'd been using this tech her whole life. The projection shimmered up, a thin glowing grid outlining the virtual surface. Jaxong flicked her fingers and tilted the surface to a slight angle, then started scribbling over it. A row of tiny numerals gradually grew into a sprawling equation as the others watched.

"I know what it was," she finally said, calmly setting down the stylus.

"Care to elaborate?" said Keeven. He pointed at the v-board. "That's not making much sense."

"It'll be hard to explain in words you'd understand." Jaxong sniffed. "But I'll do my best."

Keeven's mouth twitched, and he almost looked amused. "Appreciated, *Professor,*" he said, drawling out the word.

Jaxong sighed, picking up her stylus again and tapping it against the table. "All right. So, any phenomenon that occupies a place in space and time has to have edges, right? This Rift has edges to its influence, where the anomaly starts to take effect on other things. Like an event horizon. Do you all know what an event horizon is?"

Around the table, everyone nodded.

"When our ships entered the Rift," Jaxong continued, "it's not like we were dropped down a hole or something. No, see... if you visualize the Rift in five dimensions, it's more like a series of interlocking *slopes.* Slopes that flow from several respective locations in space-time, and they all meet *here.*" She held her hands apart, then gently brought them toward each other in a smooth downward motion. "They lead from different times, different places... to *here,* and what we're currently calling *now.* You follow?"

More nods, less convinced this time.

"Let's look at it from one specific point of view," she went on. "Pretend we're observing from Verkhoy Station. We're on the station, right before it disappears, in their subjective timeline. Just prior to its encounter with the Rift, the station starts to detect the edges of that Rift slope. The station is about to encounter the Rift's event horizon." Jaxong jotted another glowing note down on the open v-board. "Neither of our ships were equipped to detect such minute fluctuations in energy, so we didn't have any warning.

But Verkhoy, with their military-grade sensors, sweeping for nightships? They had sensors specifically looking for small traces of eversion energy where there should be none. The fact that the systems weren't sure, that it looked like a glitch, was probably because what they were recording wasn't wholly recognizable. It was traces of what we've been calling Rift energy."

"So... the thing that was approaching Verkhoy wasn't a nightship, it was the Rift phenomenon?" said Ozakka, looking awestruck.

"Sort of," Jaxong said. "Technically, the Rift wasn't approaching anything. It doesn't move. But you could say that the station was approaching the Rift, in *time*. As the time when the station's collision with the Rift—from Verkhoy's subjective point of view—grew nearer, those sensors started to detect the Rift's presence. The station staff were evacuated, and then the station was subsumed into the Rift. From the point of view of that timeline... it vanished. Just as if it had dived into subspace."

She jotted a final note, then whisked the board away. Shaan's arms prickled with goosebumps.

"Okay," said Keeven with a laugh. "I'm not sure if I'm supposed to feel better or not."

"That was an overly simplified explanation, of course," Jaxong said disdainfully. "But I'm more certain than ever that Project Last Shot is our only way out of here. We have to use the bomb."

"Then we'd better get to work, no?" Keeven clapped his hands. "We've got to present this whole plan to Captain Fransk. Lots to do. You and Mikolai need to finish up that technical spec. And I've got to go talk to Leeg—"

Director Ozakka held up both hands. "Hang on, Keeven. Stop. Stop right there. You're not going anywhere until you tell me what the rest of your damn plan is."

"I already told you," Keeven protested. "Two shuttles, one team for the S-bomb setup and one team for the maintenance switch. Shaan will open the airlock on the station, and we're in."

"And what about unlocking the control room? Switching the drive into maintenance mode? Can Shaan do *any* of that?" Ozakka insisted. "How are you getting through the inner security doors?"

She looked at Shaan, and it took all Shaan's willpower not to shrink back in her seat.

"What if I said we're not answering questions till later?" Keeven flashed his most winning smile. "Got to keep some surprises up our sleeves, no?"

Ozakka sighed. "We can keep some details on a need-to-know basis," she said. "The gods know we might not even tell the captain everything. But all of us at this table need to understand exactly what you're doing out there." She drew a circle in midair, connecting everyone at the table: Jaxong, Keeven, the two juniors, Shaan and herself.

"If we're makin' some kind of trust pact, you're missin' a member," Keeven said, pointing toward the doors. "We need *him*."

The others turned around to see Eldric Leesongronski coming into Engineering, followed closely by Dean.

"Professor Leesongronski," Ozakka said quietly, a reverent look on her face.

"Heyyy! Leeg!" Keeven shouted. "Here comes my favourite genius!'

Leesongronski was already one of the palest people Shaan had ever seen, but today he looked downright translucent. His cheeks had a sickly greyish tint, and there were dark shadows under his eyes. He shuffled grudgingly toward the table, staring straight ahead like he was walking to his own execution.

"Director Ozakka," Dean chirped excitedly. "I've been doing a little research to assist Professor Leesongronski... and we have something exciting to show you."

ELDRIC
Sëgra City, Sëgra
11 years before the Rift

"HELLO?" ELDRIC SHOUTED as he unlocked the door to the Night Palace suite. He took off his shoes, shrugged off his jacket and hung it neatly over the back of a chair in the reception room. "Jerry? Hello? You home?"

The whole hotel was furnished to such an extravagant level of luxury that Eldric found it almost embarrassing. Their suite had four large connected rooms, floor-to-ceiling windows, and a sweeping balcony with its breathtaking view over the entire city. When Eldric was here alone, the windows glittered with enough city lights to illuminate the entire reception room. But the heavy velvet curtains were drawn shut now; Jereth must've come home. The suite was seventy-nine storeys up, on the Night Palace's most decadent floor, and Jereth had never much liked looking down from it. A terrible fear of heights, he said, ever since he was a child.

"Hello? Jerry? You here?"

There was still no answer, but Eldric heard shuffling footsteps around the corner, and then the faint echoes of laughter. At least two voices—a high, nasal giggle and a lower chuckle—and neither one of them was Jereth's.

One of Jereth's fancy shoes was lying in the middle of the reception room floor, and a few other unfamiliar items of clothing were scattered down the corridor, along with a trail of glitter confetti. Swearing softly, Eldric kicked the shoe aside. He had really hoped to find Jereth at home alone tonight.

Jereth had been out more than ever lately, staggering back at unpredictable hours and in unpredictable company. Last week, he'd brought over an obnoxiously loud socialite who'd spilled half her bottle of mint liqueur into the sofa. And a couple of days ago, Eldric had come home to find a mostly-naked man standing on the balcony, unapologetically smoking one of Eldric's cigarettes.

Jereth's bedroom door opened and he stumbled out, barefoot, auburn hair in disarray, wearing only his velvet housecoat. His face shone with sweat, and his pupils were unnaturally wide.

"Oh, hey, Leeg," he mumbled, squinting at Eldric. "Why're ya dressed up, you goin' out?" His syllables all slurred together, like he'd forgotten how to pause between words.

"I've been gone for hours. I just got back," Eldric said. He glanced over Jereth's shoulder at the open door. "Can I talk to you for a minute? Or... you got someone over?"

Jereth closed his bedroom door behind him. "S'fine. We can talk. C'mon." He walked out into the main room, stopping halfway to grab the back of the sofa for balance before he stumbled forward again and threw one arm around Eldric, staring into his face. "Y'all right, Leeg? Y'look... kinda freaked out. Where were ya?"

"With Dafnë," Eldric said quietly. "She told me she *loves* me, Jerry."

"Hah!" Jereth shook his head. "Wow! How about that, huh? Listen, I was jus' about to mix up some drinks. Y'wanna drink? I'll make you a good one. Jereth special."

"Did you even hear what I said?"

"Yeah, yeah... she said she loves you." Jereth laughed. "Don't worry... it'll be fine. She'll prob'ly get over it." He walked unsteadily over to the cooler and started rummaging around in it. "Hey, y'wanna drink, Leeg? I'm gonna make you a drink. Jereth special."

"No," Eldric muttered. "I said it back to her, by the way. If you care."

"Said what?" Jereth's voice echoed from inside the cooler. "Said what to who?"

"Never mind." Eldric sighed. "I'm going to bed."

"Hey! Don't. Don't get mad at me." Jereth closed the cooler door without taking anything out, then shuffled back over to the sofa and sat down. He patted the cushion next to him. "Y'wanna talk about your love life? Okay. Look, I'm listening now! I'm listening! Sit down."

Eldric hesitated, then walked over and sat slowly down beside Jereth. The sofa still reeked overwhelmingly of sweet mint. They'd probably have to buy another one.

"So?" Jereth said. "Talk to me."

Eldric glanced behind him at Jereth's closed bedroom door. Thumping electronic music was now echoing down the hall, but he still lowered his voice to a near-whisper. "I think we should retire the Jetsetter," he said. "I don't want to work with you anymore, Jerry. I want out."

There was a long pause, and then Jereth tilted his head back and laughed uproariously. "Oh, wow!" he gasped. "Hah, wow... that's priceless! Oh, my gods!"

"What's so damn funny?" Eldric growled.

Jereth blinked. His laughter faded, his face slowly sobering. "Wait. You're *serious*?"

"Yes, actually. I am." Eldric's voice shook. "I'm out. Starting right now. I... I've been thinking about this a lot, and... I... I just don't feel right involving Dafnë in this thing. She's about to be promoted to lead animator, and I don't want to fuck anything up for her—"

Jereth sat up. "Wait, you haven't *told* Dafnë about the Jetsetter, have you?"

"Of course not! She has no idea what I do. She probably thinks I'm some kind of shady investor or whatever the fuck rich people do around here, so she doesn't ask me about it. But... I did tell her I won't be working such long hours anymore, that I'll try to spend more time with her. And I meant it."

Jereth's expression was stormy. "So *that's* what this is about, huh? You're really gonna throw away all our hard work, just 'cause of Dafnë?"

"You mean *my* hard work, Jerry! *I'm* the Jetsetter!" he hissed. "I'm the one who's been working for hours on this job while you're off your face somewhere, and you don't even appreciate it! You only do the easy parts! I'm sick of all this, and I'm fucking sick of Sëgra!" He was shouting now.

"Shhh... shhh... Leeg," Jereth said. "Stop... shhh... just listen to me." He reached out and rested his palms either side of Eldric's face. "Look at me."

Eldric did.

"You want to leave Sëgra, hmm? Sure. Okay, that's fine. But... to go where, Leeg?"

Eldric paused, thinking it over. "Well, Dafnë said she wanted a house one day. On a world with a proper sun, and plants, and rain... She said she wants to see something other than dead rocks and neon and all the fake shit in this city." He sighed. "I guess I want that stuff, too. I want to get us away from here."

"Okay. Good, that's good." Slowly, Jereth smiled. "You know, you can get founders' rights on an up-and-coming green world for about sixty million. Not just a place to live, Leeg, no, but a real, solid future! Just think, a world with all the sunshine you want, all the plants, a real nice house... And trees! You could own *land with trees on it*. Imagine that. That'd make Dafnë real happy, right?"

Eldric sighed again. "Yes, probably. But I—"

"We've got to finish this job," whispered Jereth. "C'mon, don't bail out like this. We've done all the work already. You'd be a fool to throw it away when we're so close!"

Eldric sat there in silence for a while, looking at Jereth. "Fine," he said, "We'll finish this one job. But after this, we're out. The Jetsetter is done. And we're leaving."

"It's a deal." Jereth grinned. "We'll go to a green world. Dafnë, too. You can take her anywhere she wants. Gods... we are gonna leave here so fucking rich."

Eldric nodded, but he couldn't muster a smile.

Jereth's bedroom door slid open then, and a half-dressed stranger with an absurd coif of yellow hair leaned out. It wasn't the mint-liqueur spiller *or* the cigarette thief.

"Hey! Jaymi! You still making those drinks?" the stranger yelled. "You comin' back soon?"

"Jaymi?" Jereth mumbled, looking genuinely confused. He blinked. "Ohhh. Oh, wait, hang on, Jaymi's *me*. Hah! I forgot which name I told 'em." He laughed.

"Jaymi! C'mon!" the stranger insisted.

"Be right there!" Jereth screamed back, at six times the necessary volume.

Eldric stood up from the sofa with a sigh, certain that his trousers now smelled of mint. "Right. I'll see you later, 'Jaymi.' You should probably get back to your... guests. I'm going to bed."

"Hey. Y'want me to mix you a drink first? I can make you a drink. Jaymi special."

"No, thanks."

"Wait... Leeg! Leeg. Listen." Jereth scrambled up after him, taking Eldric by the arm. "Leeg... you're my best friend. You know that, right? An' I... I want *you* to be happy."

Eldric shrugged.

"We'll leave soon," Jereth said. "I promise. Everything's gonna be just fine."

UMA
Lecture Theatre, ZeyCorp Gallion

UMA AND HER team made the presentation in the *Gallion*'s lecture theatre, where researchers usually presented findings or recorded talks. The space was overly large for their tiny group, but this room had the most sophisticated projection system and a slightly raised stage, and it seemed as good a place as any to hold the full staff meeting.

From the ZeyCorp-branded podium, Uma ran through all their carefully-rehearsed explanations, complete with a slideshow that Wazar had thrown together the night before. They pitched the two-team shuttle mission. They described the boarding of Verkhoy Station, and Noussen and Wazar showed off the improved comms relay with its repeaters mounted on hover probes. Then Jaxong came to the podium and demonstrated some of her findings about the Rift, outlining in simple terms how they intended to carry out Project Last Shot. They skimmed over all the technical details, and no one mentioned a single thing that could go wrong.

But of course, they wouldn't get away with it that easily.

"Excuse me," said Nack when Uma and Jaxong had finished. "So... how exactly are you plannin' to get that Jaxong drive into maintenance mode? Seems like you'd need some fancy high-level security permissions on the station to do that."

"Keeven? You want to take this one?" Uma glanced across at Keeven, motioning him forward.

"A most excellent question!" Keeven boomed, jumping up from his seat at the side of the stage. "But easy to explain. See, it's like this. Everyone who worked on Verkhoy Station had a set of unique passcodes, used in combination with bio-auth to verify a user's identity." Keeven pointed across the theatre at Shaan, smiling wider. "This is where it really helps us that Shaan's got a staff account on Verkhoy already."

The crew all turned to stare at Shaan.

"Without Shaan, we wouldn't be able to do anything," Leesongronski said, crossing the stage to join Keeven by the podium. "That station has no concept of guest accounts. There aren't any visitor permissions like you have here on the *Gallion*. You're either a member of Geminus staff or, as far as the station's concerned, you don't exist at all. We'd never even get inside without a Geminus ID."

Keeven gestured in Shaan's direction again. "Shaan doesn't have a very high level of access, but she does have *some*. Even with the station still on lockdown, she'll be able to get us safely through an airlock and into zone one—that's the lowest ring of the station."

"Here's where the shuttle will dock," Uma said. She activated a huge projection of Verkhoy Station that floated up over her head, and the station's lower quarter lit up. A small glowing shuttle coasted into view and docked neatly on the platform.

Leesongronski nodded. "As soon as Jereth and Shaan get inside, they'll plug in a customized transponder. We'll use that to establish a remote link between the *Gallion* and the station's mainframe. Then, I can start making some... adjustments in their database." He glanced at Uma. "I'll do an identity swap.

I'll switch Shaan's profile with someone else's... and we're going to turn Shaan into the Station Governor, Ker Marecc."

Uma scanned the crew's faces, trying to read their reactions. Most people had heard some version of the plan already, but everyone looked as anxious as she'd ever seen them. In the front row, Zel was nervously twisting one corner of his cape around and around in his hand. Director Barnabyn looked apoplectic.

"Professor Leesongronski, pardon me," said Barnabyn. "I'm no computer expert, but these systems are so much more advanced than anything you've ever worked with. How could you possibly know what you're doing?"

"The laws of mathematics haven't changed," Leesongronski said sardonically. "Dean tells us you're still using 5D transforms in your cryptography. We've found a few ways to expose that encrypted layer by using some existing exploits... so I can get you in from there."

"Yes, yes, I read the proposal document," said Barnabyn, shaking his head in annoyance. "But what does that *mean*? What kind of exploits? Dean—explain, please."

At the side of the stage, the android's eyes lit up. The AI's voice replied over the room's sound system, amplifying into the speakers high up in the walls.

"Certainly, Director Barnabyn," Dean said. "Although Verkhoy Station is modern, it disappeared from normal space six years ago relative to the *Gallion*'s time. None of the station's operating software has been updated in the years since it vanished, so we can be certain their mainframe is running with at least one known vulnerability." Dean's android head tilted to one side. "I've pulled up a list of likely exploits we could use, and I shared everything I could find in our knowledge banks with Professor Leesongronski. But once we hit the encryption layers, I can be of no further assistance."

"That'll be the easy part," Leesongronski said.

"How have you tested these... exploits?" Barnabyn asked. "Do we know for sure that they'll work?"

"No, of course not." Leesongronski sighed. "We can't test anything until somebody's out on the station. We don't even know what software they're running yet. I'm a mathematical genius, not a fucking magician."

Keeven patted Leesongronski's arm and shot him a look.

"Once the transponder is in place on the station and our remote link is active," Dean said, "we'll be able to learn more. Professor Leesongronski will be able to work on the Verkhoy computers from here."

"We considered sending Professor Leesongronski out to the station with the shuttle teams," said Uma. "But he'll need access to the *Gallion*'s processing power, so he'll stay here with us. We'll set up a console for him in Engineering."

"What about communications?" asked Fransk.

"Once the shuttles get through that boundary seam and back into a stable zone, we'll have real-time voice contact," Uma said. "We'll use Noussen's hover relay, and the shuttles will drop a few more hover probes as they go. We'll extend the relay into the boundary zone and beyond it, all the way to Verkhoy."

Uma reached up and rotated the huge projection of Verkhoy Station with a flick of her fingers. "Once Professor Leesongronski swaps Shaan's identity to make her the Station Governor, Shaan will switch off the emergency lockdown and bring the station back into normal operations. The security doors will retract, the lifts will reactivate, and our team will proceed to the control room. Where the Station Governor will put the Jaxong drive into maintenance mode."

The location of the control room, high up in the station, glowed bright green on the projection.

"Mission accomplished!" Keeven proclaimed brightly.

Fransk was frowning. "That's a lot of steps. This sounds extremely risky."

"I did raise that particular issue," muttered Leesongronski. "Not that anyone listens to me."

"I know it sounds complicated," Keeven cut in. "But hacking this station should be *way* easier than hacking any system in our own time. See, we won't need to sit around for weeks figuring out how to get at the encryption layers, 'cause Dean's software exploits will cover that."

Leesongronski nodded, stony-faced. "A hack of this type would usually involve a lot of research," he said. "We'd also need to figure out how to excise all the logs, to make sure nobody traced the incursion to us... But in this case, we don't need to erase our tracks. If your exploits get me as far as the encrypted keys, we break in the fast way."

"What if you get it wrong, though?" Barnabyn said. "We haven't even discussed the fact that our second shuttle pilot is a junior engineer with no certification to operate that shuttle."

"Director Barnabyn's right," Nack chimed in. "We're endangerin' people's lives. We gotta think about this!"

At that, Zel got to his feet, his handsome face indignant. "You want to talk about endangering lives?" he demanded. "What about the population of Etraxas? If we don't restore our proper timeline, we're condemning all those people to death! More than that, we're talking about the collapse of the Union! The ruin of the Peace! Possibly the extinction of the entire human species, and—"

"Zel, that is pure conjecture!" Barnabyn shouted back. His neck and cheeks were turning crimson. "Don't let your emotional involvement cloud your good judgement!"

Captain Fransk raised both hands, motioning for silence. "That's enough!" With a swift wave of his hand, the captain dismissed the projection of Verkhoy. "There's no sense in arguing. We've all heard the facts, and we have only two options. Either Captain Keeven goes out alone to collect those energy cells and buy us more time, or we take a chance on this two-shuttle plan, and we build Professor Jaxong's... device." His eyes flicked around the room, pausing over each of his crew. "I'd like a show of hands. Let's get a read on staff consensus."

A few murmured whispers passed between the crew, and then there was silence.

"*Gallion* crew in favour of the solo mission, with Captain Keeven collecting the energy cells?" Fransk said. "Hands, please."

Barnabyn, Nack and Macey's hands shot up. The Cordero siblings paused, looked at each other, then followed suit.

Syru hesitated, casting an apologetic look at Uma as he slowly raised his hand.

"Sy!" hissed Mikolai. "What're you doing?"

Syru didn't look over at him.

"That's... six votes for picking up the energy cells." Fransk tugged nervously on the captain's badge on his collar. "And now... *Gallion* crew in favour of Project Last Shot?"

Uma raised her hand. Then Zel. Then Noussen, Wazar, and Mikolai.

Uma held her breath... and then Shaan's hand finally went up.

The captain's eyes flicked over the group, as if he had to count them twice to be sure. "Six and six," he muttered. "Good gods almighty."

"Uh, 'scuse me," Keeven said. "Don't you think *we* should get to vote, too?" He raised a theatrical hand, gesturing toward his companions. "It's worth noting, Captain, that the *Jonah* vote is unanimous. All in favour of Project Last Shot?"

Leesongronski, Mendeg, Kva-Sova and Jaxong all raised their hands.

Captain Fransk blinked. He was silent for a long time.

"I want you to know that I'm proud of every single person here," he finally said, his voice wavering with emotion. "I appreciate the hard work you've all done over the past few days." He took a deep breath. "As the captain of this ship, my duty is to uphold ZeyCorp's good standards. To represent the company values, and encourage everything we stand for— 'research, progress, innovation.' But in a crisis situation, it also falls to me to serve the needs of our crew, our researchers, our visitors. It is up to me to ensure our ship's safety... and our survival." He paused, meeting Uma's eyes. "I value all of your voices. I have heard you. This isn't an easy decision."

Uma fixed her eyes on the captain. *Oli, please.*

There was a long, heavy silence before he spoke again.

"Project Last Shot will go ahead," Fransk said. "Make your preparations. We'll launch two shuttles as soon as we can."

ELDRIC
Sëgra City, Sëgra
11 years before the Rift

IN THE SMALL, windowless apartment, Eldric Leesongronski sat at his computer terminal, open to the Jetsetter's interface. He was staring straight ahead, but he hadn't looked at his screen for some time. A bulky commercial VR headset covered his eyes, and he held both hands out in front of him as he practiced a virtual keystroke input.

He'd perfected a series of custom micro-movements—minuscule flicks of his fingers that mapped to the standard letters and symbols. The motions he made were so slight as to be nearly imperceptible, but all it took was a delicate touch of one fingertip to another, and a torrent of tiny glowing characters flowed across his field of vision. He wore what looked like a perfectly ordinary set of gold-and-black sequinned gloves in the popular style, but inside them, a network of hair-thin filaments transmitted each keystroke to a small device clipped into his headset.

He'd built the entire system himself, and he was rather proud of it. The input method wasn't unlike the handsets he used as a jump architect, and after dozens of hours of practice, the new sequences of finger movements had become second nature. Now that Eldric had created a library of short codes to link strings

257

of keystrokes together, he was able to control his computer almost as easily as he could with a standard keyboard. The whole thing was a masterpiece.

It was almost a pity that the Grenobal job would be the Jetsetter's last.

He logged into his computer system one last time, and set up the timed program that would scrub everything from his hard drives after a delay. In a few hours' time, it would all be deleted without a trace. There was just one last thing to do, and then this would all be over.

ELDRIC STOOD AGAINST the wall in the alley outside the dreamhouse, waiting. He watched the dreamhouse performers arriving one by one, streaming toward the staff entrance, but Dafnë wasn't among them.

Was she even coming? Did he get the right show time? He was suddenly nervous. This was her first performance as a lead animator. She should have been here already.

At last, Dafnë emerged from the crowd, ducking past the people in her way. She wore the same voluminous silky robe she'd had on the day he met her, covering her familiar VR suit. She had yet to put on the close-fitting cap that completed her suit, and her sea of dark curls still bobbed loose around her shoulders. She made her way hurriedly down the alley, her arms glittering with tracking nodes.

"Dafnë!" Eldric shouted. "Hey! Dafnë!"

"Eldric?" She stopped and turned around, her face confused. "What're you doing here? I've got to get inside, I'm running really late! Transit was completely fucked."

"I know, I know. I just... I really wanted to see you before you start." He reached out and touched the orb that hung at her neck. "I wanted to... to wish you luck."

He leaned down to kiss her, but she pulled back from his embrace.

"What?"

"You've been ignoring me for days, Eldric," she said. "Where have you been? What in the five hells is the matter with you?"

"W-with me? Nothing! I said I'd be at this show for sure, and here I am. I wouldn't miss this. It's your opening night as a lead!"

She folded her glittering arms. "Then why haven't you been returning my messages? You only sent me one reply all week, and it just said you were busy. Gods. I went to your place and I talked to Jaymi, or Jude, or whatever his actual name is, and he said he didn't even know where you were! I thought we were going to spend more time together soon."

Eldric inhaled sharply. "That's right. Yes. I mean, I... yes, we are going to do that. Look, we're spending time together right now."

She examined him suspiciously. "What were you so busy doing all week that you couldn't call me back?"

"I've, uh... well... I've been working on my upload for you. For the Collectors," Eldric stammered. "Finding something to put in your Vault archive. I didn't want to tell you yet because... it's going to be a surprise."

"Oh. You were? Really?" Dafnë's shoulders relaxed slightly, her expression softening. "That reminds me, I got such a weird message from the Collectors earlier. Apparently, some anonymous contributor sent over a drive with *twelve million* new media files for the Vault archive! Books, video files, music... all of them completely unique! Can you believe that?"

"Wow. Huh." Eldric forced a laugh. "That sounds like someone scraped the City's entertainment portals for standard media formats. A hacker must've grabbed everybody's media backup troves from the cloud."

She gave him a strange look. "Right. They got into the whole City's personal storage troves, and all they did was send a bunch of music and books to the Collectors?"

"Hey, this is a great thing, isn't it?" Eldric smiled at her. "You won't need to go around begging people for contributions anymore. The Vault's all finished, you've got a copy of pretty much all the media on Sëgra. 'Course, I don't know if this City's taste in media is really what you want representing humanity. You'll probably need to make a few culls."

She laughed at that. "Yes... probably." Her eyes skirted to the performers' entrance, where two other performers were just rushing in. "Okay, Eldric, I do need to go inside now or I seriously will be late. I need to get prepped for the show." Before he could quite figure out what to do next, she'd already taken hold of his shoulders, pulled herself up onto her toes and kissed him quickly.

She started to pull away, but he held her closer, cradling her against him for a moment longer, his heart thundering in his chest.

He reached down and retrieved the tiny transmission device from his pocket, then slid his hand up Dafnë's back. Very delicately, he removed and replaced one of the VR projection nodes on her shoulder. He pressed down the tiny device, holding it tight against her suit until it stuck. And then he slipped his hand away and released her.

"Let's go out somewhere after," he said when they broke apart. "To celebrate your promotion, yeah? Let's do something fun."

She squeezed his hand and nodded. "Yes! Of course! I'll see you later." With a dazzling smile, she turned and ran to the performers' entrance, her glorious curls bouncing behind her. She disappeared into the dark.

Eldric closed his eyes, his heart still pounding. He waited

another minute before he walked around to the main entrance, went to the nearest ticketing terminal and bought a top-tier admission to the dream-play.

He pulled on his sequined gloves as he joined the stream of patrons entering the theatre.

ELDRIC WOKE UP to what sounded like pouring rain drumming against a windowpane. He opened his eyes ever so slightly, and saw a familiar gilded ceiling. He was in his room at the Night Palace. And there was definitely no rain on Sëgra.

Dafnë was asleep beside him, mumbling something unintelligible into his shoulder. Her hand brushed over his chest, and he caught a glimpse of the green ribbons that covered the fresh brand on her wrist. Then the events of the previous hours came flooding back to him.

He remembered walking up the steps into the neon-lit Temple of Everlasting Light; he remembered his arms and head being strewn with glowing flower-garlands in Sëgra's characteristically gaudy tradition. He remembered going up into one of the stone chambers... joining hands with her over the brazier... being handed the sun-brand and pressing it into her soft flesh... feeling the sharp pain on his skin as she did the same to him while they repeated the words of the Sëgran soul-bonding oath.

Bound and sealed in ember and flame, until all the Great Suns burn out. Isn't it a romantic thought, Eldric? Let's go do it!

He still hadn't fully opened his eyes, when something small and cold hit him in the face. Eldric's eyes snapped wide open, and he sat up to find Jereth standing next to his bed.

Jereth was slowly pouring thousands of credit chits out of a carry-bag. He had opened the bag just enough, so the silvery, round-edged discs cascaded out in a steady stream. They were still tumbling out onto Eldric's black sheets, half of them clattering onto the floor.

"Jerry?" Eldric mumbled. "What—"

Jereth snatched up a handful of chits from the bed and tossed them into the air, then shook Eldric by the shoulders, grinning. "Holy shit, Leeg! We *actually pulled it off.*"

"Jerry," said Eldric under his breath. "Shhh."

Jereth reached out and grabbed Eldric's wrist, holding it up to examine the ceremonial ribbons knotted over his sun-brand. "Woooow! You got some of those soul-brand things or whatever? From the temple? That's fuckin' hilarious! Can I see?"

Eldric snatched his wrist back, flinching in pain from the fresh burn. The temple acolytes had applied a numbing salve, but it had clearly worn off.

"What's going on?" Dafnë mumbled, blinking sleepily. "Eldric?"

Jereth dropped the empty carry-bag. He ran across the room and flung open the door to the balcony. "Wooooo! Fuck this city! Fuck all of this! We're done!" he screamed. Then he ran back again and jumped onto the bed.

Dafnë pulled the sheet out from under him, showering the floor with chits. "Are you out of your mind, Jaymi? Get out of here!"

Jereth just laughed, crawling between Eldric and Dafnë. "Dafnë! It's time to pick out your mansion on a green world. You earned it, fair and square." He picked up another handful of credit chits, took Dafnë's hand and dramatically pressed the silver discs into her palm. "There you go... for your much-valued contribution to the Jetsetter enterprise. Don't worry, that isn't your *whole* cut. I only cashed out a little bit." He winked.

Dafnë flung the fistful of chits at Jereth, then pointed at the door. "Get *out*, Jaymi! Now!"

This time, Jereth didn't argue. He looked at Eldric's face, and his smile disappeared. He clambered off the bed and stormed out the door.

Behind him, a few stray chits skittered across the floor.

Eldric's face was buried in his hands, and he hardly dared to look up at her. When he finally did, Dafnë was staring at her wrist, stroking the green silken bindings with her other hand.

"My contribution to the 'Jetsetter enterprise'?" she said. "What did he mean by that? Isn't the Jetsetter that hacker that's always in the news?"

"I... I have no idea." Eldric shrugged. "Maybe. I don't know. You know what he's like, he just says whatever weird thing pops into his head. He just... talks."

She was quiet for a long time. "All those media files for the Vault," she whispered at last. "You said someone must have hacked the City's personal storage troves. That was you, wasn't it?"

Eldric didn't say anything.

Dafnë picked up one of the credit chits and held it up to his face. Tears were gathering on her lower lashes. "No more lies, Eldric," she whispered. "What have you done?"

UMA
Engineering Deck, *ZeyCorp Gallion*

WHEN THE LIGHTS dimmed into night-mode, Uma was almost alone in Engineering. Most of the engineers had exhausted themselves into taking a longer break to sleep. Down in the pit, only Noussen was sitting at one of the consoles. The rest of the deck was deserted aside from Eldric Leesongronski, who had resumed his perch on the railing.

Uma leaned back in her chair and closed her eyes, contemplating getting a few hours of rest herself. But her veins buzzed with stims, and the details of Keeven's plan were still bouncing around in her brain. There was no way she could sleep right now.

She took a moment to steel herself, then walked up the stairs.

"Hey," she said. "Could I... ah, could I talk to you?"

Leesongronski raised his head and looked around. "Who, me?"

She laughed softly. "Yeah. You."

"Well, it's not like I'm doing anything else," he said. "Besides staring at this thing." He gestured at Jaxong's v-board, which was still unfolded over the table.

"Noussen's working on improving the relay stability for

you," Uma said. She pointed into the pit, where Noussen was bent intently over her console. "The new hovers will have even stronger repeaters, and the shuttles will drop one every few klicks between here and Verkhoy."

Leesongronski gave a long sigh. "Ozakka... look, I need you to understand that this whole thing's going to be unpredictable," he said. "We dressed it up real nice for your presentation, but there's a hell of a lot of unknowns here. Don't get your hopes up too high."

"Well... I believe in you," Uma said. She winced at how ridiculous that sounded. She still couldn't quite put words together in front of him.

Leesongronski made a disdainful sound. "You mean you believe what Jereth told you. Which is not necessarily the best idea." He smiled wryly, then turned back to the v-board.

"I, ah... I have a question, Professor," Uma said after a silence. "It's about Sëgra."

Leesongronski sighed again. "What about it?"

"I've always known it, but during the presentation today I... I was thinking..." She took a deep breath. "You *were* the Jetsetter hacker, weren't you? You were the one who hacked Grenobal Bank in Sëgra City."

He didn't say anything.

"It's just... I've always really wanted to know how you pulled it all off. It was one of the biggest bank breaches in history!" She leaned on the railing beside him. "One of your unauthorized biographies goes into the details of the Jetsetter case. You were always suspected of being the Jetsetter, but you were cleared because you were inside the Dome Theatre when the bank was breached, and the theatre used to jam all external communications during the dream-plays. That's why your alibi was so perfect, because the Dome was dead-zoned, so there was no way you could have sent any signals from in there."

Her fingers tightened around the railing. "So... how *did* you do it? Where did you do the hack from?"

"From inside the dreamhouse, obviously," Leesongronski said, rolling his eyes. "External comms were blocked, yeah, but the Dome didn't block *internal* signals."

Uma leaned forward. "Go on...?"

"Three of the big dreamhouses were all connected on a single internal network, linked into shared VR servers," he said. "That was my breakthrough."

"Yes!" Uma slapped the railing with both palms. "I was right! I knew it had to be the dreamhouse network somehow! But they said it was impossible for a spectator to have sent any signals out of the Dome."

This time, Leesongronski laughed out loud. "Impossible? Suuure. Let me tell you how 'impossible' it was. It turned out those three dreamhouses shared some of their infrastructure for running the plays. A bunch of the background scenery and effects for the Dome's plays came from a VR server underneath the Prismadrome, sixteen blocks away. While the play was on, the Dome would constantly send that server a stream of position data for every performer. You know, so all the little magic effects would show up in the right places." He sighed. "That hack was a fucking masterstroke. I buried my data in the position stream that flowed from the Dome Theatre back to the Prismadrome server. I got out to the Prismadrome's master network from there, and that had all *kinds* of unsecured external connections."

"Brilliant," breathed Uma. "But... wait. The encrypted key exchange for the breach into Grenobal Bank had to be done in real-time, didn't it? How could you see what you were doing to break the encryption, if you were in the dream-play?"

"I made a chip that clipped into one of their VR headsets." Something like pride flashed across Leesongronski's face.

"When I put my headset on in the Dome, instead of seeing the background scenery for the play, I was seeing my own custom display behind the performers. I made all the inputs with a special pair of wired gloves I rigged up." He held up his hand, twitching the ends of his fingers. "I replaced one of Dafnë's transmission nodes with a modified one that would capture my signal and pack my data in with her position updates. The return signal came back to me the same way, from her node to my headset." He lowered his eyes. "She had no idea about any of it. She was just performing in the play."

"Gods," Uma whispered.

"Oh, I know. I'm reprehensible, right?" He grimaced. "And then Jereth got arrested. I was so damn scared that they'd implicate Dafnë too, if they ever figured out how I did it. I got her out of the city as fast as I could. She hated me for it when she found out... I think she might've left me if we didn't have to run."

"Wait, what?" Uma said. "You mean Jereth as in *Jereth Keeven,* who's on this ship?"

"The one and only," Leesongronski said. "He and I go way back. He was with me on Sëgra, in the Night Palace, through all of that. We did all the Jetsetter jobs together."

"Oh, my gods. Wait! I think... Hang on." Uma grabbed for her lightpad, quickly logging out of her work account and flipping over to her personal trove. She flicked through folder after folder, almost missing the one she wanted in her rush, until she finally pulled up the book she was looking for.

Under Fortunate Stars: The Untold Personal History of Eldric Leesongronski.

Her favourite unauthorized Leesongronski biography, and also the one that covered his nebulous Sëgra years in the most detail. Somewhere near the middle, she found the image she was looking for.

It was a still picture, an old two-dimensional capture, with some kind of colour filter that made everything look slightly blue. And there he was. Jereth Keeven, standing with one hand on Leesongronski's shoulder, holding a glittering long-stemmed glass in his other hand and grinning straight into the camera. Keeven looked younger, his cheeks a lot fuller, his hair longer. His eyes were rimmed with dramatic gold makeup, and his temples were adorned with a string of tiny glittering stars. A single auburn braid hung over his shoulder, festooned with a tassel of bright ribbons. He and Leesongronski wore matching jackets in one of those strange vintage styles, with fluorescent sleeves covered in layers of elaborate ruffles.

"Jaymi Hanioch," she whispered. "This man right here? This is Keeven, isn't it! Without all the fancy clothes and the makeup and the hair, I didn't recognize him... but... Jereth Keeven is *your friend Jaymi Hanioch from Sëgra?*"

Leesongronski laughed. "Gods. Jereth had so many damn aliases back in those days, it's a wonder he could keep them all straight. But yeah, Jaymi was one he used a lot." He touched the image and zoomed in on it. "Wow. Those jackets were awful. Just as well those things went out of fashion."

"Of course. Of *course* Keeven has those stasis scars... because Jaymi Hanioch was arrested for the Jetsetter hacks, and he got a stasis sentence!" Uma said, still staring incredulously at the photo. How had she not put it together before? "He got handed a huge suspension term for the Grenobal Bank theft. It was basically a death sentence, so I thought... I mean, your biographers *all* said that Jaymi died in stasis prison."

Was this it? Was this the thing that had changed everything in their timeline? Jaymi Hanioch being alive instead of dead? But then, why was the *Jonah* still with Leesongronski? What were the chances—

Leesongronski slowly twirled his little fortune-charm around one finger. "Yeah, I thought he was dead for a long while too." He hopped down off the railing and went over to Charyne Jaxong's v-board. "You know, to this day I have no idea why we thought we'd get away with any of the shit we did. We must've been out of our minds to take those kinds of risks," he said. He flicked his hand through the controls, dismissing the v-board back into the table. "Looks like not a whole lot's changed, huh?"

Before Uma could say anything else, he gave her a curt nod and stalked off toward the exit.

SHAAN
Cargo Bay, ZeyCorp Gallion

THE MORNING AFTER the big presentation, Shaan stood in one of the *Gallion*'s empty cargo bays, wearing a full space-suit. It was an ultra-light model, the kind used for repair work on the ship's external instrumentation—a simple black-and-silver suit with articulated joints, a retractable helmet and a small air-recycling system curving across the shoulders. Detachable boots and gloves sealed seamlessly to the cuffs, peeling apart when a command was entered on the suit's wrist-mounted control pad.

Keeven was walking around the bay in an identical suit, bending his elbows and knees with an incredulous look on his face.

"This is amazing!" he shouted, too loudly. "Wow! Look! I can't believe the flexibility in this thing!"

"Suit tech's improved a lot since your time," Ozakka said. "Want to try out the helmet?" She walked over to him and tapped two buttons near the collar of his suit. "Press here twice, and then here."

The helmet expanded from the panel at the back of the neck, looping soundlessly over his head and covering his face with an opaque, reflective faceplate. It retracted again when she repeated the sequence.

"Well, shit!" said Keeven, his voice astonished.

"It'll only fold away if the air around you is breathable, so you can't do this in space."

"Whoa!" Keeven reached up and tapped the buttons a few more times, raising and lowering the helmet, his face alight with childlike joy. "Can I keep this when we're done?"

"We'll see." Ozakka shook her head.

He grinned. "Don't think I'll forget about it!"

The director glanced down at her lightpad. "Right, we've watched the safety demo, we've fitted everyone's suits... but we're not going to have time for much training." She exhaled, puffing out her cheeks. "Technically, you should all have had a ZeyCorp EVA certification before we even put that suit on you. Don't anyone point that out to Director Barnabyn, all right?"

"So... that's all we're getting for training?" Mikolai looked anxious.

Ozakka gave the junior a sympathetic glance. "Tell you what. I'll get Dean to dial the gravity down in here, so you and Professor Jaxong can practice manoeuvering an empty charge casing around. You should probably get a feel for it."

"Okay," Mikolai mumbled. He resumed walking carefully along one of the lines on the cargo bay floor, setting one booted foot in front of the other with painstaking precision.

"Everyone feeling comfortable enough with the suits?" Ozakka asked.

Jaxong raised and retracted her helmet once, then nodded. "I'm fine, thank you."

Keeven was hardly paying attention, still flicking his helmet up and down with that silly grin on his face. Shaan nodded wordlessly. She felt like she was about to be sick.

"Um... Director... could you show me again about the

emergency grapple?" Mikolai said. He examined the sleeve of his suit with concern, running his gloved fingers over the seams. "Are you sure mine has one?"

"I'm sure," said Ozakka with a tight-lipped smile. "Gods willing, none of you should need to deploy it."

Keeven walked over and patted the junior's shoulder.

"Hey, kiddo," he said. "Listen to me. You're gonna do great, okay? Nothing bad's gonna happen out there."

"I know," Mikolai sighed, not sounding at all convinced. He was still examining the panel that contained his suit's emergency grapple. "How do we know these tethers always work?"

"Here," Keeven said with a sly grin. "Let's check, shall we?"

He grabbed Mikolai's arm and flung it straight out in front of him. Before anyone could react, Keeven had pressed the release sequence on Mikolai's wrist. With a sharp recoil, a rounded silver grapple shot straight out of the junior's suit, trailed by a shimmering thread of tether.

There was a *thunk* and a screech as the grapple buried itself in the panelling twenty-four paces away, its claw embedded neatly in the bay wall.

Ozakka's mouth dropped open. "Keeven!"

"Ha!" screamed Keeven triumphantly, slapping Mikolai's back. "See? Nothin' to worry about." He reached out and tugged hard on the safety cord. It didn't budge. "This is quality stuff."

The shimmering tether bent and curved, then slowly started to wind itself in, pulling Mikolai toward the wall.

"It's working!" The junior yelped, taking a staggering step. "It's... ah, it's really got me!" Mikolai leaned back against the tether, but the grapple held fast. The tether retracted again, and Mikolai had to keep walking toward the wall to stop himself from falling over. "It's reeling me in! Look!" He started laughing.

Keeven whooped in delight, and even Charyne Jaxong doubled over with laughter. Shaan couldn't keep the smile from her lips as she watched the scene unfolding.

"Keeven!" cried Ozakka. "Oh, my gods! What—why would you...?" But a grin was creeping across her face, too, and she couldn't finish her sentence without laughing.

Ozakka had to run to catch up to the stumbling Mikolai, who was still trying to disengage himself from the retracting tether. She reached for his arm, pressing another sequence on his wrist to detach his suit from the grapple.

When he was finally loose, Ozakka examined the deep dent in the wall, with that shiny rounded claw embedded at its centre.

"At least Director Barnabyn's not here to tell us how much ZeyCorp budget that just wasted," Shaan said.

"Far as Barnabyn is concerned, this never happened, understand?" said Ozakka, still half-laughing. "We'll never speak of it again."

Keeven raised a finger to his lips and winked. "Speak of what?" he said with mock innocence. "I didn't see anything."

"Exactly." Ozakka composed herself and activated her bracelet. "Dean! Could you please bring us another emergency tether mechanism?" She peeked into the open panel on the arm of Mikolai's suit. "It's... model 645-1. We should have a few replacements in stock."

"Certainly," came Dean's voice. "Was there a problem? Those suits were safety-checked just a few weeks ago."

Ozakka glanced at the grapple stuck in the wall. "We, uh... had some issues in testing. Don't worry about it."

Shaan looked around at the others, suddenly realizing that the tension in the bay had all but dissipated. Mikolai stood much straighter now, his shoulders relaxed as he continued to walk along the line on the floor. Even Charyne Jaxong was still smiling.

"See?" Keeven whispered, nudging Shaan. "The kid's fine. All he needed was a bit of confidence." He slung a casual arm over her shoulder. "We're all gonna be fine."

Shaan took a deep breath and nodded, then reached out almost unconsciously and returned the gesture. They stood there in their space-suits, their arms looped over each other in a clumsy half-hug. The air recycling system on his suit jostled against hers.

"Say it out loud," he insisted. "We're gonna be fine."

"We'll be fine," she whispered. "Completely fine. All of us will be fine."

For one glorious moment, she imagined that she believed it.

And then her bracelet chimed.

She had to let go of Keeven and peel off her glove to check it, her stomach sinking as she retrieved the message from Captain Fransk.

URGENT. PLEASE SEE ME IN MY OFFICE IMMEDIATELY.

By THE TIME Shaan had extricated herself from the space suit and made her way up to the Command deck, Fransk was leaning out his office door, looking anxiously down the corridor as she approached.

"There you are!" he exclaimed, relief on his face. "Quickly, Shaan. Come in."

She stepped into the captain's office, certain that whatever was about to happen would be unpleasant. Zel was sitting there, poised on the edge of one of the square purple chairs in front of the captain's desk. He looked tense, and the black kohl from under his left eye was smudged inelegantly across one bronze cheek.

"Please, take a seat," the captain said, gesturing at the other empty chair. He leaned against his desk with a nervous smile.

"We have a problem, Shaan," Zel said, not waiting for her to sit down.

"Oh?" Shaan managed shakily. *Don't ask me anything about Geminus.* Please *don't ask me anything about Geminus.*

"The Ambassador has asked to speak with you as soon as possible."

"Me?" Shaan said, her throat tightening. "W-why me?"

"Well, now that our diplomatic guests have learned that you used to work for Geminus, I expect they may have some... questions," Fransk said. "As we all do."

Shaan didn't say anything. She just stood there numbly, her knees shaking.

"I'll go with her, of course," Zel said. His formal Etraxan accent was unmistakable in every word. "I'm the official publicity liaison for the Ambassador's visit, after all, and I need to—"

Fransk sighed. "This is not a matter of ZeyCorp publicity, Zel. The instructions we received are clear. Only Shaan is to go into the audience. Alone."

"Captain, you don't understand," Zel insisted. "The Ambassador and I have been in serious talks all morning. You see... Gida is going to accompany the *Jonah* to Etraxas. We'll be sending her along with them when they leave."

A chill crawled down Shaan's spine, a strangled gasp escaping her lips before she could bite it back.

Captain Fransk lowered himself into his chair, something between horror and disbelief dawning on his face. "Zel... what in the worlds are you talking about?"

"It makes the utmost sense, Captain. Listen to me. Keila Kva-Sova said the Voicing procedure takes *years!* Even if she were able to repeat it successfully on a new candidate when they get back, it would be far too late to save Etraxas. But we have another option right in front of us. Gida is already Voiced! If she were to accompany the *Jonah*—"

"No. *No.* Absolutely not. Gida isn't setting foot off this ship," Fransk said, shaking his head furiously. "She's our guest. She's not a pawn for you to use!"

"Tell that to the Ambassador, then!" Zel snapped. "Kva-Sova and the Ambassador have already agreed on this. They want Gida to take the place of the Decipherer."

Shaan still hadn't sat down. She imagined herself reaching forward, turning the chair and sitting down in it, but she couldn't make any of her limbs move. She just stood there numbly, clutching the back of the chair, the room spinning away under her feet.

Fransk wiped at his forehead. His sweaty hands had left fingerprints where he'd leaned on the pristine surface of the desk, and he rubbed the marks off briskly with the edge of one sleeve, as though he were scrubbing away Zel's idea. "Zel, even if Keeven somehow agreed to take Gida on the ship with them—which he won't—and both our ships got out of this Rift, and we both got back to where we came from, even if all of this was real... how could we even consider sending someone *back in time?* To a life that isn't hers?"

"She has a choice, of course," Zel said, smoothing his sash. "But it will be a great honour for her, Captain, to serve such a noble cause."

"And what about their missing Negotiator, then?" Fransk said pointedly. "I suppose *you're* going with them as well, to take the Negotiator's place?"

"Me? Into the past?" Zel looked horrified. "Of course not! How could *I* possibly replace the Negotiator? We don't even know how he—"

"My point exactly!" Fransk snapped. "We can't ask that kind of sacrifice of anyone, and we aren't going to. Gods help me, that girl isn't going anywhere! You'll tell the Ambassador that you retract the agreement." He raised a finger warningly. "No more arguments."

Zel's perfectly-proportioned face was a mask of thinly-veiled disdain. He stood and leaned over Fransk's desk.

"Watch your step, Captain," he said. His voice suddenly had a strange, steely calm to it. "I seem to recall that you've had your eye on a ZeyCorp Chancellorship, planetside, isn't that right? You wouldn't want that opportunity to slip through your fingers, now, would you?"

"What's that supposed to mean?" Fransk was indignant. "You think you're some kind of big-shot because you work for ZeyCorp Central, but none of us take orders from you. You have no authority here. I'm the captain of this ship!"

Zel reached forward then and snatched up the ZeyCorp coaster that sat on the captain's desk. He held it up with two fingers and turned to Shaan, dangling it in front of her face.

"Look at this," he said. "What does it say here? Hmm? Read it out for him!"

"ZeyCorp... Research Support," Shaan choked out, her voice shaking. "What's your point?"

"Read the rest of it," Zel snarled, shaking the coaster. Shaan willed her blurring vision to focus on the small print below the ZeyCorp logo, but Zel had already whirled back to Fransk. "It says *ZeyCorp Research Support—A Division of Yauronauf Incorporated!* See that?"

Fransk stared.

"And do you happen to know who's going to inherit the controlling share in Yauronauf Incorporated? The conglomerate that owns ZeyCorp? Me!" Zel shouted. "You have *no idea* who I am. My aunt is Eli'in Yauro. That's right. My family *runs* Yauronauf Incorporated." He tossed his cape over his shoulder. "You think they'd send just *anybody* to oversee something as important as the Ambassador's visit? Think again. This whole company is going to be mine. I could have you dismissed. I could *ruin* you."

Fransk sat back in his chair, his mouth slightly open. Zel's dark eyes blazed fury.

Finally, Fransk cleared his throat.

"My service to this company has been exceptional," he said. "You can't threaten me. And you may stand to inherit the company, but you don't sit on the ZeyCorp Board of Senior Chancellors, nor are you an executive officer. You aren't even really an employee, are you?" He reached over and snatched the coaster out of Zel's hand, throwing it back down on the desk. "You can't take any independent action within this company, much less have me dismissed, unless you want to see a lawsuit. And since you're clearly not actually a Publicity Liaison, let me teach you something. Lawsuits? Those are *bad* publicity."

Zel's face dropped. He opened his mouth to speak, but no sound came out.

"Get out of my office." Fransk pointed at the door.

"You'll regret this, Captain," spat Zel. "You're making a big mistake."

"Out. Now!"

Zel lunged out of the chair, his cape streaming behind him. He stormed out the door without so much as looking at Shaan.

When Zel had gone, Fransk wiped his forehead with the edge of his sleeve and sighed. "Shaan... I'm so sorry about that," he said, sounding shaken. "But I'll still need you to go over to the Ambassador's suite, immediately."

"Yes, Captain," she managed.

"Please do report back to me when you're through. I need to understand what's going on here." For a moment, Fransk looked like he might be about to say something else. Like he might be about to call her back, or demand to know why she lied on her ZeyCorp application, or ask her something she so desperately didn't want to answer about why she left Geminus. But whatever he'd been about to say, he abandoned it. "Just... do your best to mitigate any *situations* that may arise," he concluded with a sigh.

Shaan nodded silently, and ducked out of the office as quickly as she could.

WHEN THE DOOR to the Ambassador's apartment slid open, it took everything Shaan had in her to stay on her feet. She could barely breathe.

Gida was standing in the centre of the dimly-lit room, her hair pulled back under an iridescent headband, exposing the shining kennai symbol hanging over her forehead. Around her shoulders hung the formal green cloak of the Voiced—just like the Decipherer's in the atrium painting, right down to the wide hood folded down her back.

The Ambassador was draped in elaborate crimson robes, with sleeves that trailed nearly to the floor. The Felen was standing up this time, facing the door, watching her from under a bead-encrusted cowl that hid an angular, alien face. This was a high honour—the Ambassador was facing *toward* her.

"Hello, Shaan. The Ambassador welcomes you, and I will speak for the Ambassador," said Gida without preamble. She stood perfectly still beside the Felen, her head straight, hands flat at her sides, face devoid of emotion. "From this moment, my voice will be the Ambassador's voice."

"I understand," Shaan said.

The Voiced took a deep breath, let her head fall back and closed her eyes. When her eyelids fluttered open again, her irises were no longer visible. She had started her soundless dialogue with the Ambassador.

"We thank you for your presence," she said. Her tone was utterly neutral; any hint of her voice's natural cadence was gone. "Welcome... Shaan."

The Ambassador's head tipped slightly, and Shaan held her breath as the alien pivoted abruptly toward her, examining her closely. The Felen hadn't actually seen her when she stood in this room before, in the guise of the Director of Engineering. Perhaps that particular deception had escaped the Ambassador's notice entirely. But now, she was under the alien's undeniable scrutiny.

"I am privileged to be here," she managed in a half-whisper, her throat parched. "Thank you."

"We have learned from your colleagues that you are a loyal servant of the Peace. That you were sworn to the service of the Geminus Peace Alliance," Gida said slowly. "Is this true?"

Were. Gida had used the past tense. For a nauseating few seconds, Shaan wondered if the Ambassador might be aware of her Geminus dismissal somehow. It was beyond unlikely— the Verkhoy inquest had been so highly classified that it was doubtful this low-ranking Ambassador had so much as heard of her, much less the specifics of her dismissal—but her heart skipped a beat nonetheless.

"It is true," she said.

The Ambassador raised both arms, pale long-jointed fingers stretching majestically toward the ceiling, trailing swathes of scarlet-bright sleeves.

"We do not understand how any of these strange events came to pass. But we are overjoyed to hear that we have among us a servant of the Peace and of our continued partnership," Gida said. The Ambassador's arms stretched in Shaan's direction. "How fortunate we are, that we may call upon your help and trust you fully to assist us."

Shaan let out her breath. Of *course* the Ambassador didn't know anything.

"It is my honour to serve the Peace," she said, bowing her head. "I will do what I can."

"One hundred and fifty-two of your human years ago, our peoples both stood on the brink of destruction," Gida said. "Had the siege of Etraxas not been ended when it was, we would have suffered a devastating loss of life on both sides. The Peace may have eluded us forever. Without the truce, it would only have been a matter of time before we hunted each other to our mutual extinction."

The Ambassador shifted, crimson robes rustling. The alien's expression was invisible under the beaded cowl, but it would have been impossible to read. Felen emotions never showed in their faces.

"The siege of Etraxas—the capital of humanity's Union— was a most brilliant military victory for the Felen Starhold," the Voiced said. "And yet, if Etraxas had fallen... if the full might of the Felen fleet had been unleashed, laying waste to your capital... there is no doubt that the swift retribution from the Union would have devastated us beyond imagination. The Felen fleet was stretched too thin. We were insufficiently defended elsewhere, and the Starhold's forces in the Union Quadrant would have been greatly weakened by such losses. Our resources were scarcer than anyone knew." Gida's body shivered reverently. "We were all spared from unimaginable tragedy by the miracle of the *Jonah*. We were all saved. And so it *must* be. Without the Peace, the futures of both of our species were in dire jeopardy. Do you understand how important this is?"

"Yes. Of course," Shaan whispered. "I do."

The Ambassador's head bowed then, and Gida mirrored the action. "The Voicegiver, Keila Kva-Sova, believes that it is possible to re-create the events of our Peace. To return to the time they came from, to successfully broker a truce with the

Felen Starhold, with the help of a new Decipherer. *Gida.*" One of the Ambassador's long arms stretched out from the mass of robes, sweeping toward Gida even as the Voiced continued to speak.

"This one is willing to stand in the Decipherer's place as interpreter." Gida's voice trembled as she spoke the Ambassador's next words. "Gida must join the *Jonah*, to help negotiate the Union's truce with the Felen Starhold. Do you agree with this choice?"

"I—" Shaan's heart pounded in her throat. "I'm not sure what you want me to—"

"Shaan, as a trusted servant of the Geminus Peace Alliance, you are the only human we can confer with on this matter," Gida said. "There is no other human Geminus representative here. But before you give us your verdict, there is also something else. It is our understanding that you have made acquaintance with the one named Jereth Keeven of the *Jonah*. Do you know him well?"

Shaan nearly choked. "Keeven? I've... I've spoken to him, a little bit."

"We wish so dearly to ensure the endurance of the partnership that was forged between the United Worlds of Humanity and the Felen Starhold. We will do whatever is needed. But we must know who to trust." There was another long pause before the Voiced carried on, and the Ambassador continued to stare at Shaan intently. "The Voicegiver has made her proposal, and the one named Jereth Keeven has agreed to it. But even after seeing him before us and speaking to him face to face, we still have some doubts. Can Jereth Keeven be trusted? And from what you have seen of him... is it your belief that he would make a suitable Negotiator for the Union?"

*   *   *

She found Keeven in the canteen, sitting with his boots up on one of the chairs. He was drinking another one of those pink brews, looking like he didn't have a care in the worlds. It was all Shaan could do not to tip that damn cup over his head.

She slammed her hands flat on the table in front of him.

"Keeven. I need a word with you. *Now.*"

"Well, good afternoon to you, too, prison warden," he grinned. "What's up?"

"What's *up?* How about *you went to see the gods-damned Felen Ambassador?* I thought you said there was no way you're helping the Peace Project in the first place, and now you told the Ambassador you want to be the *Negotiator?*"

Keeven snorted a laugh. "Ohhh. That."

"This isn't funny. What the fuck, Keeven? What are you playing at here?"

He motioned for her to sit down. "So, yeah, funny story. Remember how I delivered that nice, unanimous *Jonah* vote in your ZeyCorp meeting? That bit that really tipped the scales for our Last Shot proposal?" He pointed dramatically over to the vending machines, where Keila Kva-Sova was standing and staring at them anxiously. "I made a deal with Keila in exchange for her vote. And it turns out she drives a very specific bargain."

"And you had better not be taking it back, Jereth." Kva-Sova stalked toward them. Her ears were fanned out wide from her face, her irises phasing rapidly from one hue to the next. "We are going to Etraxas, we're taking Gida with us, and *you* are going to negotiate that truce. You're the best talker out of all of us."

Keeven sighed. "Look... you know there's no *way* that kid actually wants to go with us, right? She's probably under mind control or something. Does she even have a choice about it? Ugh!" He shuddered. "This Voicing shit creeps me right out."

Kva-Sova sat down across from him and tugged on his shirt-sleeve, turning him toward her. "Jereth, you know there isn't enough time for me to try the gene splice on anyone else. Finding someone compatible with the procedure isn't easy, and the process takes years! Without my lab, I don't even have any of the necessary materials. This is our only chance. We *need* Gida."

"It's never going to work anyway," he said dismissively. "I'm no gods-damned diplomat."

"But you're a con artist, right? So you can convince them you are! Improvise! Anything has to be better than doing nothing, better than not showing up, better than letting the war carry on." Kva-Sova looked over at Shaan, her eyes filling with tears. "He promised me he would help, but I know he still doesn't really believe in the Peace. Not even when he saw the proof for himself. What more can I do?"

Shaan pressed a hand to her temple. She had a pounding headache. Her blood still coursed with adrenaline, but her body felt bone-weary, her limbs heavier than usual. She could scarcely remember what she'd said to the Ambassador, besides promising to do some further investigation into Jereth Keeven's strength of character. She hadn't reported back to Captain Fransk, either. Everything was a mess.

Kva-Sova sighed sadly. "I... I don't even know *how* to do the Voicing properly. None of my subjects were ever successful in gaining the Felen language skills. Until I saw Gida, I'd almost given up hope that a human could acquire the telepathic sense and keep their sanity."

"Your first experiments never worked," Shaan said quietly. "Not according to history. You did lose a lot of people at the beginning. Before you had your breakthrough."

"Except there *was* no breakthrough," Kva-Sova said. "Only failures. Over and over again. As soon as any of my Voiced came into contact with that Felen artifact... it slowly sapped out their minds, until there was nothing left of who they were before."

"That's what happened in the historical record, too," Shaan said solemnly. "Most of your early subjects... never recovered. And a lot of them died, before the Decipherer."

"But how did I do it?" Kva-Sova whispered. "How did I succeed? If my technique is really the same one Geminus still uses for the Voicing... what did I do differently, with the Decipherer?"

"As far as we know, nothing," Shaan said. "You made the splice on her the same way you did for all the others, and she spent more time with the Felen artifact than anyone ever had, but the degenerative effects didn't happen to her. After a while, she started to grasp more of the artifact's meaning, and then she figured out some of the deeper concepts in it. The more she studied it, the more it revealed, until she taught herself enough to communicate with the Felen."

"Some of my subjects did start to sense the artifact," Kva-Sova said. "But after a while they always started to behave... strangely. At first it was small things, little quirks in how they spoke, odd behaviour. They weren't quite themselves. But it got worse, and then... it was like... they slowly degenerated into some kind of an animal state." Kva-Sova brushed away a tear. "A living nightmare."

Shaan winced.

"Ugh!" said Keeven, looking revolted. "Why in the five hells would you keep doing it to people, if that's what was happening?"

"Because we had hope," Kva-Sova said. "Hope that we would succeed, one day. It's not an easy thing to live with, but at least I was trying. Everyone in the Peace Project was trying to make a difference, to find some way to end the war." She sniffled. "I wanted to make that difference."

"You *did*," Shaan said, suddenly longing to reassure her. "You managed to give an alien sense to a human; it was one of the most remarkable achievements in history." She looked into Kva-Sova's tear-rimmed eyes. "You went on to Voice lots of other people successfully after the Decipherer. And the Voicing probably would've worked for some of the ones you lost, too, if only they'd had proper training before they were exposed to Felen artifacts."

Kva-Sova wiped at her tears. "You know... I still have no idea what that artifact does," she said. "I meant to ask Gida about it. It was recovered from a Felen ship, and the Geminus Initiative bought it on the black market. But we had no idea what it *was*. It looks like a little greyish-white cube, like nothing at all."

"Well, the one the Peace Project had was a very common type," Shaan said. "That cube was... well, sort of like a Felen concept-holder, like what we might call a novel. Or maybe more like a poem, but one that's written entirely for the telepathic sense. Experiential."

Kva-Sova nodded, her eyes wide. "Some of my subjects said the cube was *speaking* to them," she said. "But we couldn't get an answer about what it told them. And not long after, they weren't in any state to communicate."

"Wait... fuck!" Keeven said, his face aghast. "Keila! That little white cube... I *saw* that thing. You had it in your coat pocket, it was on my ship." He stared down at his hands in horror. "Gods, I *touched* it. Should I be worried?"

"You'll be fine," said Shaan. "It's just a harmless hunk of synthetics, unless you've got Felen genetic material in your skull. Unaltered humans can't sense it."

"Oh," he said, looking sheepish. "Well, uh... good."

"I just wish I could've been there," Kva-Sova whispered. "I wish I could've seen the moment when someone *understood* it."

"Yeah, I think a lot of people would like to see that. The Decipherer is kind of a big historical mystery," Shaan said. "No one knows how she managed to teach herself enough to translate a complicated political negotiation. See, just having the telepathic sense wouldn't be enough to communicate with the Felen. That would be like... suddenly being given the ability to hear, and then immediately needing to understand a spoken language you'd never encountered. The real miracle is how the Decipherer did all that without any help, with only the artifact to learn from. She had no *alihe*."

"*Alihe*," Keeven repeated the word curiously. "What's that mean?"

"It's... a teacher, or maybe more like a guide? An experienced, older Voiced that helps a novice keep their bearings until they're totally comfortable with the telepathic sense. But since the Decipherer was the very first one to be successfully Voiced, she would've had to be self-taught. No one else has ever accomplished that except her."

"Huh," said Keeven, his face inscrutable.

"So... who was she?" Kva-Sova asked hopefully. "Could we still find her? What was her name?"

Shaan shook her head. "Her name and the Negotiator's name were never recorded, because they wanted to make it clear that they stood before the Felen as representatives of humanity, not as individuals. See, Felen emissaries and leaders never show their faces or use individual names to refer to themselves, not when they're representing the Many. So we assume that the Negotiator and the Decipherer were imitating Felen diplomatic protocols."

"I guess that's why the Ambassador was wearing that weird hat," Keeven said. "Anonymity? Huh."

"And that's *exactly* why our plan can work!" Kva-Sova said, her voice rising hopefully. "If the Decipherer and the

Negotiator had no names, no faces, no recorded history... then we're hardly changing anything if you do the negotiations and we bring Gida with us! We'll be the Fortunate Five again, and we'll go to Etraxas, and we'll—"

"Keila," Keeven interrupted, holding up one hand. "Look, can you just give it a rest? I already stood in that room and had a gods-damned conversation with that Felen for you, and I think that's enough for now. I've got a lot on my mind—"

There was a loud thump from behind them, and Keeven abruptly stopped talking.

Shaan turned to see the bulky figure of of Dargo Mendeg, the *Jonah*'s engineer. His fist was still resting against the table.

"Keeven!" he thundered. "What's this? Some sort of secret meeting?"

No one spoke.

"Did you say there's a *Felen* on this ship?" Mendeg took another menacing step forward. "Is that what you just said?"

"Listen, Mendeg, this is a misunderstanding—" Keeven began.

"Is there an alien on this fucking ship? Answer me!" Mendeg repeated. "Where is it? I swear to all the gods, if I find that thing... I'm gonna kill it. I'll kill it with my bare hands."

"Mendeg, sit down." Keeven made a pacifying gesture, sounding slightly nervous. "Let's talk—"

"No! Shut your lying mouth!" the engineer shouted. "Everything you say is lies! You told me we were only going along with this Last Shot plan so you could get Charyne to draw out the S-bomb spec! I thought that's what we were doing here! Makin' sure she gets to test that bomb so we can go back there with the bomb schematics and use it on the Felen! So we can finish this gods-damned war! But no... you're all in *league* with the fuckin' aliens, the whole damn lot of you!"

Keeven got to his feet, clenching and unclenching his fists. His hands twitched. "Mendeg—"

Before Keeven could move, Mendeg launched himself forward with a guttural roar. He clambered over the neighbouring table and leapt off the other side, kicking one of the chairs so hard that it spun off its axle with a crash. He grabbed Keeven's shirt, whipped him around and punched him square in the face.

Shaan screamed.

Keeven staggered backwards. He fought to keep his balance as he caught the front of Mendeg's vest with both hands and raised a knee sharply up into the engineer's gut.

Mendeg grunted, doubled over and dropped to the floor, pulling Keeven along with him.

There was a brief scuffle, but it took only a matter of seconds for the huge, bearded engineer to overpower Keeven. He shoved Keeven down against the purple-tiled floor, pummelling his face again and again as Keeven struggled to free himself.

"You're dead, Keeven!" Mendeg shouted, slamming Keeven's head against the floor. Blood splattered over the tiles. "You fucking traitor! Liar! Scum!"

Kva-Sova huddled against the table, sobbing, covering her eyes with her hands. Shaan continued to scream.

And then Director Ozakka was at the door.

Shaan scarcely saw her move, but in a second, Ozakka had caught Mendeg around the waist and flipped him over like a doll. Keeven crawled away to one side while Ozakka pinned Mendeg face down on the tile, her hand on the back of his thick neck, her knee pressed between his shoulder blades.

"Gods damn it!" shouted Ozakka. "What are you two doing? Have you lost your minds?"

"Rot with the demons!" Mendeg spat, struggling to extricate himself from Ozakka's hold. "You filthy traitors! You'll all be licking the floor in a Felen ship when they enslave us!"

Ozakka twisted his left arm behind his back, and Mendeg shrieked in pain.

"All right. That's enough out of you," Ozakka said. "Quiet!" With one more angry contortion, Mendeg relented and finally lay still, cursing to himself.

"Good," said Ozakka. "Now, I'm going to let you up... but if you give me another problem I'm breaking bones. You got it?" She looked over at Keeven. "Same goes for you, Keeven. Get up, sit your ass in a chair, and don't move."

Keeven scrabbled up onto his knees. His whole body was shaking, and blood was streaming down his chin. One of his eyes was rapidly swelling shut. For once, he didn't come back with some smartass retort. He braced himself against the table and staggered to his feet.

Ozakka hauled Mendeg up by his armpits, then slowly released him. For a moment the big man looked like he might be about to lunge at her. But he must've thought better of it, because he pushed past Ozakka, kicked the broken chair, and stormed out of the canteen.

As soon as he'd left, Kva-Sova bolted out after him.

"Shit," Ozakka muttered. "Where's she going?" The director reached for her bracelet. "Dean! Code 55 on the residential decks! Enact all possible security, restrict access to the corridors around the Ambassador's guest suite! No one gets near there!"

"Understood. Enacting that right away," came the AI's familiar voice. There was a brief pause, and then Dean switched to a concerned tone. "Is everything all right, Director?"

"Not really," Ozakka said. "Alert Captain Fransk and Director Barnabyn that we have a security issue. I'm on my way up to Command right now to explain."

"Yes, Director," Dean said. "I'll let them know."

Ozakka closed her eyes for a moment as if to steady herself, then looked over at Keeven. He was still trying to wipe his palm over his bloodied chin, his hand shaking uncontrollably. His face was beaded with sweat, and the front of his slightly-nicer-than-usual shirt was thoroughly spattered with blood.

"Oh, my gods," Ozakka said, staring at him.

Keeven managed a half-hearted smirk. "Can't keep your eyes off this pretty face, huh, Ozakka?"

Ozakka sighed and motioned to Shaan. "Shaan... please try to clean up this mess," she said, gesturing at Keeven. "I have to go deal with the other mess now. Otherwise known as the ZeyCorp senior administration."

KEEVEN SWIPED HIS bracelet against the door panel outside his guest apartment and stormed inside, swearing under his breath.

Shaan, following on his heels, stopped awkwardly in front of the open door. She stood there clutching a small medikit to her chest, staring into the room.

It was the kind of modest space typically occupied by a deep-space researcher: a narrow bed, a low table, some storage compartments, a small adjoining lavatory. The room looked exactly like all the others. The purple-tinged furniture was ugly but functional, the garish ZeyCorp logos were all over everything. The bed was unmade, but aside from that, the only sign of the room's current inhabitant was a large black carry-bag sitting on the floor, with Keeven's tattered jacket thrown over it.

"What're you doing? Checking I didn't trash the room?" Keeven said over his shoulder.

"No, I just—I—I was..." Shaan trailed off, not sure of the answer herself.

She took a tentative step forward, fiddling with the clasp on the medikit until it fell open and scattered some of its contents onto the floor. Gritting her teeth, she bent down and started to pick up wayward packets of healing tape and vials of stims.

Keeven didn't wait for her to finish. He went into the lavatory, peeled his blood-stained shirt over his head and dropped it onto the counter next to the sink. He paused briefly to examine his wounds in the mirror before he activated the tap and started splashing handfuls of water over his face and neck. He scooped some water into his mouth and spat it out again a few times, then tilted his head down to rinse the streaks of blood from his hair.

He leaned over the sink, his back to her. Two large, circular knots of scars gnarled down his spine—stasis port scars, matching the one on his neck.

She watched him switch off the tap, then reach behind him to grab a clean towel. When he turned around, she saw that he had the Union flame tattooed over his heart—the UWDF's hexagonal military logo, in one of those antiquated ink styles that was nothing but flat red-and-black lines on his skin.

She realized that she'd stopped moving, one hand halfway to the medikit, absently holding a packet of healing strips. She stayed half-crouched on the floor and continued to stare at him. He was wearing scuffed boots, a worn-out belt and baggy trousers, standing there shirtless with his hair dripping wet, holding a bunched-up towel to his bloodied face. She was still furious with him, but there was something familiar about him now, something comforting. She had almost cared when Mendeg started punching his face in. Still, she couldn't put Mendeg's words out of her mind, and she shivered.

Keeven glared at his reflection, muttering angrily to himself as he poked at his face. Both of his cheeks were darkening with angry bruises, and a deep gash ran from his lower lip to his chin. Blood-tinged water was still running down his neck.

"You all right?" she ventured. It was a silly question.

"I'll live." Keeven flicked the towel over his shoulder toward his scarred back. "As you might've noticed back here, I've been worse off before, huh?"

"I... I wasn't looking."

"'Course you weren't." He laughed, spotting the open medikit on the floor in front of her. "I don't need any of that stuff. I'm fine."

"Fine except for how your face is split open?" She sighed. "I think I'm obligated to patch you up. You're still our guest, right? And possibly the fucking Negotiator for the Union?"

"Language! Is it really appropriate to speak to your esteemed Negotiator like that?" He smirked.

"Oh, for the gods' sake, just shut up and let me fix your face." Shaan scrambled to her feet, gathered up the medikit and blocked his way out the lavatory door. She slammed the box down onto the counter next to his bloodied shirt. "Try not to be a child about this. I'm going to put some healing strips on you. Stay still."

She peeled open the first packet, tore a piece off and plastered it underneath his left eye, giving him no warning and making no effort to be gentle about it.

"Ow!" Keeven jerked his head back. "Damn! Guess you didn't have yet another secret life as a doctor, huh?"

She glared at him, ripped off another piece and stuck it down hard onto his other cheek.

He flinched. "Gods, would you take it easy? I think it hurt less while I was getting punched!" He took another packet of healing strips out of the medikit, holding it up to examine the label. "What is this shit, anyway? It feels like it's burning my face off."

"It's going to close up your wounds." She grabbed the packet back. "It'll take down the swelling and regenerate your skin in a few hours. There's some painkillers in it too. Would you just hold still and let me do this?" She motioned for him to tilt his chin to one side. "Turn."

Surprisingly, he didn't protest. After a moment's pause, he turned his head and cooperated.

She plastered over his chin, then applied a few smaller strips to the cuts along his jaw and bottom lip. He said nothing else, just watched her with an expression of amusement, tilting his head when told. She tried not to make eye contact with him.

"There. I'm done." She picked up one of the discarded packets to check the instructions. "It says it has to stay on for four hours. Don't touch it. Just let it dry."

"You gonna look after me till then?"

She gave him an exasperated look and folded away the medikit. "You're pretty damn lucky, you know that? This would've been way worse if Ozakka hadn't pulled him off you."

"Oh, I don't know about that. I was handling it all right."

"Mendeg was destroying you."

Keeven looked offended. "He caught me off guard, fine. But he was not *destroying* me."

"Okay, whatever." She took a deep breath. "Keeven, I... I have to ask you something. That stuff Mendeg was yelling, about the S-bomb... did you really tell him all that? That you only wanted Professor Jaxong to work on the bomb so you could go back and use it against the Felen? So you could take her schematics?"

"I don't know if those were my *exact* words..." Keeven sighed. "Anyway, who cares what I said? We needed all the allies we could get behind the Last Shot plan. Mendeg wants to believe that the Union can still crush the Felen. That's hope, for him. I told him what he wanted to hear."

"So... to get their votes, you told Kva-Sova that you'll play the Negotiator and that you'll bring Gida back to help you negotiate the Peace... but you also told Mendeg that you're going back with the plans for a doomsday device to annihilate the Felen?"

"That's right," said Keeven matter-of-factly.

"You're unbelievable."

"Look, no one knows what's going to happen when we set that bomb off. This whole thing's a dice roll. I'm not making promises under oath here! I'm just covering my back." Keeven rubbed the knot of scars on his neck. "Listen, when you grow up on a dust world, when you've seen the kind of stuff I've seen... you've got to look out for yourself first, understand? Nobody but yourself, and the handful of people you trust. If you can trust anyone at all."

Keeven examined his face in the mirror one last time, then went back out into the main room. He sat down on the edge of the bed and rummaged in his black carry-bag. He tugged a crumpled grey shirt out of the bag, shook it out a couple of times and pulled it over his head, nearly dislodging one of the salve strips from his chin in the process.

"Did you know the Negotiator was from a dust world, too?" Shaan blurted. "He was born on Desmoën, same as you."

Keeven looked up, his face almost startled. "What?"

"It's true. Almost nothing is known about him... except for that one thing. His homeworld."

"Well, shit." Keeven pressed the healing strip on his chin back into place with the palm of his hand, then raked his fingers contemplatively through his damp hair. He brought his hand to his chest, his fingers brushing over his heart, where the Union flame rested under his shirt. "There was only one way off that rock during the war. The UWDF youth recruitment program. So... I guess that means your Negotiator was lifted by the deffies when he was a kid. Just like me."

"Yeah," Shaan said softly. "Just like you."

ELDRIC
Dylham Settlement
7 years before the Rift

ELDRIC WATCHED DAFNË from the doorway, committing her image to memory: her curly hair swept into an elaborate coil, the tiny iridescent chains streaming from her temples, the headband that glittered as she moved. Her eyes were fixed on the mirror in front of her as she arranged the holograms around her head. When she turned, a cascade of tiny lights followed the curve of her shoulder.

"Eldric. There you are." She gave a flicker of a smile when she saw him. "You ready?"

He didn't say anything, he just kept staring at her face. There was a sadness in her gaze when she looked at him, a crushing disappointment that he wished he could erase. They hardly spent any time in the same room lately, and the sheer size of their house meant they could go entire days without actually seeing each other.

"I wish we didn't have to go to this," he said. "I hate these things."

"Well, I don't like them either. But we have obligations, Eldric." She sighed. "This is *your* Cornerstone. Everyone will be expecting you tonight."

She motioned him closer and reached up to smooth back his hair. He closed his eyes, and for a fleeting instant, he imagined them back in her tiny apartment in the lower city. He imagined them lying in her too-narrow bed with all the plants hanging overhead, her fingers twining into his hair as he kissed her.

Things had been so unimaginably different then. Before they ran from Sëgra City, before Grenobal Bank, before Jereth got arrested, before—

He pushed the thought away.

"Eldric, let's *try* to be sociable tonight." She reached for his hand. "Please. I need you to stay with me, to keep me company. I never know what to say to these people."

She made a final adjustment to her headband, then stood up and kissed him lightly on the cheek. It was the most affection they'd exchanged in weeks.

On the landing pad outside their sprawling house, a private transport sat in wait.

ELDRIC LOATHED THE lavish Founder parties. They reminded him too much of Sëgra, of all the things they'd lost, of the awful mistakes he'd made. The minute he stepped into that glitter-encrusted gala room, he always felt ill.

Most of the other Founders of Dylham came from new money. Some of them were so-called 'wartime heirs,' who'd come into a fortune when some distant relative got wiped out by the war. Some were Latter-Worlders with little in the way of lineage, not quite rich enough or famous enough to pull off a land claim on their homeworlds. They'd all been waiting for their opportunity, waiting until an up-and-coming settlement was ready to invite new Founders.

Founders were the benefactors of arts and culture, the wealthy investors who came when a settled world was established enough to support some semblance of high society. In exchange for extravagant sums of money, Founders were granted land and—most importantly—a *legacy*. These people didn't just want to be rich; they wanted to make a name for themselves, to have libraries and theatres named after them, to leave monuments for generations to come.

Eldric didn't want to make a name for himself. All he wanted was to disappear, and these ridiculous obligations wore on him like a yoke. Couldn't they just take his money and leave him alone?

For the most part, he'd become something of a philanthropic recluse, but the season opening of the dreamhouse was the one occasion he couldn't avoid. The dreamhouse was his Founding Cornerstone, his personal contribution to Dylham's blossoming society, funded directly from the money he'd paid for his Founder's rights. He'd made his forced appearances at each season-opening gala, but he'd never actually set foot inside the theatre, not even when Dafnë performed. *Especially* not when Dafnë performed.

Sometimes he wondered if it hurt her that he didn't watch the plays, but she always seemed relieved when he said he wasn't going. The dreamhouse was his gift, after all—not to the settlement, but to her. He'd given her back at least one thing she'd lost.

And he'd given her a place to weave a world without him in it.

AT THE GALA, Dafnë did her best to compensate for Eldric's awkward silences. He orbited her, smiling politely, laughing when she laughed. But each time they did this, the pretense felt exponentially heavier.

She barely looked at him, and after a while, she drifted away. She was drawn into a conversation that he never joined, pulled away by some acquaintance who wanted to introduce her to a newcomer. She was a pace away from Eldric, then three paces, then five, and then she was a glimmer of gold in the moving crowd. She didn't look back for him, and he didn't follow her. Instead, he made his way to the bar, and pointed at the first drink on the menu.

It was a strong, sweet blue liquor, served in an ornate chalice, and it tasted as unbearably artificial as this room felt. He choked it down and ordered another one.

Dafnë didn't come back.

He ordered another.

By the time his fifth chalice was empty, Eldric was no longer bothered by the swell of noise in the room. He watched other people sliding past him as though through an invisible force field. The cacophony of voices, the glitter and feathers and holograms and clinking glasses, it all flowed past him like he wasn't even there. He imagined the calming permutations of a subspace stream behind his eyelids, picturing the 5D transforms surrounding him as he dropped a ship neatly into the stream, and the image soothed him.

Through his half-closed eyes, he could see the little flicker of gold in the crowd, and he knew exactly where Dafnë was standing. He remembered the first time he'd recognized her from a distance on Sëgra… the first time he'd seen her outside a dreamhouse illusion.

I'm Dafnë Valay.

She seemed as unreachable as one of her illusions now, as ethereal and insubstantial as that wood-nymph, and the pain tightened in his chest. He felt lonelier than he'd ever been.

His island of tranquillity evaporated; all around him the room was spinning with chaos again. The noise was deafening, his senses swam with too many colours and reflections. He needed to get out.

Scrambling to his feet, he abandoned his table and went in search of an exit. After he'd circled half the room, he came upon the door to a small terraced balcony, mercifully empty. Eldric shouldered the fancy door open and stumbled outside.

He hadn't noticed just how drunk he was until now, but he had to hold the balcony rail to keep the ground from spinning away under him. What in the five hells was he even doing here? Why had he come to this planet?

He could almost hear Jereth's voice in his head: *Oh, come on, Leeg. Don't be so melodramatic. Everything's gonna be fine.*

He leaned against the railing and looked up into the night, where the blurred halos of a few stars broke through in a mostly-overcast greyish sky. They glowed down at him, their ancient stares indifferent.

He could hardly believe that he'd once been somewhere among them. His life before Dylham felt like a half-remembered fever dream. And yet that life had existed. Sëgra City, The Night Palace, the gambling-houses, the little apartment, Grenobal Bank, the Dome Theatre... and *Jereth*.

Jereth was still out there somewhere, a ghost that might never wake. A number on a casket in a stasis prison. A frozen body as lifeless as Eldric felt.

This time, Eldric didn't push the thought away. He held onto the rail for balance, tilting his head up toward the stars.

None of this was worth it, was it, Jerry... What a waste. What a gods-damned fucking waste.

How bitter it tasted, this freedom Eldric had been gifted.

THE SOUND OF the balcony door opening startled him, and Eldric turned unsteadily. He saw a flash of gold, then he felt Dafnë grabbing his arm as he lost his balance.

"Eldric! Where've you been? I was looking everywhere for you!"

"Sorry... I was... I just..." He staggered against her, all too aware that he was slurring his words. "Ah, shit, Dafnë. I... I was coming right back—"

"Oh my gods. How much have you had to drink?"

"Not that much," he said weakly.

"We need to go home," she whispered. "Come on. You're a mess. Follow me, and *please* try to walk in a straight line."

WHEN ELDRIC OPENED his eyes again, he was back in their transport. He couldn't recall getting in, but he was slumped over in one of the plush seats, his head resting against the window. The blur of Dylham's rolling hills was rushing past in grey shadows, and they were almost back at home.

He vaguely remembered exchanging goodbyes with a few guests at the gala. He remembered Dafnë's hands guiding him down the stone stairs out of the building.

And he remembered how upset she'd looked.

In the adjoining seat, she sat with her shoulders stiff, her expression unreadable. Her holograms glinted under the transport's ambient light.

He reached for her hand. "Hey... I... I'm sorry about the party. I didn't mean to—"

"Eldric, sometimes you're just so bloody selfish." She sucked in a breath through her teeth. "Honestly, you're starting to remind me of Jaymi."

"Don't," Eldric mumbled, bitterness welling in his throat. "Don't talk about'm like that. He was... my best friend."

"Oh, please." Dafnë sighed. "Jaymi Hanioch was his own best friend. He did exactly *one* selfless thing in his entire life, to get you out of the mess *he* fucking caused in the first place!" She tugged on Eldric's sleeve. "Why did you do that to me tonight, Eldric? I said I needed you to keep me company, and you just... *left* me out there with those people!"

"I told you I didn't want to go," he said quietly. "We could have stayed at home."

"You think I like this any more than you do? You're the one who wanted to be a fucking Founder, Eldric! You brought us here! Take some gods-damned responsibility!"

She turned away and looked out the opposite window. Eldric's vision swam, and he slumped over in the seat, trying not to throw up.

When the transport glided to a stop in front of their mansion, he was crying into his hands. Dafnë disembarked first, and when he made no effort to get out, she took him by both shoulders and hauled him out the door.

He dropped to his knees on the slim strip of grass between the landing pad and the walkway, still sobbing. She knelt on the walkway beside him.

"Eldric, please. Come on, stand up and walk to the house. Please."

At last, he let her pull him back to his feet and nudge him in the right direction. She looped her arm around his waist and they stumbled together into the house.

The nearest room to the entrance hall was the downstairs salon, an entertainment room full of VR systems that were never turned on and stacks of decorative blankets that hadn't even been unrolled. With just a few gestures at the salon's control panel, the ceiling could glow with stars and galaxies, the floor could be carpeted with emerald moss surrounding a twinkling river. And yet it remained as empty and silent as the day it was installed.

Eldric hated that room, as unfinished as everything they'd ever tried to do in this house, but she steered him in there and sat him down on one of the plush sofas. She rested her hand on his back.

"Gods. What are we doing with our lives, Eldric?" Her voice sounded small and defeated.

"A damn good question."

She didn't look at him. "I thought you wanted us to be happy."

"I tried, Dafnë! I thought... you said you wanted to leave Sëgra City. You wanted to live on a green world, to see rain and real grass and all that shit. I tried to give you what you wanted!"

"What *I* wanted?" She looked incredulous. "Eldric, I lost everything! My friends, my career, everything I worked for! It took me *years* to get promoted to lead animator! I had so much left to do... I had a life there! And you took it away from me!"

"But—"

"I asked you to send me your favourite song for that archive because I wanted to save a piece of you. I wanted to *know* you! Instead, you hacked the central data portal and gave me everyone *else's* favourite songs. You never understood a damn thing about what I wanted, did you?"

"Dafnë, that's not fair—"

"I said it would be nice to live on a green world *someday*. I don't remember asking to become a fucking Founder, or asking to get smuggled off Sëgra like some kind of fugitive because *you* got led on by that asshole Jaymi—"

"Don't!" Eldric shouted. "Don't you say that. He could've turned me in, but he didn't. He saved my life!"

"He *ruined* your life!" she screamed back. "This isn't your burden to bear! You don't owe him anything. You have to let this go."

Eldric staggered to his feet unsteadily. "I wouldn't be here if it wasn't for him."

"And? Is this really such a good place to be?" she whispered.

"I... I just wanted to be where you are." Eldric could barely choke out the words. "Because I loved you."

She was silent for a long time before she spoke again. "Do you still love me now?"

"You know I do, Dafnë." He paused. "Do you still... love me?"

She avoided his eyes. "I'm trying, Eldric. But sometimes, I think I might have been happier without you."

She dissolved into heaving sobs then, curling into a ball on the sofa cushion. He rested his palm against her tear-stained cheek, his fingers tangling in the golden chains at her temples.

"I'm so sorry, Dafnë. I... don't know what to do. I just—"

He bent his head toward her hesitantly. Before he could finish his sentence, she took him by the shoulders and kissed him hard, taking him by surprise. She wrapped her arms around him, pressing her body into his as though to close the invisible distance between them.

"I want it to be like the good times," she murmured against his ear. "Make it like the good times again, Eldric, please..."

He pulled her close to him and kissed her. As his hands followed the familiar curves of her body, the vise of regret in his ribcage eased for just a moment. He closed his eyes and imagined himself back in Sëgra City, where the future had seemed limitless and the sun never rose.

ELDRIC WOKE UP on the sofa. He lifted his pounding head, looking around. A cold rain was sleeting against the window, a mass of low-hanging grey clouds obscuring the rolling hills in the distance.

Dafnë was sitting on the windowsill, looking out at the rain, her legs tucked up under her. Her dark hair spilled past her shoulders, half of her curls still caught up in yesterday's web of holograms, the rest of them cascading down her back. She'd wrapped herself in one of the decorative blankets, pulling it up to her chin against the chill. Her gold sheath was on the floor, next to Eldric's rumpled clothes.

He sat up, and her eyes met his. She'd been crying again.

"Eldric," she said quietly. "I think... maybe we should take some time apart."

His skin turned to ice; her words froze in the air in front of him.

"What?"

"Please don't look at me like that." She sighed. "You know you aren't happy either. We can't go on like this. All we do is argue."

He nodded silently, feeling as though he was disconnecting from his body.

"I don't mean forever, Eldric. Just for a little while. To get our bearings again."

He didn't speak for a long time. He stared at the floor, wondering what he should feel. It didn't seem possible he would ever feel anything besides the crushing numbness in his chest.

"Say something," she pleaded.

"Fine," he said at last. "I... I can probably get a jump job. I'll go into space for a few months. Is that far enough apart for you?"

Eldric was sorely out of practice—he hadn't done a single subspace jump since right before he met Jereth—but his commercial record would still be impressive enough to land a new contract. Jump architects usually had short careers, and with wartime trade sanctions still on, there was always somebody looking to replace one.

"Oh, not a jump job! No, that's too dangerous." Tears filled Dafnë's eyes. "You've got enough money to last the rest of your life. Why would you go back into space, Eldric?"

"I thought you said you'd be happier without me." He leaned down to pick up his clothes, crumpling the fancy shirt in his hand. "I might be just out of practice enough to solve our problems for good."

UMA
Common Deck, ZeyCorp Gallion

UMA AND THE engineers sat together in the canteen, but the conversation was minimal. A crackling, nervous tension hung between them. Keeven and Leesongronski sat a couple of tables over, looking equally maudlin. The rest of the *Jonah* crew were nowhere to be seen.

The healing strips had done their work on Keeven's face, but the skin under his eyes was still marred with fading bruises, and a faint reddish line ran down from his mouth where his lip and chin had been split open. With his rumpled shirt and dishevelled hair, he looked so unlike the majestic Negotiator. It wasn't *possible*. But then... something like a sliver of hope crept into the corners of her mind. Maybe Zel was right about sending Gida with the *Jonah*. Even Fransk couldn't deny that it all made some kind of sense, despite his continued protestations. What were the chances of everything lining up just like this? The *Gallion* happened to be carrying a Felen diplomat with a Voiced interpreter on board. The *Jonah* had the supplies they needed to make an escape attempt. And what about the fact that there was a Geminus station out there, a symbol of the living Peace? It *had* to mean something. That the Peace wasn't unreachable. That their future wasn't dead.

"So... what should we do now, Director Ozakka?" Syru asked, startling her out of her thoughts.

"I could go up to the lounge and practice on *MeteoRacers Ultimate* one more time," Mikolai said, pushing away his empty food wrapper.

"I should double-check the repeater settings on the relay," said Noussen.

"No. No more work," said Uma, holding up both hands. "Captain's orders. We regroup in seven hours. You need to relax. Sleep. Talk to each other about... anything other than this."

"A strong drink would be nice," Leesongronski muttered from the next table. "Anyone got a bottle of decent agnathe?"

No one answered.

A moment later, Keeven stood up. He said something to Leesongronski, then patted him on the shoulder, flashed an encouraging smile at the Engineering team, and walked out.

Leesongronski slumped over in his chair as he watched Keeven leave. He didn't look away until Keeven had turned the corner, and then he went back to staring at his untouched dinner, his expression dejected.

One by one, the *Gallion* crew also disappeared off into the corridor. The engineers hugged each other tightly as they each departed, whispering words of hope and encouragement. It felt strangely like a goodbye.

Mikolai and Syru were the last to go, and Uma waved over her shoulder as the two of them walked hand in hand to the exit.

When she turned around again, only Leesongronski remained in the canteen. A half-finished beverage sat in front of him, next to the still unopened box with *ZeyCorp Food Services* printed across the top. He had lit up a cigarette, and he was gazing intently into the smoke that drifted in front of his face, slowly swirling one finger through it.

Watching him, she was seized with that familiar wave of awe that had never quite worn off. That was Eldric Leesongronski—*the* Leesongronski, the Pathfinder, captain of the *Jonah*. The Last of the Greats.

In quiet moments, it still seemed as unbelievable as it had on the first day. She continued watching him as he carefully unsealed the food container, prising it open along three sides. He ashed his cigarette into the hollow lid, then looked over at her.

"What're you staring at, Ozakka? This?" He held up the cigarette, rolling his eyes. "You can let me off for breaking the rules this one time, hmm?"

Uma laughed softly. "It's fine. All ZeyCorp regulations are currently suspended."

"Come sit here, would you? Don't just stare at me." Leesongronski motioned at the chair across from him. "I'm about to eat my dinner. I'm sure it's going to be absolutely riveting."

He sucked on the cigarette and leaned back in his chair, half-closing his eyes. When he lifted his hand to his mouth, Uma caught sight of the sun-seal scar on his wrist, the doubled ray coiling out from under the edge of his black sleeve.

She sat down slowly. "Professor Leesongronski... would it be all right if I asked you another personal question?"

He gave a long, pained sigh. "Go on, then."

"You're sure you don't mind?"

"Would it stop you if I did?" He flicked the cigarette again.

She gave him a small smile. "So... well, I... I'm curious what your relationship with Dafnë Valay was like."

Leesongronski's eyes snapped wide open, his face disquieted.

"See, all the major biographies of you have such different opinions about her," Uma continued. "About your relationship. And... I've always wondered what the truth really was."

Leesongronski gave a mirthless laugh.

"The truth?" he said derisively. "I still ask myself the same damn thing, and I was there. What *is* the truth?" He took a long drag from his cigarette. "Dafnë was a celestial being. She was too good for me. She loved me, but we were a mistake, and I never deserved her. I lied to her, I disappointed her, and then I left her to die alone. That enough truth for you?"

He didn't say anything else for a long time. He sat there looking straight through Uma, twirling the dwindling cigarette between his fingers, gazing up into the bluish smoke. She thought about getting up and leaving, but that felt far too awkward.

"I was going to turn back to Dylham, you know," he finally said, his voice nearly inaudible. "I boarded the ship that was taking me to meet the company that hired me, but then I changed my mind on the way. Decided I'd try one more time to make things right with Dafnë." He blinked, pausing to wipe a palm over his eyes. "I was going to get off the ship and turn back. But when we docked at the next outpost, there was something wrong. People were in a panic, everyone was gathered around the news-kiosks, watching the feeds coming in. It was all over every news network... *disaster, tragedy, deadly strike*. The Felen destroyed one of our planetary settlements. Everything levelled, no survivors on Dylham."

"I'm... so sorry," Uma whispered.

"Don't be sorry. Not for me, anyway. I'm an asshole."

He stubbed the end of his cigarette into the lid of the food container, then lifted one of ZeyCorp's dry, flavourless grain buns out of the other half of the box and started eating it.

Uma sat and watched him eat in silence. When he'd finished his dinner, he went over to the vending machine and collected another beverage. He stood there for what felt like ages, and when he turned back around, she was sure he was going to walk away and never speak to her again. But instead, he returned to the table and sat back down across from her.

"So, Ozakka," he said, lighting up another cigarette. "You sure do know a hell of a lot about my life story. But what about you?" He gestured toward her wrist, pointing at her sun-seal scar. "What was *your* relationship like, with... whoever has the other half of that?"

"Uh..." She blinked, taken aback. "It's, uh, not that interesting."

"No excuses. It's your turn now," Leesongronski said. "Tell me about them."

He twirled the cigarette with a self-satisfied look on his face, waiting.

"Okay, ah... let's see." Uma cleared her throat, wishing she had something to drink. "Her name is Halli. She's from Anvaelia, like me. And... she also loves history."

Leesongronski looked amused, waving his hand for her to continue.

"More? What else... um... Halli's a peacekeeper. She works for Border Security." Uma took a breath. "She works for Geminus."

"Oh, great. Another one," Leesongronski said. "Does everybody in the whole damn Union work for Geminus now?"

"Not at all," she said, almost laughing. "I've never met anyone from Geminus besides Halli. Well, and now Shaan. It's just another one of our strange coincidences, I guess."

Leesongronski rolled his eyes. "So, how'd you two meet?"

Uma glanced down at the table. "War History Society. She was the president of our chapter, because of *course* she was." Uma smiled. "See, Halli is one of those incredibly annoying people, the type that's just so damn good at *everything* that you wanna hate them, you know? Brilliant artist, talented at her job, great public speaker, stunningly good-looking, amazing in bed..."

Leesongronski smirked. "And let me guess, a bit of a smartass? Kind of stuck up about it?"

Uma laughed despite herself. "Hah. Well, maybe a little bit. But she's actually one of the kindest people I've ever met. Always looking for ways to serve humanity." Uma sighed. "Sometimes I wished she *was* more of a jerk, so I could make sense of what happened. The thing is... Halli always had this absolute, clear vision about what she wanted to accomplish in life. She believes in destiny, like every little thing that happens was *meant* to be that way. She doesn't compromise. And... well, I'm not so great at it either. Compromise, I mean."

Leesongronski puffed on his cigarette, then blew the smoke out slowly. "How come you two broke up?"

"Oh, lots of reasons. Different life goals, being long distance... Halli got stationed out on the border, so we were apart for months at a time. After she got back, she got promoted again, and we could hardly ever communicate because the work she was doing was classified. She was always on a comms blackout." Uma leaned on the table, resting her chin on her hand. "She got offered a permanent posting, way out in the far reaches of the border zone. But I stayed in the Anvaelian system, because I was working on some restoration projects with my father. Papa and I used to restore vintage ships. We specialized in rebuilding and modernizing war-era models, equipping them with modern jump systems to make them spaceworthy."

"Oh. Wow," Leesongronski said.

Uma paused, swallowing hard. "Then six years ago, after my father died, I guess I... kind of went into a spiral. I couldn't face staying in our family home without him, so I closed our restoration workshop down. I said I wanted to go into space for a while. Halli told me she wanted to get back together, and she asked me to come out to the border zone and be with her. Geminus was recruiting engineers for the watchfleet at the time. I was more than qualified, and she wanted me to apply, but... I couldn't do it. I applied to work for ZeyCorp instead. We argued badly, and... we just never talked again. That was it."

Leesongronski arched a dark eyebrow. "Why didn't you want to apply for that Geminus job?"

"Because their engineering jobs were all on armed ships. The Geminus peacekeeping watchfleet has weapons. And I'm a Pledged engineer."

He looked at her blankly. "Which means...?"

Uma hesitated. "I can explain, but, um... it's got to do with the end of the war with the Felen. Will it bother you if I talk about the war?"

Leesongronski waved his hand impatiently. "Just talk, Ozakka."

She took a long breath. "So, right before the Peace happened, the Union was planning a counterattack to try to break the siege of Etraxas. The UWDF was gathering a specialized assault squadron to attack the Felen siege fleet. It would've been a suicide mission, and the Union probably knew that." She paused. "Most war historians think the UWDF could've forced the Felen back, but not before the Felen unleashed everything they had on Etraxas. The whole surface population would've been lost if the UWDF engaged the Felen inside the Etraxan system. This is the outcome that Zel's worried about... if the *Jonah* had never arrived."

Uma watched Leesongronski's face as she spoke. He flinched when she mentioned the potential casualties, but when she stopped talking, he waved his hand again for her to continue.

"Well, fortunately, that assault on the siege fleet never happened," she said. "It was called off because of an incident on one of the big Union bases. A team of UWDF subspace engineers objected to the attack plan, and they refused to work on the assault fleet. They said they weren't willing to risk the destruction of Etraxas, to sacrifice all the human lives on the Capital for one strike on the Felen. Their refusal caused a delay to the launch of the Union's fleet... and in the meantime, the *Jonah* had arrived. The Negotiator and the Decipherer managed to secure the truce."

"Hm," said Leesongronski. He ashed his cigarette.

"The siege of Etraxas was withdrawn peacefully. Not a single life was lost on the planet. The peace talks went on for a while yet before a lasting partnership with the Felen was established, but the end of that siege was effectively the end of the war. Those engineers saved billions of lives when they refused their orders, knowing they could be tried for treason."

She paused, but Leesongronski said nothing.

"After the Peace, most of those engineers vowed never to work on an armed ship again," she said. "And since then, some engineers choose to become Pledged when they graduate. We make the same oath, never to use the skills we learned on an armed ship. Not even a peacekeeping vessel. I never could've worked for the Geminus watchfleet and kept my oath."

Leesongronski frowned, seeming to contemplate her words. "So... what was your relationship with Halli really like, then?" he asked pointedly. "Is all that, what you just said, *the truth?* Are you really sure that's exactly what happened?"

"Point taken." Uma winced. "I'm sorry. Really. I shouldn't have asked you that before."

"Don't worry about it."

"Gods. I haven't talked about Halli in such a long time," Uma whispered. "The thing about me and her is... that I... I still..." She choked on the words, and had to wipe at unexpected tears with the back of her hand. "Shit. Wow, this is really embarrassing."

Leesongronski leaned back and pointed the stub of his cigarette at her with a searching look. "You still love her."

Uma shrugged. "What does it matter now?"

"That's a 'yes,' then." Leesongronski gave a smile that was just a little too sad to be smug. "Got some regrets after all, hmm? Well, maybe you should say something to her. When you get back."

Uma shook her head, blinking back tears. "We haven't spoken in six years. And if the timeline has changed... then Halli... she might not even..." Uma squeezed her eyes shut, the unspoken possibility closing around her heart like an icy fist. "We don't know if the people we love even *exist* anymore, do we? We don't know if *anything* will be the same." One determined tear escaped from under her eyelid then, and she slapped it angrily from her cheek. "Fuck."

When she opened her eyes, Leesongronski was staring down at his left wrist. He pushed back his sleeve and ran one finger over the rays of his lopsided sun-seal scar, then swiftly crushed his cigarette into the empty food container and closed the lid.

"Well," he said quietly, "if you do get another chance to talk to her... don't waste it."

He took his black jacket from the back of the chair and folded it over his arm, standing to leave.

"Hey—ah, hey. Wait! Professor—about that drink..." Uma grabbed the edge of his jacket. "I do have a nice bottle of agnathe. In my apartment. If you... still want...?"

He looked at her for a long time, then gave a small bob of his head.

"Yeah," he said. "Yeah. That would be good."

She got up. They walked out to the nearest lift together and she called it.

As the lift doors slid open, she turned to him. "Thank you," she whispered. "For agreeing to help us out, with the station and everything.... I know you don't think it's a great plan."

"Oh, well," he said. "What's one more terrible decision at this point?"

She looked at him, unsure if he was joking or not. He didn't crack a smile. When they stepped out of the lift, he walked a half-step behind her down the deserted hallway, following her silently until they reached the door to her apartment.

Uma unlocked her door.

"Well... here we are," she said with an awkward laugh. "Décor courtesy of ZeyCorp." The lights came on, illuminating the garish purple logo on the storage hutch next to the door.

Leesongronski looked around the room and chuckled. "Wow. This is half the size of our ship's whole living space." He swung his arms around and turned in a slow circle. "You should see the inside of the *Jonah*. We were sleeping on the *floor* in that damn thing."

"I *would* like to see that, you know," Uma said. "I'd love to get on board the *Jonah* and just... take a look around."

The look Leesongronski gave her was unimpressed, bordering on pitying.

"Hey, I'm serious!" she protested. "It's the *Jonah*! We have songs and poems about that ship."

"Ugh." Leesongronski grimaced. "Believe me, it'll be a letdown. You could ask Jereth if you want to go on board that badly, but—"

He trailed off mid-sentence, staring into the room over her shoulder.

"Oh, you've got to be kidding," he growled. He strode past her into the middle of the room and snatched up her model *Jonah* from the table where she'd left it, flipping the little ship over in his hands with an expression of faint disgust. "Gods. You have a *model* of our ship?"

"Hey, be careful!" she gasped. "I built that years ago! It's delicate!"

"A model *Jonah*," he repeated. He didn't put it down. Instead, he lifted the little ship up over his head, tracing a fingernail over the seams on the miniature hull. "Shit. This is actually pretty accurate."

"I've been interested in the *Jonah*'s voyage for a long time," Uma said, holding her hands out protectively underneath the model. "Ever since I was a child. You know, ah... *you* were one of the reasons I decided to study subspace. It was partly because of you."

Leesongronski's dark eyebrows knitted together, and he lowered the ship.

"Because of *me?*"

"My father wasn't just an expert on restoring vintage ships. He was a historian of the *Jonah*'s voyage. He was a curator of the *Jonah* Museum on Anvaelia, so I've known about your life pretty much forever." She paused. "Professor Leesongronski, I've watched every university lecture you ever recorded, dozens of times. And... gods, you were such an inspiration to me, always. That incredible life you lived, the way you talked about the subspace jumps, it was just so beautiful..."

Leesongronski set the model ship back down on the table, then wiped his hands off on his trousers like he'd touched something dirty.

"I don't know what you're talking about," he said. "I taught first-year students the basic principles of subspace physics and 5D mathematics. They were hardly awe-inspiring lectures."

"Oh, not those. I meant the lectures that you did after the *Jonah* voyage," she said. "I guess you haven't done any of those yet. But after the Peace was made, you were *famous*. Everyone wanted to meet you. You gave talks all over the Union. My great-grandfather met you once, when you visited your old university campus on Anvaelia. He was there in the crowd, and you looked right at him. When you came down from the stage, you touched his shoulder... He told that story all his life."

Leesongronski said nothing for a long time.

"What did I *do*, exactly?" he finally asked. "Why was I so famous? I mean... the others negotiated the Peace, and Keila did the Voicing, and Charyne built some kind of infinite energy drive. I get that stuff, but... what's it all got to do with me?"

Uma looked at him and took a deep breath. "Well, you found the miracle jump, for one thing," she said. "The *Jonah* found a brand new jump route. That's how you got to Etraxas so quickly."

He gave a brusque laugh. "A new jump route, with that junker? No chance. The *Jonah* doesn't even have the right dive shielding for exploratory jumps. That hull would go to pieces if you went the slightest bit off-stream."

She sighed. "Well, I guess in our timeline the *Jonah* was a little different, then," she said quietly. "You jumped it to Etraxas through the Girum Vela subspace stream."

"Never even heard of that one."

"Oh... well, of course you wouldn't have. The Union hadn't discovered it yet," she said. "It was uncharted! You did that, too." She smiled. "After the Peace, you discovered loads more new jump routes. You found more new pathways than anyone in ten generations. You revolutionized travel, linked so many Union systems in new ways..."

"Hm," he said, his face inscrutable.

"They called you the Pathfinder, the Last of the Greats. They say you were just as good as the jump architects who discovered the Latter Worlds."

"You do know I've never found a totally new stream before, right?" Leesongronski looked doubtful. "And that I haven't jumped professionally in years? Sure, I agreed to go with Jereth when he needed a jump architect, but that was... more of a personal favour."

She frowned. "Agreed to go with Jereth where?"

"To Fedraya," Leesongronski said. "That's where we were heading, with the *Jonah*. We were supposed to be meeting a ditch ship there. That's the ship I was going to jump with. We were going to leave Union space."

"Gods," she whispered. "So you *were* taking all those weapons to a ditch ship."

He nodded solemnly, skimming his fingers over the top of the model *Jonah*.

"I have missed it, you know. Working as a jump architect," he said. "I went back to commercial jumping for a while after Dylham... after Dafnë was gone. I took that job with the shipping company after all. But the big corporations were starting to get nervous about Felen hostilities, and they started closing down their inter-system operations. After a couple years, the company I was jumping for shut down, so I ended up going to work at this shitty little tech university in the Almant system." He wrinkled his nose. "'First Foundations and Principles of Subspace'... that was the course I taught. Ugh. I fucking hated teaching, but at least it was something to do. I ended up staying at that university for four or five years, or whatever it was, and then..."

He trailed off, seeing Uma's expression. "Shit. You already know this," he said. "You knew that entire story, didn't you?"

"Yes. You were teaching for five years," she said quietly. "You left Dylham seven years before the Peace, and then you worked for the shipping company for two years before they shut down, and you got the job at the university right after that, so... it must've been five." She stopped herself. "Oh, gods. I'm sorry. This must be really weird."

"How about we have that drink, huh?" he said grimly. "What've you got?"

Uma went over to the shelf where the intricately carved bottle of Etraxan agnathe rested on its ornate stand. She lifted it out carefully and looked at the inscription on the label, her neck prickling as she passed it over to Leesongronski.

"It's a rare vintage," she whispered. "Look."

He took the heavy bottle from her hands and held it up to the light, examining the golden liquid inside before he squinted at the date on the inscription.

"Next year," he said. "This was made... next year?"

"The season after the Peace," Uma said. "One hundred and fifty-one years ago."

"Damn."

"This came from Etraxas, from Denarba Vineyard. It's made from the fruit that was growing during the siege... the harvest that never would've happened if it hadn't been for the Fortunate Five," Uma said. "When I finished university and I officially became a Pledged engineer, my father gave it to me. He got it from a friend, who got it from her grandmother, whose uncle got it from an Etraxan client..." Her voice shook. "After my father died, I... I gave away most of his things. I was too sad to talk about it, too sad to think about it... I just couldn't stand to be reminded that he was gone. This bottle is one of the only things of his that I have left."

Leesongronski traced the crystal base. "You really sure you want to open this?"

"Yeah," she whispered. "I'm sure."

She pressed two fingers to her lips, then reached out and touched her father's image on the shelf. He stood as resolute as ever in his museum uniform, gazing silently out from his frame.

"Papa gave me that bottle to remind me to stand by my convictions," Uma said. "He told me, 'Never forget that if those engineers hadn't followed their instincts, then this fruit would never have been picked, and the vines of Denarba would've been ashes.' He said that when you know you're doing the right thing, you have an obligation to stand your ground, even if everyone says it's impossible. And that's exactly what we're doing right now, isn't it?" She straightened the frame. "He would want me to open it."

Leesongronski examined the picture. "That's him there, huh?

Curator of the *Jonah* Museum... damn. No wonder you're so into all this."

"Papa taught me so many things. Everything, really. How to respect the workings of the universe, how to code dive shielding for vintage ships, how to be a good person... I could always count on him."

"You look a lot like him, too."

"Oh, I know. It's that distinctive nose, right?" She smiled tearfully, then looked back at Leesongronski. "I wish I could tell him I'm opening this agnathe with the Last of the Greats."

Leesongronski shuffled back to the table and set the bottle down next to the little *Jonah*. Uma retrieved two small reusable ZeyCorp drinking-glasses from her storage cupboard.

They sat down across from one another, both silently staring at the bottle between them.

She nudged it toward him. "Please. You do it."

With delicate precision, Leesongronski lifted one corner of the silver foil around the bottle's neck and peeled it away. He activated the uncorking mechanism.

There was a click as the cork rotated up and out. An old-fashioned hologram floated up from the cork: a spinning globe of Etraxas, all its cities lighting up and painting the map in hues of white and gold. The location of Denarba Vineyard glowed with a single bright blue dot on the coast of the smallest continent. Uma caught her breath.

Leesongronski poured two drinks, filling each glass to the bottom edge of the ZeyCorp logo.

Somehow, she managed to reach out and lift her glass to her mouth, her heart pounding. She tipped it back just enough to let the agnathe touch her lips. The Etraxan vintage was extremely strong, bittersweet, with a hint of spice that she couldn't quite place.

Leesongronski lifted his own glass and drank at the same

time. He nodded appreciatively and took another little sip.

The two of them sat in reverent silence, drinking slowly, neither of them speaking. After a while, Uma let her eyelids flutter closed, her head swimming with exhaustion and the rush of strong alcohol in her veins.

When she opened her eyes, Leesongronski had picked up the bottle again. He had switched off the hologram, but now the ambient light was catching the carved crystal in the bottle's base, making luminous lines dance across his face.

"You went to visit Denarba Vineyard, you know," Uma said quietly. "On Etraxas, after the Peace... right before this harvest. There's a beautiful image of you walking between the vines with one hand out, like this... with your head tilted back like you're looking toward the sky..." She leaned her head back. "It's on the cover of my favourite biography of yours—*Under Fortunate Stars*. I've always wondered what you were thinking about, at the exact moment when that picture was taken."

"Well, I can tell you what I'm thinking about right now," he said. "I'm thinking... you're telling me this is a vintage bottle, and it sure does taste like a well-aged agnathe, but that year on the label there is *next year*." He paused. "Tomorrow, Jereth's gonna fly out into that void, in a shuttle using experimental shield mods, moving through a form of energy none of us have seen before. I'm going to hack a space station that shouldn't be here, to get Charyne access to a drive she hasn't invented yet, so that she can turn it into a superweapon she *has* already invented... and here we are, sitting on a ship from the future, having this conversation... drinking this drink."

He reached for his glass, tipped back the last mouthful of agnathe, then set it back down on the table with a *clink*.

"Maybe it *is* destiny," said Uma. "That's what Halli would say. I mean, you being here, the station being here, the Ambassador, the Voiced... it all fits together. You even had weapons-grade lenanium cabling, for fuck's sake!" She gave a decisive nod. "If we're all fated to be here, then the mission must be meant to succeed. And our plan has to work. There's nothing to worry about, right?"

"That almost sounds like it makes sense," Leesongronski said. "Maybe I'm drunk already, huh? This is strong stuff."

"It's a nice agnathe, isn't it?"

"Mmm-hmm. A damn nice agnathe."

"Shall we have one more for luck?" She picked up the bottle.

"There's no such thing as luck." Leesongronski reached up to his collar and pulled out the fortune charm, twirling the chain around his finger. "But... it's worth a shot, right?"

"Oh, definitely," she whispered.

He nudged his empty glass toward her with the ghost of a smile. "Go on, then. One more for luck."

She topped up his glass, then hers, and they drank.

JERETH

Nightship *Aeglaca*
5 years before the Rift

When Jereth awoke, the first thing he was aware of was the darkness. It wasn't the kind of dark you see when you're blindfolded. It wasn't the empty, soulless dark of deep space. No, this darkness was thick and cold and liquid, and it poured over him like syrup. It poured into him, freezing his lungs, filling him with a desperate panic. He couldn't tell if his eyes were open or not. He was choking for air. He thought he was screaming, but he couldn't even be sure of that; his ears detected nothing but a still, impenetrable silence.

He realized with terror that he couldn't feel any of his limbs. Did he even *have* a body anymore? Was he dead?

His mind was chaotic with disjointed images, flashes of memory—but that was the only thought he managed to unravel before he lost consciousness again. Everything disappeared for a long while.

The next time Jereth woke, he struggled to open his eyes. His eyelids felt heavy. He still couldn't move his head, and he could distinguish nothing but vague shapes. It was still dark, but the darkness no longer held that syrupy weight. He could hear sounds again: the soft rasp of his own laboured breathing, the hum of an air vent, the distant thrum of engines.

He was on a ship, then. And he was *alive*.

"Would you relax?" came a low, amused voice from somewhere to his right. "Don't make me sedate you again. Relax."

As Jereth's eyes adjusted to the dim light, he saw that he was lying on a narrow bed, his body covered with a blanket. His arms and legs were immobilized; his head and shoulders were propped up, almost in a sitting position.

The bed was in a small room with a sloping ceiling, its walls edged with orange-tinted ambients. There were some cluttered shelves on the far wall. He moved his eyes slowly around the room, concentrating on each shape until he could make it out.

He tried to remember what had happened just before this, but his memories were nothing but fleeting, unconnected images. *The dreamhouse—Leeg—the apartment—Sëgra City—the money—Grenobal Bank—*

The voice that had spoken to him. Where had it come from? There was someone else in the room, sitting beside the bed. At least, he *thought* there was someone sitting beside the bed. He couldn't turn his head, and rolling his eyes as far as he could gave him only the vaguest impression of the person's shape.

Jereth tried to speak, but all that came out was a dry croak. He felt a trickle of cold water running down his throat from a hydro-tube taped to his cheek. His throat hurt, and it was hard to swallow.

"Relax," said the stranger's voice again, distinctly closer now. "It looks like you're gonna come out all right. You'll probably regain full use of your limbs, and that makes you one of the lucky ones."

"Who... in the... five hells... are you?" Jereth choked out.

"Hmm. At least you're talkin' now instead of screaming," said the stranger, ignoring the question. "Had about enough of that. I was starting to worry. You've been down for six years, that's more than enough to mess up your head."

"Who *are* you? Wh—what ship is this?"

The hydro-tube dispensed more water into Jereth's mouth. He coughed painfully, spitting it out.

"I'll be the one asking questions, for now," the stranger said, dabbing a warm towel over his chin. "I saved your life, Jaymi Hanioch—if that's even your name. But I haven't decided if you were worth my time yet."

Jereth was silent for a while, contemplating this. What *was* his name? How did he even get here? What was he doing on this ship? He should feel enraged, but everything felt so distant, so difficult to pin down, even his emotions. He felt like he was reaching down a deep well to find words, pulling them slowly out of the darkness, uprooting them, examining them for meaning.

The fragments of memories pouring back into his mind were taking clearer shape now. He remembered the arrest— the interrogation—the trial on Sëgra—*Jaymi Hanioch, you are hereby sentenced to twenty-four years in stasis. Your confinement is to be served at Grimm Parukh.*

Twenty-four years. Stasis.

Jereth mumbled the words to himself incoherently.

"That's right, they sent you down for twenty-four years," the stranger's voice said. "It's all coming back to you now, isn't it? Those assholes."

Jereth stopped his mumbling, swallowing hard.

"Sounds like they wanted to make an example of you real bad," the voice continued. "That's as good as a death sentence, hmm? Not much chance you'd walk away from a twenty-four. But fortunately, we were able to negotiate you an... early release of sorts. Hah!" A hand slapped against Jereth's shoulder, but Jereth couldn't feel anything.

"You... *you* broke me out of Grimm Parukh?" he whispered hoarsely. "You got me out of a maximum security prison orbital?"

"Yep. Grimm Parukh's gone. Obliterated! You're *all* freed now—one way or another," chortled the stranger. "But you? You're something special." The stranger stood up and walked slowly around Jereth's bed. Each footstep sounded heavy, metallic—almost mechanical. He heard a low whirring noise, something that stirred memories of his childhood in the Desmoën desert.

A rattler-snake.

Jereth felt suddenly chilled.

"I had a look at your prison record," the stranger said. "You got yourself arrested for some kind of big bank heist, hmm? Had a list of previous cybercrimes so long they didn't even fit on one screen. Called yourself *Jetsetter.* Heh."

Jereth didn't respond. He fixed his eyes on the ceiling.

"You were accused of diverting a hundred and twenty-nine million creds from Grenobal Bank in Sëgra City with a false transaction. Gods alive, you didn't really think *that* would go unnoticed, did you? You absolute fool." The stranger laughed. "Looks like you're a real risk-taker, hmm? You've either got some kind of death wish or you just don't know when to quit. And those are both excellent qualities in my line of work." A hand reached over and tapped Jereth's chest, just over his heart. "I see you've got some military ink, too. Squadron Leader... impressive. So you're a defector, I suppose? Bet you've still got some decent piloting skills."

The stranger leaned in closer, near enough for Jereth's eyes to finally focus on her. She was at least twice his age, but her deep-set eyes were knife-sharp, her gaze unyielding and steady. Her brown, weathered skin was peppered with pale freckles, and her thick eyebrows met without a gap above a nose that looked like it had been broken more than once.

When she tilted her head, Jereth glimpsed the gnarled round scar on the side of her neck—a port scar, like the ones Jereth would now bear as well. She'd been in the freezer, too.

"Just tell me what the fuck you want from me," mumbled Jereth, closing his eyes.

The stranger walked back to the other side of the bed, her footsteps echoing on the metal flooring. There was that soft rattling sound again as she moved. Jereth shuddered internally.

"Why don't you tell me about your friend Eldric Leesongronski?" she said. "You only went down because you wouldn't give him up. That's why they hit you so hard with that sentence, isn't it—because you wouldn't break? All you had to do was say his name, and you would've walked away." She leaned in closer again. "So why'd you do that, hmm? Why'd you protect him?"

"Eldric Leesongronski... didn't... do anything wrong," said Jereth through clenched teeth. "He had *nothing* to do with the Grenobal hack. I acted alone."

The stranger snorted. "Alone," she repeated mockingly. "So... you're telling me *you* pulled off a complicated encrypted-systems intrusion against the biggest bank on Sëgra, a hack involving real-time 5D calculations, using algorithms that even a supercomputer couldn't crack? The notes from your trial say you failed a basic mathematics test. And meanwhile, your best friend just happens to be a mathematical genius. What a *coincidence*. I can see why the prosecution was so—"

"Leeg didn't do it, all right?" growled Jereth. "His alibi checked out, the security recordings confirmed it. He was in a dream-play inside the Dome Theatre at the time of the hack. They had nothing on him."

"Which was exactly why they needed you to confess, to tell them how he did it. All you had to do was *say his name*, and you could've been free."

Jereth inhaled deeply, the dry air scraping against his aching lungs. "Did you really wake me up just to question me about this shit?" he rasped. "'Cause you're about to get real disappointed."

"Watch it." The stranger shook a warning finger at Jereth's face, pressing the palm of her other hand against his throat. "You can't even take a piss on your own right now, you little corpse-worm, so you'd better think real hard about this." She leaned in harder, crushing Jereth's airway. "I'll ask you one more time. Did Eldric Leesongronski hack Grenobal Bank?"

Jereth blinked, unable to do anything but gasp for air. He tried to will his arms to move, but his body wouldn't obey. The shadows in his peripheral vision darkened, then everything turned to bright white as he suffocated.

This was it, then. This was how he would die.

At last, the stranger pulled her hand away, allowing Jereth a few choked breaths.

"Well? You gonna tell me now?" She smiled cruelly, unclipping a plasma pistol from her belt and lowering it toward his face. "Or have you still got that death wish?" She dragged the weapon delicately across his cheek.

"Eat with the hell-hounds, asshole," Jereth spat.

The stranger raised her arm abruptly, as if she was about to strike him in the face with the weapon. Her hand shook. "You're making a huge mistake."

"Gods, would you just kill me already? I'm not gonna tell you *shit*."

The stranger started to chuckle as she slowly lowered her hand. Then she tossed the plasma weapon over her shoulder, and it clattered away past the foot of the bed.

It was a long time before she spoke, her low voice serious again. "Want to know how I ended up in the freezer? Hmm?" She touched the scar on the side of her neck, tracing a finger over the gnarled, mottled brown skin where the stasis port had been inserted.

He didn't say anything, but she didn't wait for an invitation to continue.

"I went down for nine years because my so-called friend sold me out after a job," she said bitterly. "Someone I trusted turned me in to save their own hide, understand? Someone I loved. And I never saw it coming." She leaned in close, bringing her face right up to Jereth's. "You've got to be careful who you call *friend* in this life. Real careful. 'Course, when I got out of the freezer, I got my revenge, don't you worry. I took back what was mine in the end. But nothing I did could bring back those nine years I lost. And it sure didn't make my gods-damned legs work like they used to."

The stranger stood up and walked to the end of the bed, and Jereth squinted at her silhouette. That sound he'd been hearing—that soft whirring, the distinctive rattle—was coming from a bionic exoskeleton. A sleek, armoured walk-suit encased her from the waist down. Its plates were painted with the red-and-brown stripes of a deadly desert-snake, with the sound effects to match.

"I like your determination," she said, "and I admire your loyalty, Jaymi."

"My name's... Jereth," he choked.

"Ahhh. Well, then, *Jereth*. Thank you for your honesty." There was a smile in her gravelly voice. "To answer your earlier questions: you're on the nightship *Aeglaca*. My ship. My name is Azeran Guillem. I'm an arms dealer and the main weapons supplier for most of the ditch ship launchyards this side of the Gedringa system." She patted his shoulder again. "And from now on... you can call me your friend."

UMA
Engineering Deck, ZeyCorp Gallion

THE MORNING OF the mission launch, Uma spoke little, and Leesongronski said even less. From the moment the two shuttles left the safety of the *Gallion*'s bay, it was as if everyone on the ship was holding their breaths.

In Engineering, the crew sat in complete silence, watching two pale blue dots crawl along on the main viewscreen. The shuttle trackers blinked steadily from one square in the grid to the next, dropping further and further away from the *Gallion*.

Shuttle One, slightly ahead: that was Keeven and Shaan. Shuttle Two, six minutes behind them: that was Mikolai and Jaxong. Uma tried to calm her mind, but she couldn't focus. She looked over at Leesongronski again.

It was strange to see him down here in the pit, instead of perched in his usual place on the railing. He looked mildly uncomfortable at the console they'd set up for him between Wazar and Noussen. The screen in front of him was still closed—there was nothing for him to do yet—and he was spinning his little fortune charm between his fingers.

"Shields doing okay?" Syru broke the silence, leaning forward in his chair. "Wazar, could you give us another shield update?"

"Shieldforms still stable," Wazar said. "I'm seeing a few minor energy impacts, but the shuttles are moving out of the boundary zone now. I was a bit worried some of the nav systems would get fried with that energy load, but looks like we're clear now."

"Great," Uma said, silently thanking Wazar for keeping that particular fact to herself until now.

Syru smiled faintly, but none of the anxiety left his face.

"Comms signal strength is fluctuating within expected range. The relay's holding," Noussen said. "All good over here, too."

Zel continued to hover around the proceedings, though he was trying very hard to make it look like he wasn't, like he just *happened* to be standing casually at the edge of the Engineering pit for some unrelated reason. Every so often, he ventured a little closer and peered over the engineers' shoulders.

Uma was just opening her mouth to ask him to stop it, when he suddenly froze in his tracks, staring at the top of the staircase. She followed his gaze.

At the top of the stairs stood Keila Kva-Sova, her braids tied up in a purple ZeyCorp scarf. On her arm was the Ambassador's young, frightened-looking Voiced. Today, Gida was swathed in delicate yellow robes. Her headpiece was a shimmering dark gold, two finely curled points framing the kennai symbol on her forehead. Beneath it, her face looked haunted and drawn, as if her olive skin were stretched too tightly over her cheekbones.

Zel managed something of a contorted smile that looked more like a wince.

"Gida!" he gasped. "I didn't know you'd be in attendance! I should have escorted you!"

The Voiced held up one slender hand. "Formalities are not necessary. The Ambassador isn't here." Her eyes darted around the pit. "I hope you don't mind if I stay a while. To... observe?"

"Of course! You are most welcome!" said Zel with exaggerated enthusiasm. He swept his hand toward one side of the pit. "Come! There are seats over here."

Kva-Sova and Gida walked down the stairs, moving slowly to avoid stepping on the hem of Gida's over-long robes. Everyone's eyes remained glued to them as they descended.

Kva-Sova led Gida over to the empty chairs Zel had indicated.

"Please carry on," Gida said to the engineers. "Pretend I'm not here." She carefully arranged her robes around her and folded her hands into her lap.

Kva-Sova was gazing at Gida like a parent watching over a precocious child, but Gida didn't look at the Voicegiver. She just sat there with her shoulders turned inward, her mouth set in a tense line.

Uma tried to imagine Gida in the mantle of the Decipherer, shrouded by the famous green cloak. The nameless heroine, standing alongside the Negotiator and making that historic overture to the Starhold's Envoy.

The thought should have lifted Uma's spirits, but it felt too heavy to contemplate. Her stomach clenched with doubt when she looked at Gida sitting there, clearly holding back tears. Could this young, scared girl really take the fate of humankind on her shoulders? Could they ask that of her? But on the other hand... was it any different than asking the same thing of Leesongronski? Of asking Keeven to take on the mantle of the Negotiator?

Uma tried to tell herself that it wasn't different. But Fransk had a point. Sending Gida back to the wrong time to live out a life that definitely wasn't hers... that felt worse, somehow.

Gida was on her first solo assignment, new to her diplomatic role and inexperienced as a political interpreter. Of course she wouldn't feel ready to translate a complex truce negotiation under that kind of pressure, much less to mentor the whole next generation of Voiced.

And yet the Decipherer herself had been even less experienced than Gida. She had supposedly never even met a living alien before she made that fateful trip on the *Jonah,* and she was reported to have taught herself the Felen telepathic language solely from interactions with an artifact. Of course, most serious scholars doubted that was the *whole* truth. No one that inexperienced could possibly have undertaken a translation as complicated as the peace talks.

Some historians theorized that—unsavoury as the idea may be—the Decipherer must have practiced her telepathic language skills with live Felen prisoners on a secret base somewhere. But to have grasped the language without a human Voiced teacher was still an unparalleled achievement.

Uma looked at Gida again, dismissing her doubts. Gida may not be the prodigy that the Decipherer had been, but she was a skilled translator who had ample experience interacting with the Felen. She knew their customs and peculiarities... and most importantly, she was *here*, against all the odds.

If Gida agreed to go back with the *Jonah,* then there was still a chance, however slim, that history could be set right. The Decipherer's mysterious life could become Gida's. Maybe Jereth Keeven of the ramshackle *Jonah*—Jaymi Hanioch of Sëgra City—really could pull off the ultimate con and become the Negotiator. The Peace could still be made.

And the Fortunate Five would be complete again.

Shuttle One
Mission Time: 1.4 hours

THE MISSION TEAMS had taken the *Gallion*'s two smallest cargo-transports: compact, utilitarian vehicles with minimal interiors, two seats up front, and a good-sized cargo space behind. The rest of the space inside was occupied by the embedded emergency airlock.

Shaan wasn't quite used to the lack of gravity. She shifted in her seat, trying to find a comfortable way to sit. In the pilot's seat, Keeven was uncharacteristically quiet, and the silence was starting to wear on her. She tried not to think of the *Gallion* falling further and further away behind them. But she didn't want to contemplate what was ahead, either.

She huddled against the seat and watched Keeven at the controls, staring at his hands moving back and forth. When he was piloting, his hands didn't shake as much.

The expression on Keeven's face now was the same as when he threw his red ball: a calm but distant focus, like he was *mostly* paying attention to what he was doing, but probably also thinking about something else. Periodically, he would flick out the command to drop another hover probe for the comms relay. The little machine would uncouple from its anchor point on the shuttle's underside, spinning out into the void to join the others. Most of the time, Keeven hadn't needed to do anything except check on a rotating sequence of graphs, occasionally making a tiny adjustment to the shuttle's course. But every so often the shuttle bobbed and shook, and Shaan closed her eyes.

She had no idea how much time had passed when Keeven reached over and opened a comms channel. "*Gallion*, this is Shuttle Team One," he said, startling her. "We're on approach to Verkhoy Station, landing in a few minutes."

"We hear you, Shuttle Team One!" came Director Ozakka's voice. "Comms signal holding strong. Let us know when you're inside. Good luck!"

*   *   *

Verkhoy Station
Mission Time: 2.1 hours

UNDER NORMAL CIRCUMSTANCES, the shuttle would have docked with the station directly. One of the crescent-shaped bays should have lit up, sliding open to welcome Verkhoy's visitors—and as they approached the station, Shaan almost expected it to happen. But the bays remained unlit and sealed, and Keeven brought the shuttle down on one of the external landing platforms.

It was only about a dozen paces from the shuttle to the emergency airlock, but each step was agony. Shaan stepped as delicately as she could in her heavy boots, as if, at any time, the station might recoil from her unsanctioned return.

The station knew nothing of her transgressions, she reminded herself. As far as these buttons and panels were concerned, she was still Shaan from six years ago. Shaan who still worked for the Geminus Peace Alliance. Shaan before the shuttle accident.

Shaan who hadn't yet made any decisions quite bad enough to *kill* someone.

She gritted her teeth, grateful that Keeven couldn't see her through her reflective faceplate. She was aware of him walking along beside her, an EVA harness linking his suit to hers.

And then they were at the airlock. Shaan pulled down the emergency hatch and opened the outer door. They stepped in, and it sealed behind them.

Scarcely breathing, Shaan reached for the access panel. She removed her glove and placed her hand on the mirrored surface. The system chirped, processing her bio-auth, then prompted her for her security access sequence. For a brief moment she wondered if she'd actually remembered it correctly, but the movements were burned into her muscle memory, and her hand formed the shapes without hesitation.

The inner airlock glowed blue.

Auth accepted: SHAAN NORTE, GEMINUS PEACE ALLIANCE.

The door telescoped open, admitting them to a small service passage. Shaan exhaled, her pulse pounding behind her eyes as she flipped down her helmet.

Keeven flipped his own helmet down and peeled off his black gloves with a grin. "Well! That was pretty damn easy, huh?"

Shaan didn't reply. She was shivering, her whole body shaking with a cold sweat, and she had to brace herself against the wall to keep her knees from buckling. Luckily, Keeven's attention was already captivated.

"Woooaaa." He looked around in wide-eyed amazement.

The grey corridor around them was gently curved, and the walls had an organic quality to them, rough and pebbled like bark. Where the walls met the dark-tiled floor, the angles were slanted and irregular. The effect was that of standing in a deep underground tunnel, or inside a giant tree. The ceiling was studded with clusters of pale globular ambients the shape of mushrooms, arranged in random patterns.

"Uh.... is this floor *tilted?*" Keeven frowned, finding his footing. "And the walls? Does the gravity still feel a bit weird to you?"

"It's supposed to be that way," Shaan said reassuringly. "This lower level is inspired by the way the Felen lay out their living spaces. This is what their habitat-vessels look like inside. Everything here is coded to Felen preferences."

Keeven looked perplexed. "I feel like I'm drunk."

"Yeah, the Felen don't really do straight lines. You get used to it."

Shaan looked to her left. A thick security door glowed at the end of the corridor, flashing with ominous orange messages in human standard text: *NO ACCESS—DANGER—STATION*

LOCKDOWN IN EFFECT. To her right, the cavernous passageway carried on until it curved out of sight.

The words *death, darkness, only death* flashed through her mind, and she shuddered.

"Somethin' wrong?" Keeven asked.

"I... don't have the best memories of this place," she mumbled.

"Well, hopefully Leeg gets this thing done real quick, so we can get the fuck out of here." Keeven looked around with concern. "But I don't see any consoles. Where exactly are we supposed to plug in this transmitter?"

"There should be an info-point somewhere around here." Shaan trailed one hand along the wall, exploring the knotted surface with her fingertips. Keeven watched curiously as she slid her fingers along a nearly invisible groove in the wall. "Ah! Here it is."

A panel no wider than her palm slid out from the wall, a virtual console projection unfolding from it. The Geminus intranet login appeared.

"Console. There you go," she whispered. Her chest constricted at the aching familiarity of it.

Keeven set his small cargo-pack onto the floor and lifted out the data transmitter, along with a handful of coiled connection leads: some blue, some green, one black.

"Check this out," he said, holding up the fistful of cables. "Dean gave me *seven* different leads to try." He laughed. "A hundred and fifty-two years and still no standardized data ports, huh?"

Shaan managed a smile. She felt for the shape of the port on the underside of the wall panel. "Round port, one flat side. You got one like that?"

Keeven examined the leads, narrowing them down to two before he handed them over to her. The second one fitted, and Keeven clipped the other end of it into the transmission device.

He grinned gleefully as the device blinked to life, then grabbed the comms receiver hanging from his suit's chestplate. "*Gallion*, this is Shuttle Team One. Transmitter's live! We're in business!"

Verkhoy Station
Mission Time: 3.2 hours

"I'M GETTING KINDA bored," Keeven said, sighing dramatically.

Shaan shrugged. *Bored* wasn't the word she would've chosen. The two of them were still standing in the same corridor, not far from where the transmission device was blinking away, but it felt like half a year had passed since they got here. Out on the power annex, Jaxong and Mikolai were probably wiring up the diffractor charges for the bomb's primer by now. As for what Leesongronski was doing back on the *Gallion*, Shaan had no idea.

Keeven kicked at the edge of the wall, walked over to the locked security door, then circled back to her again.

"How 'bout you tell me a story?" he said. "You got any scandalous company gossip?"

Shaan forced a laugh. "ZeyCorp's not that exciting."

"Oh, there's always something," he said, his eyes mischievous. "C'mon, give it up. Like... what's the deal with Ozakka and Fransk, hmm? There has to be a story with those two."

Shaan shrugged again. "They've known each other for ages. Met at university, then both ended up working for ZeyCorp."

Keeven looked disappointed. "That's it?"

"I think so. Fransk has been with the company for years, but he hates working in space. He's just waiting to finally get named a Chancellor so he can work planetside. All he wants is a job at Central HQ, with a nice office overlooking the ocean."

"Can't say I blame him," said Keeven.

"Director Ozakka joined ZeyCorp around the same time as me," Shaan said. "She's way overqualified, though. She's actually a double-certified subspace engineer, she used to build whole custom jump systems before. I don't know why she puts up with this company." Shaan sighed. "You know, sometimes I think Fransk and Ozakka hate their jobs almost as much as I do. I doubt they would've made it this long without each other."

Keeven smirked. "You reckon they ever...?" He made a suggestive gesture with his hands. "I bet they have."

Shaan rolled her eyes. "They were together a really long time ago, like back at university. But they broke up way before either of them worked here." She shrugged. "Honestly, I can't see Fransk being Ozakka's type. He seems a bit too boring for her. But... maybe he was different back then."

Keeven looked contemplative. "Hmm. Well, what about me, then?"

"What *about* you?"

"Am I Ozakka's type?"

Shaan rolled her eyes again. "Definitely not."

"Ah, damn. Shame, 'cause I'm *not* boring. And I'd sure let Ozakka tie me up and spank me."

Mercifully, he was quiet for about half a minute after that. Then he turned back to Shaan again.

"So, what about the super hot, fancy-dressed Etraxan, hmm? There *has* to be some good gossip about him."

"You mean our fake Publicity Liaison?" Shaan grimaced. "Ugh, I forgot about him. *There's* a nice ZeyCorp scandal for you."

Keeven looked intrigued. "Oooh. Tell."

"Well, apparently, Zel secretly owns the company or something? At least, that's what he said when he threatened to get Fransk fired... right before Fransk threatened to sue him if he tried it."

Keeven's eyebrows shot up. "What?"

"Zel's family has a controlling interest in the conglomerate that owns ZeyCorp. He was here to oversee the Ambassador's visit, pretending to be a Publicity Liaison from Central HQ. But he's not just a Blessed Scion of Etraxas, he's also the heir to Yauronauf Incorporated, which I guess makes him, like... a multi-billionaire."

"Well, shit." Keeven grinned. "Multi-billionaire, huh? You know, if he really wants to convince me to save his planet, he's got quite a few angles to work with." Keeven tapped his chin. "What d'you figure he looks like with his clothes off? Think it's true what they say about Etraxan men? That they—"

Shaan smacked his arm.

"Hey, ow!" Keeven laughed. "Okay, okay. I get it. You saw him first, right? He's all yours." He gave Shaan a look of mocking sincerity. "I promise, I won't let one ridiculously attractive Etraxan billionaire ruin our friendship. Although, for the record, I'm pretty sure he's into me."

Shaan rolled her eyes. "Can you please just stop *talking?*" she snapped, more harshly than she'd meant to. "I can't deal with this right now."

Keeven mimed sealing his lips, that ridiculous grin still plastered over his face. He walked over to lean on the opposite wall. Shaan looked the other way, staring down the dim corridor. She tried to think of anything else besides being on this station, but it was impossible. Her skin crawled, and unbidden memories stirred painfully in the back of her mind. After a few minutes, the silence was overwhelming.

Maybe it was better when Keeven was still talking.

"Hey... Keeven?" she said. "Why don't *you* tell me something scandalous? I'm sure you've got stories actually worth telling."

*   *   *

Verkhoy Station
Mission Time: 4.4 Hours

"So THEN, I went over to The Apartment... 'cause we still kept that old flat we had in the middle city, for business purposes," Keeven said.

He was lying on the floor with his booted feet against the wall and the cargo-pack propping up his head. He couldn't be comfortable like that, but he didn't seem to care. Shaan sat next to him with her back against the wall. It had to be at least four hours gone now. Still no word from the *Gallion*. She forced herself not to look at the time.

"Business purposes? Do you mean the crypto-hacking, or the con jobs?" she said.

"Oh, come on, don't say it like *that!*" Keeven protested with a laugh. "It was a fine art, Shaan. I had *ideas*. And I did loads of work, no matter what Leeg might tell you. Who do you think came up with using the dreamhouse for the Grenobal job?"

"You, I'm guessing?"

"Damn right. And I'm the one who found our target, too. That guy Antiem? Ugh, what an asshole. Scamming him was poetry." Keeven gave a wistful sigh. "A big-time ripoff artist gets done in by a better one, there's something beautiful about that. It's just like in nature. You do your thing until a bigger critter comes along and snaps your neck." He flicked his wrist. "Just like that."

Shaan made a disgusted face.

"Hey, Sëgra City is not a nice place," he said. "Nobody's innocent. You either play the game or you get played." He held up three fingers. "On Sëgra, they say there's three ways to get what you want: buy it, steal it, or win it. But that's not entirely true. Because you can also convince somebody to *hand it to you.*" He sat up to look at her. "How do you think we got this mission approved, hmm? We played them, Shaan, and we won! It worked like a charm."

"Minus the part where you nearly got your head caved in by Mendeg?"

"Hey, even a good plan has at least one hitch." Keeven winked. "But me and Mendeg, we're fine now. We talked things over."

She looked at him incredulously. "You *talked* to Mendeg? After he almost killed you?"

"Sure. I showed him Charyne's Last Shot plans, all drawn out and finished. Told him we're still gonna find a way to get that stuff to the Union forces, so they can find another physicist to build the bomb. He believed me. He even *apologized* for punching me."

Shaan's mouth dropped open. "Wha—but—*no!*"

"Relax, don't look so worried! Charyne told me this version of the bomb will only work in Rift-space. Those plans are useless anywhere else. But Mendeg doesn't know that. So he's happy, for now."

"Until he finds out you lied again, and actually kills you this time."

Keeven laughed. "Well, *that* is a problem for another day."

He hauled himself to his feet, walked to the locked security door again, then meandered back after checking on the blinking transmission device.

"So... what happened with that Grenobal Bank hack, anyway?" Shaan asked. "How'd the Jetsetter get caught?"

"Bad luck," Keeven said with a wince. "It was just plain bad luck. We were no amateurs, believe me. We had everything covered: sent the money into an anonymous account, transferred it offworld a few hours later. It should've been untraceable."

"But... even a good plan has a hitch?" Shaan said.

He gave her a cynical smile. "Wait till you hear this one. See,

Leeg did an identity swap in the Grenobal customer database—exactly like the one we're gonna do here, for you and your Station Governor Marecc. But first, I had to open a legit Grenobal business account, so Leeg would have something to swap Antiem's details with. During the hack, I was supposed to become Antiem temporarily, and Antiem was going to become me."

Keeven clenched his fists. "We watched Antiem's activity for weeks, and he never paid for anything out of that account. There were no small transactions, no purchases. All that account ever did was hold the escrow money and dole out those big payouts to his clients, like I told you... and he did that at the same time every week. So it should've been safe, right? Our details were only switched for *three minutes*." He smacked one of his fists against the wall. "But here comes the hitch. While we were doing the hack, Antiem was in a bar entertaining some clients... and get this, he used his Grenobal account! He logged in from a bar terminal during that exact three minutes, an' he used his business account to pay for a fucking round of drinks! You believe that?"

Shaan leaned forward. "Oh, gods. So... what happened, Antiem's bar transaction got declined?"

"If only," said Keeven grimly. "His transaction did go through, but it came out of *my* account. Because according to that database, as soon as Antiem logged in, *he was me*. When he paid for his drinks, his transaction went through against *my* legit Grenobal account. I'd used a fake ID at the bank, of course—Jaymi Hanioch, that was the name—but that account was never supposed to come into play at all. It had my actual photo and biometrics on it. So they had me dead to rights."

"Oh my gods."

"Yep." Keeven laughed bitterly. "Antiem had no idea anything strange happened, and neither did I. He bought his drinks, I finished the transfer, and a couple minutes later Leeg switched everything right back to the way it was. Sweet success." He gave a pained sigh. "Leeg edited the logs and deleted all the evidence, so they would never have known about the identity switch if it wasn't for that gods-damned round of drinks. It should've just looked like Antiem sent those millions out of his account himself."

Keeven paused and shook his head. "You know, sometimes I still can't believe that happened," he said. "*Three fucking minutes*. 'Course, when Antiem figured out his money was missing, he contacted the bank, and they contacted the City authorities. They started investigating, and someone must've noticed that the payment Antiem claimed he made at that bar wasn't showing up on his account. So they started digging... and oh, look! At the exact same time as Antiem's hundred and twenty-nine million was sailing out of his account, Jaymi Hanioch's account was paying for Antiem's drinks. They worked out that the two accounts must've been swapped... and that was it."

"They arrested you," Shaan concluded.

"It only took 'em twenty-two hours to grab me," he said. "Apparently, the City had me and Leeg on some kind of watch list, but they were waiting for us to do something they could actually prove. And once they had *me*, they thought I'd turn him in. They never really believed I was the Jetsetter all on my own."

"Did you ever consider it?" Shaan asked. "Naming him, so they'd release you?"

"Nah. No way, I couldn't do that to Leeg. I said I acted alone, and I just kept on sayin' that, no matter what they threatened." Keeven's eyes misted over. "Gods, I was just hoping he'd have enough sense to take the money and run. I knew I was probably gonna die in the freezer... an' I didn't want it all to be for nothing."

Shaan sat quietly, not sure what to say.

"Best not to think about that stuff, I guess," Keeven said. "It's ancient history." He rubbed at the scars on his neck. "You know... I think Sëgra City might be the worst place I've ever been. And I've been in some pretty shit places."

Shaan thought about checking the time again, but she resisted.

"So where's the *best* place you've ever been, then?" she asked him.

"Ah! The best? Ajuen Island, on Gedringa, no question. They call Gedringa one of the most beautiful green worlds in the Union." He sighed, then a worried frown flitted over his face. "It's still there, right? Gedringa?"

"Oh, yeah," Shaan said. "Gedringa's still there. And they still say that about it." She looked at the floor. "I've never been on any of the green worlds, though. I've been in space for most of my life."

"Well, Gedringa's incredible," he said. "Most of the planet's one huge ocean, but there's all these tiny green islands... thousands of 'em." He leaned back against the wall, tucking his hands behind his head. "You ever heard of an arms dealer called Azeran Guillem?"

Shaan shook her head. "I don't think so."

"Ah, well. She's a good friend of mine, and she has a house on Ajuen Island. Absolutely beautiful. It's up on a hill, looking over a private beach." Keeven smiled fondly. "You know, I think you'd like Guillem if you met her. She's real fun. And her beach house is gorgeous."

"An arms dealer's beach house, sounds entertaining." Shaan sighed. "Gods, though, I'd go just about *anywhere* right now. I'd rather be anywhere but here staring at this wall."

"Well, why don't we take a little look around?" Keeven got up. "You said we can get all the way around this zone, right? So let's go explore!"

He didn't wait for her to reply before he picked up his cargo-pack and started walking down the corridor, away from the locked security door. He moved slowly, looking up and down each wall at the strange arrangements of fungi-lights. He kept following the tilted passageway until it curved away sharply to the left and out of her sight.

Swearing under her breath, Shaan scrambled to her feet and rushed to catch up with him.

Keeven carried on walking until the corridor ended, its walls opening out into a huge, cave-like reception room. Here, the dark floor tiles stopped. The greyish walls turned to midnight black, their surfaces knotted and gnarled, rising up to a high ceiling dotted with luminescent constellations. On the floor, a delicate swath of pale foam-cloth had been laid out like carpet.

Instinctively, Shaan stopped at the edge, fighting the impulse to remove her boots. Keeven walked out onto it, his corrugated soles leaving indentations in the fragile surface.

"Whoa, this is weird," Keeven said, looking down at his feet. "The floor's kinda... squishy."

"You're meant to take your shoes off," she muttered. "This is the reception area for welcoming diplomatic visitors."

"Oh, so I don't count, or what? The Negotiator for the Union is visiting today!" He laughed. "I get no respect around here."

"Well," she said drily, "if it makes you feel any better... look at this."

She touched a hair-thin switch beside the door, and bright blue light flooded out of the far wall, illuminating an enormous statue that towered far above them.

Keeven sucked a breath between his teeth as he took in the majestic figure, four times larger than life: a representation of the Negotiator for the Union, carved from polished stone.

"Shiiiit," he whispered.

The stone Negotiator stood back-to-back with a matching figure of the Decipherer in her sweeping cloak and cowl. Their marble hands were raised over their heads, and together they held up the Geminus crest.

Keeven slowly circled the statue. *"The Negotiator,"* Keeven read from the inscription on the base. *"Representing the United Worlds of Humanity, a True Hero of the Union. We Give Eternal Thanks for his Ultimate Sacrifice, to Bring an End to our Days of War..."*

"May he Inspire all our Days of Peace," Shaan finished from memory.

Keeven's face was as unreadable as the statue's. "Ultimate sacrifice?" he said. "Well... damn."

Shaan's body went cold. Maybe no one had told Keeven exactly what happened to the Negotiator in their history. But even if no one had specifically mentioned the Negotiator's untimely demise during the Peace talks, Keeven couldn't have missed the implication in that inscription.

"Hey, it's okay," Keeven said, looking almost amused. "I figured it out already. I know your Negotiator didn't make it out alive."

"I'm sorry," Shaan whispered. "I don't know if you actually intend to go through with it—with going back, with trying—but..."

He cleared his throat. "Yeah, well... you know what? Just don't tell me how it happened, okay? I don't fucking care. He's not me. *That* is not me." He pointed up at the statue.

She nodded, trying frantically to think of something else to talk about. Nothing came to mind.

Keeven was looking back at the inscription again. She watched him trail one trembling hand along the inscription from start to finish, tracing the rounded grooves of each letter and lingering over the word *Hero*. With his other hand, he touched two fingers to his lips, then pressed them to his chest, right over his heart.

"So... how come you left the UWDF?" Shaan asked. "You're a defector... aren't you?"

Keeven jerked his hand away from his chest. A flash of anger crossed his face. "Let's be clear, I didn't *defect*. The UWDF kicked me out. 'Insubordination,' that's what they said. I made it twelve years in the service, but gods... I just couldn't take it anymore." His shoulders slumped. "Taking all those kids off the dust worlds, telling us we were gonna be heroes? Only to stick us on these useless patrols around the Prime Worlds, protecting the rich, while the outer systems were getting decimated by the Felen." He sniffed. "It was my older brother who always wanted to go fight so badly. Joining the UWDF was all he dreamed about. Just as well he didn't live to see what serving the Union was really like, huh? It would've broken his heart."

"I didn't know you had a brother," Shaan said quietly.

"Well, I did. His name was Ludyth. He died way back when I was a kid," Keeven said. "When the UWDF recruiters came, they marked him to go train as a pilot. You had to be sixteen years old to qualify, an' he was so damn excited to go." Keeven wiped imprecisely at his eyes with a clenched fist, his hand shaking. "I was a year too young for the cutoff. But when Ludyth died, I took his intake chit an' I lined up for the recruiters instead of him. Do you think they even gave a damn to check if they took the right kid or not? Hells, no. I showed 'em Ludyth's intake chit, I looked enough like him, and they took me. Fifteen years old. One dust world kid was just the same as another to them. We were nothing, just fodder to be thrown to the aliens while our worlds still didn't have any damn clean water."

"What happened to him?" Shaan whispered. "Your brother. How did he die?"

"Gods. It was such a fucking pointless death, out in that desert." Keeven lowered his eyes. "We were just messin' around on the machinery for the water delivery system, out in the gorge. We jumped the fence, but I was too shit-scared to run across the spar."

He pointed up at the statue again.

"*That* is *not* me, understand? I'm no gods-damned hero, Shaan. I haven't done a damn thing in my life that's worth being proud of," he choked. "It should've been me lyin' dead in that gorge instead of Ludyth. It was *my* fucking fault! He died pushing me out of the way. He died for *nothing!*"

Keeven's face crumpled, tears falling over his flushed cheeks. He pressed a fist to his mouth and walked away. A few paces from the statues, he dropped to his knees in the middle of the delicate reception-carpet and buried his face in his hands, sobbing silently.

It didn't feel right to stand there and stare at him crying, but Shaan wasn't sure what else to do. She walked slowly around the statues and looked up. The stone Decipherer seemed to be staring at her accusingly, watching her with unseen eyes buried somewhere in that stone cowl. *Death, darkness, only death.* Disconcerted, Shaan looked away.

After a while, Keeven stood up again and came back to Shaan's side. His cheeks were still wet, but he had composed himself.

"I'm, uh... sorry 'bout that," he muttered, swiping a palm over his face. "Sorry. I'm good now."

A deep hurt was still evident in his eyes. What did he want from her? Understanding? Forgiveness? Absolution?

Or was that what *she* wanted?

"It's okay. I... I do understand," she said. She took a steadying breath. "Keeven... there's something I've never told anyone about what happened on this station."

Her own words shocked her, echoing in the empty room. She hadn't planned to tell him any more of the truth than had already been necessary. But she was strangely drawn to him just then. It seemed wrong to have witnessed his rare moment of honesty without offering some truth in return.

And where else could she ever talk about this, if not here, on Verkhoy Station?

"There was an accident during the evacuation. Someone died," Shaan whispered. "Her name was Ashlish. And... it was my fault."

"Shit." Keeven's face dropped. "What happened?"

"Ashlish was Voiced. And... she was sick." Shaan's heart pounded, her mouth suddenly parched. "You remember what happened to all of Kva-Sova's subjects, before the Decipherer? That awful way they lost their grip on reality? That's called *detachment*. And it happened to Ashlish."

Keeven grimaced.

"Ashlish had an episode during the evac. She was totally disoriented, I had to drag her into a shuttle to get her out of here. She was hitting and scratching me, screaming... I was so distracted during the launch sequence that I must've accidentally switched the shuttle over to manual controls. I overshot the clamps when we were docking with the evac vessel, and I crashed the shuttle." Shaan's voice faltered, the words catching in her throat. "Ashlish died on impact."

"Wow," Keeven said softly. "Well, that sure as all hells doesn't sound like it was your fault." His forehead creased with concern. "But, uh... I thought that *detachment* shit doesn't happen anymore in your time? Because the Voiced are all getting properly trained now, or whatever?"

"Detachment still happens sometimes," Shaan whispered. "It's rare, but it can happen."

"Ugh." He glanced up at the statue of the Decipherer. "You really think it's ethical to keep doing this to people? If they still haven't found a way to make it... safe?"

"It *is* safe. Usually." Shaan sighed. "Detachment is mostly caused by untrained exposure to a Felen artifact. That's what happened to Kva-Sova's early Voiced. They had no idea what they were experiencing, and they couldn't process the information they were getting from the artifact. That kind of detachment doesn't happen now, because no Voiced would just be handed a Felen artifact if they're untrained. Ever. There's strict rules against that."

Keeven nodded, still looking extremely uncomfortable.

"But there's a rarer form of detachment that can be triggered by learning too much, too fast," Shaan continued. "It can happen to a Voiced who's overworked with high-concept artifacts. That's what happened to Ashlish. She was an *ailukh*... a novice Voiced who was still learning. She was only seventeen years old."

"Gods." Keeven winced. "Almost the same age as Ludyth."

"She'd been Voiced less than two years, but she was learning way faster than normal. Everyone on the station called her 'the prodigy,'" Shaan whispered. "They said she was tracking to become the most gifted telepath of her generation. But she was always under so much pressure... and her *alihe* was horrible to her, always pushing her further, harder, wanting more from her. Ashlish was burning out. She needed help."

"And nobody did anything?"

"People tried, but Ashlish begged everyone not to intervene," Shaan said. "She said she was fine, that she *wanted* to work harder. But I... I knew the truth, Keeven, I knew she wasn't fine. And... I knew other things, too. Awful things. Her *alihe* edited the records to hide the fact that Ashlish was practicing outside of approved hours. Ashlish wasn't taking rest days like the logs said." Shaan took a ragged breath. "When Ashlish started getting sick... I didn't do anything. I didn't tell the Governor, not even when he asked me point blank if Ashlish was acting strange. Ker Marecc and I never got along, and I thought he'd.... he'd fire me for not telling him sooner. I didn't want to risk my career with Geminus, so I lied to him. It was such a mistake, Keeven! I lied right to his face, and I told him Ashlish was fine."

She gulped back a sob. "But I really thought she *was* going to be fine! Her *alihe* paused her training to give her time to rest. She probably would've recovered if it hadn't been for that evacuation. She'd still be alive if I hadn't crashed that shuttle! She's dead because of me!"

Keeven didn't say anything, but he reached out and put one arm around Shaan. That small gesture of compassion cracked something in her, and she started sobbing uncontrollably into his shoulder.

They stayed that way for a long time, her cheek resting against the cool plating of his space-suit as tears streamed unapologetically down her face. When she finally let go of him, Keeven was looking at her with something almost like tenderness.

"I used to think about my brother's accident all the time," he said. "It was just so fucking unfair how he died. I kept thinking, if only I'd done something different, it wouldn't have happened. I'd play it over and over in my mind, beating myself up, asking myself why *I* didn't die instead of him."

"Me, too," Shaan whispered. "Exactly that."

"But one day I realized... whether it's fair or not, *I'm still alive*. And I've got to keep living my life." He brushed a tear from Shaan's chin. "I've made mistakes, Shaan. But I kept living. And I kept getting back up. That's what Ludyth would've wanted me to do."

Shaan nodded quietly.

"You, uh... gonna be okay?" he asked. "You want some water?"

She shook her head. "I don't want anything, except not to be on this station anymore."

"No kidding. I'm getting pretty damn tired of the place myself."

Shaan glanced at the silent comms receiver hanging on his suit. "Why hasn't the *Gallion* called us for so long? What if something's wrong?"

"Nothing's wrong." Keeven sounded unworried. "Leeg's doing his thing. They'll call soon."

He leaned against the base of the statue of the Decipherer, dropped his cargo-pack and slid down next to it. He took a water bottle out of the pack and drank, then pulled out a ZeyCorp-branded energy bar.

He offered the bar to her first, and when she declined it, he peeled it open and shoved it into his mouth whole. He chewed contemplatively, staring up at the constellation-studded ceiling. After a while, he looked back at her.

"Hey, what do you say we go somewhere else for a bit?" he asked.

She stared at him. "Um... like where? This is the most interesting place we can get to."

"Oh, is it?" Keeven's eyes twinkled with the hint of a smile. He patted the floor next to him. "Sit down. We'll see."

Shaan leaned against the statue's base and let herself slide down, just like Keeven had. It was hard to find a comfortable way to sit, with the curved arch of her suit's air recycling system digging into her shoulders.

"I'm gonna show you this thing I do whenever I'm stuck somewhere terrible," he said. "Okay?"

She nodded.

"So... pick an amazing, beautiful, happy place. Say the first one that pops into your head," he said. "Go!"

"Umm... Gedringa?" Shaan mumbled.

Keeven beamed triumphantly. "Aha! A fine choice! I should be getting a commission from the Gedringa tourism board, huh?"

She managed a tiny smile.

"Right. So, since you haven't been to Gedringa, I'll have to tell you every detail I remember about it. I might be talking for a long time."

"Keep talking," she whispered. "Please."

"Got it." He smiled. "Ever been on a boat? Guess not, huh?"

"No. Never."

"Well, that's perfect, then. You're in luck, because I'm *the* only person who's allowed to borrow Guillem's boat. And it's a beauty. Picture this: a sleek hoverboat, three levels, silent propulsion... barely leaves a ripple on the water. And I'm gonna take you out on it."

He pointed at an arbitrary spot in front of him. "Up here. Come on board with me."

"Right," she said. "Okay..."

"Just imagine it. We climb all the way up to the top deck, and we're standing on the roof. Here, look over the side." He took both her hands and held them out in front of her. "Put your hands on the rail and look at the water. Now... tell me what you see."

"Ummm... I guess... islands?" she said. "Pretty little islands."

"You bet," he said. "We took the boat out right at sundown, so we've got this nice, golden light coming over the ocean... and in the distance, you see lots of little islands rising above the water." He made a sweeping motion with his hand. "Over that way... there's Ajuen Island. You see the beach curving away, with green hills behind it." He nudged her. "Can you imagine that?"

"Yeah," she said, closing her eyes. "I... I think so."

"Gedringa has the most amazing sand. You pick it up and it's like stardust, like something out of a dream-play, only it's real," he said. "It stays warm even after sunset. Maybe we can go for a walk on that beach later." He gently turned her head to the left. "Look up the hill there, and you'll see Guillem's house. There's the lights from the terrace, just through those trees."

He took hold of Shaan's left hand again and unfolded her arm.

"You see that little sparkle there, in the water?" He pointed her hand down. "Know what that is? Glow-fish! Dozens of little fish, right near the surface. If you put your legs over the side of the boat, they'll swim right up to your feet."

"For real?"

"Absolutely! Gedringa has a bunch of bioluminescent species. I don't even have to make this up!"

He sat quietly for a while, but she didn't open her eyes.

"Want to put your feet in the water?"

Shaan nodded without saying anything.

"We'll have to climb down to the back." He squeezed her shoulder like he was holding her steady. "Careful here... it's going to be four, maybe five steps down... and... there we go! Now we're on a little platform on the back of the boat. C'mon, take your shoes off." He waited a few seconds, then asked: "Did you?"

"Did I what?"

"Did you take your shoes off?"

"Yeah," she whispered. "I did."

"Good. Now, picture this. The boat's stopped. You sit down on the edge and lower your feet... the water's nice and cool. Relax and breathe." He inhaled deeply, then exhaled with a sigh. His arm was still around her. "Waves splashing, warm breeze on your face..."

Shaan tilted her head back and breathed in. The air really did feel warmer on her face. She wriggled her feet inside her boots, trying to imagine what ocean water might feel like.

"The islands are over to your left now. To your right, it's ocean as far as you can see. You can hardly tell where the water stops and the sky starts, because everything's twinkling. The sun's gone, but you've got the stars, and the lights from the hills, and the glow-fish." He tilted her head to one side. "There's two moons out. A big golden one, and a smaller pinkish one... just over there. The sky's fucking beautiful. You can see the tail of the Union Quadrant from here, all those stars sweeping across the sky..."

He leaned back further, pulling her along with him. He was lying nearly flat out on the floor now, propped up on one arm.

Shaan lay her head against his chestplate.

"There's something about looking up at space from a green world that makes all your problems feel small," he said. "*Especially* when all your problems are out in space, right?" His laugh rumbled in his chest. "You can't help but feel better, lookin' at stars like these."

He *was* right. That awful, suffocating panic was slowly draining out of her, and she was breathing evenly again.

"Don't stop talking," she whispered.

"Hmm, all right," he said with that smile in his voice again. "Well... I guess it's getting pretty late. I'm thinking about bringing the boat back in, so I can take you to see the house. Or we *could* just spend the night here on the boat. Tough choice, huh?"

At once, Shaan realized that she felt extremely warm, and that she was very, very close to Keeven. His chin was resting on top of her head; she could feel his soft breath against her hair as he spoke. His fingers were idly stroking the back of her neck, and she didn't want to let go of him.

Who *was* he, this person she was holding? Not the revered, magnanimous Negotiator. Not Keeven, the self-centred liar and con artist. No, this was someone else. Someone flawed, and broken, and contradictory, and complicated... and as real as she was.

Jereth. She had never called him by his familiar name.

He was still talking. "So I'm sitting on the back of the boat, thinking to myself... boat or house? Boat or house? What should we do? I turn around to ask you what you think..." He rearranged his arm around her. "And we're sitting real close, just like this..."

Shaan turned her head, her eyes still closed.

"Jereth..." she whispered.

"Mmm-hmm?"

His fingers slipped into her hair as she leaned toward him. For an instant, their lips brushed together. Her breath hitched.

And then, she realized their comms receiver was buzzing.

"*Gallion* calling Shuttle Team One!" came Ozakka's voice. "You hear us? We're ready!"

JERETH
Ajuen Island, Gedringa
3 months before the Rift

JERETH STOOD ON the terrace of Azeran Guillem's beach house, staring out over the ocean. The last rays of sunlight had just disappeared over the horizon, leaving lingering pink halos around the islands. As Jereth watched, the glow of sunset faded, too, giving way to a perfectly clear star-studded sky.

He breathed in, his lungs filling gratefully with sea air. After weeks in space, there was nothing like putting his feet on the ground again, especially here. The moment he saw that beach as the lander was coming down, he felt... *alive.*

Maybe it was some deep-seated memory of his recovery all those years ago, when Guillem had brought him here to recuperate from stasis. But whatever shitty outpost he was sleeping on, whatever claustrophobic ship bunk he was hunkered down in, the knowledge that this place existed always soothed his spirits. Landing on Gedringa was the closest thing to a homecoming that he'd ever experienced.

He watched the waves and tried to clear his thoughts, but couldn't find the peace of mind that usually came so easily here. There was a strange unease in Guillem, and he had the distinct feeling that the boss wanted to talk to him about

358

something important.

As Jereth stood staring at the water, the wide terrace doors slid open, and light from the house spilled over the polished stone tiles. In the doorway, Guillem paused to fold away a portable comms device, then slowly made her way out across the terrace.

She wasn't wearing her exoskeleton, or the body armour she donned when she met business associates. Instead, she was dressed in one of the simple tunics that she favoured at home. Her face and neck were bare, her weathered brown skin unornamented, and her silver hair was pulled back into a round knot. Without the suit, Guillem was a hand shorter, and she leaned heavily on an ornate walking-stick. She shuffled her sandal-clad feet over the smooth stone.

There were very few people that Guillem would allow to see her without her fearsome guise. And whenever she dispensed with the imposing uniform, Jereth knew the conversation wouldn't be entirely business-related.

She came to the railing beside Jereth and stared out at the water, her expression grave.

"What's the word, boss?" Jereth said, searching her face. "Something wrong?"

Guillem looked up at the bright belt of the Union Quadrant, cascading across the sky. "*Everything's* wrong, Jer," she said. "The whole Union's burning."

"It's getting worse out there, for sure," Jereth said. "Nothing but orange zones from here to Baedenoch. I heard they torched two more outposts this week."

"Outposts?" Guillem gave a rueful chuckle. "Tch. That's just a distraction. It's all a distraction. You think the Felen give a damn about raiding cargo ships, about blowing up some piss-useless deep space junk? They could've been doing that all along, but they choose right now to step it up?" She shook her head. "No way. This is a cover. Something big is about to happen, mark my words. And when the Prime Worlds start to fall, this thing's as good as over. The Union's finished."

Jereth looked back down at the shore, watching moonlight glint softly off the beach. A dread he hadn't felt in a long time sank into his bones.

"This is the beginning of the end," Guillem said. "It's only a matter of time. This war's been going on since I was a suckling babe. And if the Union forces haven't turned it around by now..." She laid a hand on his shoulder. "I'm saying it might be time to get out, Jer. Sooner rather than later."

Jereth stared at her. "You're talking about skipping Union space," he said, uncertainly. "You mean... getting on a ditch ship?"

Guillem nodded solemnly. "Not *me*. I've still got the business to run, for as long as there's business. But I'm sending Tyamuki and Aylenki out, as soon as I can. The arrangements are already under way." She'd used the diminutive forms of her grandchildren's names, the affectionate baby names they hadn't gone by in years.

"Shit," Jereth said. "You're sending them to Baedenoch?"

Guillem laughed. "Are you kidding? You know as well as I do that Baedenoch's a fucking scam. Those jumps don't go anywhere."

"Then where?"

"I have a lead," Guillem said. "There's a new venture-ship being built over in the Wayan cluster. They're planning to jump from the Fedraya system into the outer territories, and go on from there. Sources say it looks good. This ship's five times the size of the Baedenoch ships, and it's a live haul! They can go for months before they have to use the stasis pods. Plus, the pods they have are all new tech. They call it *lightsleep*—they say it won't do the damage, that you could stay under for sixty years with minimal risk."

"Huh," said Jereth. "You really believe all that?"

"Comes to a point, you've got to believe *something*." Guillem's face was pained. "This isn't the future I wanted for them. But I don't want to wait until it's too late. I have to get them out."

"When?" Jereth asked.

"The ship will be ready in three months, if construction stays on schedule." She inhaled deeply. "Jereth... listen. I locked down an extra place on that ship. It's yours if you want it."

"What?" Jereth's limbs tensed. "No way! I mean, if you're not going, why would I? You'll need me here if you're still running the business—"

Guillem held up one hand. "Jer, please. You've done enough for me." She sighed. "Truth is... I was planning to give you the business when I was done. I thought one day I'd hand everything over to you, maybe retire while I still had a few good years left. But now..." She looked out over the water again, her eyes misting over. "I think you should get out, Jer."

Jereth swallowed hard. "I don't know. A ditch ship? I just... never thought..."

"Relax. There's no pressure," Guillem said. "You can stay here till the bitter end and keep running things with me, if you want. That's your choice. You know I'll always have your back. But before that ship leaves from Fedraya, I need you to do a job for me. A personal job, understand? One for the family."

"What job?" Jereth's hands shook on the railing.

Guillem cleared her throat. "Well... a few weeks ago, I cast the net for a jump architect," she said. "This ship's gonna have my grandkids on it, I'm not fucking around here. I want it jumped by someone I vetted personally. Someone with a long record. Experienced, reliable... *trustworthy*." She looked up at the stars again. "Gods damn it, though, that's hard to find. Most of the decent architects are long dead or retired, and the ones that volunteer for these kinds of missions are usually...

not right in the head. Nobody sane wants to go into space right now."

Jereth nodded. "Guess it's a tough sell, as jump jobs go," he said. "So did you find anyone?"

"I was passed the names of a few candidates," Guillem said. "But I've narrowed it down to just one. He's a retired commercial jumper. More jumps on his record than anyone else I've come across. He's a professor now, apparently, working at some shit little university in the Almant system." Guillem fixed her piercing gaze on Jereth. "I want you to go out there and pick him up, then bring him to Fedraya and get him on that ship. You can make a cargo pickup at Pilar in the same trip. I've got supplies coming in."

"Okay," said Jereth, nodding. "What's the cargo?"

"A hundred and twenty crates of high-yield assemblage. There's no payment to collect—I'm trading it straight up for the kids' passage on that ship. And yours," Guillem said. "But you need to get that jump architect first, understand? That's priority number one."

"Got it. Almant, the university professor. So... you've made contact with him already? He knows I'm picking him up?"

"Nope," said Guillem. "I thought I'd leave it to you to persuade him."

Jereth's eyebrows went up. "He has no idea?"

"This is the job, Jereth," said Guillem. "You'll have to convince him to go."

"Okay, but we're talking about *leaving Union space* here. It's a one-way trip, and like you said, no one sane wants to go into space." Jereth frowned. "What if he says no? Am I supposed to, like... kidnap him or something?"

"I doubt you'll need such drastic measures," Guillem said, amusement in her voice. "He's an old friend of yours. Name's Eldric Leesongronski."

"*What?*" Jereth gripped the railing with both hands, his heart pounding. "But—no, Leeg's dead! He died on Dylham while I was in the freezer!"

"Did he?" Guillem smiled enigmatically.

"I checked the census records years ago," Jereth said. "Leeg was still on Dylham the month before it got levelled. And his name was in the list of the dead Founders…"

"Well, I guess he must've left the system just before the attack," said Guillem. "He took a job as a jump architect. According to his commercial record, he was still doing jump work for some shipping company *two years* after Dylham blew. He fell off the map when that company shut down, but one of my contacts finally managed to track him down."

"He's alive," Jereth breathed incredulously. "You're really sure it's him?"

"No doubt about it. *Professor* Eldric Leesongronski. Your old pal Leeg is teaching the basics of subspace physics to first-year students."

"What the *fuck?*" Jereth shook his head, a grin spreading across his face. "I can't believe it. He's really alive."

"Yeah, well, I'm sure he'll get a surprise and a half when he sees you out of the freezer," Guillem said. "He probably thinks you're dead, too, since Grimm Parukh's gone. Seems some gods-damned coffin-robber got to it and blew it all to bits. Some of these arms-dealing assholes have no shame, huh?"

Jereth laughed, then threw his arms out and embraced Guillem, tears filling his eyes.

"You're welcome, Jer," Guillem said, patting his back affectionately. "You just get his ass onto that ditch ship, okay?"

"I'll figure something out," Jereth said, still catching his breath. "I'll plot the quickest route to Almant without crossing too many orange zones. I'm gonna need a fresh ship. Something fast, and unmarked—"

"I'm way ahead of you," Guillem said. "Your ship's called *Enigma,* and it's already waiting in orbit. I think you'll like this one. It's real nice inside, loads of interior space."

"And you've got an engineer for me?"

"Yep. Name's Mendeg, already vetted and paid. Word has it he's reliable and he keeps to himself, doesn't ask too many questions. He'll go with you for the whole trip—first to Almant to pick up Leesongronski, then to Pilar to get our cargo and onward to Fedraya."

"Got it," said Jereth. "So... what's *supposed* to be in the cargo this time?"

Guillem grinned. "Permit says you're hauling live deep-water squid. The assemblage crates are all marked as *exotic aquatics,* sealed self-sustaining eco-containers, scan-exempt. They'll be on Pilar in a few weeks."

"Aquatics, nice," said Jereth, whistling softly.

"I told you I'm not fucking around," said Guillem, her eyes clouding over again. "I'll take the kids up to Fedraya myself, on *Aeglaca.* And I'll meet you there, three months from now. At the shipyards."

Jereth nodded solemnly. "It's a deal."

"Mendeg will be at the orbital in two days. You can leave then." Guillem scanned the sky again before she looked back at Jereth. "I'm not gonna tell you what to do, Jer. But for what it's worth, I think you should get on that venture-ship. Get the fuck out of here... while anybody still can."

UMA
Engineering Deck, ZeyCorp Gallion
Mission Time: 5.6 hours

UMA STOOD NEXT to Leesongronski, watching a stream of data flowing across his viewscreen. Whatever he was looking at, he was unimpressed. He swore, then switched to a different data set, then back to the first one again, while everyone stared at him.

Most of the engineers had turned their chairs toward the console where Leesongronski was working. The rest of them were sitting on the floor near the bottom of the stairs, their own consoles abandoned. Mercifully, Kva-Sova and the Voiced had already gone. Several hours of staring at nothing but scrolling lines of code had apparently been enough for them.

"Leeg? You there?" said Keeven over the comms. "We're gonna try one more time. Sixth time lucky, right?"

"Doing the same thing again is *not* going to achieve a different result," Leesongronski muttered under his breath. He hadn't bothered to open the comms line.

"It's still not working," came Shaan's tense voice. "I'm seeing all of Marecc's files... and when I log in it says *STATION GOVERNOR MARECC—GEMINUS COMMAND.* But when I go into the security panel to deactivate the lockdown, that error comes up."

"Same message again?" said Keeven.

"Same one," Shaan said. "'Co-authorization not entered. Security status update failed.'"

Leesongronski sighed, rolling his eyes. He still didn't open the comms line.

"Gods damn it!" shouted Keeven. "Leeg! You there?"

Leesongronski finally slapped the comms switch. "What do you want?"

"Some help would be nice," Keeven said. "Nothing's happening here."

"That's right, and it's never going to," Leesongronski said. "See what it says there, Jerry? 'Co-authorization.' Marecc didn't have a solo auth on this. He hasn't got the permissions. We assumed the Station Governor alone could remove the station from the lockdown state, but we were wrong."

"So... what are we gonna do?"

"Nothing," said Leesongronski flatly. "From what I can tell, Marecc needs at least two senior staff members to co-authorize it with him if he wants to reverse that lockdown. We'd need three accounts on the system, all logged in at the same time."

"Shit," said Keeven. "But... you're gonna find a way around it, right? Make more accounts?"

"Oh, sure, yeah. I'll get right on that, Jerry." Leesongronski gave a bitter laugh. "Wait right there for a month or two, and I'll go do some research. No problem."

Keeven exhaled loudly. "Thanks for the sarcasm. Real fucking useful."

"Don't you start with me," Leesongronski snapped. "I *told* you. I said, Jerry, this is a risky idea, there's too many unknowns. But you never listen—"

"There's always a way," Keeven interrupted. "We have to get these damn security doors up and get to that control room! So... just... come up with something!"

Leesongronski switched off the comms line without replying. He leaned back in the chair and rubbed his eyes with his palms. Uma took a step toward him, but before she could get a word out, Captain Fransk was motioning her to one side.

"What's going on?" Fransk whispered. "I thought this was meant to be simple."

"It's fine. Don't worry," Uma whispered back. "I'm sure Professor Leesongronski will find a fix. The other team's not even finished with the physical setup on the annex; we still have time to think."

"What is there to think about?" Fransk's voice was strained. "If the Station Governor can't raise those security doors, then... what are we even doing?"

Eldric Leesongronski was silent, still covering his eyes.

"Captain, might I suggest we fall back to our other plan?" Nack said. "We could tell Shuttle Team Two to forget about building Last Shot and just bring back some of those energy cells instead."

"Absolutely not," said Uma. "You bloody well stay out of this, Nack."

Fransk looked appalled. "Director Ozakka, please."

"The first plan failed, Captain, it's time to face it," Nack continued. "But if we get those cells, at least we'll have something to show for our—"

Just then, Leesongronski sat bolt upright in his chair, startling them all. He leaned over the console and made a few frantic keystrokes, then scrolled through the resulting data before he flipped open the comms channel.

"Jerry! You there? I think I found something!"

"Hah!" came Keeven's voice. "I was right, huh? Hit us with the good news! You got Marecc those permissions, or what?"

"Forget Marecc, he's useless," Leesongronski said. "I only gave Shaan that profile because it's the one you asked me for...

but Marecc isn't the most powerful profile in the database."

"There was someone on Verkhoy with *more* permissions than the *Station Governor*?" Shaan sounded confused.

"There's a sub-section in this database called Sector Command," Leesongronski said. "And there's a profile in here that outranks your Governor by an order of magnitude. I'm looking at dozens of extra override permissions."

"That's a winner!" Keeven enthused. "Swap it in, Leeg! Go!"

Leesongronski flicked out a few more hectic keystrokes. "There," he said. "It's done."

Uma let out her breath, relief flooding her body. *Thank the gods.*

"Shaan, if you log in again, you should be able to reverse that lockdown without any co-auth now," Leesongronski said. "You've just become Geminus High Commander Kehallian Sifyer."

"High Commander Sifyer?" Over the voice line, Shaan gasped aloud. "Oh! I've *met* her before! She was at the Verkhoy inquest!" Shaan's voice was high and incredulous. "She was with Border Security... so she must've had these override permissions on every Geminus facility in the sector!"

Uma was clutching the back of Leesongronski's chair with one hand, her other hand clasped to her mouth. "Oh my *gods...*" she breathed, almost inaudibly. "I..."

Leesongronski turned to look at her, his face concerned. "What?"

"High Commander Kehallian Sifyer," she repeated in a whisper, pointing at the open profile on his display. "That's *Halli!*"

Over the comms, they heard three long, shrill beeps, then a triumphant whoop from Keeven.

"Clearance accepted. Security status updated." Shaan said. "It's working now!"

"Security doors are going up!" yelled Keeven. "Yeaaah! Leeg, you're a fucking genius!"

The whole *Gallion* Engineering pit erupted into a chorus of joyous shrieks and cheers, the engineers all hugging each other jubilantly. And in the midst of it, Uma and Leesongronski stared at each other in wide-eyed disbelief.

Engineering Deck, ZeyCorp Gallion
Mission Time: 6.7 hours

As UMA WATCHED the monitor, Shuttle Two's blue light peeled away from the annex and started blinking back toward the *Gallion,* and she finally allowed herself to feel just a little bit triumphant.

It had taken a little more than an hour for Shuttle Team One to make their way up to the control room and work out how to set the Jaxong drive into maintenance mode. Jaxong's state changes had only taken a matter of minutes to upload, and when the drive had been restarted, they had transferred remote control of the Jaxong drive to the *Gallion.*

The mission had been more of a success than even Uma had dared to hope.

She patted the edge of Leesongronski's black sleeve. "Thank you," she whispered. "Thank you so much."

Leesongronski didn't respond. He remained motionless, his eyes fixed on the projection in front of him. Only his finger moved, scrolling the lines of code.

"Hey, Noussen," Leesongronski said. "Did you shut down the hover relay?"

Noussen turned in her chair. "No. I didn't do anything. Why?"

"The remote connection just dropped out. I've got no data stream."

Noussen frowned. "The relay should definitely still be live. We need it to keep voice comms to the shuttles." She reached over and activated one of the voice lines. "*Gallion* to Shuttle Team Two, are you hearing us?"

"We hear you, *Gallion*!" came Mikolai's excited voice. "We're on course, heading home!"

Noussen's frown deepened. She flicked over to the other comms band. "*Gallion* to Shuttle Team One, you hear us? What's your status?"

"We've got you, *Gallion*!" said Keeven. "We're still in the station, on our way back down to the shuttle."

"Weird. It's only the data stream that's gone," Wazar whispered to Noussen. "The relay's fine. Maybe it's the data transmitter on Verkhoy Station that went down."

"Something strange is going on here," Leesongronski muttered, more to himself than to anyone else. The pale rectangle of his virtual screen was gradually filling up with garbled red characters. "This is the last data we received... what the fuck's all this stuff?"

Macey leaned over and examined the rows of wavy red lines. "Corrupted data, maybe?" he ventured. "Random noise?"

"Not random," said Leesongronski. "There's a pattern. See here? This part's repeating. And this string up here is exactly the same as this one."

Uma stood behind Leesongronski, parsing the half-familiar symbols.

"Wait," she said. "I think these might be Felen short-notation characters!" She traced a finger over the uppermost line. Leesongronski scrolled again before she'd reached the end, and she had to chase the characters down the screen. "I've seen this character before... and this one's a numeral..." She drew the shape in the air.

"Felen text?" said Noussen, wide-eyed.

Uma turned to Leesongronski. "The Felen didn't use a written script before the Peace, and they still don't, but these short-notations were developed for tech-sharing with the Union. This is Felen computer code."

"Alien code strings," Leesongronski said, his face amazed. "Well, shit."

"The station must've had some Felen code integrated with their mainframe," Uma said. "Dean! You know anything about Felen computer code?"

The android in the charging port awoke and hurried toward Leesongronski's console, adopting an apologetic expression. "The *Gallion*'s local knowledge bank contains nothing on this subject," Dean said. "Without network access, I'm afraid I can't help."

Leesongronski continued to examine the scrolling red lines. "We have no idea what these Felen programs are doing. I don't know what logs they could see, or what independent verification checks they were running..." He trailed off, his expression dark. "I think the station knows it's been hacked from the outside. It cut off our remote data connection to safeguard itself."

Dean's head bobbed. "We did not take this scenario into account."

"Oh, well. It's no big deal now, is it?" said Wazar. "We're done already. The Jaxong drive changes are done, we don't need the data stream anymore, so.... we'll just call this lucky timing. Right?" She peered hopefully at Leesongronski.

"Yeah. Sure," Leesongronski mumbled, not raising his head. He activated the comms line to Shuttle Team One.

"Jerry, you there?"

"Yeah," Keeven said. "What's up, Leeg?"

"Listen, we just lost the data stream. Some Felen system's coming online over there, and it's cut us off. I'm guessing it's a security sentinel, so I'd suggest you get out of there quick."

Keeven laughed. "Don't worry, we're goin'! Not like we're hanging around on purpose." There was a clicking sound in the background, like someone was repeatedly pressing buttons. "Might be a long walk down, though. Looks like the lifts just stopped working. Guess we're heading to the emergency stairs."

"Fuck," Leesongronski said under his breath. "Hurry up, Jerry. I'm keeping this channel open."

There were a few seconds of silence, except for the muffled, distant sounds of Keeven and Shaan's booted footsteps. The *Gallion* crew closed in around Leesongronski's console again, listening.

Then, abruptly, the footsteps stopped.

Keeven's voice was back over the comms. "Uh, Leeg... something's happening," he said uncertainly. "The lights are all changing colour."

"What lights, Jerry?"

"Oh, shit! And now... *Shit!* Gods damn it!"

In the background, there was a loud, metallic thump, then another one. Shaan screamed.

"What was that? Jerry!"

Fransk pushed to the front of the group. "Shuttle Team One, this is Captain Fransk. What's going on over there?"

"The security doors are coming back down!" Keeven shouted. "They're all closing!"

"Oh my gods, oh my gods..." Shaan was repeating breathlessly. "The system won't recognize me anymore! It's declining Commander Sifyer's auth... oh my *gods*."

Then Keeven again: "Leeg! Do something!"

"Damn, damn, damn," Leesongronski muttered. "Okay... there must've been a separate staff identification cache inside that Felen system. One we didn't edit." His fingers tapped nervously on the edge of the console. "So the mainframe's telling that security sentinel that Shaan is Kehallian Sifyer... but the sentinel knows that isn't true... and if this thing can *also* see everything our fake Sifyer did, which now seems increasingly likely..."

"Leeg!" Keeven interrupted. "Listen, you'll just have to crack into it, right? You can get into that Felen system somehow, and edit that cache?"

"No!" shouted Leesongronski. "No, I *can't* do that, Jerry. Get *real*. You think I can just unravel a fucking *alien codebase*, just like that? And besides, the station cut off our remote data connection. All we've got left is voice comms. I can't do anything. You need to get out."

"Did you not hear me when I said the gods-damned security doors are down?" yelled Keeven. "We're stuck in the upper levels, nowhere near the shuttle. How can we—"

The rest of his sentence was drowned out by a blaring alarm.

"Oh, gods. Now it's saying... 'critical security breach detected'!" Shaan's panicked voice was muffled by the background noise. Uma could hardly make out what she said next as the voice line stuttered. "It says... breach... engaging grey destruct ... self-destruct protocol ... get out—"

And then, the line cut off. Dead silence.

"We lost the voice line," gasped Uma. "Noussen!"

A sick-looking Noussen shook her head. "The hover relay's intact," she whispered. "The station is jamming our voice comms."

"Damn it!" Uma grabbed Leesongronski's arm. "We have to get them out of there! Please, you have to fix this!"

Leesongronski's face was grim. "Fix it?" he growled. "Fix it *how*?"

"What if we called for the Ambassador?" Fransk suggested. "It's a Felen alarm system, right? So maybe there's something the Ambassador could do."

"No!" Leesongronski stood up, shouldering Uma's hand

away. "It's too *late,* the remote connection is *dead.* We can't connect to the station anymore, and now it's jamming our voice comms, too. It knows full well it's been hacked from outside, so the last thing it's going to do is accept any more remote commands from us. If Kehallian Sifyer herself was standing right where you are, she still couldn't do *shit* from here, understand? It's *over.*"

"Professor—" Uma began, but Leesongronski pushed past her and marched to the stairs.

He stormed halfway up before he stopped and turned back to the group. "Did anybody think to tell me there might be alien code in that thing? Did you even consider that possibility?" He glowered down at Uma. "I told you this wouldn't be easy, and you accepted the risks! This was *your* choice—yours and Jereth's—so don't shout at me to fix it like it's somehow my fault!"

"Wait! W-where are you going?" Fransk said hoarsely. "Professor Leesongronski—"

Leesongronski held up a cigarette. "I'm going for a smoke," he spat. He pointed the cigarette at Macey, who was frantically repeating a prayer gesture. "Which is exactly as useful as what *he's* doing."

Verkhoy Station
Mission Time: 6.8 hours

SHAAN SANK ONTO the floor and folded herself into a ball, hugging her knees as best she could in the space-suit. It seemed fitting that she would die here, on Verkhoy Station. Just as she should have died six years ago. It was almost too poetic.

Around her, the alarm continued to blare at ear-splitting volume. She couldn't hear Keeven shouting at her at first, not until he came closer and waved his hand to get her attention.

"Shaan!" he screamed. "Shaan, listen to me! What's the quickest way to a space-facing airlock?"

She squinted at him in confusion. "What?"

He crouched down and bent his head close to hers, his face bathed in orange from the warning lights. "I might be able to get us out!" he shouted. "I've got scarab grenades! In my pack!"

"You brought those here?" she gasped. "Why?"

"Contingency!" He gestured around him as if to make his point. The alarm shrieked on. "I've got two of 'em, so I can blow out two doors to get us to an airlock!"

Shaan's heart sank. "That won't work, Keeven! There's more than two doors in the way—"

"Then we need to get to an outer wall!" he shouted. "I'll set a scarab to do hull damage, we'll take cover, put up our helmets, seal our suits... an' when the wall blows, we should get sucked out into space!"

She gave him an incredulous look. "*What?*"

Keeven was rummaging in his cargo-pack as he spoke. He threw his water bottle and two ZeyCorp snack bars over his shoulder before he retrieved what he was looking for: a small, insect-shaped object, shiny and black. As Shaan looked on in horror, he fiddled with a setting on the underside, then flicked it with his fingernail. The scarab unfolded on his palm like a winged beetle.

"The first door we blow has to be this one!" He pointed at the nearest security door. "The outer wall's got to be that way! I'm doing it!"

Before she could say a word, Keeven flung the little device at the security door. A bright light pulsed from its centre as it stuck, then the wings spun and the scarab started to burrow its way into the door's surface. It emitted a screeching, high-pitched tone that almost drowned out the station's alarms.

"Twelve seconds! Run!" Keeven grabbed Shaan by the shoulders and turned her away from the security door. They started running, getting halfway to the opposite end of the corridor before he stopped abruptly and crouched down, pulling her down with him. They huddled together against the wall.

"We are *not* going to die," he insisted. "We're getting out of here."

The floor vibrated with the explosion at the end of the corridor, and searing hot air rushed against Shaan's face. When she looked back, a gaping hole had appeared where the sealed security door used to be, and smoke was pouring into the corridor. Bits of metal and shattered panelling were falling from the ceiling, and blue cooling fluid sprayed from a broken pipe. Part of the wall sagged into the gap with a creak.

The station's alarm screamed on.

"C'mon!" Keeven hauled Shaan to her feet. "Through there!"

"We're too far in," Shaan protested as she bolted down the corridor. "This is pointless! There's more doors, Keeven—"

He didn't slow down. She followed him through the jagged gap, dodging the leaking pipe and protruding metal. They skidded out into a wider passageway, and Keeven carried on down the corridor. But there was nowhere for them to go. Another sealed security door would be waiting around the next corner.

"Come on!" he shouted, pulling her down an adjoining hallway. "Outer wall's this way!"

And then Shaan suddenly realized exactly where they were, and her stomach lurched.

In front of her were two small, bloody handprints on the wall. *Two bloody handprints. The tracks of each finger trailed from somewhere around shoulder height all the way down to the dark-tiled floor, where the blood was no longer visible.*

No *no no no no no*—

Shaan slumped against the wall, each breath an agony in her aching lungs. She looked down the empty hallway, willing herself into motion. She had to find Ashlish and get her to the evac vessel.

Over the public address channel, a repeated message looped round and round: 'All Geminus personnel, evacuate immediately. Please make your way to the nearest evacuation point. This is not a drill. All Geminus personnel, evacuate immediately.'

And then—oh, gods, no—she saw Ashlish far down the corridor, crawling on all fours.

No *no no no no*—

Shaan bolted down the hall, dived onto the floor and grabbed Ashlish by one ankle. Ashlish jerked away, kicking out with her other foot, squirming loose. She shrieked like some injured animal, her body thrashing on the floor before she scrambled to her feet and started running again.

Shaan ran too, following Ashlish through the next bulkhead. How long had it been since the evac order? Was everyone else out already? And how long before the security doors started sealing?

Then Ashlish bolted into a service nook, a small alcove with wide, flat-handled panels on every wall. On each panel, a glowing display listed what equipment it held.

Ashlish backed into the alcove, holding her bloodied hands against her chest, her eyes wild. She was still screaming. Dark patches of red soaked through her clothes where her fingers gripped the fabric, and her head swung from side to side, her frightened eyes desperately seeking an escape route. But she was cornered.

Shaan took a step toward her.

Ashlish swivelled toward the nearest panel, grabbed the

handle with both hands and pulled. The equipment-box inside swung out on its stout wheels, and Ashlish shoved the heavy box at Shaan.

It clipped Shaan just below the ribs, and she stumbled back in pain.

'All Geminus personnel, evacuate immediately. Please make your way to the nearest evacuation point. This is not a drill. All Geminus personnel, evacuate immediately.'

Shaan wrestled Ashlish against the wall, seizing her by both slender wrists, and managed to drag the girl back a few steps. The whole time, Ashlish continued to shriek in terror, her bloodied hands clutching helplessly.

When they stumbled into the loose equipment-box, Shaan kicked it hard, propelling it out of her way. She locked her arms around Ashlish and kept pulling her.

The equipment-box rolled all the way to the end of the empty corridor. It rolled in a straight line, but the cavernous passage curved sharply here, and one wheel caught the edge of the gnarled wall. The box wobbled and tipped over, and the equipment inside shattered over the hard floor.

In Shaan's arms, Ashlish continued to scream.

"Oh my gods," breathed Shaan.

"Whoa!" Keeven had stopped in his tracks, his hand closing around Shaan's. "Holy astral mother! Do you see *that*?"

Lying at the edge of the corridor was an overturned equipment-box, its former contents scattered around it. The box had been crushed flat on one side by a lowering security door. The heavy door was bent off its tracks, its descent halted by the splintered box—stuck open, jammed with its bottom edge sitting slightly above the floor.

Keeven punched the air with a victorious shout. He grabbed Shaan's hand again and took off in a breakneck run toward the door. They both squeezed under it and hauled themselves through to the other side.

Suddenly—impossibly—a space-facing wall was within their reach. Right ahead. Shaan could hardly breathe, could hardly think, could hardly feel anything. Her stinging eyes filled with tears.

"Here!" Keeven pulled up the EVA harness on the back of Shaan's suit. "Find your clips and make sure they're facing up, okay? Right before the blast, I'm gonna clip us together so we don't get separated! Check your gloves and boots!"

Shaan didn't reply. Stars danced at the edges of her vision, and her heart felt like it was tunnelling through her ribcage. She fumbled to untangle the harness, then leaned down and slid her fingers along her boot-seals. She tugged her suit's black gloves back into place.

"You good?" Keeven shouted. "Ready?"

She gave him the tiniest nod.

He checked the seals on his own suit, then tinkered with a setting on his remaining scarab grenade. Before he activated it, he motioned to Shaan, pointing out the small service nook that opened off the corridor behind them. There was a gap in the wall there; one panel stood open where a single equipment box had been removed.

"That gap there, see it?" he shouted. "We'll take cover in there while the wall blows!"

Shaan clenched her eyes shut. Her boots suddenly felt unbelievably heavy.

Keeven threw the scarab grenade.

"Twelve seconds!" he yelled as it started burrowing into the wall. "It's set to hull damage. Go!"

Shaan ran to the alcove. She crouched down and backed her way into the narrow space, and Keeven squeezed in right after her. His hands were shaking hard, but he managed to link the clips on the front of his EVA harness to hers. Then he reached behind him and pulled the panel shut, leaving them with only a sliver of light.

The grenade's screeching warning escalated, keening over the alarms.

"Luck be with us!" Keeven roared over the noise. "Put your helmet up, Shaan!"

Shaan knew she needed to move, but her arms were both wedged behind her. She wriggled one hand up from behind her back, edging her fingers toward her suit's helmet release.

Keeven hadn't put his helmet up yet, either. She could just make out the contours of his shadowed face, his eyes fixed on her in the dark. He rested his hot forehead against hers.

And then he leaned forward and kissed her on the mouth.

Shaan's eyes opened wide in surprise, warmth flooding into her cheeks as his lips pressed against hers. A second later, he pulled back, holding down the buttons on her suit's collar at the same time as he tapped his own.

Both of their helmets snapped up.

Shaan's faceplate slipped into place, and the suit's HUD lit up. The row of lights at eye level flashed blue as her oxygen scrubber engaged.

And then the scarab grenade exploded.

There was an agonizing sound: creaking metal, splintering beams and hissing pipes, the very bones of the station being wrenched apart. The flimsy panel behind Keeven was sucked away, and light poured into their little hideaway as the panel clattered off.

Keeven was pulled away from her until her linked harness caught up, and then she was dragged along after him. Their bodies slid across the floor and toward the huge, irregular breach that had opened in the outer wall.

For a few horrifying seconds, everything was deathly silent. Keeven's suited form tumbled alongside her as they spun out into space. They crashed into each other and then spun apart, over and over again.

Her helmet's display lit up with a spray of orange warnings: a tear in one of the joints of her suit, dropping oxygen levels, some problem relating to pressure, and the gods only knew what else. Blood rushed to her head, her ears ringing.

And then she felt a terrible, lurching jerk. The harness crushed her chest, knocking the air from her lungs.

Keeven had fired his emergency grapple. Their free-fall had stopped, and a thin, gleaming tether ran from his space-suit back to the station's outer hull.

"Keeven!" she screamed. Were their suit-to suit comms still online? "Jereth! Are you okay?"

"Yeah," he said. His voice was raw. He reached out and pulled Shaan toward him. "Just as well we rehearsed the tether thing, huh?"

"My suit's saying it's critical," Shaan said. "It's losing oxygen."

"Same here," Keeven said. "But we won't be out much longer."

She couldn't see his face through the reflective faceplate, but she watched him look back toward the station, and something about the way he tilted his head sent a chill of dread into her. He was assessing the situation, and it wasn't good.

"Damn. We're still pretty far up," he said. The glimmering tether was retracting now, hauling them both back toward the station. His grapple had struck the station about two decks lower than where they'd been before. "We need to climb all the way down to that docking platform, and we probably haven't got a lot of time."

He nodded down to where their shuttle's rounded little roof gleamed on the platform. It seemed alarmingly distant, so far below.

"We'll have to fire your grapple, too," he said. "We'll fire it straight down, right into that platform, if we can hit it.... hopefully the tether's long enough! We'll detach my line and follow yours straight down. Yeah?"

She bobbed her head wordlessly.

"Aim it for me, okay?" he said. "Aim right at the platform. Hold it real steady."

Shaan levelled her arm. She could hardly bear to look as he pressed the release sequence at her wrist and fired the grapple.

The tether was long enough. The little silver claw found its mark less than a pace from the edge of the platform, next to the airlock where they'd first stepped onto the station.

"Whoa! Nice shot!" Keeven yelled.

He detached his own safety line, and the grapple mechanism fell away from his suit.

As Shaan's safety line started to reel them in, pulling them down toward the docking platform, she tilted her head back to look at the station's upper levels. The gaping hole where they'd blown the wall out was clearly visible; bright white light spilled out of the station's wound.

But there was something else happening up there. The top levels of Verkhoy Station were imploding. The uppermost decks were slowly crumpling, like a ball of foil being crushed underfoot.

The station was deconstructing itself piece by piece, its own nanotechnology consuming it, reducing it to a viscous grey pulp.

"Look!" Shaan gasped. "Up there! The grey destruct is starting."

Keeven followed her gaze.

"Oh, *shit*," he said. "Guess we're in a real hurry now! We're just gonna have to..."

Without finishing his sentence, Keeven did something to the

control panel on the wrist of her suit. Shaan felt a sharp tug, and then the silvery tether was retracting at quadruple speed. They hurtled into motion, faster and faster, down toward the platform where their shuttle sat waiting.

The descent took only seconds, but there was no way to stop when they reached the bottom. As they approached the platform, the station's gravity field grabbed them, and they were both flung into the flat metal surface at speed.

The air was knocked out of Shaan's lungs again as her body collided with the platform. She felt a brutal impact, a searing pain in her skull... and then everything went black.

JERETH

**Long Range Cargo Hauler *Enigma*
8 weeks before the Rift**

JERETH WAS HALF-ASLEEP, his head leaning back against his headrest, his booted feet resting on the *Enigma*'s navigation console. They'd exited the last orange zone before Almant, and there hadn't been a trace of Felen activity in any of the danger sectors. They hadn't run across a single UWDF patrol, either, and they were on course to reach the Almant system within two weeks.

And so, when Jereth was suddenly startled by a sensor screaming about Felen ships on an intercept course—with a UWDF patrol in pursuit, no less—his first reaction was stunned disbelief.

"You believe this?" he said to Mendeg when he'd roused the engineer. "We've got serious traffic up ahead, and it's coming right for us. Felen thorn fighters. All the way out here?"

The burly man lowered himself into the chair next to Jereth, watching the approaching ships on their scanners with narrowed eyes. "Shit. Seven of 'em... no, eight. Think they've seen us?"

"Chances are they've got their hands full," Jereth said. "That UWDF patrol's probably firing on them. We're out of range, so we're best off laying low. I'm shutting us down."

Jereth quickly cut all the engines and activated the diversion generators to mask the ship's energy signature. The *Enigma* had no external weapons, and although it was equipped with the strongest military-grade defensive shield grid that money could buy, it would still be no match for Felen thorns at close range. They couldn't outrun a whole Felen formation; their best hope was to remain cloaked and to go unseen.

Silently, the powered-down *Enigma* drifted along, disappearing into the anonymous depths of space, impossible to distinguish from random, drifting space-junk.

Onscreen, Jereth and Mendeg watched the Felen ships circle and regroup twice before they looped back and surrounded the pursuing UWDF patrol. For a long time, the ships all held position at a standoff, and nothing much happened. And then the Felen ships were sweeping into motion again, changing formation. Three of the thorns converged on the larger of the UWDF vessels.

There was a perfunctory exchange of fire, and the *Enigma*'s instruments recorded four explosions in the distance. A mass of pale, contorted spheres appeared all over the scanner.

"Shit! They take 'em out?" hissed Mendeg, leaning forward. "Was that a Felen ship, or one of ours?"

"Not sure," Jereth said. "One of each, maybe? There's a few thorns going off that way now..." He traced a finger over the engine signatures fading on the grid in front of him. "I think they blew up the big UWDF cruiser. But there was a smaller one there, too. Where did it—?"

The control panel flashed bright, and the view refreshed. *PROXIMITY ALERT.*

Two Felen thorn ships were moving directly toward the *Enigma* at alarming speed, with the smaller UWDF vessel in pursuit. Jereth and Mendeg watched in dismay as the three ships closed in... closer... closer...

And then, the UWDF ship started firing in their direction.

The floor rumbled, and the sleek white chairs shook. The two Felen thorns neatly swerved around the *Enigma*, and the full force of the UWDF ship's assault struck the cloaked ship's back end.

"Oh, shit!" shouted Jereth. "Shit, shit, shit!"

The shield grid monitor lit up with a rainbow of impact warnings.

"That UWDF ship's shooting at *us?*" Mendeg screamed, jumping to his feet. "What the fuck!"

"Damn it! They can't see us, with all these masks up and no engine signature... I think the Felen are using us as *cover!*"

The Union vessel tore past, still firing as one of the Felen thorns suddenly looped back around and re-targeted, firing directly at the *Enigma* as they passed.

"Okay, the Felen *definitely* see us!" Jereth shouted.

Their warning systems howled as the Felen ship dodged around them and fired again. The assault shredded the *Enigma*'s secondary grid, penetrating to the hull in several places. The UWDF vessel fired back, and a volley of weaker impacts flared across their grid monitor.

Then the UWDF ship abruptly changed course and sped away. The Felen thorn circled one final time before it was gone, too, tailing the retreating Union vessel into the oblivion of space.

The entire exchange had taken less than a minute, but the *Enigma*'s shield grid was in tatters.

"Fuck. You've got to be kidding me!" Jereth buried his head in his hands as the two ships' engine signatures blinked away. "We were *way* out of the orange zone! What *was* that?"

"It's worse than you think," Mendeg said. "We've still got one on our back. There's a thorn stuck in our bloody hull."

"*What?*"

Jereth brought up the *Enigma*'s external view on his screen, and a shiver of horror went through him. The Felen ship had embedded itself near the top of the *Enigma*'s cargo hold, its landing claws biting into the surface of the damaged hull. Soon, it would use a powerful beam weapon to carve a hole through the *Enigma*'s hull and bore its way in.

They were about to be boarded by the Felen.

Felen boardings of this kind were entirely unpredictable. Sometimes, the aliens stole cargo or towed away the ship, and sometimes they torched it, regardless of its contents or value. Sometimes they executed all or some of the human crew; sometimes, they took human prisoners alive.

Jereth shuddered.

Mendeg stood there for a few seconds, staring at the foreboding thorn silhouette on the viewscreen. Then he stalked to the weapons cabinet on the back wall and grabbed the biggest plasma gun on the rack. He checked that it was fully charged and slung it over his shoulder.

"I'm gonna wait by the cargo airlock," Mendeg said. "If one of those things comes in here, I'll roast its fucking face off. Just you watch."

"You won't be able to shoot 'em with that." Jereth sighed. "Their suits have force-fields that can take a dozen times that charge without a flicker."

"Well, I'll be damned if they're taking me prisoner," Mendeg said. "Hells, no! I'll shoot myself first, before I let 'em take me." An unhinged gleam came into his eyes. "I'll overload one of our engines and blow up this whole damn ship! Dargo Mendeg goes down fighting!"

"Listen, Mendeg—"

The engineer shook his fist in the general direction of the cargo hold. "You hear me, hell-beast? Come at me! I'm not afraid to die; I'll blow this whole ship up! I'll—"

"Whoa, whoa!" Jereth shoved Mendeg back. "First of all, it can't hear you. It can't fucking understand what you're saying, so you can stop screaming in my ear. Second of all, we're not blowing up our own damn ship." Jereth gave the engineer a warning look. "Put that gun down and let me deal with it, okay? Let me think."

Jereth took a few steps back into the bridge. He went to the weapons cabinet and retrieved a tiny black scarab grenade. He turned it over in his hands, weighing up the likelihood that its charge would tear through the alien's shielding against the possibility that it would also take a chunk out of the *Enigma*'s external wall if he used it.

"Hey... Keeven?" Mendeg said, sounding marginally calmer now. "C'mere and take a look at this thing, would you?"

Jereth walked back and leaned over the engineer's station. Mendeg was looking at the overview of the embedded thorn again.

"It's not chewing through us yet," Mendeg said. "I don't see any beam weapons, nothing. The ship's just... *sitting there*. What the fuck's it waiting for?"

Jereth shrugged. "We picking up any signals from it?"

"Nope. Nothin' we can read, anyway. Looks dead as dirt," Mendeg said. "But that doesn't mean it's not—you know—doin' the thing they do..." The engineer tapped the side of his head. "Maybe it's waitin' for backup."

Mendeg isolated the area of the hull that had been pierced by the thorn ship, initiating a direct scan on it. Most of the Felen ship was impermeable to their scanning tech, but the density scan illuminated a large, jagged irregularity on the left side of the thorn's hull.

"I think it's been hit," Jereth said. "Look at the side there."

"Yeah," Mendeg agreed, his voice rising hopefully. "That's damage!"

"Gods bless the UWDF. They managed to get one shot on target while they were hammering innocent bystanders," Jereth said, rolling his eyes.

The two sat in silence for a few more minutes, looking tensely from each other to the screen and back to each other again. Jereth's shaking hands gripped the arms of his chair so tightly that his knuckles cracked. Still, the Felen ship didn't do anything.

Jereth sat back in the chair and gave a nervous laugh. "Well, I'll be damned," he said. "Looks like it might be dead. Our lucky day after all, huh?"

Mendeg jabbed a finger at the *Enigma*'s damage report on his other screen. "I'm not sure I'd say that," he said gruffly. "We've got at least two shield breaches, bad ones. I'll try to get the hull regen system back online, but we're gonna need repairs."

Jereth frowned. "One problem at a time. There's no way we can dock up anywhere with a Felen thorn on our back." He shook his head. "This ship's compromised."

"So... what are we s'posed to do?" Mendeg looked perplexed. "It's got its damn claws stuck in our hull."

Jereth thought about it. "I could take a walk out there in a suit, see if I can get it off us."

"Get it off *how*?"

"I'm still thinking about that part," Jereth said. "We can't use scarabs, that would tear up our hull worse than it already is. The last thing we need is another hole in us. I'd have to use something more localized... what if I cut it off with the beam torch?"

"You fucking serious, Keeven?"

"We don't have a lot of choices here; we need to get rid of this thing." Jereth squinted at the screen, examining the smaller craft's neat perforations through the *Enigma*'s hull. "I can probably cut into those landing claws a bit, try to weaken 'em. Then we'll start up the engines, give ourselves a little spin... hopefully it'll just fall away."

"Right," said Mendeg uncertainly. "Well... watch your back. This could be some kind of trap. What if the critter in there isn't dead?"

Jereth shrugged off his jacket, tossed it over the back of the chair and tucked in his shirt.

"Get me the beam torch," he said. "I'm puttin' a suit on."

UMA
Engineering Deck, ZeyCorp Gallion

UMA PACED BACK and forth in Engineering, her footsteps marking out the passing seconds. Anxiety thrummed in the pit like a heartbeat. The engineers were all wringing hands, nervous glances, eyes glued to empty tracking screens.

Verkhoy Station's grey destruct had triggered a cascading shockwave of Rift energy pulses that rippled all the way into the boundary zone. There had been alarming spikes across all the *Gallion*'s monitoring systems as the Rift reacted to the station's implosion.

The Rift seemed to be stabilizing again now, but the shuttles had been out of contact for a long time. Too long.

"Director Ozakka," Syru whispered when she passed. "We're going to find them again, right?"

Uma patted his shoulder, avoiding his eyes. "We'll keep scanning, Syru. Just keep scanning."

"The hover relay's unrecoverable," Noussen said, slumping in her chair. "There's not a blip of signal from any of them. Their chips've all fried. There's no way we're getting voice comms back."

It wasn't too late, Uma told herself. On impact, the shuttles' power should have been redirected to auxiliary shielding. And if they'd survived the initial blast—if a shieldform collapse hadn't taken out their life support—then they could hold for a while. There was still time to find them.

A small commotion of voices from Engineering's upper level interrupted her thoughts. Captain Fransk was back, and he was hurrying down the stairs with Zel and Barnabyn close behind him. Uma's jaw clenched.

"Anything new to report, Director?" Fransk asked. "What's happening?"

"I've been stalling as best I can with the Ambassador, but I need *something*," Zel said at the same time. "Tell me you found something!"

"Still scanning," Uma said. "Dean is expanding our search area. We're doing the best we can, but the hover relay is gone. We have limited range beyond the boundary zone."

"I'm pretty sure Shuttle One cleared the shockwave," Noussen said. "We got a burst of telemetry showing the shuttle was powered on, and their tracker was still moving for a few seconds after the station imploded. Airlocks were sealed, and Keeven got the shieldforms up. They must've made it out. We still had their signal just before the hover relay went out."

"And the other shuttle?" Fransk pressed.

"Shuttle Two... I'm not so sure." Noussen winced, looking away from Syru when she spoke. "They were right in the boundary zone, smack in the worst of it. Last telemetry showed a huge spike on the forward shield."

"A gods-damned direct hit," Wazar said. "Just about the worst luck possible."

"I have been focusing the search on the area surrounding Shuttle Two's last contact," Dean said. "But it is possible that the shuttle has drifted, pushing it further back into the boundary zone. As Director Ozakka said, without the hover relay, our scanning range is indeed minimal."

Syru's face was tear-stained, his voice barely above a whisper. "Shields on Shuttle Two took an impact of five-point-two thousand mitzwols," he said. "You all saw the sims. Seven out of eight times, anything over five thousand on the forward shield is unsurvivable. This is all my fault."

"It's not. We all saw the same numbers. We accepted the risks," Uma said. "This was an *extremely* unlikely case; no one could've known the station's grey destruct would set off a shockwave like that."

"Seven out of eight means there's a chance they're still alive," Fransk said firmly. "So we need to get back to work. Catastrophic systems failure is certain, but shieldform collapse is not." He took a ragged breath. "If they are alive, we need to find them as fast as we can."

"Dean, redirect all available power to the scan efforts," Uma said. "Can we get any more hover probes out? Wazar, how many do we have left?"

"Captain, this is pointless," Nack said. "They could've been hit a dozen more times by now with their shields down! It's a damn shame, but they're probably gone already. And while you're wishin' for miracles, we're wastin' power we can hardly afford to lose. We have to think of the rest of us!"

"*No,*" Uma snapped. "We keep searching. All we need is a lock on their location, then we can reach them with a concentrated tractor beam, like we did when we brought in the *Jonah*." She dropped her fists to her sides, swearing under her breath in Anvaelian.

"It isn't too late," Fransk said. "It isn't. We just need to find them."

SHAAN
Shuttle One, Rift-Space

SHAAN FOLDED HER arms against her chest, her teeth chattering. She was freezing cold, and uncomfortably aware that her entire body ached with the slightest movement. Her head throbbed where she'd struck the station's platform, and she felt like she was going to throw up. Her vision blurred as she tried to focus on Keeven in the pilot's seat beside her.

Somehow, she was still breathing.

They'd made it into the shuttle.

They were alive.

She watched Keeven working at the shuttle controls with his usual half-distant focus, repeating his familiar motions with outward calm. But the growing lines of tension in his face were impossible to ignore.

"*Gallion*, are you receiving this?" Keeven was saying. "Shuttle Two, come in. This is Shuttle One calling Shuttle Two. Mikolai, are you receiving? *Gallion*, come in, this is Shuttle One calling *Gallion*."

"It's been ages, Keeven," she whispered. "Why aren't they answering us?"

"I'm pretty sure the hover relay's gone," he said, shaking his head. "All those little hover probes are unshielded. Shockwave probably knocked 'em right out..." He trailed off. "Gods *damn* it. Look at this!"

Shaan leaned forward as far as her safety harness would let her, and he flicked a grainy proximity scan image toward her. There was the clear outline of a ZeyCorp shuttle, spinning in a slow circle. Shuttle Two, in the boundary zone just ahead of them.

Ice spilled into her chest. "Are they... are they hit?"

"Trying to find out." He flicked at the controls, changing the shuttle's heading. "Hang on. I'm angling back to match Mikolai's trajectory. Let's see if we can get close enough to hail them on close-range comms."

He made another change on the control panel and the shuttle's tinny engine hum escalated.

Shaan curled up in her seat and turned toward the window, trying not to think about how far away the *Gallion* was. She shivered, peering out into the dark. And she *hoped.*

Keeven opened a close-range comms channel. "Shuttle One calling Shuttle Two... you hear me? Mikolai? Charyne? Shuttle Two, come in!"

There was no answer.

"Mikolai! You hear me? Shuttle One calling Shuttle Two, hello! Come in, Shuttle Two."

Still nothing.

"I don't think they're receiving," Keeven said. "We're so close to 'em. We should be getting *something*..."

He tapped a few more options on the control panel. A moment later, he grinned triumphantly as a spray of text messages appeared over the console. "Yes! Got 'em."

SHUTTLE TWO CALLING GALLION! *ARE YOU THERE,* GALLION? *SHUTTLE TWO CALLING SHUTTLE ONE, IS ANYONE RECEIVING THIS? WE'VE TAKEN A*

DIRECT HIT. SHIELDFORMS ARE DOWN. EMERGENCY LIFE SUPPORT IS HOLDING, BUT WE HAVE SOME SERIOUS SYSTEMS DAMAGE. REPEAT, WE HAVE NO SHIELDS AND NO POWER. SHUTTLE TWO, CALLING GALLION! SHUTTLE ONE, ARE YOU THERE? CAPTAIN KEEVEN? COME IN, SHUTTLE ONE! GALLION, THIS IS SHUTTLE TWO CALLING—

"Yes!" Shaan's pulse thudded under her skin, and she nearly leapt from her seat with a shriek. "Yes! They're alive! I knew it!"

"They're in a real bad way, though," Keeven said, the elation fading from his face. "We haven't got a lot of time. We need to get that shuttle out of the boundary zone and move it back toward the ship before they take another hit." He tapped his chin with one gloved hand. "I'm gonna clamp onto them, and we can tow them back. Hopefully we can signal the *Gallion* once we're out the other side of the boundary zone."

Keeven turned back to the controls. He was quiet for a long while after that, and Shaan watched him staring intently at the screen. He flicked through what looked like a tech readout, his frown deepening.

"What?" she whispered. "Is something wrong?"

"Yeeeaaah... we've got some seriously inconvenient technical problems." He sighed. "Looks like all our external automated systems are down. We must've taken more damage than I thought when we rode out that shockwave." He thumped a fist against the side of his seat. "Damn! See, this was exactly the reason we needed live pilots on these missions."

"External automated systems down... what's that mean, exactly?"

Keeven scrolled to the bottom of a long list of errors. "Navigation and auto-steering systems are gone. We've lost the docking calibration, too," he said. "Means our docking clamps won't self-align to them, and they sure aren't gonna line up to us. They've got no power at all!" He dusted his hands together with something like grim determination. "Well... guess I'm just gonna have to take a walk out there."

"You're *what?*" She stared at him incredulously.

"I've got to lower the clamps manually." Keeven tapped at his helmet-ring. "EVA. It's the only way. I'll bring 'em down by hand just like I would've done it if I went to tow back those energy cells."

Shaan frowned. "But... if you're going to be outside... then how...?"

"I'd be seriously screwed if I was out here alone." He gave her a wry half-smile. "Lucky for me, I've got some help. You're gonna drive for me."

"No. No way, I can't do that," Shaan whispered.

"You can. Trust me, Shaan, you can. I'll go out the airlock and climb over to the clamps, while you reverse us toward them, nice and slow. You'll line up the docking mechanism for me and I'll bring our clamps down on them."

"No..."

"Come over here, and I'll show you." He unbuckled his safety harness, slipping out of the pilot's seat and motioning for her to slide over. "I'll show you exactly what you need to do."

"Keeven, no! Stop. The last time I did this, *I killed someone,*" she said. "I fucked it up, I misaligned the docking clamps. Remember that?"

"I remember," he said with a grave nod. "This time, you won't. Don't worry. You're gonna be moving real slow."

"With you outside, hanging on to the gods-damned *roof?*" She looked Keeven up and down. "Your grapple is gone! And our suits had all those critical warnings... How long is the oxygen scrubber going to last on that thing, if it starts up at all? What if you lose your grip—?"

He looked at her, raw emotion in his eyes. "Shaan, I'm sorry... but there isn't another way," he said. "Look... I... I don't know if I'm gonna be able to help save Etraxas, or negotiate for the Union, or rescue humanity. But I'm damn well getting this shuttle back to the *Gallion*, or I'll die trying, understand? We're getting out of here, all of us or none of us. But I need you right now, Shaan. You've got to do this."

A chill squirmed down Shaan's spine, and she nodded slowly. "Okay," she whispered.

"I'll be real careful out there, I promise," he said. "And I'll be quick. Believe me, this *isn't* the most dangerous EVA I've ever done." He reached across and unbuckled her harness, then patted the pilot's seat. "Come over here. We're gonna practice."

Shaan grabbed the handholds between the seats and pulled herself over to the pilot's side, letting him buckle her into her new seat.

"Show me what to do."

He must have noticed how terrified she sounded, but he didn't let on. Instead, he took her hands and placed them gently over the controls. Her ears rang, her heart pounding in her throat as he narrated the process of lining up the docking clamps. He showed her the directional view on the screen and re-positioned her hands, going through each of the sequences several times.

Left, down. Up, right.

She felt like she was watching from outside her body, the scene unfolding in slow motion.

"Left, down. Up, right," he said. "Like this." His hands were on her wrists, guiding her fingers from side to side through the three-dimensional grid. "And again. Left, down. Up, right. You've got it."

"How will I know when?" she whispered.

"Count half a minute after I'm out the airlock. I'll be ready," he said. "Then start backing toward them, real slow. That

shuttle's got some spin on it, so I'll need to time it carefully."
He squeezed her shoulder. "You'll probably feel an impact
when the clamps come down, but don't worry. That's normal.
As soon as it's done, I'll come right back in."

She nodded tearfully.

He reached across her and opened the advanced controls.
"There's one last thing," he said. "You aren't going to like this,
but... I have to take our shields down temporarily."

"Wait, *what?*"

"It won't let me open the airlock with shieldforms active," he
said. "We'll have to switch the shields off. You'll see a bunch of
warnings about shields, but just ignore them. Okay?"

"But what about the Rift energy pulses? If we don't have
shields... if we get hit—"

"We won't," he said. "Luck's holding. We made it this far. We
won't get hit."

She nodded, tears blurring her vision. "Okay," she mouthed.

"Say it."

"We... we won't get hit."

"Good."

Keeven entered a sequence into the control panel. Behind them,
the shuttle's airlock chirped and lit up with its 'ready' icons. At
the same time, every orange warning light came on in the cabin,
along with a spray of terrifying messages: *SHIELD FAILURE—
PRIMARY SHIELDING DISENGAGED—SHIELD FAILURE
—SECONDARY SHIELDING DISENGAGED—SHIELD
FAILURE*

Shaan tried not to look.

"You can do this." Keeven patted her shoulder.

He had been crouched in the small gap between the two
seats, holding himself in place by wedging one foot against the
passenger seat. Now, he turned to face the small airlock. She
watched him check over the seals on his gloves and boots before

he lifted one hand to his neck, feeling for the helmet release.

"Keeven!" she said, before he could put the helmet up. "Jereth... wait."

He stopped and looked over his shoulder.

From where she was sitting, he was half-hidden in shadow. The reflected lights from the control panel and the glowing airlock cast strange shapes over the curves and angles of his space-suit, but she couldn't see his face. She unbuckled one side of her harness so she could turn around, bracing her knee against the back of the seat.

"Luck be with us," she whispered.

Then she reached out and pulled him back to her, and her mouth was on his before she could second-guess herself.

Keeven leaned toward her as best he could in a cramped space with no gravity. He kissed her back softly at first, his tongue slowly tracing hers, surprisingly gentle. He slid one gloved hand over her shoulder, drawing her closer.

For an instant, Shaan's rational mind protested—what was she doing? But she couldn't finish a coherent thought before their mouths collided again, fiercely, hungrily. Her veins lit up with heat, her heart slamming against her ribs as he tipped her head all the way back.

She kissed him like everything depended on it, like they were both about to die, like there was nothing else left. Maybe they'd already failed. Maybe nothing they'd done would matter, and he would never become the Union's glorious Negotiator... but she wanted him anyway.

She wanted *him*, Jereth Keeven, Jaymi Hanioch, whoever he was.

When their lips parted, Shaan was holding the back of her seat with one hand and clutching him with the other, her fingers still curled around the arm of his suit. She slowly pulled her hand back to her chest, her face flushing hot.

He stared at her with a lingering smile, his eyes intense with longing.

"Count half a minute, then start reversing," he whispered. "I'll be back real quick."

He flipped his helmet up. Shaan couldn't see his face anymore, but she was sure that his eyes hadn't left her as he backed toward the airlock. He was still looking over his shoulder when the inner door sealed behind him.

Then he opened the outer door... and then he was gone.

All the warmth drained from Shaan's body, her jumble of emotions obliterated by the reality of the situation. She shivered with dread as she turned back to the controls, re-clipped her harness and tightened it. Warning messages were still blinking on every lit surface: *SHIELD FAILURE—EMERGENCY MODE ON—WARNING—SHIELD FAILURE—EMERGENCY MODE ON*

She counted out the seconds of a half-minute as she raised her hands to the correct positions.

Time crawled.

...six... five... four... three... two... one.

Shaan straightened her shoulders, gritted her teeth, and started to reverse the shuttle.

JERETH

Long Range Cargo Hauler *Enigma*
8 weeks before the Rift

THE FELEN SHIP'S landing claws were sunk into the *Enigma* like teeth. Jereth had been outside for a half-hour, hacking away at them with the beam torch, moving as quickly as he could in his bulky grey space-suit. He could think of nothing more unnerving than standing in the empty void of space, with that alien craft so damn close that he could touch it.

He fought back his revulsion and kept working. He'd already hacked through the main claw at the front of the ship and three of the four supporting barbs. One more to go. He tried not to think about the nightmarish creature that had been piloting this craft. He had to keep his focus.

Jereth had worked all his life to shake off his childhood fear of heights, but being out on the hull of a ship in deep space still evoked something of that old feeling, that nauseating certainty that if he made one wrong step he would never stop falling.

C'mon, Jereth, just do it. Don't look down.

He was moving carefully around to the Felen ship's other side when he glimpsed a flicker of motion from the corner of his eye.

He switched off the torch and took a step back from the

thorn. His heartbeat thundered through his skull. Had the ship really just moved?

No, of course it hadn't—it was just his nerves playing tricks on him.

Go on, Jereth. It's easy.

He studied the smooth black hull. There was a thin, silver-bright seam running along the ship's side now. Had that always been there? He really wasn't sure.

Very slowly, he walked along the small ship's length, following the seam. The hairfine fracture angled along the flank, then curved over the top of the ship and down the other side, where it disappeared into the twisted, jagged crater where the deadly shot had hit.

The tiny line flowed with an elegant symmetry that suggested a design feature more than battle damage. The edge of a door, maybe?

Jereth stared at it for a few more moments until he was satisfied that nothing was going to happen. Just as he reactivated the beam torch, the tiny silver line on the ship's flank flared and the fracture grew to a finger's width. The Felen craft's external running lights all switched on.

Jereth staggered back, grabbing frantically at his safety line. He dropped to his knees and pulled himself flat against the *Enigma*'s hull, raw panic rising in his chest.

He lay motionless, listening to his own breathing echoing inside his helmet. When he finally willed himself to turn his head and look up, he recoiled.

The Felen craft had opened, splitting along the side like a mollusc. The door had struggled to unseal itself on the ship's damaged side, and the force of its opening had wrenched away part of the ship's corrupted hull. It left a grotesque mass of coiled tendrils on that side, like peeling metal skin.

Now, the ship sat motionless again, its open maw gaping

into space. The running lights were still on, but nothing else had changed. He must have interfered with some mechanism on the outside of the ship, he told himself. He'd cut through something that made the door open. That had to be it.

Get up, Jereth. Come on, move!

Slowly, he got to his feet and stood back up on the *Enigma*'s hull. His shaking hands still clutched the beam torch, but he attached it to his safety harness and retrieved the plasma gun instead. He'd taken the weapon out with him, clipped to his suit. Useless as it was against a Felen body shield, it still comforted him to have it there.

It took several attempts to steady his hands enough to manipulate the gun's controls, but Jereth eventually managed to arm the weapon. He took a tentative step toward the Felen ship. Then another one.

Nothing happened.

He was going to have to climb up the side of the ship if he wanted to look inside—he'd have to put his foot on it, and take a step up. He was still anchored to the *Enigma*, the tether trailing behind him like an umbilical cord. The rational thing to do was to back away and follow the line back to the airlock. The rational thing to do was to get back in his ship, start the *Enigma*'s engines, and see if he'd done enough to let them shake the thorn off.

But something about the Felen ship drew him in as surely as it repelled him. He had to look.

He rested a gloved hand against the side of the ship. A glossy step had unfolded from the side of the craft as the door opened. He shuddered, then took a deep breath and hauled himself up.

Like just about everyone, Jereth knew what the Felen looked like. He'd seen enough images and videos, models and caricatures. He'd even seen a couple of dead ones during his military training—disgusting, dissected things that he'd tried not to remember in too much detail. But what he saw when he looked over the edge... this was different.

There was a single alien inside, strapped into what remained of the pilot's seat. And it was *alive*.

The creature was looking straight back at him. Four round, shining eyes peered from behind a translucent faceplate.

Jereth froze.

The Felen's body had been crushed badly when the ship was hit. One of the alien's arms was pinned under the mass of melted hull, and its lower limbs were twisted at an angle to the rest of it. Its suit and shielding still held, protecting it from the cold reach of space—although Jereth couldn't imagine it would survive much longer.

He watched the violet glow of the defensive body shield pulsing around the alien's armoured suit, reminding him that the plasma gun in his hand was useless. Still the Felen stared at him, and Jereth found himself unable to turn away. Despite the extra eyes and the hooked mandibles, he was struck by how *human* it looked. He couldn't quite identify the horrifying emotions it evoked in him.

He held the gun as steady as he could, but his hands shook. The Felen moved its free hand toward its chest, and the pale aura around the creature's suit grew fainter and disappeared. It must have switched its defensive shielding off.

The Felen made a slight motion with its head, then slowly extended its long arm, raising a palm as if in imitation of the human greeting. Its pitch-black eyes glittered wetly.

Jereth climbed the rest of the way into the ship. He was standing right over the Felen pilot now, both hands on the gun, his arms stretched out in front of him. He willed himself to pull the trigger and kill the thing. Its body shielding was switched off. There was no reason not to.

Just do it, Jereth.

He rested the gun against the Felen's faceplate.

Jereth! Do it!

But as he looked down at the alien, a memory surfaced and spilled into his chest like liquid ice. He recognized the look on the Felen's face. The look of someone who knows the end is near; the same look Ludyth had when he lay broken and dying on that spar.

For an instant, Jereth saw his brother's eyes behind the faceplate, and he choked back a sob.

The creature raised its free hand toward him again. It closed its long, gloved fingers around the gun, its hand brushing against his own. Jereth drew back, tears welling up in his eyes, and he realized with a shock that he had released his grip on the weapon.

The Felen pilot lifted the gun out of his hands.

Jereth stood frozen, but the alien didn't shoot him. It just continued to stare at him as it took hold of the gun and held down the trigger, unleashing a plasma shot directly into the centre of its own chest.

The bright light from the shot seared painfully against Jereth's eyes. He turned away as a terrible, blood-curdling scream rang in his ears, but after a few seconds he realized it was his own voice.

He stopped screaming then, catching his breath in short, pained gasps. He staggered out of the Felen ship, following his tether hand over hand until he was lying flat on the hull of the *Enigma* again.

Then he put his head against the hull and sobbed, his tears falling onto the inside of his helmet.

"KEEVEN!" MENDEG SHOUTED over his suit's comms line. "Keeven, answer me! What in the name of the Suns are you doing so long?"

Jereth lifted his head, his trembling hand fumbling for the comms switch at his neck.

"Keeven, damn it! Are you alive out there?"

"It's done," Jereth choked out. "I cut it loose. One spin and we should be rid of it."

Mendeg exhaled loudly. "Well, thank fuck for that. Took you long enough. Did you see any of the critters out there? How many?"

"Just the one. It was dead already," Jereth said.

"You real sure? 'Cause if it's faking us out, you know it's probably gonna—"

"Mendeg, I just fucking told you, okay? It's dead." Jereth rolled onto his back, facing the void of the cosmos above him, and tried to steady his breathing. "Update me on the hull regen situation," he said. "How's it look? Think we can hold off on repairs till we get into the Almant system?"

"Not a chance," Mendeg said. "That other Felen ship took out the main regen system *and* the backup. We can't self-repair at all. I can hold us together for a while with shield redirection, but there's no way we're makin' it to Almant like this. We'll have to get this fixed somewhere close by."

Jereth laughed bitterly. "We're in the middle of nowhere, Mendeg. The nearest outpost is a tiny shit-hole, population fifteen—if they're even still on it. Who's gonna repair something like this?" He sighed. "We're on a serious deadline. I need a working ship, and I need it *now*."

"So... uh, what do you want me to do about it? This ship's wrecked to all hells."

"Then we'll just have to get a different ship," said Jereth. "We'll trade this one, to whoever we can, for whatever else we can get our hands on. One damaged but obviously very expensive ship to trade, straight up, for whatever solid spaceworthy junker we can take right away. I'll take anything as long as the engines are good and it has room for a hundred and twenty crates of cargo."

Jereth heard the familiar beeps of the navigation system echoing over the comms line, as Mendeg opened up a sector directory and flicked through it. "Hmm. There's some little scrapyard just a few hours' skim from here," the engineer said. "Says they pick up abandoned junk from the orange zone an' refurb it. They might have something there."

"Good," Jereth said. "Great. Fantastic. Let's do that. We'll head for that scrapyard, find a replacement ship, then get right back on course for Almant."

Mendeg grunted. "Fine."

"I'll try to make it quick with the Almant pickup. And our cargo crates should be ready by the time we get to Pilar Outpost," Jereth said. "Hopefully we can make up some time if we get in and out of Pilar smoothly."

"Sure," said Mendeg. "As long as we don't hit any more detours."

Jereth dragged himself up to his feet. For a moment, he stood facing the crumpled Felen ship, the beam torch heavy in his hand. He looked away from it again, forcing his voice back into lightness. "If we stay on schedule here, it'll be a damn miracle," he said. "But who knows. Maybe we'll get real lucky."

UMA
Residential Deck, *ZeyCorp Gallion*

UMA SAT WITH her head on the table in her apartment. She'd left Engineering for a few moments to clear her head, but she could scarcely remember why. She could hardly think about anything.

Rage burned in her chest unlike anything she'd felt in years, tinged with a bitter disappointment. She dug her fingernails into her palms, slammed her fists on the tabletop, bit down on the inside of her cheek until she tasted blood.

How could they possibly have come so close, only to have it all fall apart? It didn't make any sense. She had been so sure. *Why, why, why, why, why?*

She thought about Halli, working somewhere out on a border zone base. Geminus High Commander Kehallian Sifyer, always so sure of her destiny, had sworn her life to serving an Alliance that might no longer exist. Without the Alliance, who was Halli? Who was Uma? Who was *anybody* who'd been born after the Fortunate Five spared the Union from destruction?

And what of her great-grandfather's proud moment at that lecture, the day when Eldric Leesongronski, the Last of the Greats, touched him on the shoulder?

The bottle of Etraxan agnathe still sat on the table, next to two empty glasses and the model *Jonah*. Uma tried to picture Leesongronski sitting here across from her, but it felt like a lifetime ago. She pulled the half-empty bottle toward her and closed her fingers on it, tightening her grip until her knuckles ached. When she touched the stopper, the map of Etraxas glowed softly over her palm, illuminating the location of the Denarba vineyard.

At once, the knot in her chest loosened slightly. She looked over at the picture of her father, gazing serenely out at her from his frame, and she knew exactly why she had come back to her apartment.

She stood up slowly from the table, then crossed the purple carpet and picked up the frame.

"Papa," she whispered. "Papa... I... I need your advice. I don't know what to do now. We've tried everything we could, but... I'm afraid it wasn't enough. I really thought I was doing the right thing... but... now I'm scared. I'm scared that we won't make it out of this. Papa, please, help me see how it can still count for something. Show me how this can still *matter*."

She pressed two fingers to her lips and touched the edge of the frame.

And then, for the first time since her father died, Uma whispered an Anvaelian invocation. The one that came to mind was Halli's favourite, the one Halli always chose when they clasped hands over the week's end meal.

No matter how far apart we wander,
No matter where we lay down to rest,
May we find our way back together,
May we find a way home.

Her eyes swam with tears as she set down the picture of her father. *May we find a way home.*

She lowered her head as the tears spilled over her cheeks, and for the first time in years, she allowed herself to cry freely. She sank to her knees on the carpet and sobbed: all the tears she'd been holding back, all the anger, all the grief that had still never quite settled in her ribcage. She cried until she couldn't breathe, until her shoulders heaved, until she couldn't cry any more.

And then, there was a buzz at her apartment door.

Uma hauled herself back up to her feet, smoothing down her wrinkled uniform. She opened the door without checking who was there, mopping at her burning eyes with one sleeve.

Captain Fransk was standing in the entry, looking at her tear-stained face with concern.

"Olghan, I—" she began.

"Director Ozakka. I need you back in Engineering immediately," he said, a tired smile breaking across his face. "We just got a lock on Keeven's shuttle. They're clear of the boundary zone. And it looks like they're towing the other one."

SHAAN
Residential Deck, *ZeyCorp Gallion*

SHAAN STOOD IN front of the sink, looking at her face in the lavatory mirror. She blinked slowly, staring at her own reflection like she wasn't sure she recognized herself. She looked exhausted, her eyes red-rimmed. Her head still ached badly.

But she was *alive.*

She pinched at the tender skin on the back of her hand, twisting it between her fingers. She splashed handfuls of freezing water on her face and neck, then cupped her hands and drank some down.

She could feel all of it. She was really here.

She thought back to that agonizing moment when she'd lined up the shuttle docking clamps in the boundary zone, that terrifying silence before the clamps rumbled down. Forty-eight seconds had elapsed before the airlock engaged again, and Keeven finally came back in. She wasn't sure if she'd taken a breath that entire time.

But their luck had held. He came back. They survived. It had all really happened.

She'd really hugged her dear friend Mikolai in the shuttle bay, safe and alive and astonished, as a tearful, overjoyed Syru ran to meet them. She'd been surrounded by the congratulatory shrieks and cheers of all her *Gallion* colleagues. Even Director Barnabyn had gone out of his way to praise her.

The Cordero siblings had belted out an off-key victory chant, while Wazar and Macey had lifted Professor Jaxong onto their shoulders, managing to hold her aloft for about two seconds before they all collapsed into laughter on the cargo bay floor.

And Keeven... well, Keeven had been Keeven, grinning maniacally at Ozakka and Fransk while shouting, "See! Look at that! Didn't I tell you nothing would go wrong? Easy!"

After the exhausting disaster that was the Verkhoy mission, Captain Fransk had declared that Engineering wouldn't be setting off the bomb until the next day. No one seemed in any rush to take their lives into their hands again, and a few more hours wouldn't change a thing.

Today, they would all rest. Tomorrow, they'd push the *Jonah* back to the other side of the boundary zone, back to exactly where they'd found it. Then the *Gallion* would broadcast the signal to set off Last Shot. And after that... no one knew *what* would happen.

Some part of Shaan was grateful for a short reprieve from potential doom, but another part of her just wanted it all to be over already, so she could finally put all this behind her.

Leave the past in the past. That was the goal, wasn't it? Jereth Keeven and the *Jonah* crew belonged to the past, too, she reminded herself. It was almost time to let them go.

She and Keeven hadn't got a moment alone together since they got back to the *Gallion*, but Shaan's mind still kept wandering back to him. The way he smiled, the way his hair always fell over his eyes, the way he'd kissed her on that shuttle... gods. Of all the unreasonable, irrational things she had done in the past few days, getting weak-kneed over Keeven had to be the most ridiculous. And yet, it was nearly impossible to ignore.

Whatever happened tomorrow would happen, she told herself. There was no point in worrying about any of it. But before then—at least for one more day—she and Jereth Keeven were both in the same place, at the same time.

She looked back at her reflection in the mirror again.

And for the first time in a long time, she smiled at it.

UMA
Cargo Bay, ZeyCorp Gallion

ELDRIC LEESONGRONSKI WATCHED in silence as Uma stood in the cargo bay, looking up at the *Jonah*. She stepped slowly onto the metal ramp, pausing with each reverent step as she climbed up to the ship's hatch. Her knees nearly buckled as she climbed.

"Oh my gods," she whispered. "The *Jonah*. I can't believe it. These vintage hulls.... incredible. They take a beating, but stay as solid as they come."

She stood at the top of the ramp for a good two minutes before she made up her mind to cross the threshold into the ship. When at last she went inside, Leesongronski ducked after her into the low enclave, and waited again while she spun in a slow circle, looking around.

It wasn't until she turned to look at him that he finally said something.

"See that plasma shot up there? That was courtesy of Charyne," he said drily, pointing at a dark, burnt-out gash in the ceiling just above her head. "The rest already looked this bad when Jereth got it from that junkyard. Charming, isn't it?"

Uma walked around the whole interior of the ship, trailing her hands over each of the flimsy bunk doors. The look on

Leesongronski's face as he watched her was somewhere between amusement and mild disgust.

She walked up to the control panels in the bridge, a distance of no more than a few paces. The living area was minuscule, and part of the ship's original hab zone appeared to have been sectioned off and converted into additional storage space. Behind the small sitting area at the back of the bridge, where she had assumed that two more sleeping bunks would be, there was only a row of dented, grubby-looking metal storage panels, and the narrow door that led into the lavatory.

She stood facing the *Jonah*'s controls for a long time, staring at the antiquated flat screens and manual switches, wiping at her eyes.

"You, uh, want to sit down?" Leesongronski indicated the left seat. "That's where Jereth sits."

"And... this one's yours?" Her voice wavered as she indicated the other seat.

"That would be Mendeg's," he said. "Absolutely no part of this garbage heap is mine. I even got kicked out of my damn bunk."

He saw the look that crossed Uma's face, and after a moment he rolled his eyes and sighed defeatedly.

"Oh, fine, fine, all right," he said. "Maybe I sat in that one a couple of times. I guess it could be mine, if you want it to be."

Uma touched the back of the chair. It was upholstered with cheap blue synthetics, discoloured with wear, bits of the edging peeling away. One of the armrests was visibly loose.

She lowered herself onto the seat and turned the chair around so she was facing the control panels. She half-closed her eyes and tilted her head back as her fingers traced each of the worn console buttons and switches.

"So... um... anyhow..." said Leesongronski awkwardly, leaning against the neighbouring chair. "Jereth's gonna come down soon to unlock this for you, so you can install our new dive shielding."

Uma nodded, her head still tilted back.

"Who's bringing the equipment?" he asked.

"There is no equipment. I have the patterns right here. I'll do it myself." She fished in her pocket and pulled out a portable data drive, along with the special adapter they'd printed.

"That's it?" Leesongronski said sceptically. "*That's* gonna give us dive shielding?"

"Yep. And for once, we're doing something that's been tested *very* thoroughly." She smiled. "I've done this before, believe it or not."

Leesongronski raised an eyebrow. "You've uploaded fancy futuristic dive shield mods to an ancient, piece-of-crap ship?"

"I have, in fact," she said. "I did it on a ship exactly like this one, the same base model as yours. The War History Society of Anvaelia built a historically accurate *Jonah* replica for a documentary, and my father and I both worked on it."

The chair emitted a loud squeak when she moved.

He laughed. "Did you find high-quality furnishings like that?"

"Nope," she said, smiling. "We had no reference. See, this type of cargo hauler was originally sold unfurnished, with no interior fittings or navigation consoles. The only thing these hulls came with, aside from engines, was the main shield grid and the operating system. So we just started with an authentic vintage hull and made up what it might've looked like inside." She pointed across the small room. "We put the bridge over there, facing the other side. There was an extra seat for you in the bridge, too—a jump architect's station. And... we thought there were five sleeping bunks."

"That would be nice," said Leesongronski sarcastically.

"We put two more bunks over there, where those storage panels are."

There was another long silence before Leesongronski spoke again. "So, ah... what happened to the *Jonah*?" he asked. "I mean the original ship, the *Jonah* in your history? I guess it's not around anymore, if you were just guessing what the inside looked like."

Uma lowered her eyes. "The *Jonah* was destroyed, not long after the truce. Historians aren't sure what happened, but it caught fire or something... and then the UWDF supposedly scrapped it." She sighed. "There are some pretty big gaps in what we know about this stuff."

"Huh," Leesongronski said. "Well, say the word and I'll gladly set fire to this thing myself."

Uma half-smiled at the joke, then let his words sink in.

"You know, maybe that's not a bad idea," she said. "You'll have anachronistic shield patterns in your grid, after all. You could delete the patterns afterwards, but that won't explain how you survived an exploratory jump without external dive shielding." She locked eyes with him. "You probably *should* try to get rid of this ship after you get to Etraxas, so it doesn't raise any strange questions."

"How are you giving us dive shielding without any hardware upgrades, anyway?" Leesongronski asked. "And how can whatever you're uploading even *run* on this hardware?"

"Not easily. It took bloody ages to figure out a patch, but my father did it. We wrote this code together," she said proudly. "We knew the original *Jonah* must've had dive shielding installed on a separate external grid, since this stuff I'm about to give you didn't exist yet. But the historically accurate shielding is considered too unstable to be safety-certified now, so we weren't allowed to be *that* accurate. We installed the right hardware on the outside to make it *look* right, but we did the actual dive shielding with pattern mods patched into the main grid." She smiled and held up the drive. "Works with your ship's original operating system."

"Anyone ever make any exploratory jumps with your replica?" Leesongronski asked.

"Hah, no. It was mostly just an experiment, to see if we could get the modern patterns to run on such an antiquated system. A personal triumph. I dug through my trove for the code, and I still had it." She looked away from him. "Anyway. I'm going to upload these patterns. Shouldn't take more than an hour, and then you'll be safe to jump. Safer than the historical *Jonah*, even!"

"Right," said Leesongronski. "When you're dealing with an uncharted jump, I don't know that 'safe' applies by any definition."

Footsteps clattered up the metal ramp, and Jereth Keeven climbed into the enclave.

"Hey, Ozakka! How's the ship tour going?" Keeven said with a grin. "I forgot to tell you, there's an extra fee for sitting on the furniture."

Uma laughed. "How about I give you some free dive shielding?"

Keeven walked up into the bridge and leaned on the chair next to her, swinging it around with a creak. He activated an ancient-looking bio-scanner and put his hand on the dome. One by one, the console lights came on and the *Jonah*'s controls blinked to life.

"There you go, it's all yours," he said, still grinning. "Try not to break anything that isn't already broken."

Keeven sat down next to Uma and propped his feet up on the console, watching her as she accessed the core of the ship's OS and initiated the upload. The system was painfully slow, and the viewscreens glitched concerningly, but soon a circular progress bar was creeping along its track.

"Is that really it?" Keeven marvelled. "The shielding's just... a computer program?"

She nodded. "Yeah, that's it! We'll need to reboot your OS when this is done, but that should do it. I'll show you both how to switch into dive mode from inside your shield controller... and then... you'll be able to..."

Her voice faltered as her gaze landed on Leesongronski. He'd moved to the little table behind the bridge, where he was carefully unpacking a jump kit from a slim black case. He delicately removed each piece from its slot, examined it, then set it on the tabletop.

"Wow," she breathed in a whisper.

Leesongronski looked up with a sigh. "What now?" He shook his head, looking mildly annoyed. "Yes, this is my jump kit. You want to come over here and see it?"

"Your... that's your *own* kit?" she managed. "Your *actual* jump kit?"

"Absolutely. I've always brought my own," he said. "You wouldn't believe the crap some of those shipping companies tried to pass off as professional equipment." He ran a finger along the lid of the box. "These handsets are perfect, tuned and calibrated by *me*. I've done almost two hundred halvers with this kit, and I've never lost an envelope."

Uma descended from the bridge and approached the table, her heart in her throat.

"Your name," she whispered, indicating the box and swallowing hard. "Is... is your name painted on the outside of that case?"

Leesongronski didn't answer, but he lifted the lid of the case and slowly turned it to face her. There, in a neat, tilted script, were the hand-painted letters:

L E E S O N G R O N S K I.

"That's in the *Jonah* Museum on Anvaelia!" Uma gasped. "That box! Papa was the one who acquired it for the collection. I've *seen* it. You used that exact jump kit to get the *Jonah* to Etraxas, and you used it so many times afterward... for all your other discoveries, for all the paths you found..." She reached out and touched the edge of the box. "You're going to become the Pathfinder, the Last of the Greats. With those handsets."

There was a strange expression on Leesongronski's face. He

slowly set down the piece that was in his hand and sank onto one of the stools.

In the bridge, Keeven stood up. "Hey. Ozakka, could you give us a minute?"

Uma nodded. She stepped away from Leesongronski and returned to the bridge as Keeven took her place next to the table.

Leesongronski had gone back to staring at the half-assembled jump kit, his face haunted.

"Leeg. Hey, pal? You all right?" Keeven put a hand on his shoulder. "Leeg. C'mon... I think we need to talk about this."

"About what?" Leesongronski said. His voice sounded choked.

"About all of it. All this." Keeven gestured around, up at the open console where the progress bar still blinked along. He touched the top of the black case in front of Leesongronski. "You think this'll really work? I mean... can you actually jump this ship to Etraxas?"

Leesongronski slowly closed the case, lifting Keeven's hand aside. "Jerry, I don't know how I can possibly answer that," he said. "We're talking about an undiscovered subspace stream here, right? Well... when you find a new stream, first of all, you don't know if it's stable. You don't know if it's navigable, or even where it goes. It's not like you can just sit down one day and say, 'Hey, I need to get to Etraxas real quick, go find me a new stream for that.' It doesn't work that way. You don't set out to find a completely new stream to get to somewhere specific. You find a new stream and then *you figure out where it goes.*"

Keeven nodded. "I know."

"Maybe you get killed trying that first jump," Leesongronski went on. "Maybe the stream's unstable, or you hit a bad patch, or you just plain make a mistake. But if you manage to stay alive, and the stream is both stable and useful? Well, that makes you amazing. And if you do that more than a handful of times in your entire life? Then you're one of the Greats."

He sighed. "After you've proven the stream's stable, the long work starts. You start refining the potential routes through the stream to find the faster ones. Eventually you might get more architects out there doing halvers, like I did with those shipping rigs. You experiment, and you explore, and you refine your routes until you find the best ways through. It takes years."

"Right," said Keeven. "I got it. But—"

"Look, all we can do is go to where they *say* this stream should be. And if there's really a stream there, then I could try to jump it and we'll see where it goes. Just like I would've done with that ditch ship if we'd found something. But there's no guarantees, Jerry." He fixed his eyes on Keeven. "You know damn well this is risky. And if we survive the jump, and we do end up at Etraxas... we could fly right into the middle of a fucking alien siege fleet! But there's no point talking about it, is there? Because once you've made up your mind, you never listen to me—"

Keeven reached out and put a hand on Leesongronski's arm.

"Leeg," he said softly. "I'm asking you. Should we do this?"

Leesongronski closed his eyes for a moment, and when he opened them again, something in the hard edges of his face had softened.

"Jerry... are you actually asking me what *I* want to do?"

"Yeah. I am," Keeven said. "I made a lot of mistakes, Leeg. I know that. I fucked everything up, for both of us... and I'm sorry." He squeezed Leesongronski's arm. "Honestly, if you'd punched me in the face when you saw me in that lecture-hall on Almant, I would've deserved it."

"Jerry—"

"I need to know you're with me on this one, okay?" Keeven picked up one of the loose nodes from Leesongronski's jump kit and held it up. "Tell me what we should do, and I'll listen.

Hand to the gods, Leeg. I don't want to fuck anything up this time. This one's your call... Captain Leesongronski."

Leesongronski glanced up into Uma's tear-filled eyes as she watched them from the bridge, then he slowly turned back to Keeven.

"I think we should do it," Leesongronski said. "If we find that stream, I'll try to jump it." He paused, then took the node out of Keeven's hand. "And if we do make it to Etraxas with Gida... I guess you're going to negotiate us a truce with the Felen."

"Okay, pal." Keeven's voice was quieter than usual. "That's exactly what we'll do."

Uma held her breath until Keeven turned back to look at her.

"Hey, Ozakka. So, uh... you planning to tell us what we're s'posed to do when we get there?" he said. "I'm assuming that Felen siege fleet doesn't just send someone over to say 'hi' to some random civilian-looking human vessel. How come the Felen didn't shoot the *Jonah* down?"

"Well, actually... I... don't know," Uma said. "Nobody knows for sure."

"Right." Keeven looked dubious. "So we just show up somewhere in the Etraxan system, which is under alien siege, and then we..." He gave an exaggerated quizzical shrug. "Any ideas here?"

Uma sighed. "This has always been one of the most contentious points about the *Jonah*'s voyage. How did they evade the Felen scouting ships when they reached Etraxas? There's the transponder theory, which I always thought was plausible... but it's not like we can replicate that..."

"What's the transponder theory?" Keeven's face creased into a frown.

"Some historians think the Peace Project might've acquired a working Felen transponder somehow," Uma said. "There were ways to get Felen tech on the black market—usually it was salvage from war wrecks. From a distance, if the *Jonah* had a Felen transponder, it would've been identified as a Felen warship, so it wouldn't have attracted any attention. And, because it came out of that unknown subspace stream, in a part of the outer system that wasn't under close scrutiny... that disguise could've worked just long enough to let the *Jonah* get closer to the siege line."

"Huh," Keeven said.

"Eventually, the *Jonah* did get spotted by the Felen fleet," Uma continued, "but because of the Felen transponder signal and the *Jonah*'s willingness to approach, the Felen would've assumed it was a captured human ship under Felen command. The *Jonah* had no weapons, and it didn't seem to be a threat, so they didn't destroy it. They decided to board it, and when they did, the Decipherer opened telepathic contact with the boarding party. And the Negotiator got to work."

Leesongronski leaned forward, listening with consternation.

"The thing is, none of us have *any* clue how to re-create that situation," Uma said. "Our Ambassador does have a couple of Felen communication devices on board, but they're modern. That's not going to help us fake a Felen warship transponder from a hundred and fifty-two years ago. We don't even know what kind of military codes a transponder should've been broadcasting..."

While she was talking, Keeven stood up and circled behind Leesongronski to one of the storage panels. He kicked at the join in the panels until one loosened, then he shoved it open with a loud, metallic scrape.

"Jerry?" said Leesongronski. "Are you listening?"

Keeven reached into the storage space and dragged something out: an orange containment crate, with the icons for 'danger' and 'contamination' emblazoned over the side.

Leesongronski looked horrified. "What the fuck is *that?*"

"Oh, ignore the box. This was the only sealable container

I could find." Keeven pushed the crate over the uneven floor with his foot. "You remember what I told you about how we lost the *Enigma*? When we ran into those Felen fighters on the way to pick you up?"

"Yeah..." said Leesongronski. "You got shot at, and the ship was damaged, so you traded it for the *Jonah* at the junkyard. And?"

"We got a bit more than just shot at," Keeven said. "I didn't tell you before because I knew it'd freak you out, and I didn't want to scare you off coming with us. The *Enigma* got snared by one of those thorn ships."

Leesongronski gasped. "Shit! You were *boarded*?"

"No, luckily we weren't. I did have to go out in a suit and chop that thorn off our hull, though. And when I finished up out there... I took a few things out of the Felen ship." Keeven patted the lid of the box. "I was planning to give this to Guillem as a goodbye gift, when we met up with her at Fedraya. She collects this stuff. Felen tech's worth a fortune."

Keeven undid the containment seals, peeling back the box's lid. Uma stepped closer. Inside were two handheld Felen weapons, a mass of wiring and damaged computer chips, and a pile of miscellaneous electronics.

On the top of the pile sat a shiny black half-sphere the size of a fist, adorned with a thin silver coil.

The thing was perfectly intact.

A vivid image flashed in front of Uma's eyes then: the same object, shown from three different angles and again in a cutaway.

Figure 71—A Felen fleet-leader's identification transponder. A similar type of transponder may have been used by the Jonah *to evade the scouting ships at the perimeter of the Etraxan system.*

"Keeven," Uma whispered. "I think... oh, gods. Maybe this really is going to work."

Maybe it always *had* worked.

*   *   *

BACK IN HER apartment, Uma gently set the half-empty agnathe bottle back into its ornate little stand. She paused for a moment to smile at her father's portrait, as he gazed back from his place next to the model *Jonah* that she'd returned to the shelf.

"We did it, Papa," she whispered. "We really, actually did it."

Her father's serene expression didn't change, but in her mind, she saw him smile.

What the *Gallion* crew were about to do tomorrow was terrifying... and yet, Uma felt lighter and more confident than she had in years. What had been a frayed hope had become a fervent certainty. They would get the rest of the way.

She sat down at the table and flicked open her lightpad, navigating to the ZeyCorp knowledge bank. Her fingers flew over the display, summoning the section she wanted. She read quickly, skimming from entry to entry, following the generally-accepted timeline of the *Jonah* voyage up to the end of the Contact War.

ZEYCORPnet KNOWLEDGE BANK

End of the Felen Conflict

SEARCH RESULTS
Peace of Etraxas
Truce Negotiations at Etraxas

The <u>Siege of Etraxas</u> had been ongoing for forty-nine days when the Capital's <u>Roundhouse</u> received a message from the Felen flagship in orbit above the Northern Continent. A short text in two human languages was transmitted to the surface, stating that the Felen Starhold would accept the terms of the truce as proposed by the Union's Negotiator, and that the Felen siege fleet was to be withdrawn peacefully from Etraxan orbit while further negotiations continued.

Initially, the message was met with skepticism and disbelief. No official negotiator had been appointed, and no one had been given authority to broker a truce on behalf of the Union. The unsigned message was the first known attempt at communication from a Felen war fleet. The <u>United Worlds Defense Forces</u> initially denied knowledge of any attempted peace overtures, and suspicions on the planet's surface quickly grew. Most of the Peers and sitting senators believed that the Felen must have anticipated the imminent attack by the UWDF's <u>Liberation Fleet</u>, and that they were attempting to throw the UWDF forces into confusion.

The Roundhouse, in conference with two UWDF bases, voted in favour of immediately calling in the Liberation Fleet to decimate the retreating Felen siege fleet. However, the Liberation Fleet was still at half-strength following the <u>rebellion of the subspace engineers</u>. The UWDF advised against deploying the fleet as originally planned, stating that there was insufficient time to assess a fallback strategy in the event of the attack's failure.

Over the following two days, the Felen siege fleet disassembled from low orbit around Etraxas, and retreated as far as the <u>Etraxan outer system</u>. Several Union vessels were allowed to leave Etraxan planetary space to rendezvous with the Felen flagship around the far-orbiting ice planet <u>Girum Vela</u>.

An Etraxan ambassadorial vessel, the *Esprin*, carried six Blessed Scions of Etraxas to Girum Vela, as well as numerous other planetary representatives from the

Union's Planetary Senate who had been among those sitting in the Roundhouse during the siege. (See also: List of UPS senators in Esprin Peace Delegation) The convoy departed from Etraxas at low speed, taking a further three days to make the journey to the outer system— during which time some of the Liberation Fleet arrived to stand guard during the negotiations.

In orbit around Girum Vela, the Etraxan delegation met with the two human representatives who had brokered the initial truce: the Union's Negotiator and his translator, later known as the Decipherer. She was the first human to be successfully modified with Felen genetic material, allowing her to learn the Felen telepathic language. (Related: Voicing).

As they had agreed before leaving Etraxas, the UPS senators on board the Esprin all feigned knowledge of the existing negotiations, and confirmed that the Negotiator had been sent by the UWDF—a decision hotly disputed, but later credited for the success of the early peace talks.

In reality, the Negotiator had no previous affiliation with the senators, and had entered the negotiations with no official authority to speak for the Union or the UWDF. Unbeknownst to the Felen, the Negotiator was actually a civilian peace activist who was working for the Geminus Initiative, on the illegal Peace Project that the UWDF had spent several months trying to quell.

It is thought that the Negotiator owed his initial success to the Felen's shock at the Decipherer's fluency in communication, rather than the quality of his diplomacy. The Starhold's Envoy had not previously been convinced of full sentience among the human species, and was said to be emotionally affected 'beyond measure' by the Decipherer's telepathic overture. The <u>Felen peace statement</u> included reference to the Envoy's 'deep and profound regret at the lack of understanding between us, and sorrow for the loss of sentient life that could surely have been avoided with more clarity of communication.'

Attempting unsanctioned communication with the Felen carried a death sentence for civilians under <u>contemporary wartime laws</u>, but the Roundhouse insisted the six Etraxan senators had collectively sanctioned and secretly funded the Peace Project, granting all remaining members of the Geminus Initiative <u>political immunity</u>. The UWDF upheld the Senate's testimony, stating that at the request of the Roundhouse, they had enlisted the anonymous Negotiator to help broker the truce.

It is now well-known that the Peace Project was never sanctioned nor funded by the Etraxans, nor by any of the Roundhouse Peers. The UWDF had in fact arrested and executed several other members of the Geminus Initiative in the preceding months with the Roundhouse's approval, and none of the senators had been aware of the *Jonah's* mission to Etraxas. The initial truce negotiations with the Felen Starhold's Envoy were entirely improvised by the Negotiator, without input from the Roundhouse, the UWDF or any other Union body. However, this fact did not become public knowledge until well over sixty years after the Peace.

The <u>earliest accounts</u> of the Peace of Etraxas elided the issue of the Negotiator's background and affiliation, but the Union eventually addressed the question in a series of official statements released after his death. The statements explained that the UWDF had decided to send an undercover peace activist rather than a military commander to the table for strategic reasons: since the Negotiator truly had no knowledge of the UWDF's current operations or classified information, he could not have been compromised through torture or mind-control if he had been taken prisoner by the Felen.

Some historians still believe that the Negotiator was more likely a trained undercover operative for the UWDF, and that he was specially selected and coached for the *Jonah* mission. They maintain that the alternate narrative—that he was a civilian peace activist acting on his own—is the fiction. It was reported by some contemporary sources that the Negotiator bore a military tattoo, indicating that he was UWDF-affiliated. However, the Negotiator's anonymity has been preserved, and his identity—if known at all—remains strictly classified.

After the Peace of Etraxas, members of the Fortunate Five were deemed exempt from civilian law in the matter of the unauthorized alien contact. Leesongronski, Kva-Sova and Jaxong were all cleared of treason charges and lauded as heroes of the highest order.

Many historically tantalizing mysteries still surround the Fortunate Five's journey into the Etraxan system. The improbable events leading to the *Jonah*'s arrival have prompted some to hail the voyage as an act of fate or even a 'miracle,' while scholars continue to scour the historical record for concrete evidence to answer the remaining questions—

Uma's head snapped up at the sound of someone buzzing at her door. Olghan Fransk's ZeyCorp ID flashed on the ident-panel, and she swiped out the unlock command.

"Are you ready, Director?" Fransk stood straight in the doorway, his purple blazer immaculate, buttons gleaming. "Director Barnabyn and Zel are already there. We should go."

"I'm ready," she said, and she meant it.

Fransk glanced at her open lightpad on the table. "I thought you knew all that historical stuff inside and out," he said with a teasing smile. "You really still need to study it?"

"Hah, no. And I wouldn't advise studying the ZeyCorp knowledge bank for your primary source, either." She paused, holding his gaze. "Oli, I know you still have your doubts about all this, about Gida... But the thing is, the more I go over it... I don't think there are actually *that* many historical changes we need to worry over. I don't think much is going to change at all if we send Gida back with them."

"Oh?" Fransk's eyebrows rose. "Well... I don't really know how you can say that, or how we expect this to work. Sending Gida back in time won't magically fix history, will it? There's already too many discrepancies! There's so much wrong, so many changes... Like, what about the fact that the *Jonah* never made another stop after Pilar Outpost? And our Negotiator never worked for the Geminus Initiative? And—"

"Absolutely none of that matters, Olghan," she interrupted. "The last documented stop on the *Jonah*'s voyage was at Pilar. No one has *ever* found any hard evidence of their exact route between Pilar and the Girum Vela stream."

"What?" Fransk frowned. "But... they must have stopped again, to pick up the Negotiator, right? Where did they stop?"

Uma held up one hand. "Let me finish. Listen. Historians have confirmed that the *Jonah* docked at Pilar Outpost sometime in the month before the Peace, because the ship name was listed on a docking manifest that was recovered post-war. But that's all we have. No one knows what cargo they actually picked up there, or what crew or passengers boarded that ship at Pilar. After that, the ship did make one more stop: Zora Outpost, where the Negotiator came on board." She paused, searching his worried face. "But, Oli, there's no material record of the *Jonah*'s docking at Zora. That outpost was destroyed by the Felen right after the *Jonah* stopped there, and the docking records simply don't exist."

Fransk stopped walking, and his frown deepened. "So... wait, how do we know the *Jonah* really docked at Zora Outpost in the first place?"

Uma smiled. "That's just it. We don't! We've never known any of this for sure. There *is* no proof. The Fortunate Five themselves are the source for almost all the facts we know. How and why they each boarded the ship... how the Five knew each other... the fact that they were working for Geminus... all that information comes from the personal accounts of exactly three people." She held up three fingers. "Eldric Leesongronski, Charyne Jaxong and Keila Kva-Sova. History will record *whatever they say*."

Fransk's worried eyes met Uma's. "But if they go back there and try to lie about what happened... it'll never work. They're bound to make mistakes, to say something wrong, or contradict themselves, or—"

"Yes, and they did! Conspiracy theorists have been talking about all the weird discrepancies in the Fortunate Five's stories for years!" Uma squeezed his arm. "The *Jonah* voyage has always had that certain... strangeness about it. Things that can't be explained by any logic. Why do you think it's called 'the miracle flight'?"

Fransk was nodding slowly, comprehension dawning in his eyes.

"People always ask why no one questioned any of the oddities at the time," Uma said. "But I think it's simple. The Union was desperate. They were ready to accept absolutely anything, no matter how outlandish. Gods, the UWDF actually pretended they'd sent a Negotiator they'd never even heard of! The *Jonah* history is already full of strange contradictions, believe me. That's part of what makes it all so fascinating."

Fransk stared at her for a long time, then sighed. "I... guess I just wish I understood..."

"Shhh. It'll be all right," she whispered. "They can do this, Oli. And so can we. Come on. Let's get to this audience."

She reached out and took his hand, and they went together to the Ambassador's guest suite.

WHEN UMA AND Fransk stepped into the dimly-lit room, Zel and Barnabyn were already there. Leesongronski, Keeven, Jaxong and Kva-Sova were assembled in a small semi-circle, all facing the Ambassador. Gida stood to one side, her expression serene, the kennai symbol glinting on her forehead.

Uma caught her breath at the sight of them—the Fortunate Five, all of them, together at last. The living embodiment of that critical moment in human history. And she, *Uma Ozakka*, was here witnessing it... on a corporate science ship, wearing the rumpled Engineering uniform she'd had on for two days straight.

She looked at Eldric Leesongronski and thought of her great-grandfather, staring up in awe at the Pathfinder's lecture. She had never been more sure that they were doing the right thing.

Gida took her usual place next to the Ambassador. Her eyes rolled slowly back, her irises disappearing into her eyelids. At the same time, the alien's thin arms swept apart, awash in pearlescent blue sleeves.

"We rejoice," Gida said. "Captain Fransk, Director Ozakka... thank you for coming to witness this important moment. Is everything prepared?" The Ambassador's eyes weren't visible under the beaded headpiece, but the alien's gaze was undoubtedly fixed on the captain.

"Yes, Ambassador," Fransk said. "We're ready to broadcast the detonation command and set off the bomb." He shifted his feet nervously. "Of course, we still have to push the *Jonah* back to their original side of the boundary zone before we do. And assuming the... ah, Rift inversion works... and we return to our own time, and..." He trailed off, clearing his throat. "Well, suffice to say that we are all as ready as we can be."

"That is most welcome news," Gida said. "Our gratitude is boundless. Thank you."

The Ambassador turned toward the *Jonah* crew, and the beaded headpiece jingled. One arm moved toward Keeven, spindly fingers fully extended.

"Jereth Keeven," said Gida. "You will become the Union's Negotiator. You must negotiate the truce with the Felen Starhold, and speak on behalf of the United Worlds of Humanity to bring an end to our days of war. Are you still willing to undertake this mission?"

"I'll do it," said Keeven, lifting his chin with determination. "I'll give it my best shot."

"Charyne Jaxong," Gida continued. "You shall become the Inventor. You will deliver the gift of limitless energy, and the Negotiator will offer your schematics to the Starhold's Envoy as part of the Peace negotiations. You will work with the Felen scientists to complete the Jaxong drive, and we will begin to share our technologies peacefully. Are you willing?"

"Yes," said Jaxong quietly. "I'll do that."

"Keila Kva-Sova... you will be the Voicegiver. Through your genetic modification procedure, you will create more translators for the Alliance. You will open the lines of communication between our peoples, allowing us to understand one another at last. Are you willing?"

Kva-Sova nodded. "I'm willing," she whispered. "With all of my heart, yes."

"Eldric Leesongronski... you shall become the Pathfinder," Gida said. "Captain of the great ship *Jonah*. You will make the miracle jump. You will navigate a subspace stream never before discovered, and guide the *Jonah* to besieged Etraxas. Are you willing?"

Leesongronski bobbed his head. "Yes."

Gida blinked, and her monotonous voice suddenly returned to her own.

"I am also willing," she said. "I will translate the Peace negotiations... and I will mentor the next generation of the Voiced." She lifted the hood of her green cloak and pulled it up over her head, shrouding her face. "I will become the Decipherer. The first teacher, the original *alihe*."

Then Gida approached Keeven, laying one hand delicately on his arm. She turned to stand beside him, now facing the Ambassador.

"Representatives of ZeyCorp, we hope you have come to understand our decision, and why it is so clear to us," Gida said, resuming the Ambassador's flat monotone. "There is no higher calling, no greater gift than the preservation of the Peace. We must do all in our power to protect it. We thank you for your help."

Fransk glanced at Uma before he spoke. "You have our support, Ambassador," he said. "And... thank you, Gida. We owe you more than we can possibly express."

"We thank you also," Gida said. The Ambassador's head tilted reverently toward the *Jonah* crew. "Now, the Fortunate Five must walk together into history. And they shall be remembered for all time as the truest heroes of humanity."

SHAAN
Common Deck, ZeyCorp Gallion

SHAAN FOUND KEEVEN in the canteen, standing in front of the vending machine—in what had somehow become their usual meeting spot. There wasn't much time left to get Keeven alone, to say some kind of proper goodbye to him. Yet in all this time, she still hadn't figured out exactly what she wanted to say.

What words would make any sense at all? *I'm really sorry you're probably going to die not long after you get to Etraxas and negotiate that truce, but it was really nice kissing you? Have a good trip back to the past? Thanks for saving humanity? Guess I'll see you around... in the mostly-incorrect history texts?*

Keeven looked up and noticed her standing there. His mouth quirked into that cheeky half-smile, and her face instantly flushed hot. Something still buzzed between them like electricity, every time their eyes met. *Gods damn it.*

Keeven held up the ZeyCorp-branded cup in his hand. "Look at me, just out here getting one last cup of... whatever this stuff is," he said. His voice was amused. "Guess you'd better give me that feedback form soon, huh? I've gotta leave my good review before we go."

"Ha. Yeah, sure. I'll, uh... I'll send one over to you." Shaan

435

walked to the vending machine, grabbed a cup and shoved it into the dispenser. "That'll be great for the press-releases. Food services officially endorsed by the Negotiator for the Union. I'm sure ZeyCorp Central would *love* that." She rolled her eyes.

Keeven smiled again, but he didn't say anything back. His gaze was contemplative, and she could hardly blame him for being quiet. Was he thinking about his looming death? The truce he had to negotiate with the Felen? The bomb detonation? It all felt too heavy to handle, and she tried to keep her thoughts away from any of it.

They stood side by side in silence for a while, sipping from their cups, glancing at each other. Keeven was wearing his usual garb: a faded shirt with the sleeves rolled up, those scuffed unlaced boots, the dark trousers. His worn-out jacket was tied around his waist, and his chaotic hair looked slightly wet, like he hadn't quite bothered to finish towelling it off after he got out of the shower. A faint line still ran from his bottom lip down his chin where she'd patched up his face, and he smelled like the standard-issue ZeyCorp soap.

He didn't look much like the Negotiator just now... but he looked like *Jereth*, and her heart skipped. He had been dead for a hundred and fifty-two years, and he was also standing here in front of her. Both things were true. And both things were equally unnerving.

"Hey. You all right?" Keeven finally asked, turning to look directly at her. "How're you doing? I mean, impending superweapon detonations aside?"

"Me? I'm... okay." As the words left her mouth, she was surprised to find that she actually meant them. "I think I really am going to be okay."

"Good." He tilted his cup toward her with a smile.

"What about you, though?" She searched his face. "Are you sure *you're* really okay? I mean, with... the whole... knowing the Negotiator's supposed to *die*..."

Keeven shrugged. "Shaan, I've been supposed to die ever since I was born two generations into an interstellar war. I was supposed to die growing up on a dust world with no supply chain and a failing water system. I was supposed to die in stasis. I was supposed to die at least a dozen times while I was hauling weaps for Guillem. But I didn't." He took the empty cup from her hand and stacked it into his own before he discarded them both into the disposal, dropping them with a flourish as though he was throwing away the notion of his own death. "I'm still alive, aren't I?"

"But... this is different, Jereth."

He shook his head. "No. It's not. Look, no matter what happens, I'm gonna do this thing. We're gonna try to get to Etraxas with Gida, and we'll try to make this peace deal. And maybe it works, maybe it doesn't. All I can do is give it my best shot. But one thing's for sure." He fixed his eyes on hers. "As long as I'm still living, Shaan... I'll always keep taking my chances while I've got 'em."

She looked into his face, and for a split-second, she saw every version of him at once: the resolute, majestic Negotiator, the stoic statue on Verkhoy, the radiant paragon of history... and *this* version. Jereth Keeven, real and tangible and present, with his gold-flecked brown eyes and that smile that did strange things to her insides.

"I'm still alive," he repeated.

"Yeah," she whispered. *And so am I.*

He leaned forward, one hand braced against the vending machine, and cupped her chin with the other. Shaan's heart was pounding. Then he trailed his hand slowly down the side of her neck, until his fingers rested on the staff badge at her collar. Their lips were nearly touching.

"So... you're the Facilities Coordinator, huh?" he murmured, leaning closer. "That's good. 'Cause... y'know... I was actually wondering if... maybe you needed to... like, inspect the facilities or something in my apartment..."

It was all she could do to keep from grabbing him and kissing that smirk off his face, right there in the *Gallion* canteen. Instead, she looked down and mimed checking her bracelet.

"Oh, look at that," she said, a grin spreading across her face. "Says your guest apartment inspection is due right now. *You* need to report back to your apartment to meet with your Facilities Coordinator. Immediately."

"Mmm," he said. "Sounds about right. I do love me some of that ZeyCorp protocol."

KEEVEN'S APARTMENT DOOR had barely closed behind them and they were already entwined. Whatever Shaan might have wanted to say to him, the words dissolved on her lips and turned to frantic kisses. Keeven kicked away his boots and dropped his jacket; Shaan stepped out of her shoes, and they collapsed onto the narrow single bed together, a mess of entangled limbs.

She pushed him back onto the sheets, unzipping his shirt and discarding it onto the floor as she climbed into his lap. Meanwhile, he was fumbling over the clasps on her ZeyCorp uniform. After several failed attempts to undo them with his shaking hands, he just laughed and tugged the top half unceremoniously over her head, leaving her in her black camisole. And then he was kissing her newly-exposed skin, touching her everywhere he could, his mouth hungrily following the contours of her neck down to her collarbone.

If either of them had envisioned a slow, elegant seduction, they abandoned that idea along with their self-control. There was nothing graceful about it. They'd slipped halfway off the bed in their rush to undress, dragging most of the sheets along with them, but Keeven made no move to remedy the situation. Instead, he let himself fall and sprawled out onto the floor, pulling her down on top of him, still kissing her.

Her impatient fingers found his belt buckle, swiftly unfastening his trousers. She shifted her weight off him while he kicked them the rest of the way off. She pulled off the black camisole and threw it over her shoulder. And then his hands were sliding down her thighs, and he was freeing her of her remaining clothing.

When they were both thoroughly naked, she took hold of his shoulders and straddled him. He held her by the hips as she rocked against him, their bodies colliding again and again in unbridled triumph. She gasped for breath, clutching fistfuls of his hair as he moaned into her neck. They tumbled over the floor together, unselfconscious and uninhibited, and it was nothing short of glorious.

It didn't take them long to find the release they'd been craving, and they made no attempt whatsoever to delay the pleasure. They got there hard and fast, writhing blissfully in each other's arms until they both collapsed onto the purple carpet.

Afterwards, she lay next to him in stunned silence, her legs still tangled up in the fallen sheets, her exhausted body glowing with the aftershocks. When she looked over at him, he was as out of breath as she was, staring up at the ceiling with the biggest grin on his face.

After a while, he pulled her closer and started stroking the back of her neck with his fingertips, exactly the same way he'd done on Verkhoy Station. She pressed her cheek against the Union flame on his chest, focusing on the brush of his trembling fingers over her skin as his heartbeat slowly came back to normal.

She closed her eyes and imagined the deck of a boat, and an endless starry sky.

UMA
Command Deck, *ZeyCorp Gallion*

WHEN UMA CAME up to the Command deck, the captain's office door was open. Inside, Fransk was sitting at his desk, turning that ZeyCorp coaster over in his hands, deep in thought.

"Olghan?"

He looked up, dropping the coaster. "Uma."

"Some of the crew are having a little goodbye gathering in the staff lounge." She smiled. "Might be nice if the captain made an appearance, hmm? I thought you'd want to make a speech."

"Sure. Yeah." He sounded distracted. "I'll, ah... I'll be down in a minute, okay? Just go on without me."

She paused at the door for a moment, then stepped into the office and came over to the desk. She sat down in the chair across from him without waiting to be asked.

"You need to talk about something?" She nudged his arm. "What're you up here pondering so seriously about?"

He gave a half-hearted laugh. "Oh, nothing much. Not like we might be erased from existence tomorrow or anything... or blow ourselves up when that bomb goes off..."

She reached out and put her hand over his. "Well, how about you come ponder all that down in the staff lounge with

440

a nice glass of fizz? It's like Wazar said: if we're going to dread our imminent demise, we might as well do it with a good soundtrack. Right?"

He didn't laugh. He picked up the coaster again, turning it over slowly in his hands. "I've been thinking about what you said before," he said. "About how the history isn't going to be all that different in the end. I keep trying to convince myself... I mean, I'm thinking about all the coincidences we've had, about how strange it is that we were all here. Maybe you're right, and it's going to be fine."

"I'm right about a lot of things," she said teasingly. "Like the Verkhoy mission. Hmm? You going to admit how right I was about that?"

"Any reasonable person would've voted against it."

"I actually couldn't believe you went along with it," she said with a smile. "I thought you'd nix it for sure when you saw how complicated it was."

"Oh, I *know*." He gave a deep sigh. "It looked like a disaster in the making."

"Then why *did* you go ahead?"

"Isn't it obvious? Because I trust you," he said. "Besides, if I'd gone against you, you probably would've staged a gods-damned mutiny and airlocked me."

She half-laughed, letting out her breath. "Nah. Maybe just locked you into your office."

"Seriously, though... I know how you work, Uma. You get your ideas and you stick with them, even if you go down fighting tooth and claw." He squeezed her hand. "You think I don't know how damn stubborn you are, after all these years?"

"Fuck," she whispered. She stared down at the desk, shocked at the sudden tears that were welling in her eyes. "I know. I... I really do the same thing every time, don't I? I make a decision, good or bad, and I just... run with it. I run straight ahead, no looking back, and no one can tell me otherwise. I did the same thing when I stopped speaking to Halli... and when I closed the workshop after Papa died. Gods, I even did it when I broke up with *you*, way back in first year at the U." She looked up at him, blinking the tears back. "It's a miracle you and I are still friends, huh?"

"Well, I honestly don't know if breaking up with me was one of your good decisions or one of your bad ones," he said with a tired smile. "But one thing's for sure, Uma. If we survive this thing, if we do get back home... it'll be because of *you*." He reached over and wiped her teary cheek with the pad of his thumb. "Everything you've ever done, you've done with your whole heart. You throw yourself into things. And, yes, sometimes it's a disaster... but sometimes it's the only way to get it right. I trust you more than anyone else I've ever met."

"You... Really?"

"Absolutely. It's why I had no hesitation to recommend you to ZeyCorp when you applied. Of course, I never thought you'd actually suffer the corporate life for more than one rotation. Or that you'd get assigned to *my* ship." He laughed. "You must be the most overqualified engineer in the fleet. When are you finally going to get another job?"

"Oh, believe me, when we get out of here, my resignation will be the first thing in your message box," she said. The knot in her stomach eased, and she managed a laugh.

"Good. It's about time. You thinking of going planetside, or what?"

"I..." She paused. The answer was fresh and new in her mind, but as solid as if it had been waiting to be spoken for years. "Olghan, I... I think I might go back to the Anvaelian system. I mean, I could reopen the workshop... and work on vintage jump systems again... maybe see if the *Jonah* Museum needs a volunteer." Her chest flooded with warmth, the *rightness* of it settling over her. "I think I'm ready to do it."

"Good. That's really good, Uma."

Fransk stood up and came around the desk to sit in the chair beside her, holding his arms out to her. She leaned forward and lay her head against his shoulder, and he held her there for a long time, hugging her tightly.

"I'm glad you were here," he said quietly. "For this, and... for all of it. We would never have made it this far without you. *I* would never have made it."

"I'm glad you were here too, Oli. So glad." She patted his back. "Gods, nothing like a near-death experience for us to get sentimental, huh?"

He pulled back, fixing his gaze on her with his hands firmly on her shoulders. "Look, just promise me one thing, when we get home," he said. "Promise that you're finally going to talk to Halli, instead of just writing all those messages you never send."

"Gods." Uma sighed. "Halli and I haven't spoken in six years. I deleted all her messages, I never called her back when she tried. I told her never to contact me again. I... I said so many awful things... I don't think she's going to care what I say now."

"You were the love of her damn life, Uma," he said. "Just *talk* to her. Forgive each other. You'll feel better for it." He smiled. "Promise me you'll call her. That's an order, Director. Possibly the last one I'll ever give you."

"I promise." Uma smiled back softly. "Order acknowledged, *Captain*."

Fransk stood up from the chair. "Right. How about we get over to this party, then?"

And then, both their bracelets trilled at once, high and loud, with an urgent alert. They lit up with the same message: *SHIP EMERGENCY.*

An instant later, everything was awash in flashing orange lights, and an alarm tone started screaming into the room. Dean's eerily calm voice echoed from the ship-wide address channel. "Attention, *Gallion* crew and visitors. This is not a drill! Please move toward the nearest emergency gathering point on your deck, following the illuminated guides in the corridor. Move as quickly as possible. This is not a drill."

"What's happening?" Fransk shouted over the alarm. "Dean, this is the captain. Report! What's the problem?"

"I do not yet know," the AI said. "I am working to find out. The state of emergency has been manually triggered on Command authority."

Over the ship-wide channel, a second instance of Dean's voice was still repeating the same warning: "Attention, *Gallion* crew and visitors. This is not a drill! Please move toward the nearest gathering point on your deck—"

"Dean, on *whose* authority?"

"On Director Barnabyn's authority, Captain."

Fransk swore, fumbling with his bracelet. "Dean, connect me to Director Barnabyn."

"Impossible, I'm afraid," Dean said. "Director Barnabyn's bracelet has become inoperative."

"Where is he right now?"

There was no answer from the AI.

"Dean! Where is Director Barnabyn?"

The other instance of Dean's voice was still on a loop. "Attention, *Gallion* crew and visitors. This is not a drill! Please move toward the nearest gathering poi—" There was a single, ear-splitting beep, then the AI's voice cut off abruptly. The blaring alarms all shut off. Dead silence.

"Dean!" Fransk shouted. "Report!"

"*Ship's AI is offline*," the ship's computer replied in a digitized voice. "*Please use manual inputs*."

"What?" Uma's heart jumped into her throat. "But... Dean can only be switched off from Engineering! And that would need Command-level codes..."

"Dean, report!" Fransk persisted, a shred of desperate hope in his eyes. "Dean!"

"*Ship's AI is offline. Please use manual inputs.*"

Uma shoved Fransk toward the open door. "The bridge! Quick!" she shouted. "I can connect to Engineering from there!"

She grabbed his hand, and they ran.

The *Gallion*'s aesthetic bridge was just down the corridor on the Command deck. Though it was technically functional, it served mostly decorative purposes. Uma couldn't remember when she'd last seen anyone go in there, except to give tours or take pictures with visitors. It was equipped with a row of fancy navigational consoles and a few overhead displays that showed the ship's status, the active scientific missions and the flight time remaining to their next destination.

In the centre of the room were three wing-backed purple chairs on a raised platform, the headrests inscribed with the names of the captain and the directors. It looked exactly like the bridge backdrop in all the ZeyCorp advertisements.

"Can you open comms to Engineering, and get the security feed onscreen here?" Fransk shouted. "We need to see what's going on!"

"On it!" Uma jumped into the Engineering chair and spun up a screen. With Dean offline, the connection process was unnecessarily slow. Every second felt like it dragged for an eternity as she brought up a command prompt and started opening a link to the Engineering security system.

"You got it?" Fransk asked anxiously.

"Got it. Here." She flicked out a final command, and threw the Engineering feed up to the main viewscreen. As soon as it came into focus, her heart dropped.

Director Barnabyn was standing in the Engineering pit next to an open console. On the floor in front of him, the Ambassador's

Voiced was on her knees with her hands clasped behind her neck, her voluminous Felen robes enshrouding her.

Dargo Mendeg, the *Jonah*'s engineer, was holding a plasma gun to the back of Gida's head.

"Oh, gods," breathed Uma, ice flooding her veins. "He's got *Gida!*"

"Can they hear us?" Fransk whispered.

She managed a nod. "Audio link is on."

"This is the captain speaking!" Fransk yelled. "What is going on down there? Director Barnabyn, explain this!"

Barnabyn's head snapped up at Fransk's voice. "H-he had Gida at gunpoint, Captain," Barnabyn cried, pointing helplessly at Mendeg. "He must've grabbed her in the corridor! H-he said he was going to shoot her unless I entered my override codes and took Dean offline. I tried to engage the emergency alarm, but—"

"Shut *up!*" Mendeg bellowed, brandishing the gun toward Barnabyn. He looked directly up into the security camera. "You can see me? Good. I want you to watch this. The *Jonah*'s not gettin' anywhere near Etraxas, 'cause I'm gonna kill every one of your famous traitors." He reached down toward Gida with his free hand, grabbing her roughly by the collar of her robes. "Starting with this monstrosity…"

"Please, no… please…" Gida whimpered.

"There will *never* be peace between the Union and the Felen. Never! The Union will fight back until the Felen are dead or the Great Suns are dust!" Mendeg shouted. "We'll hunt down and eliminate every last one of them. And this—this *Voicing*? This won't be happening. This is an abomination!" He snatched the kennai jewel from Gida's forehead and threw it on the floor.

"Mendeg," said Fransk nervously. "Can we… maybe… talk about this—?"

"No! I'm done talking to you assholes. You're all Felen

sympathizers and traitors!" Mendeg smiled, an unhinged grin spreading across his face. "But... if you want your Director Barnabyn back alive, you'll bring me the rest of the Five. I want *all* the rest of 'em, understand? Send 'em down here. And the alien, too."

"Don't do it!" said Barnabyn. "Captain Fransk, don't listen to him!"

"You have *five* minutes to send them down," Mendeg said, staring into the camera. His eyes were wide and wild as he held up the weapon. "Victory for the United Worlds! Strength to the Union! Humanity prevails!"

While Mendeg was distracted, Uma saw Gida glancing furtively over to her left. Barnabyn had caught her eye and was gesturing to her surreptitiously, motioning toward the stairs that led to the top floor of Engineering.

"Strength to the Union!" Mendeg was still ranting. "Long live humanity! Death to the Felen! The Union will not surrender!"

Barnabyn kept his hand close to his body, still looking at Gida, and held up three fingers.

Then two fingers.

Then one.

When Barnabyn closed his fist, Gida suddenly jumped to her feet, ducked away from Mendeg and bolted to the staircase, holding up her long robes as she ran.

At the same moment, Barnabyn launched himself in the other direction, flinging himself onto the big engineer's back with a shout. He grabbed Mendeg's wrist with both hands, shoving the barrel of the plasma gun toward the floor.

Mendeg swore furiously as he kicked out at the director.

"Run!" Barnabyn screamed as Gida started climbing up the stairs. "Go! Run!"

Uma held her breath. The door on the top level of Engineering was still standing open. Every vital door on the ship would have opened with the emergency sequence; ZeyCorp safety protocol in action. But the Voiced girl would never make it to the exit, not across that expanse of open space, not before—

Barnabyn managed to keep hold of Mendeg's wrist just long enough for Gida to get to the top of the stairs, but the Director of Administration was no match for Mendeg's strength. Mendeg shook Barnabyn loose, shoving the director to the floor.

Barnabyn scrambled back to his feet just as Mendeg brought the gun up and pulled the trigger, unleashing a close-range plasma shot into the director's neck.

It was a merciless execution. As Fransk and Uma watched in horror, Barnabyn's head lolled to one side, the collar and shoulder of his purple blazer melting around him. He stood there swaying for a half-second before the rest of his body collapsed, and he crumpled slowly to the ground.

"Gods almighty," Fransk gasped. "No..."

Uma couldn't make a sound, bile rising in her throat.

Gida had started running across the upper level of Engineering, but as the shot went off, she doubled back and dove beneath the oblong meeting-table. She was huddled out of the camera's view now, invisible except for the trailing hem of her long robes.

"Too bad," Mendeg said sarcastically, stepping over Barnabyn's body. "Guess I'm gonna have to go get them myself. You think any of you can hide from me? No chance." He barrelled up the stairs after Gida. "I'm coming for you, you little vermin."

In the bridge, Fransk sank down into the captain's chair. He reached over and clutched Uma's hand as Mendeg leaned over to look under the meeting-table. There was absolutely nothing they could do but watch.

Mendeg lowered the gun under the table. He aimed at Gida and pulled the trigger.

Nothing happened.

Mendeg shook the gun, pulling the trigger again and again,

but the weapon hadn't recharged yet after his first shot. He shoved the weapon back into his belt, muttering to himself. "Fuckin' piece of junk."

Gida had started to crawl away from him, moving even further under the table, her robes slowly disappearing from view. For an instant, Uma dared to hope that somehow she could tuck herself just out of Mendeg's reach. But Mendeg stomped down on the edge of Gida's robe, grabbing the cloth in his fist.

He dragged Gida out roughly, yanking her back as she sobbed and struggled. He pulled her up and slammed her body hard into the table, then threw her against the railing.

With a strangled yelp, the Voiced fell to her knees at his feet. Mendeg easily hefted her up, holding her slender body aloft for one nauseating moment before he flung her right over the rail into the pit below.

This couldn't be happening. Fransk was staring at the feed in horrified disbelief, still clutching Uma's hand. Tears were streaming down Uma's face. *Oh, please, oh, no, no, no...*

Mendeg looked over the railing and laughed. He pulled the plasma gun out of his belt, checking the charge indicator before he marched back down the stairs into the pit. He stepped past Barnabyn's body again and walked to Gida's motionless form, brandishing the weapon as he looked up into the security camera.

"You still watching?" he shouted. "Witness this: all traitors will die. Your 'Fortunate Five' are finished!" With a gruesome smile, Mendeg pointed the gun directly down at Gida's head. "This is for humanity..."

And then, suddenly, Mendeg froze. His feet rose slightly off the floor and his body arched back, his face contorting in silent agony.

The Felen Ambassador was standing at the top of the stairs, one hand raised in Mendeg's direction. A tiny round weapon glinted from the middle of the alien's palm.

Mendeg's body spun once, then folded over and dropped, his corpse landing toe-to-toe with Barnabyn's. The plasma gun clattered out of his hand onto the floor.

There was silence from the security feed.

"C-captain Fransk? Uh... Director Ozakka?"

Uma turned to look behind her. Zel was standing in the doorway, wearing an elaborate red silk suit with the ubiquitous Etraxan sash still pinned over it. The rest of the crew who had been at the farewell gathering were all clustered behind him. Some of the engineers were in casual dress, and the Cordero siblings wore ridiculous party hats that seemed eerily incongruous in the moment. Leesongronski, Kva-Sova and Jaxong were with them.

No one else said a word. They all filed slowly into the bridge, assembling into a somber half-circle as they stared at the open feed. The Felen Ambassador was still standing at the top of the stairs. There were three bodies on the pit floor. Uma could hardly breathe.

"What do we do?" Zel croaked. "What do we...?"

"I think we have to go down there," Uma whispered. "Someone needs to go to Engineering."

"We'll all go," Captain Fransk said, his voice shaking. "All of us. We'll go together."

Single file, they all followed Fransk out into the atrium, and Uma couldn't bear to look up at the image of the Fortunate Five as they passed it.

When the group reached Engineering, the Ambassador was no longer standing on the top level, and Uma couldn't see down into the pit from the door.

Fransk advanced into Engineering's upper level, proceeding

with infinitesimal slowness, one tiny step at a time. She stepped in alongside him, while the others hung back near the doors. Some of them were craning their necks to see, others were averting their eyes. Syru and Mikolai held each other silently. Kva-Sova was crying into Jaxong's shoulder.

"Where's Jereth?" Leesongronski whispered behind her. "Anyone seen Jereth?"

Where *was* Keeven? Uma didn't have time to think about it.

Fransk had already shuffled almost all the way to the railing, edging slowly toward the spot where Leesongronski usually sat on the corner. Uma took a deep breath, steadied herself, and looked over the side of the rail.

The Felen Ambassador was crouched next to Gida, cradling her unmoving body. The alien was lost in a sea of ocean-blue robes, looking unusually vulnerable without the ubiquitous headpiece. One pale hand clutched at Gida, rocking her slowly back and forth. The other held her fallen kennai symbol, the gold chain glittering between long, greyish fingers.

Fransk nudged Uma. "Do you remember there being anything in the guidelines about... you know, communicating with gestures?" he whispered frantically. "Was there anything in the rules? How do we show we're *friendly?*"

The Felen's head suddenly jerked up. Four glistening black eyes stared intently up toward the stairs as the alien's head tilted to one side.

Fransk startled back from the rail, knocking into Uma. He instinctively raised both hands in defense, as if the Ambassador might be about to shoot at them with the same tiny weapon that had killed Mendeg. "We mean no harm!" he shouted. "Ambassador, we... we mean no harm..."

But the Felen was staring past Fransk, looking somewhere to the left of the stairs.

At the same time, Uma heard a flurry of whispers from behind her. She turned and looked over her shoulder. The gathered crew had parted to admit Keeven and Shaan, who were standing just inside the entrance.

"Jerry!" Leesongronski exclaimed under his breath, his shoulders lifting with visible relief. "There you are."

Keeven's shirt wasn't done up properly, the zip hanging halfway open. Shaan was bare-shouldered in a black camisole and her uniform trousers. Both of them were barefoot.

"Hey! What's goin' on?" Keeven asked, his face concerned. "System said Dean's offline, an' there was some kind of alarm going off! We ran around but we couldn't find anybody else, and..." He looked around at the crew's stunned faces, trailing off as he realized everyone was dead silent. "What?"

But Shaan wasn't looking at any of them. For some reason, she chose this precise moment to push past everyone in the group and walk directly toward the Engineering stairs.

"Stop!" Uma hissed. "Shaan, don't go down there!"

Uma looked back down at the Ambassador. The alien's glassy gaze was now fixed firmly on Shaan.

"I don't think that's a good idea, Shaan," Fransk said warningly. "We should stay up here."

Shaan ignored them both and continued walking. She started calmly down the staircase, her bare feet soundless on the steps.

The Felen didn't move. She kept walking.

Before anyone thought to stop him, Keeven had elbowed his way past the crew and followed Shaan to the top of the stairs, stopping short when he saw the scene below.

"Ohhh, *shit!*" he gasped. He reached down the stairs to take hold of her arm. "Shaan..."

She turned around and looked back at Keeven, gently pushing his hand away. She motioned for him to step back, giving him a reassuring nod.

Keeven looked confused, but he let her go. He stayed on the

stairs watching her as she descended the rest of the way, one hand resting on the railing, her eyes on the Ambassador.

The rest of the crew approached now, gathering close around Uma and Fransk, clustering at the top of the stairs and along the rail. Uma's heart pounded in her throat.

In the pit, the Felen Ambassador gently lay Gida's head back down onto the floor, one pale finger trailing over her face.

The alien stood up. Shaan made a half-turn to face the stairs.

And then, Shaan's irises slowly rolled back into her eyelids.

"Oh... my... *gods,*" Uma whispered, her hands gripping the rail.

"Friends, we are in need of your help," said Shaan in a flat, toneless voice unlike her own. "Our companion needs medical attention. She is alive, but her injuries are serious."

Keeven's mouth dropped open.

"We are in great disbelief at such a terrible tragedy," Shaan said as the Ambassador moved toward her. "We fear for our injured companion. We express a heavy sorrow at the loss of your courageous colleague, who defended this one's life with his own. And yet..."

The Felen's long fingers opened to reveal the kennai ornament. The Ambassador held the jewel aloft over Shaan's head, then lowered the ceremonial symbol of the Voiced onto her forehead.

"And yet, somehow... it seems that we may still be fortunate."

SHAAN
Geminus Base, Border Zone Sector W1F
6 years before the Rift

SHAAN HELD STILL as the flat, cold sensors were applied to her shorn skull. The scanning ring descended until it stopped just above her shoulders, beeped softly, then rotated. After six images, the machine gave a longer beep, and the ring retracted. The clinician pulled off the sensors.

"Hmm," the clinician said with a frown. She looked away from the scan, tapping at a message that had blinked up on her lightpad. "I've just received a message from High Command... and it looks like they're clearing you to leave this base." She swivelled her chair to face Shaan. "This says your patient record is to be closed, effective immediately."

Shaan nodded, tears pooling in her eyes. "Yes. I know."

"Really?" The clinician scowled at the lightpad, looking offended. "I should have been consulted on this. Did they tell you where you're being transferred, or who your new clinician will be?"

"No," Shaan said in a near-whisper. "I'm not being transferred. I'm... I'm being dismissed. Because of what happened. They want me to leave Geminus... for good."

The clinician's eyebrows went up, and her mouth formed

a small, shocked circle. Something like sympathy crossed her face, then disappeared just as quickly.

"Well. For what it's worth," the clinician huffed, "I think that's a ridiculous decision. An unusual case like yours would make an invaluable scientific study in the long term!" She tapped at the lightpad again. "But I suppose it has been several months with no improvement in your condition. They aren't interested in carrying on with your rehabilitation."

Shaan didn't say anything back.

The clinician held up the lightpad. "It seems the Council wants you released as an unaltered civilian," she said. "They won't be flagging up your genetic mods on your new background file. They want me to sign an affidavit declaring that your condition is permanent, and that in my professional opinion, you will never recover your telepathic abilities." She frowned. "Now, Shaan... This comes direct from the Council so, I'm going to have to sign off on this. But to be clear, I don't think it's *impossible* for your abilities to one day—"

"It doesn't matter," Shaan interrupted. "I'm barred from all future contact with the Felen, or the Voiced, or any member of the Geminus Peace Alliance. Forever." She blinked back tears. "I'll never work for Geminus again."

The clinician pursed her lips, her face betraying no emotion. "Be that as it may... I've noted my opinion in my final report," she said. "The injuries you sustained in the shuttle crash were not insubstantial. You suffered a severe blow to the head in that accident, and there was enough physical trauma to cause you lasting brain damage. However, I remain unconvinced that this is the sole cause of your condition."

She fixed Shaan with a searching gaze. "The brain is one thing, but the *mind* can be entirely another. I still think some form of trauma-induced amnesia is a factor here, Shaan. It's not inconceivable that some of this is psychological, and that you've somehow suppressed your abilities. What with the tragic death of your student..." She looked away. "Even a normal human mind still holds many mysteries. And when you add an alien genome to the mix... well, even after all these years, we've hardly begun to understand the peculiarities of the Voiced brain."

The clinician produced a small green data disc and held it out to Shaan.

"Here. It's a copy of your full history. All your medical records, and the neural scans from the day after the shuttle crash and onwards. If you need it." She nodded toward the door. "Someone's here to collect you."

Shaan looked over, and her heart sank. Ker Marecc was standing at the door in his Geminus uniform, holding an unmarked grey carry-bag. Of course Marecc was still here. He would have remained to hear the final verdict in the Verkhoy inquest.

She willed herself not to flinch as she slid out of the chair with a respectful nod.

Like everyone who had spent the last few months sitting in that inquest hall, Verkhoy's former Station Governor was a spectre of his old self. His gaunt, pallid face was even thinner than usual, and two violet-tinged rings of exhaustion had formed under his eyes, but his gaze was as cutting as ever.

Marecc wore his full Alliance insignia. He must have pulled out every ribbon, pin and piece available, as though to make some kind of point. A row of four service emblems hung heavy on his collar: one many-pointed star for every twelve years of service to Geminus.

Marecc had been working for the Geminus Peace Alliance longer than Shaan had been alive. And he would continue to, long after she had been completely forgotten.

"You're here for me, Governor?"

"Oh, yes. I insisted on escorting you to your transit personally," Marecc said. "We haven't said our goodbyes yet."

He snatched the data disc out of Shaan's hand, snapped it in two, and handed it back to the clinician.

"Thank you for your hard work, doctor," Marecc said. "Pity it was all such a waste of time." He flicked his hand at Shaan. "Come."

He took Shaan by the elbow and led her into the corridor.

"If you're feeling sorry for yourself right now, don't," he said coldly. "You got off a lot easier than you should have. Seems someone *important* took up your cause, and decided to meddle in the Council's affairs. The gods only know why she bothered."

"What are you talking about?"

"That Border Security commander from the inquest. Kehallian Sifyer." Marecc sniffed indignantly. "Your dramatics and professions of contrition must've impressed her. She gave a big speech to the Council, said she thought you'd suffered enough already, and recommended your unconditional release. Evidently, she has a much more forgiving heart than I."

"Governor, I'm so sorry," Shaan whispered. "I never meant for—"

"I don't care how sorry you are," Marecc spat. "Ashlish should never have been your student! I knew it was a mistake to pair you two! She was our most promising novice in years... ah, but it seemed so natural to give her to you, didn't it? You, our most talented teacher! What a dream! Our brilliant *ailukh* with such a gifted *alihe*! How could that be anything but a triumph?"

His icy eyes glared into Shaan's. "Ashlish needed a teacher who would temper her! Not encourage her with their own delusions of greatness!" he hissed. "But you never could see past your godsforsaken narcissism, could you? And now here we are, bereft of you both. You accomplished *nothing*."

Tears spilled over Shaan's cheeks, and she didn't try to hide them.

"Believe me, there is no solace when so much has been lost," Marecc said. "But as sorry as you may be, you'll never be *alihe* again. For the rest of your life, you'll be an absolute nobody. And that, at least, brings me some peace."

They reached the end of the corridor, and Marecc led her into a waiting room. There was nothing in the room except a wide airlock and three benches, all of them empty.

"Your transit will pick you up shortly," Marecc said. "Goodbye, Shaan. I only wish I could forget you as quickly as Geminus will."

He shoved the grey carry-bag into Shaan's hands, then turned and stalked out to the corridor without a backwards glance. The door locked behind him.

Shaan sank onto the nearest bench and opened the bag, examining what was left of her life. A change of clothes. A pair of shoes. A clear sleeve of toiletries. A small pack of credit chits and a cheap, unregistered comms device.

There was a digital info-card sitting on top, holding a list of civilian job openings. Shaan clutched the card in her hands, tears blurring her vision as she scrolled the list back and forth without reading it. She screwed her eyes shut, her shoulders heaving pitifully.

When she opened her eyes again, her finger was resting on the sixth job on the list.

Facilities Coordinator
ZeyCorp Research Support
(A Division of Yauronauf Incorporated)

SHAAN
Common Deck, ZeyCorp Gallion

SHAAN WALKED DOWN the deserted corridor, her eyes half-closed, Gida's hooded cloak trailing behind her. The weight of the green fabric was familiar over her shoulders, the heavy cowl hanging down her back as if she'd never stopped wearing it. Beneath the long hem, her feet were still bare, and her footsteps were silent on the cool floor tiles.

She remembered the first time she'd worn the cloak of the Voiced, so many years ago in a ceremonial hall. She remembered bowing to her own proud *alihe* as the kennai was laid on her head, appointing her a fully trained translator, a spiritual successor to the Decipherer.

Shaan had felt the same awe laying the cloak and kennai on her own students. She had cloaked every *ailukh* she ever taught—all except for Ashlish, the most brilliant of them all; Ashlish, who died without ever receiving her cloak.

Shaan's footsteps faltered, and she paused to wipe tears from her face. She pressed two fingers to her lips and raised them in the remembrance to the dead, whispering Ashlish's name.

At that exact moment, someone switched off the artificial engine hum, and the ship was left entirely silent.

Shaan's skin prickled. She swiped the green sleeve over her face, glancing behind her.

The corridor was still empty.

All she'd wanted for so long was a chance to make amends, impossible as it had seemed. Nothing could ever bring Ashlish back, but Shaan would be *alive* again. She was about to walk into history itself.

Shaan shivered. She straightened her shoulders, and kept walking through the ship: past the guest apartments, past meeting-room doors emblazoned with that omnipresent ZeyCorp logo. She walked into the canteen, trailing her hands along the empty tables and chairs.

She sat down at one of the tables, just as Jereth Keeven appeared in the main doorway.

Keeven wore his unlaced boots and battered jacket. He dropped his black carry-bag at the door and walked to her, his footsteps echoing over the floor. He paused beside the table, thinking it over for a long time before he swung out the chair next to hers and sat down.

"It was you, wasn't it?" Keeven said when he finally spoke. "That story about Ashlish's teacher, on Verkhoy Station... that was about *you*."

"Yes," she whispered. "Ashlish was my student."

Keeven nodded slowly.

"Everything Ker Marecc said about me was right." Shaan lowered her head. "I *was* overconfident. And narcissistic, reckless, arrogant—that was all true. I made so many mistakes..."

"Gods, didn't we all," Keeven said. He slid one arm around her, pulling her head against his shoulder. "Didn't we all."

"After the accident, I lost my telepathic sense," Shaan continued quietly. "They weren't sure why, or if I could ever get it back. They gave me so many tests, but I... I just couldn't sense anything anymore. Nothing at all. Right up until that moment in Engineering, when the Ambassador was calling out for Gida..."

Keeven squeezed Shaan's hand. "Gida's okay, you know. She's got a bunch of broken bones, and they've got her sedated, but she should recover. Your people have some real amazing med-tech."

Shaan didn't say anything. She just buried her face in his tattered jacket and hugged him tightly, and she stayed that way for a while, eyes closed, as if she could somehow suspend time.

"We *are* gonna do this, Shaan. I'll do whatever it takes," he said. "And as long as we're alive... we'll keep taking our chances."

She nodded against his chest.

"Say it out loud, Shaan."

"We're gonna do this," she whispered. "We'll keep taking our chances."

"Damn right." He smiled. "We're not quite out of chances yet."

Then he tilted her chin up and kissed her hard, and in that moment, she couldn't imagine that Jereth Keeven would ever cease to be. She might even have believed that they were both immortal.

THEY WERE STILL embracing when Zel walked into the canteen, dressed in the same red suit he'd been wearing in Engineering. His family crest glinted on the elaborate Etraxan sash. His hair was pinned into those two perfect coils behind his ear, his bronze skin shone, and he seemed even taller than usual.

He cleared his throat loudly. "Captain Fransk calls for the Fortunate Five," he said, enunciating every word as if he were reading some kind of proclamation. "The crew would like to exchange a formal goodbye with all of you, and thank you on behalf of ZeyCorp. Come with me."

On a different day, Shaan might have rolled her eyes. Today, she just got to her feet, pulling Keeven up with her.

They started walking together toward Zel, synchronizing their steps without having intended to. Shaan thought of the statue in the reception hall on Verkhoy Station—the magnificent Negotiator and his cloaked companion, holding up the Heart of Geminus—and something shifted in her chest. She held her head straighter.

Zel watched them approach with an awed smile.

They reached the doorway, Keeven leaned down to pick up his black carry-bag. But just as he was straightening back up, Zel stuck out his hand and placed his palm on the top of Keeven's head.

Keeven stopped in surprise, his head still tipped forward, auburn curls shrouding his face.

"As a Blessed Scion of Etraxas," Zel said, "I confer upon you political immunity in perpetuity. I appoint you, Jereth Keeven, as our Negotiator. And I sanction the peace mission." Zel closed his eyes. "My great-grandparents spoke the truth: *Etraxas sends you*. We call on you to save us."

He slowly lifted his hand from Keeven's head, his eyes glimmering with emotion as he turned to Shaan. "Etraxas owes you both an unimaginable debt of gratitude. As does all of humanity. It has been a great honour to meet the Decipherer."

Keeven pushed his hair back behind his ear, shifting the bag onto his shoulder.

"We'll look after Etraxas. Don't worry," Keeven said. "But I need you to take care of your people right here, understand? The *Gallion* crew. Make sure they're okay. Ozakka, Fransk, the juniors, and all the rest of 'em." Keeven lowered his voice. "I heard you've got some connections up high in this company, is that right?"

Zel's eyes widened. "Uh... yes. Yes, you could say that."

"Then listen here," said Keeven. "When you get back, all this"—he waved expansively at the ship around them—"isn't gonna look pretty for ZeyCorp. Your shuttles are wrecked. You've got people dead and injured under some real suspicious circumstances, while you had a Felen Ambassador on board. Shaan here will be missing, and you'll be carrying all my crates of you-don't-even-want-to-know-what." He gave a wry smile. "I hear it's bad form to take a hold full of illegal weapons to a peace negotiation, so the rest of my shipment is gonna be staying here with you."

Zel nodded solemnly. "Oh. Of... of course."

Keeven leaned closer, whispering now. "Look, Zel. What I'm saying is... anybody with a financial interest in this company would be smart to cover this whole thing up. Use your influence. Find some way to just... sweep it all away." He brushed his hand swiftly through the air. "You got me?"

Zel nodded again, smoothing his sash down with determination. "I'll contact my aunt privately, as soon as we have working comms again," he said. "You save the Union, and I'll see that the *Gallion* matter is... ah, taken care of."

"It's a deal." Keeven grinned.

He looked over at Shaan with a wink. Then he took her hand, and they all started walking together to the nearest lift.

UMA
Cargo Bay, ZeyCorp Gallion

UMA AND SOME of the *Gallion* crew stood in the cargo bay in front of the *Jonah*, waiting for Captain Fransk to come and give his farewell address before the Five embarked. Near the boarding ramp, Eldric Leesongronski, Charyne Jaxong and Keila Kva-Sova were clustered together, deep in conversation.

Sometimes, it was still difficult to believe they were all really here, that they'd really been standing in front of their own portrait, learning about their future accomplishments. Uma could hardly imagine a history text without a picture of the Five. How many times had she seen them in paintings and statues since she was a child? How many times had she wondered about their secrets?

"Director Ozakka!" Kva-Sova called. "Can we speak to you a moment?"

As she walked across the bay to join them, Uma thought of all the images on the *Gallion*'s atrium wall, all those framed portraits of history's most-revered. Every day she'd been on this ship, she'd walked past the faces of scientists and theorists, space explorers and philosophers. She'd never dreamed it possible to come face to face with the most famous of them all.

The Fortunate Five.

"We're just talking about what we're going to tell them... you know, when we get back," Kva-Sova said. "We obviously have to pretend that Shaan was one of my subjects, and that I did my gene-splice on her... but... what about the rest of it?" She looked at Uma, her pointed ears twitching. "Do you think we should say that Shaan and I both boarded the *Jonah* at Pilar Outpost, like your history says? And that we went to pick up the Negotiator at Zora before it was destroyed?"

Uma smiled slowly. "You won't just be making history. You'll be *writing* it," she said. "Almost everything we know about the *Jonah* voyage, we know because of you three. Whatever you decide to tell them, that's exactly what history will record."

Jaxong sighed grudgingly. "I suppose if we can agree on a story, it doesn't really matter what that story is. It sure as all hells can't be the truth," she said. "As long as it makes some kind of consistent sense—"

"Sense?" Leesongronski laughed. "Please! Most of what they think happened makes no sense at all! All those coincidences... all those *miracles*? What are the chances their so-called history was accurate in the first place?"

"Slim to none," Jaxong said acerbically. "After all, they seem to think that *you* were a genius."

Leesongronski looked affronted for a moment, but then Jaxong cracked a smile, and gradually they all started laughing.

Uma stared at Leesongronski, the emotions suddenly catching in her throat. She thought of her favourite image of him: walking in the vineyard at Denarba, his head tipped toward the sunset-tinged sky, his arm outstretched, that inscrutable expression on his face. Out of everything history had retained of Eldric Leesongronski—the lectures, the biographies, the portraits and statues, the pictures and films and recordings—she'd always thought that simple snapshot in the vineyard had captured the part of him that felt the most real. *Under Fortunate Stars.*

He'd been more than the legendary Pathfinder, more than the captain of the *Jonah*, more than what he would accomplish. And he was more than that *now*, as they all were, standing there laughing in the *Gallion*'s cargo bay.

Then the doors to the corridor opened, and Zel, Keeven and Shaan came into the bay.

The Decipherer's green cloak billowed behind Shaan as she ran to Uma and threw her arms around her. A moment later, Keeven ran up and put his arms around both of them. The rest of the Five and the whole *Gallion* crew surrounded them, until they were all holding one another, a mass of clutched hands and fervent hope.

One by one, Shaan's former colleagues approached and embraced her. Syru and Mikolai and Noussen, Wazar and Macey, Nack and the Cordero siblings. And then Fransk was there with his words of farewell. He stood on the *Jonah*'s ramp, reading out some variation on the speech he always made for leaving researchers, although she'd never seen him make it quite so tearfully.

Zel looked on from a distance, one hand pressed reverently to his family crest. "I commend you all!" he proclaimed. "I appoint you all by the lifeblood of Etraxas, and I send you to negotiate peace on behalf of the United Worlds of Humanity!"

Uma clutched the fabric of that green cloak and cradled Shaan's head against her shoulder, standing underneath the great ship *Jonah*.

Then the Fortunate Five ascended the *Jonah*'s flimsy metal ramp, and one by one, they entered the ship. First went Kva-Sova, her cold-weather coat bunched under one arm. Then Jaxong in her oversize sweater. Next went Keeven, holding his carry-bag with one hand while he reached back for Shaan's hand with the other. The cloak trailed up the ramp behind her, and Shaan stopped to raise one hand to her friends.

Leesongronski was the last one to go up to the ship. He looked back longer than the others had before he stepped onto the ramp. His eyes locked onto Uma's, and she realized with a start that he was standing in exactly the same place where she'd first seen him.

He reached under his collar and drew out his fortune-charm, holding it up as he flicked the orb once with his thumb. Then he dropped the chain against his chest, walked up the ramp, and disappeared into the hatch.

CAPTAIN FRANSK STOOD at the front of the *Gallion*'s bridge, facing the assembled staff.

"Crew of the *Gallion*... I won't bore you with another speech, but I do feel I have to tell you this," he began when the room had quieted. "The ZeyCorp recruitment adverts like to tell us that we're offered a chance to make history, as we support scientific progress and innovation. Working for this company, we have a unique opportunity to be there when a stunning discovery is made about our universe. When a new subspace particle is found, or when a research team proves a theory about the nature of the cosmos." He paused. "But what this crew has done—what we're about to do—is so much more important than that. We were given a mission we didn't ask for, one nothing could have prepared us for. A mission to *restore the past*... and to save our own future. And I'd like to think that every one of us rose to that mission most admirably." He reached up to his collar and removed his ZeyCorp captain's badge. "What I say next, I say not as your captain, but as your colleague and friend. Whatever happens, I am proud of you. All of you. We existed. We made a difference. And we will *all* be remembered and recognized... even if it's only by each other, for as long as we have left."

Fransk walked slowly up the Command platform to the three wing-backed chairs. He placed his hand on Barnabyn's empty chair, and set his captain's badge there. "Thank you, friend," he whispered.

Then Fransk sank into his own chair, his hands tightening around the armrests as he looked over at Uma. "Director Ozakka, are we ready for detonation?"

"We are," she said softly.

"The *Jonah* is in perfect position," Mikolai said, checking something at one of the Engineering consoles. "I'm preparing the detonation sequence now, Captain. Are we clear to go?"

"Do it," said Fransk.

There was a long, fraught silence. No one moved.

"It, ah... it might take a minute before the drive picks up the signal," Noussen said. "We've still got a lot of interference, and we didn't have any hovers left to deploy a relay."

"Yeah," Mikolai said nervously. "This is normal. The primer reaction will take a little while to build. The same Rift-energy anomalies that kept our engines from starting are going to dampen the blast... That's why we needed all the energy cells."

Another long silence.

"So... ah... what do you think's going to happen when this goes off?" Macey asked. "From what Professor Jaxong said, this thing could rip a hole right through the lower subspace layers."

"No one really knows," Syru said. "It's not like anybody's done this before."

Wazar shrugged. "Technically, mate, I think just about anything could happen. It could create subspace anomalies, space*time* anomalies... or..."

Next to Mikolai, Noussen was looking at a lightpad, frowning down at one of the old Rift energy scans. "Hey. Remember way back when we were theorizing about what could've caused the Rift?" she said slowly. "Mikolai was looking at all these anomalous energy graphs... and... that was when Professor Jaxong first brought up the subspace bomb."

Uma sat up suddenly.

"A violent event in the subspace layer could cause an aberration in spacetime," Mikolai said, whirling around in his seat. His eyes were wide. "Director Ozakka—"

"Like an S-bomb detonation," Uma whispered, her heart pounding. "Like *this*. I think... What if... *we're* creating the Rift? That event is about to happen, right now."

"Detonation is imminent," Dean's voice said. "I would strongly advise that you hang on to something. We may lose gravity with the impact."

Wordlessly, the crew obeyed.

The engineers who weren't at a console sat down on the floor and looped their arms through the low railing that surrounded the Command team's chairs. In the silence, one of the Cordero siblings started a quiet, warbling rendition of one of the *Jonah* folk songs, and one by one, the rest of the crew joined in, their off-key voices filling the room.

> *So tonight, toast the mighty flight of the Jonah,*
> *The ship and the jump and the beauty of being alive!*
> *Human and Felen, peace now prevailing,*
> *Lift your voice and your glass to the sky, to the Fortunate*
>   *Five...*

And then, somewhere out in the void, the S-bomb detonated.

The floor shook. The bridge lights all went out, and the *Gallion* pitched and rumbled. The artificial gravity glitched, and the room tilted sickeningly away.

Uma held onto her chair as they hurtled sideways into the dark.

*　*　*

IT TOOK A few moments for the overhead lights to flicker back to life, and the gravity slowly normalized. Uma opened her eyes and sat up, blinking in disbelief.

They were still alive.

"Dean! Report!" Fransk shouted. "Do we have hull damage?"

"Only minor damage, Captain. Shieldforms are stabilizing."

"And... did we... have we exited the anomaly? Are we back on the network?"

The AI adopted the chirpiest, most cheerful voice in the repertoire. "Sensors detect no sign of anomalous energy, Captain! Our network connections are back and stable. Navigation data is available. Engine diagnostics are normal." There was a short silence. "And we appear to be exactly where we were before we entered the Rift anomaly, Captain."

Fransk exhaled, leaning against the back of his chair. "Thank the gods."

"The *Gallion* received one final voice transmission from the *Jonah* before we cleared the anomaly," Dean added. "It came in just a moment before the detonation impact."

"Dean, play back the transmission," Uma said, wiping tears away with the back of her hand.

There was a slight crackle, and then Leesongronski's familiar voice.

"*ZeyCorp Gallion...* This is Captain Eldric Leesongronski of the Union vessel *Jonah,* on a mission to negotiate peace on behalf of the United Worlds of Humanity. Thank you all for your assistance." He paused, then added: "Luck be with us all."

ZeyCorp Internal Memorandum
Subject: *RV ZC-2812 ZeyCorp Gallion*
[Incident number: 27150]

RELATED DOCUMENTS
ZeyCorp Incident Report #27150 / status CRITICAL
Affidavit, Olghan Fransk [Captain]
Affidavit, Uma Ozakka [Director, Engineering]
Deep Space Forensics Report [re: Incident 27150]

It is with both regret and relief that this Committee submits our final review of Incident 27150, in the matter of the loss of our flagship scientific vessel *RV ZC-2812 ZeyCorp Gallion*.

As detailed in the attached Command affidavits and incident report, a crisis event occurred during a routine transit through deep space at skim speed. The *Gallion* encountered an energy anomaly, resulting in complete systems failure, shieldform collapse and core explosions in the forward and rear engines. This accident resulted in the destruction of the ship, the deaths of the ship's Director of Administration and Facilities Coordinator, and serious injuries to one human diplomatic passenger.

While we deeply regret the loss of two valued ZeyCorp colleagues, we must acknowledge the extraordinary performance of the *Gallion* crew during this incident. Were it not for the ship's quick-thinking and highly trained team, it is likely that such an accident would have resulted in more injuries and claimed more lives. We remain awed and grateful that the remaining crew and visitors were successfully evacuated from the ship by ejecting the *Gallion's* isolated emergency module.

Unfortunately, we cannot ascertain exactly what happened on board the *Gallion* in its final moments. Due to the catastrophic damage to the vessel, the *Gallion*'s digital records, sensor logs and mainframe drives were all irreparably damaged or irretrievable. The sections of the ship that were retrieved by the deep space forensics team had been ravaged by the ensuing fire, and yielded no further information. While the ship's android and a partial copy of the *Gallion*'s AI instance were preserved in the evacuation, the AI-OS memory cells were not backed up and could not be recovered.

Our review of all available facts has ruled this incident a tragic accident, the specific circumstances of which are extremely unlikely to reoccur. All ZeyCorp vessels have undergone an extra round of safety evaluations as a precaution, and no concerns were identified. ZeyCorp's safety record remains exemplary for a fleet of our size, and there is no evidence of wrongdoing on the part of any staff member or at any level of the fleet maintenance crew. We remain proud of our record, and of the overall success of our emergency procedures as demonstrated in this incident.

The Geminus Peace Alliance has extended its profound thanks to ZeyCorp, lauding the *Gallion* crew's professional conduct. The Felen Ambassador involved in the incident has expressed nothing but praise for the ZeyCorp staff, and we are told that the Voiced interpreter who was injured in the incident will make a full recovery.

ZeyCorp will provide the results of our findings to the Geminus Diplomatic Affairs Department, and we will comply fully with any additional requests for information by Geminus High Command. However, we have been assured that there will be no legal charges laid against ZeyCorp in this matter.

With the well-being of our staff in mind, we have extended two months of paid leave to all crew members involved in this traumatic incident. After such time, we will happily welcome the *Gallion* crew back into a similar position with ZeyCorp, or accept any resignations with a generous compensation package and the highest recommendation.

Captain Olghan Fransk of the *Gallion* has already been recommended for a transfer directly into the open Chancellorship at our planetside head office. This promotion will be confirmed by the Board in a following session.

In conclusion, while we remain deeply saddened by the loss of two colleagues on the *Gallion*, we are grateful for an extraordinarily fortunate outcome. Finding any survivors in a disaster of this scale is nothing short of a miracle.

ELDRIC
Northern Continent, Etraxas
4 months after the Rift

ELDRIC SAT ALONE at a stone table in the terraced back garden of an Etraxan country house. The place belonged to a cousin of one of the Roundhouse peers, or so he'd been told. It was in a quiet, hilly northern village, crucially just far enough from the nearest town to avoid media interest.

Late in the afternoon, a page in Etraxan livery brought Eldric some fancy spiced tea in an irregularly-shaped cup, served with what looked very much like a stick of wood. Eldric had stared at it for some time, contemplating what exactly he was meant to do with it. Finally, he picked up the stick and used it to poke at the leaves that floated around in the cup.

Thankfully, the stuff tasted a lot better than it looked, and he drank most of it before he set the cup down. He lit up a cigarette, turning his attention back to the letter on the table in front of him.

There were three hand-written pages, both sides of the thin paper filled with Charyne Jaxong's spidery calligraphy. On the final page was a long, elaborate equation. Eldric solved it with a marking-pen, circling the nineteen-digit solution. Then he turned back to the first page and skimmed over each line of the letter, underlining some of the words and striking out others as he decoded the message.

When he'd finished, he folded the paper into a triangle and set it on the little plate that had come under the teacup. He held the lit end of his cigarette to one crinkled corner, and the paper caught fire quickly.

He used the tea stick to shepherd the burning paper around the plate as the letter curled in on itself and disintegrated. When the last shred of paper had crumbled into greyish ash, Eldric tipped the plate and brushed it into the cup.

He watched the ash sink slowly among the tea leaves at the bottom of the cup.

When he looked up again, he was startled to discover that the young page was standing a few paces away, staring at him in bewilderment.

"Professor Leesongronski?" the page said hesitantly. "I'm sorry to disturb you again, but—"

"But what?" Eldric sighed. "What do you want now?"

"I, ah... Well... Unfortunately, the news media figured out that you're here." The page's eyes skirted away. "There are a *lot* of them out looking for you, over in town. It seems the Union authorities finally went public with the news of the Negotiator's death."

Eldric nodded slowly, saying nothing.

"And what with all the rumours that the *Jonah* has been destroyed... well, everyone is waiting for a statement on that, too," the page said. "There are a lot of questions for you, Professor."

"I'm not talking to any news media," Eldric said curtly. "How in the five hells should I know what happened to the *Jonah*, anyway? I've got no idea. Tell them to ask the UWDF."

"Understood."

"I'm due to leave in the morning," Eldric said after a brief silence. "Is everything still in order?"

"Yes, Professor. Your ship will be in orbit tomorrow, and we'll arrange to take you up discreetly," the page said. "It's an exploratory vessel, brand new, with top-of-the-line dive shielding. Everything is exactly as you requested. I'm told that at least a dozen makers have sent you their best jump kits, so you'll have the most exquisite handsets to choose from—"

Eldric held up a hand. "No, thank you. I won't need those. I have my own handsets."

"Understood." The page's head bobbed in acknowledgement. "I'll not trouble you any further, Professor, but... as this will be your last evening on Etraxas, is there anything more we can do for you?"

Eldric looked out at the bright green hills that stretched as far as he could see. The sun was low in the sky, sinking lazily toward the tallest of the hills, and sunlight was reflecting from gold-limned roofs in the distance.

"Could you secure me a personal transit?" he said after a moment. "I'd like to go out."

"Out?" The page looked surprised. "If you go into town, you'll certainly be swarmed by the media—"

"Not to town." Eldric pointed down into the valley. "I want someone to take me down there."

"That's Denarba Vineyard, Professor."

Eldric nodded. "Yes, I know. I hear they're famed for their excellent agnathe."

"The best on the northern continent," said the page with a proud smile. "The vines are nearly ready for harvest now. Despite all that's happened, this has been one of the most fruitful years in recent memory. I suppose you could say we've had a very fortunate season."

Eldric pushed back his chair and reached for his jacket.

"Yes," he said. "I suppose we all have."

ACKNOWLEDGMENTS

SO MUCH GRATITUDE goes out to everyone whose insight and energy helped make this book possible. There are so many of you who encouraged and uplifted me throughout this journey.

To Michael, my love, my first reader and best friend. This book (and so many of my wildest dreams) literally would not exist without you. Words are not enough. I love you, forever and always.

To my family, thank you for your endless support. To Mummy, who has read and loved every single version of this story, and all the ones that came before it. I would be absolutely lost without you. To Dad, who has always had unwavering confidence in me and my work. To Gab, for penning my first imaginary book blurb (yes, I kept it).

To my editor David Thomas Moore, thank you so much for seeing the magic in this story right alongside me, and for supplying the keen editorial vision that summoned the book's final form. Thanks also goes to Jess Gofton, Rosie Peat, Paul Simpson, Bridette Ledgerwood, Amy Borsuk, Hanna Waigh, and the whole team at Rebellion/Solaris for their hard work and dedication, and to Dominic Forbes for creating my gorgeous book cover!

To my agent Bridget Smith and the team at JABberwocky Literary, thank you for believing in this book from the start, for championing it and shepherding it to a wonderful home.

To my dear friends and critique partners Kerbie Addis, James Nutting, Harry Jones, Kate Murray and Claire Winn, and to my fabulous beta readers Allison, Rebecca, Amelia, Samantha, Kate P. and Luna. Thank you for the immense care you've shown to this world and these characters (and for always reminding me to put in descriptions of things!) One day in the not-so-distant future, we'll raise a glass together to all the stories and dreams yet to come.

To the indomitable Team B, who made the bad times into good ones. I could not have asked for a better squad.

To the Dionysus crew, thank you for the perpetual hive of positive energy, manifestation and passion.

To my beloved Chaos Bakery, your creativity is mindblowing. You are the bright stars in my sky and I'm so lucky to have met every one of you.

To Chance and Monica, your friendship has meant more than you can imagine. I'm so glad we get to build worlds together.

To my whole incredible writing community—you inspire and sustain me.

To Mike Mammay and Mike Chen, for so much invaluable advice and encouragement. To Saritza Hernandez and Kat Howard, for giving feedback on an early version of the story that became this book. To Jamie Dexter, for nerding out with me about writing and storytelling. To June Hur for the brilliant suggestion that fixed my first chapter, and to Rae Loverde for teaching me so much about craft and publishing. To everyone else who has ever given caring and constructive critique on this story or on any of my writing, I am eternally grateful.

To Mathias Kom, the most talented bard who immortalized the Jonah in song.

To Kevin and Amanda and Rita, who were there at the beginning of everything.

To Clea, my first ever writer friend – I hope you've kept creating universes.

And to Mr. Allgood, who told me to consider this as a calling.

FIND US ONLINE!

www.rebellionpublishing.com

/rebellionpub   /rebellionpublishing   /rebellionpublishing

SIGN UP TO OUR NEWSLETTER!

rebellionpublishing.com/newsletter

YOUR REVIEWS MATTER!

Enjoy this book? Got something to say?

Leave a review on Amazon, GoodReads or with your
favourite bookseller and let the world know!